MEMOIRS OF THE LIFE OF
HENRIETTE-SYLVIE DE MOLIÈRE

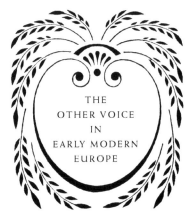

THE
OTHER VOICE
IN
EARLY MODERN
EUROPE

A Series Edited by Margaret L. King and Albert Rabil Jr.

RECENT BOOKS IN THE SERIES

GABRIELLE DE COIGNARD
Spiritual Sonnets: A Bilingual Edition
Edited and Translated by Melanie E. Gregg

MARIE LE JARS DE GOURNAY
*"Apology for the Woman Writing"
and Other Works*
Edited and Translated by Richard Hillman
and Colette Quesnel

ANNIBAL GUASCO
Discourse to Lady Lavinia His Daughter
Edited and Translated, and with an
Introduction by Peggy Osborn

ANNE-MARIE-LOUISE D'ORLEANS,
DUCHESSE DE MONTPENSIER
*Against Marriage: The Correspondence
of La Grande Mademoiselle*
Edited and Translated by Joan DeJean

OLYMPIA MORATA
*The Complete Writings of an
Italian Heretic*
Edited and Translated by Holt N. Parker

ISOTTA NOGAROLA
*Complete Writings: Letterbook, Dialogue
on Adam and Eve, Orations*
Edited and Translated by Margaret L. King
and Diana Robin

JACQUELINE PASCAL
*"A Rule for Children" and Other
Writings*
Edited and Translated by John J. Conley, S.J.

FRANÇOIS POULLAIN DE LA BARRE
Three Cartesian Feminist Treatises
Introductions and Annotations by
Marcelle Maistre Welch
Translation by Vivien Bosley

MARÍA DE SAN JOSÉ SALAZAR
Book for the Hour of Recreation
Introduction and Notes by Alison Weber
Translation by Amanda Powell

MADELEINE DE SCUDÉRY
The Story of Sapho
Edited and Translated by Karen Newman

ARCANGELA TARABOTTI
Paternal Tyranny
Edited and Translated by Letizia Panizza

ELISABETTA CAMINER TURRA
Writings on and about Women
Edited and Translated by Catherine M. Sama

Madame de Villedieu
(Marie-Catherine Desjardins)

MEMOIRS OF THE LIFE OF
HENRIETTE-SYLVIE DE MOLIÈRE:
A NOVEL

࿓

Edited and Translated by
Donna Kuizenga

THE UNIVERSITY OF CHICAGO PRESS
Chicago & London

Madame de Villedieu (Marie-Catherine Desjardins), 1640–83

Donna Kuizenga is professor of romance languages and associate dean of the College of Arts and Sciences at the University of Vermont. She is the author of *Narrative Strategies in "La Princesse de Clèves"* and coeditor of *Women Writers in Pre-Revolutionary France*.

The University of Chicago Press, Chicago 60637
The University of Chicago Press, Ltd., London
© 2004 by The University of Chicago
All rights reserved. Published 2004
Printed in the United States of America
13 12 11 10 09 08 07 06 05 04   1 2 3 4 5

ISBN: 0-226-14419-4 (cloth)
ISBN: 0-226-14420-8 (paper)

Library of Congress Cataloging-in-Publication Data

Villedieu, Madame de, d. 1683.
  [Memoires de la vie de Henriette-Sylvie de Molière. English]
  Memoirs of the life of Henriette-Sylvie de Molière : a novel / Madame de Villedieu (Marie-Catherine Desjardins) ; edited and translated by Donna Kuizenga.
    p. cm. — (The other voice in early modern Europe)
  ISBN 0-226-14419-4 (cloth : alk. paper) — ISBN 0-226-14420-8 (pbk. : alk. paper)
  I. Kuizenga, Donna. II. Title. III. Series.
PQ1794.D5A6813 2004
843'.4—dc22

2003022130

For Joan, who shares Sylvie's will and love of laughter

CONTENTS

Acknowledgments ix
Series Editors' Introduction xi
Madame de Villedieu, a Woman on Her Own 1
Volume Editor's Bibliography 19

Memoirs of the Life of
Henriette-Sylvie de Molière: A Novel 25
Fragment of a Letter 25
Part One 26
Part Two 50
Part Three 74
Part Four 99
Part Five 123
Part Six 152

Series Editors' Bibliography 183

ACKNOWLEDGMENTS

Bringing Sylvie's story into modern English in the hope of gaining a wider audience for Villedieu's innovative novel has been a joy. It has also taken hard work, and I owe many debts of gratitude. The international community of scholars of seventeenth-century French literature has for many years offered me collegiality and constructive feedback on my work with Villedieu's texts. My colleagues in the Dean's Office of the College of Arts and Sciences at the University of Vermont, with their friendship and their ability to laugh at the foibles of academic life, have sustained me through my struggle to remain a scholar while serving as an administrator. Albert Rabil, coeditor of The Other Voice in Early Modern Europe series, has offered encouragement and constructive suggestions. I am grateful to the National Endowment for the Humanities for financial support and to the University of Vermont for time, in the form of a sabbatical leave. George F. Held offered invaluable editorial assistance.

Donna Kuizenga

THE OTHER VOICE IN EARLY MODERN EUROPE: INTRODUCTION TO THE SERIES

Margaret L. King and Albert Rabil Jr.

THE OLD VOICE AND THE OTHER VOICE

In western Europe and the United States, women are nearing equality in the professions, in business, and in politics. Most enjoy access to education, reproductive rights, and autonomy in financial affairs. Issues vital to women are on the public agenda: equal pay, child care, domestic abuse, breast cancer research, and curricular revision with an eye to the inclusion of women.

These recent achievements have their origins in things women (and some male supporters) said for the first time about six hundred years ago. Theirs is the "other voice," in contradistinction to the "first voice," the voice of the educated men who created Western culture. Coincident with a general reshaping of European culture in the period 1300–1700 (called the Renaissance or early modern period), questions of female equality and opportunity were raised that still resound and are still unresolved.

The other voice emerged against the backdrop of a three-thousand-year history of the derogation of women rooted in the civilizations related to Western culture: Hebrew, Greek, Roman, and Christian. Negative attitudes toward women inherited from these traditions pervaded the intellectual, medical, legal, religious, and social systems that developed during the European Middle Ages.

The following pages describe the traditional, overwhelmingly male views of women's nature inherited by early modern Europeans and the new tradition that the "other voice" called into being to begin to challenge reigning assumptions. This review should serve as a framework for understanding the texts published in the series the Other Voice in Early Modern Europe. Introductions specific to each text and author follow this essay in all the volumes of the series.

TRADITIONAL VIEWS OF WOMEN, 500 B.C.E.–1500 C.E.

Embedded in the philosophical and medical theories of the ancient Greeks were perceptions of the female as inferior to the male in both mind and body. Similarly, the structure of civil legislation inherited from the ancient Romans was biased against women, and the views on women developed by Christian thinkers out of the Hebrew Bible and the Christian New Testament were negative and disabling. Literary works composed in the vernacular of ordinary people, and widely recited or read, conveyed these negative assumptions. The social networks within which most women lived—those of the family and the institutions of the Roman Catholic Church—were shaped by this negative tradition and sharply limited the areas in which women might act in and upon the world.

GREEK PHILOSOPHY AND FEMALE NATURE. Greek biology assumed that women were inferior to men and defined them as merely childbearers and housekeepers. This view was authoritatively expressed in the works of the philosopher Aristotle.

Aristotle thought in dualities. He considered action superior to inaction, form (the inner design or structure of any object) superior to matter, completion to incompletion, possession to deprivation. In each of these dualities, he associated the male principle with the superior quality and the female with the inferior. "The male principle in nature," he argued, "is associated with active, formative and perfected characteristics, while the female is passive, material and deprived, desiring the male in order to become complete."[1] Men are always identified with virile qualities, such as judgment, courage, and stamina, and women with their opposites—irrationality, cowardice, and weakness.

The masculine principle was considered superior even in the womb. The man's semen, Aristotle believed, created the form of a new human creature, while the female body contributed only matter. (The existence of the ovum, and with it the other facts of human embryology, was not established until the seventeenth century.) Although the later Greek physician Galen believed there was a female component in generation, contributed by "female semen," the followers of both Aristotle and Galen saw the male role in human generation as more active and more important.

In the Aristotelian view, the male principle sought always to reproduce

---

1. Aristotle, *Physics* 1.9.192a20–24, in *The Complete Works of Aristotle*, ed. Jonathan Barnes, rev. Oxford trans., 2 vols. (Princeton, NJ: Princeton University Press, 1984), 1:328.

itself. The creation of a female was always a mistake, therefore, resulting from an imperfect act of generation. Every female born was considered a "defective" or "mutilated" male (as Aristotle's terminology has variously been translated), a "monstrosity" of nature.[2]

For Greek theorists, the biology of males and females was the key to their psychology. The female was softer and more docile, more apt to be despondent, querulous, and deceitful. Being incomplete, moreover, she craved sexual fulfillment in intercourse with a male. The male was intellectual, active, and in control of his passions.

These psychological polarities derived from the theory that the universe consisted of four elements (earth, fire, air, and water), expressed in human bodies as four "humors" (black bile, yellow bile, blood, and phlegm) considered, respectively, dry, hot, damp, and cold and corresponding to mental states ("melancholic," "choleric," "sanguine," "phlegmatic"). In this scheme the male, sharing the principles of earth and fire, was dry and hot; the female, sharing the principles of air and water, was cold and damp.

Female psychology was further affected by her dominant organ, the uterus (womb), *hystera* in Greek. The passions generated by the womb made women lustful, deceitful, talkative, irrational, indeed—when these affects were in excess—"hysterical."

Aristotle's biology also had social and political consequences. If the male principle was superior and the female inferior, then in the household, as in the state, men should rule and women must be subordinate. That hierarchy did not rule out the companionship of husband and wife, whose cooperation was necessary for the welfare of children and the preservation of property. Such mutuality supported male preeminence.

Aristotle's teacher Plato suggested a different possibility: that men and women might possess the same virtues. The setting for this proposal is the imaginary and ideal Republic that Plato sketches in a dialogue of that name. Here, for a privileged elite capable of leading wisely, all distinctions of class and wealth dissolve, as, consequently, do those of gender. Without households or property, as Plato constructs his ideal society, there is no need for the subordination of women. Women may therefore be educated to the same level as men to assume leadership. Plato's Republic remained imaginary, however. In real societies, the subordination of women remained the norm and the prescription.

The views of women inherited from the Greek philosophical tradition became the basis for medieval thought. In the thirteenth century, the

---

2. Aristotle, *Generation of Animals* 2.3.737a27–28, in *The Complete Works*, 1:1144.

supreme Scholastic philosopher Thomas Aquinas, among others, still echoed Aristotle's views of human reproduction, of male and female personalities, and of the preeminent male role in the social hierarchy.

ROMAN LAW AND THE FEMALE CONDITION. Roman law, like Greek philosophy, underlay medieval thought and shaped medieval society. The ancient belief that adult property-owning men should administer households and make decisions affecting the community at large is the very fulcrum of Roman law.

About 450 B.C.E., during Rome's republican era, the community's customary law was recorded (legendarily) on twelve tablets erected in the city's central forum. It was later elaborated by professional jurists whose activity increased in the imperial era, when much new legislation was passed, especially on issues affecting family and inheritance. This growing, changing body of laws was eventually codified in the *Corpus of Civil Law* under the direction of the emperor Justinian, generations after the empire ceased to be ruled from Rome. That *Corpus*, read and commented on by medieval scholars from the eleventh century on, inspired the legal systems of most of the cities and kingdoms of Europe.

Laws regarding dowries, divorce, and inheritance pertain primarily to women. Since those laws aimed to maintain and preserve property, the women concerned were those from the property-owning minority. Their subordination to male family members points to the even greater subordination of lower-class and slave women, about whom the laws speak little.

In the early republic, the *paterfamilias*, or "father of the family," possessed *patria potestas*, "paternal power." The term *pater*, "father," in both these cases does not necessarily mean biological father but denotes the head of a household. The father was the person who owned the household's property and, indeed, its human members. The *paterfamilias* had absolute power—including the power, rarely exercised, of life or death—over his wife, his children, and his slaves, as much as his cattle.

Male children could be "emancipated," an act that granted legal autonomy and the right to own property. Those over fourteen could be emancipated by a special grant from the father or automatically by their father's death. But females could never be emancipated; instead, they passed from the authority of their father to that of a husband or, if widowed or orphaned while still unmarried, to a guardian or tutor.

Marriage in its traditional form placed the woman under her husband's authority, or *manus*. He could divorce her on grounds of adultery, drinking wine, or stealing from the household, but she could not divorce him. She could neither possess property in her own right nor bequeath any to her children upon her death. When her husband died, the household property passed not to her but to his male heirs. And when her father died, she had no claim to any family inheritance, which was directed to her brothers or more remote male relatives. The effect of these laws was to exclude women from civil society, itself based on property ownership.

In the later republican and imperial periods, these rules were significantly modified. Women rarely married according to the traditional form. The practice of "free" marriage allowed a woman to remain under her father's authority, to possess property given her by her father (most frequently the "dowry," recoverable from the husband's household on his death), and to inherit from her father. She could also bequeath property to her own children and divorce her husband, just as he could divorce her.

Despite this greater freedom, women still suffered enormous disability under Roman law. Heirs could belong only to the father's side, never the mother's. Moreover, although she could bequeath her property to her children, she could not establish a line of succession in doing so. A woman was "the beginning and end of her own family," said the jurist Ulpian. Moreover, women could play no public role. They could not hold public office, represent anyone in a legal case, or even witness a will. Women had only a private existence and no public personality.

The dowry system, the guardian, women's limited ability to transmit wealth, and total political disability are all features of Roman law adopted by the medieval communities of western Europe, although modified according to local customary laws.

CHRISTIAN DOCTRINE AND WOMEN'S PLACE. The Hebrew Bible and the Christian New Testament authorized later writers to limit women to the realm of the family and to burden them with the guilt of original sin. The passages most fruitful for this purpose were the creation narratives in Genesis and sentences from the Epistles defining women's role within the Christian family and community.

Each of the first two chapters of Genesis contains a creation narrative. In the first "God created man in his own image, in the image of God he created him; male and female he created them" (Gn 1:27). In the second, God created Eve from Adam's rib (2:21–23). Christian theologians relied principally on Genesis 2 for their understanding of the relation between man and woman, interpreting the creation of Eve from Adam as proof of her subordination to him.

The creation story in Genesis 2 leads to that of the temptations in Genesis 3: of Eve by the wily serpent and of Adam by Eve. As read by Christian theologians from Tertullian to Thomas Aquinas, the narrative made Eve responsible for the Fall and its consequences. She instigated the act; she deceived her husband; she suffered the greater punishment. Her disobedience made it necessary for Jesus to be incarnated and to die on the cross. From the pulpit, moralists and preachers for centuries conveyed to women the guilt that they bore for original sin.

The Epistles offered advice to early Christians on building communities of the faithful. Among the matters to be regulated was the place of women. Paul offered views favorable to women in Galatians 3:28: "There is neither Jew nor Greek, there is neither slave nor free, there is neither male nor female; for you are all one in Christ Jesus." Paul also referred to women as his coworkers and placed them on a par with himself and his male coworkers (Phlm 4:2–3; Rom 16:1–3; 1 Cor 16:19). Elsewhere, Paul limited women's possibilities: "But I want you to understand that the head of every man is Christ, the head of a woman is her husband, and the head of Christ is God" (1 Cor 11:3).

Biblical passages by later writers (although attributed to Paul) enjoined women to forgo jewels, expensive clothes, and elaborate coiffures; and they forbade women to "teach or have authority over men," telling them to "learn in silence with all submissiveness" as is proper for one responsible for sin, consoling them, however, with the thought that they will be saved through childbearing (1 Tm 2:9–15). Other texts among the later Epistles defined women as the weaker sex and emphasized their subordination to their husbands (1 Pt 3:7; Col 3:18; Eph 5:22–23).

These passages from the New Testament became the arsenal employed by theologians of the early church to transmit negative attitudes toward women to medieval Christian culture—above all, Tertullian (*On the Apparel of Women*), Jerome (*Against Jovinian*), and Augustine (*The Literal Meaning of Genesis*).

THE IMAGE OF WOMEN IN MEDIEVAL LITERATURE. The philosophical, legal, and religious traditions born in antiquity formed the basis of the medieval intellectual synthesis wrought by trained thinkers, mostly clerics, writing in Latin and based largely in universities. The vernacular literary tradition that developed alongside the learned tradition also spoke about female nature and women's roles. Medieval stories, poems, and epics also portrayed women negatively—as lustful and deceitful—while praising good housekeepers and loyal wives as replicas of the Virgin Mary or the female saints and martyrs.

There is an exception in the movement of "courtly love" that evolved in southern France from the twelfth century. Courtly love was the erotic love between a nobleman and noblewoman, the latter usually superior in social rank. It was always adulterous. From the conventions of courtly love derive modern Western notions of romantic love. The tradition has had an impact disproportionate to its size, for it affected only a tiny elite, and very few women. The exaltation of the female lover probably does not reflect a higher evaluation of women or a step toward their sexual liberation. More likely it gives expression to the social and sexual tensions besetting the knightly class at a specific historical juncture.

The literary fashion of courtly love was on the wane by the thirteenth century, when the widely read *Romance of the Rose* was composed in French by two authors of significantly different dispositions. Guillaume de Lorris composed the initial four thousand verses about 1235, and Jean de Meun added about seventeen thousand verses—more than four times the original— about 1265.

The fragment composed by Guillaume de Lorris stands squarely in the tradition of courtly love. Here the poet, in a dream, is admitted into a walled garden where he finds a magic fountain in which a rosebush is reflected. He longs to pick one rose, but the thorns prevent his doing so, even as he is wounded by arrows from the god of love, whose commands he agrees to obey. The rest of this part of the poem recounts the poet's unsuccessful efforts to pluck the rose.

The longer part of the *Romance* by Jean de Meun also describes a dream. But here allegorical characters give long didactic speeches, providing a social satire on a variety of themes, some pertaining to women. Love is an anxious and tormented state, the poem explains: women are greedy and manipulative, marriage is miserable, beautiful women are lustful, ugly ones cease to please, and a chaste woman is as rare as a black swan.

Shortly after Jean de Meun completed *The Romance of the Rose,* Mathéolus penned his *Lamentations,* a long Latin diatribe against marriage translated into French about a century later. The *Lamentations* sum up medieval attitudes toward women and provoked the important response by Christine de Pizan in her *Book of the City of Ladies.*

In 1355, Giovanni Boccaccio wrote *Il Corbaccio,* another antifeminist manifesto, although ironically by an author whose other works pioneered new directions in Renaissance thought. The former husband of his lover appears to Boccaccio, condemning his unmoderated lust and detailing the defects of women. Boccaccio concedes at the end "how much men naturally surpass women in nobility" and is cured of his desires.[3]

---

3. Giovanni Boccaccio, *The Corbaccio, or The Labyrinth of Love,* ed. and trans. Anthony K. Cassell, 2nd rev. ed. (Binghamton, NY: Medieval and Renaissance Texts and Studies, 1993), 71.

WOMEN'S ROLES: THE FAMILY. The negative perceptions of women expressed in the intellectual tradition are also implicit in the actual roles that women played in European society. Assigned to subordinate positions in the household and the church, they were barred from significant participation in public life.

Medieval European households, like those in antiquity and in non-Western civilizations, were headed by males. It was the male serf (or peasant), feudal lord, town merchant, or citizen who was polled or taxed or succeeded to an inheritance or had any acknowledged public role, although his wife or widow could stand as a temporary surrogate. From about 1100, the position of property-holding males was further enhanced: inheritance was confined to the male, or agnate, line—with depressing consequences for women.

A wife never fully belonged to her husband's family, nor was she a daughter to her father's family. She left her father's house young to marry whomever her parents chose. Her dowry was managed by her husband, and at her death it normally passed to her children by him.

A married woman's life was occupied nearly constantly with cycles of pregnancy, childbearing, and lactation. Women bore children through all the years of their fertility, and many died in childbirth. They were also responsible for raising young children up to six or seven. In the propertied classes that responsibility was shared, since it was common for a wet nurse to take over breast-feeding and for servants to perform other chores.

Women trained their daughters in the household duties appropriate to their status, nearly always tasks associated with textiles: spinning, weaving, sewing, embroidering. Their sons were sent out of the house as apprentices or students, or their training was assumed by fathers in later childhood and adolescence. On the death of her husband, a woman's children became the responsibility of his family. She generally did not take "his" children with her to a new marriage or back to her father's house, except sometimes in the artisan classes.

Women also worked. Rural peasants performed farm chores, merchant wives often practiced their husbands' trades, the unmarried daughters of the urban poor worked as servants or prostitutes. All wives produced or embellished textiles and did the housekeeping, while wealthy ones managed servants. These labors were unpaid or poorly paid but often contributed substantially to family wealth.

WOMEN'S ROLES: THE CHURCH. Membership in a household, whether a father's or a husband's, meant for women a lifelong subordination to others. In western Europe, the Roman Catholic Church offered an alternative to the career of wife and mother. A woman could enter a convent, parallel in function to the monasteries for men that evolved in the early Christian centuries.

In the convent, a woman pledged herself to a celibate life, lived according to strict community rules, and worshiped daily. Often the convent offered training in Latin, allowing some women to become considerable scholars and authors as well as scribes, artists, and musicians. For women who chose the conventual life, the benefits could be enormous, but for numerous others placed in convents by paternal choice, the life could be restrictive and burdensome.

The conventual life declined as an alternative for women as the modern age approached. Reformed monastic institutions resisted responsibility for related female orders. The church increasingly restricted female institutional life by insisting on closer male supervision.

Women often sought other options. Some joined the communities of laywomen that sprang up spontaneously in the thirteenth century in the urban zones of western Europe, especially in Flanders and Italy. Some joined the heretical movements that flourished in late medieval Christendom, whose anticlerical and often antifamily positions particularly appealed to women. In these communities, some women were acclaimed as "holy women" or "saints," whereas others often were condemned as frauds or heretics.

In all, although the options offered to women by the church were sometimes less than satisfactory, they were sometimes richly rewarding. After 1520, the convent remained an option only in Roman Catholic territories. Protestantism engendered an ideal of marriage as a heroic endeavor and appeared to place husband and wife on a more equal footing. Sermons and treatises, however, still called for female subordination and obedience.

THE OTHER VOICE, 1300–1700

When the modern era opened, European culture was so firmly structured by a framework of negative attitudes toward women that to dismantle it was a monumental labor. The process began as part of a larger cultural movement that entailed the critical reexamination of ideas inherited from the ancient and medieval past. The humanists launched that critical reexamination.

THE HUMANIST FOUNDATION. Originating in Italy in the fourteenth century, humanism quickly became the dominant intellectual movement in Europe. Spreading in the sixteenth century from Italy to the rest of Europe, it fueled the literary, scientific, and philosophical movements of the era and laid the basis for the eighteenth-century Enlightenment.

Humanists regarded the Scholastic philosophy of medieval universities as out of touch with the realities of urban life. They found in the rhetorical discourse of classical Rome a language adapted to civic life and public speech. They learned to read, speak, and write classical Latin and, eventually, classical Greek. They founded schools to teach others to do so, establishing the pattern for elementary and secondary education for the next three hundred years.

In the service of complex government bureaucracies, humanists employed their skills to write eloquent letters, deliver public orations, and formulate public policy. They developed new scripts for copying manuscripts and used the new printing press to disseminate texts, for which they created methods of critical editing.

Humanism was a movement led by males who accepted the evaluation of women in ancient texts and generally shared the misogynist perceptions of their culture. (Female humanists, as we will see, did not.) Yet humanism also opened the door to a reevaluation of the nature and capacity of women. By calling authors, texts, and ideas into question, it made possible the fundamental rereading of the whole intellectual tradition that was required in order to free women from cultural prejudice and social subordination.

A DIFFERENT CITY. The other voice first appeared when, after so many centuries, the accumulation of misogynist concepts evoked a response from a capable female defender: Christine de Pizan (1365–1431). Introducing her *Book of the City of Ladies* (1405), she described how she was affected by reading Mathéolus's *Lamentations:* "Just the sight of this book . . . made me wonder how it happened that so many different men . . . are so inclined to express both in speaking and in their treatises and writings so many wicked insults about women and their behavior."[4] These statements impelled her to detest herself "and the entire feminine sex, as though we were monstrosities in nature."[5]

The rest of *The Book of the City of Ladies* presents a justification of the female sex and a vision of an ideal community of women. A pioneer, she has received the message of female inferiority and rejected it. From the fourteenth to the seventeenth century, a huge body of literature accumulated that responded to the dominant tradition.

The result was a literary explosion consisting of works by both men and women, in Latin and in the vernaculars: works enumerating the achievements

---

4. Christine de Pizan, *The Book of the City of Ladies,* trans. Earl Jeffrey Richards (New York: Persea Books, 1982), 1.1.1, pp. 3–4.

5. Ibid., 1.1.1–2, p. 5.

of notable women; works rebutting the main accusations made against women; works arguing for the equal education of men and women; works defining and redefining women's proper role in the family, at court, in public; works describing women's lives and experiences. Recent monographs and articles have begun to hint at the great range of this movement, involving probably several thousand titles. The protofeminism of these "other voices" constitutes a significant fraction of the literary product of the early modern era.

THE CATALOGS. About 1365, the same Boccaccio whose *Corbaccio* rehearses the usual charges against female nature wrote another work, *Famous Women*. A humanist treatise drawing on classical texts, it praised 106 notable women: 98 of them from pagan Greek and Roman antiquity, 1 (Eve) from the Bible, and 7 from the medieval religious and cultural tradition; his book helped make all readers aware of a sex normally condemned or forgotten. Boccaccio's outlook nevertheless was unfriendly to women, for it singled out for praise those women who possessed the traditional virtues of chastity, silence, and obedience. Women who were active in the public realm—for example, rulers and warriors—were depicted as usually being lascivious and as suffering terrible punishments for entering the masculine sphere. Women were his subject, but Boccaccio's standard remained male.

Christine de Pizan's *Book of the City of Ladies* contains a second catalog, one responding specifically to Boccaccio's. Whereas Boccaccio portrays female virtue as exceptional, she depicts it as universal. Many women in history were leaders, or remained chaste despite the lascivious approaches of men, or were visionaries and brave martyrs.

The work of Boccaccio inspired a series of catalogs of illustrious women of the biblical, classical, Christian, and local pasts, among them Filippo da Bergamo's *Of Illustrious Women*, Pierre de Brantôme's *Lives of Illustrious Women*, Pierre Le Moyne's *Gallerie of Heroic Women*, and Pietro Paolo de Ribera's *Immortal Triumphs and Heroic Enterprises of 845 Women*. Whatever their embedded prejudices, these works drove home to the public the possibility of female excellence.

THE DEBATE. At the same time, many questions remained: Could a woman be virtuous? Could she perform noteworthy deeds? Was she even, strictly speaking, of the same human species as men? These questions were debated over four centuries, in French, German, Italian, Spanish, and English, by authors male and female, among Catholics, Protestants, and Jews, in ponderous volumes and breezy pamphlets. The whole literary genre has been called the *querelle des femmes*, the "woman question."

The opening volley of this battle occurred in the first years of the fifteenth century, in a literary debate sparked by Christine de Pizan. She exchanged letters critical of Jean de Meun's contribution to *The Romance of the Rose* with two French royal secretaries, Jean de Montreuil and Gontier Col. When the matter became public, Jean Gerson, one of Europe's leading theologians, supported de Pizan's arguments against de Meun, for the moment silencing the opposition.

The debate resurfaced repeatedly over the next two hundred years. *The Triumph of Women* (1438) by Juan Rodríguez de la Camara (or Juan Rodríguez del Padron) struck a new note by presenting arguments for the superiority of women to men. *The Champion of Women* (1440–42) by Martin Le Franc addresses once again the negative views of women presented in *The Romance of the Rose* and offers counterevidence of female virtue and achievement.

A cameo of the debate on women is included in *The Courtier,* one of the most widely read books of the era, published by the Italian Baldassare Castiglione in 1528 and immediately translated into other European vernaculars. *The Courtier* depicts a series of evenings at the court of the duke of Urbino in which many men and some women of the highest social stratum amuse themselves by discussing a range of literary and social issues. The "woman question" is a pervasive theme throughout, and the third of its four books is devoted entirely to that issue.

In a verbal duel, Gasparo Pallavicino and Giuliano de' Medici present the main claims of the two traditions. Gasparo argues the innate inferiority of women and their inclination to vice. Only in bearing children do they profit the world. Giuliano counters that women share the same spiritual and mental capacities as men and may excel in wisdom and action. Men and women are of the same essence: just as no stone can be more perfectly a stone than another, so no human being can be more perfectly human than others, whether male or female. It was an astonishing assertion, boldly made to an audience as large as all Europe.

THE TREATISES. Humanism provided the materials for a positive counterconcept to the misogyny embedded in Scholastic philosophy and law and inherited from the Greek, Roman, and Christian pasts. A series of humanist treatises on marriage and family, on education and deportment, and on the nature of women helped construct these new perspectives.

The works by Francesco Barbaro and Leon Battista Alberti—*On Marriage* (1415) and *On the Family* (1434–37)—far from defending female equality, reasserted women's responsibility for rearing children and managing the housekeeping while being obedient, chaste, and silent. Nevertheless, they served the cause of reexamining the issue of women's nature by placing domestic issues at the center of scholarly concern and reopening the pertinent classical texts. In addition, Barbaro emphasized the companionate nature of marriage and the importance of a wife's spiritual and mental qualities for the well-being of the family.

These themes reappear in later humanist works on marriage and the education of women by Juan Luis Vives and Erasmus. Both were moderately sympathetic to the condition of women without reaching beyond the usual masculine prescriptions for female behavior.

An outlook more favorable to women characterizes the nearly unknown work *In Praise of Women* (ca. 1487) by the Italian humanist Bartolommeo Goggio. In addition to providing a catalog of illustrious women, Goggio argued that male and female are the same in essence, but that women (reworking the Adam and Eve narrative from quite a new angle) are actually superior. In the same vein, the Italian humanist Maria Equicola asserted the spiritual equality of men and women in *On Women* (1501). In 1525, Galeazzo Flavio Capra (or Capella) published his work *On the Excellence and Dignity of Women*. This humanist tradition of treatises defending the worthiness of women culminates in the work of Henricus Cornelius Agrippa *On the Nobility and Preeminence of the Female Sex*. No work by a male humanist more succinctly or explicitly presents the case for female dignity.

THE WITCH BOOKS. While humanists grappled with the issues pertaining to women and family, other learned men turned their attention to what they perceived as a very great problem: witches. Witch-hunting manuals, explorations of the witch phenomenon, and even defenses of witches are not at first glance pertinent to the tradition of the other voice. But they do relate in this way: most accused witches were women. The hostility aroused by supposed witch activity is comparable to the hostility aroused by women. The evil deeds the victims of the hunt were charged with were exaggerations of the vices to which, many believed, all women were prone.

The connection between the witch accusation and the hatred of women is explicit in the notorious witch-hunting manual *The Hammer of Witches* (1486) by two Dominican inquisitors, Heinrich Krämer and Jacob Sprenger. Here the inconstancy, deceitfulness, and lustfulness traditionally associated with women are depicted in exaggerated form as the core features of witch behavior. These traits inclined women to make a bargain with the devil—sealed by sexual intercourse—by which they acquired unholy powers. Such bizarre claims, far from being rejected by rational men, were broadcast by intellectuals. The German Ulrich Molitur, the Frenchman Nicolas Rémy, and the Italian Stefano Guazzo all coolly informed the public of sinister orgies and midnight pacts with the devil. The celebrated French jurist, historian, and political philosopher Jean Bodin argued that because women were especially prone to diabolism, regular legal procedures could properly be suspended in order to try those accused of this "exceptional crime."

A few experts such as the physician Johann Weyer, a student of Agrippa's, raised their voices in protest. In 1563, he explained the witch phenomenon thus, without discarding belief in diabolism: the devil deluded foolish old women afflicted by melancholia, causing them to believe they had magical powers. Weyer's rational skepticism, which had good credibility in the community of the learned, worked to revise the conventional views of women and witchcraft.

WOMEN'S WORKS. To the many categories of works produced on the question of women's worth must be added nearly all works written by women. A woman writing was in herself a statement of women's claim to dignity.

Only a few women wrote anything before the dawn of the modern era, for three reasons. First, they rarely received the education that would enable them to write. Second, they were not admitted to the public roles—as administrator, bureaucrat, lawyer or notary, or university professor—in which they might gain knowledge of the kinds of things the literate public thought worth writing about. Third, the culture imposed silence on women, considering speaking out a form of unchastity. Given these conditions, it is remarkable that any women wrote. Those who did before the fourteenth century were almost always nuns or religious women whose isolation made their pronouncements more acceptable.

From the fourteenth century on, the volume of women's writings rose. Women continued to write devotional literature, although not always as cloistered nuns. They also wrote diaries, often intended as keepsakes for their children; books of advice to their sons and daughters; letters to family members and friends; and family memoirs, in a few cases elaborate enough to be considered histories.

A few women wrote works directly concerning the "woman question," and some of these, such as the humanists Isotta Nogarola, Cassandra Fedele, Laura Cereta, and Olympia Morata, were highly trained. A few were professional writers, living by the income of their pens; the very first among them was Christine de Pizan, noteworthy in this context as in so many others. In addition to *The Book of the City of Ladies* and her critiques of *The Romance of the Rose*, she wrote *The Treasure of the City of Ladies* (a guide to social decorum for women), an advice book for her son, much courtly verse, and a full-scale history of the reign of King Charles V of France.

WOMEN PATRONS. Women who did not themselves write but encouraged others to do so boosted the development of an alternative tradition. Highly placed women patrons supported authors, artists, musicians, poets, and learned men. Such patrons, drawn mostly from the Italian elites and the courts of northern Europe, figure disproportionately as the dedicatees of the important works of early feminism.

For a start, it might be noted that the catalogs of Boccaccio and Alvaro de Luna were dedicated to the Florentine noblewoman Andrea Acciaiuoli and to Doña María, first wife of King Juan II of Castile, while the French translation of Boccaccio's work was commissioned by Anne of Brittany, wife of King Charles VIII of France. The humanist treatises of Goggio, Equicola, Vives, and Agrippa were dedicated, respectively, to Eleanora of Aragon, wife of Ercole I d'Este, duke of Ferrara; to Margherita Cantelma of Mantua; to Catherine of Aragon, wife of King Henry VIII of England; and to Margaret, duchess of Austria and regent of the Netherlands. As late as 1696, Mary Astell's *Serious Proposal to the Ladies, for the Advancement of Their True and Greatest Interest* was dedicated to Princess Anne of Denmark.

These authors presumed that their efforts would be welcome to female patrons, or they may have written at the bidding of those patrons. Silent themselves, perhaps even unresponsive, these loftily placed women helped shape the tradition of the other voice.

THE ISSUES. The literary forms and patterns in which the tradition of the other voice presented itself have now been sketched. It remains to highlight the major issues around which this tradition crystallizes. In brief, there are four problems to which our authors return again and again, in plays and catalogs, in verse and letters, in treatises and dialogues, in every language: the problem of chastity, the problem of power, the problem of speech, and the problem of knowledge. Of these the greatest, preconditioning the others, is the problem of chastity.

THE PROBLEM OF CHASTITY. In traditional European culture, as in those of antiquity and others around the globe, chastity was perceived as woman's quintessential virtue—in contrast to courage, or generosity, or leadership, or rationality, seen as virtues characteristic of men. Opponents of women charged them with insatiable lust. Women themselves and their defenders—without disputing the validity of the standard—responded that women were capable of chastity.

The requirement of chastity kept women at home, silenced them, isolated them, left them in ignorance. It was the source of all other impediments. Why was it so important to the society of men, of whom chastity was not required, and who more often than not considered it their right to violate the chastity of any woman they encountered?

Female chastity ensured the continuity of the male-headed household. If a man's wife was not chaste, he could not be sure of the legitimacy of his offspring. If they were not his and they acquired his property, it was not his household, but some other man's, that had endured. If his daughter was not chaste, she could not be transferred to another man's household as his wife, and he was dishonored.

The whole system of the integrity of the household and the transmission of property was bound up in female chastity. Such a requirement pertained only to property-owning classes, of course. Poor women could not expect to maintain their chastity, least of all if they were in contact with high-status men to whom all women but those of their own household were prey.

In Catholic Europe, the requirement of chastity was further buttressed by moral and religious imperatives. Original sin was inextricably linked with the sexual act. Virginity was seen as heroic virtue, far more impressive than, say, the avoidance of idleness or greed. Monasticism, the cultural institution that dominated medieval Europe for centuries, was grounded in the renunciation of the flesh. The Catholic reform of the eleventh century imposed a similar standard on all the clergy and a heightened awareness of sexual requirements on all the laity. Although men were asked to be chaste, female unchastity was much worse: it led to the devil, as Eve had led mankind to sin.

To such requirements, women and their defenders protested their innocence. Furthermore, following the example of holy women who had escaped the requirements of family and sought the religious life, some women began to conceive of female communities as alternatives both to family and to the cloister. Christine de Pizan's city of ladies was such a community. Moderata Fonte and Mary Astell envisioned others. The luxurious salons of the French *précieuses* of the seventeenth century, or the comfortable English drawing rooms of the next, may have been born of the same impulse. Here women not only might escape, if briefly, the subordinate position that life in the family entailed but might also make claims to power, exercise their capacity for speech, and display their knowledge.

THE PROBLEM OF POWER. Women were excluded from power: the whole cultural tradition insisted on it. Only men were citizens, only men bore arms, only men could be chiefs or lords or kings. There were exceptions that did not disprove the rule, when wives or widows or mothers took the place of men, awaiting their return or the maturation of a male heir. A woman who attempted to rule in her own right was perceived as an anomaly, a monster, at once a deformed woman and an insufficient male, sexually confused and consequently unsafe.

The association of such images with women who held or sought power explains some otherwise odd features of early modern culture. Queen Elizabeth I of England, one of the few women to hold full regal authority in European history, played with such male/female images—positive ones, of course—in representing herself to her subjects. She was a prince, and manly, even though she was female. She was also (she claimed) virginal, a condition absolutely essential if she was to avoid the attacks of her opponents. Catherine de' Medici, who ruled France as widow and regent for her sons, also adopted such imagery in defining her position. She chose as one symbol the figure of Artemisia, an androgynous ancient warrior-heroine who combined a female persona with masculine powers.

Power in a woman, without such sexual imagery, seems to have been indigestible by the culture. A rare note was struck by the Englishman Sir Thomas Elyot in his *Defence of Good Women* (1540), justifying both women's participation in civic life and their prowess in arms. The old tune was sung by the Scots reformer John Knox in his *First Blast of the Trumpet against the Monstrous Regiment of Women* (1558); for him rule by women, defects in nature, was a hideous contradiction in terms.

The confused sexuality of the imagery of female potency was not reserved for rulers. Any woman who excelled was likely to be called an Amazon, recalling the self-mutilated warrior women of antiquity who repudiated all men, gave up their sons, and raised only their daughters. She was often said to have "exceeded her sex" or to have possessed "masculine virtue"—as the very fact of conspicuous excellence conferred masculinity even on the female subject. The catalogs of notable women often showed those female heroes dressed in armor, armed to the teeth, like men. Amazonian heroines romp through the epics of the age—Ariosto's *Orlando Furioso* (1532) and Spenser's *Faerie Queene* (1590–1609). Excellence in a woman was perceived as a claim for power, and power was reserved for the masculine realm. A woman who possessed either one was masculinized and lost title to her own female identity.

THE PROBLEM OF SPEECH. Just as power had a sexual dimension when it was claimed by women, so did speech. A good woman spoke little. Excessive speech was an indication of unchastity. By speech, women seduced men. Eve had lured Adam into sin by her speech. Accused witches were commonly accused of having spoken abusively, or irrationally, or simply too much. As enlightened a figure as Francesco Barbaro insisted on silence in a woman, which he linked to her perfect unanimity with her husband's will and her unblemished virtue (her chastity). Another Italian humanist, Leonardo Bruni, in advising a noblewoman on her studies, barred her not from speech but from public speaking. That was reserved for men.

Related to the problem of speech was that of costume—another, if silent, form of self-expression. Assigned the task of pleasing men as their primary occupation, elite women often tended toward elaborate costume, hairdressing, and the use of cosmetics. Clergy and secular moralists alike condemned these practices. The appropriate function of costume and adornment was to announce the status of a woman's husband or father. Any further indulgence in adornment was akin to unchastity.

THE PROBLEM OF KNOWLEDGE. When the Italian noblewoman Isotta Nogarola had begun to attain a reputation as a humanist, she was accused of incest—a telling instance of the association of learning in women with unchastity. That chilling association inclined any woman who was educated to deny that she was or to make exaggerated claims of heroic chastity.

If educated women were pursued with suspicions of sexual misconduct, women seeking an education faced an even more daunting obstacle: the assumption that women were by nature incapable of learning, that reasoning was a particularly masculine ability. Just as they proclaimed their chastity, women and their defenders insisted on their capacity for learning. The major work by a male writer on female education—that by Juan Luis Vives, *On the Education of a Christian Woman* (1523)—granted female capacity for intellection but still argued that a woman's whole education was to be shaped around the requirement of chastity and a future within the household. Female writers of the following generations—Marie de Gournay in France, Anna Maria van Schurman in Holland, and Mary Astell in England—began to envision other possibilities.

The pioneers of female education were the Italian women humanists who managed to attain a literacy in Latin and a knowledge of classical and Christian literature equivalent to that of prominent men. Their works implicitly and explicitly raise questions about women's social roles, defining problems that beset women attempting to break out of the cultural limits that had bound them. Like Christine de Pizan, who achieved an advanced education through her father's tutoring and her own devices, their bold questioning makes clear the importance of training. Only when women were educated to the same standard as male leaders would they be able to raise that other voice and insist on their dignity as human beings morally, intellectually, and legally equal to men.

THE OTHER VOICE. The other voice, a voice of protest, was mostly female, but it was also male. It spoke in the vernaculars and in Latin, in treatises and dialogues, in plays and poetry, in letters and diaries, and in pamphlets. It battered at the wall of prejudice that encircled women and raised a banner announcing its claims. The female was equal (or even superior) to the male in essential nature—moral, spiritual, and intellectual. Women were capable of higher education, of holding positions of power and influence in the public realm, and of speaking and writing persuasively. The last bastion of masculine supremacy, centered on the notions of a woman's primary domestic responsibility and the requirement of female chastity, was not as yet assaulted— although visions of productive female communities as alternatives to the family indicated an awareness of the problem.

During the period 1300–1700, the other voice remained only a voice, and one only dimly heard. It did not result—yet—in an alteration of social patterns. Indeed, to this day they have not entirely been altered. Yet the call for justice issued as long as six centuries ago by those writing in the tradition of the other voice must be recognized as the source and origin of the mature feminist tradition and of the realignment of social institutions accomplished in the modern age.

We thank the volume editors in this series, who responded with many suggestions to an earlier draft of this introduction, making it a collaborative enterprise. Many of their suggestions and criticisms have resulted in revisions of this introduction, although we remain responsible for the final product.

PROJECTED TITLES IN THE SERIES

Isabella Andreini, *Mirtilla*, edited and translated by Laura Stortoni

Tullia d'Aragona, *Complete Poems and Letters*, edited and translated by Julia Hairston

Tullia d'Aragona, *The Wretch, Otherwise Known as Guerrino*, edited and translated by Julia Hairston and John McLucas

Giuseppa Eleonora Barbapiccola and Diamante Medaglia Faini, *The Education of Women*, edited and translated by Rebecca Messbarger

Francesco Barbaro et al., *On Marriage and the Family*, edited and translated by Margaret L. King

Laura Battiferra, *Selected Poetry, Prose, and Letters*, edited and translated by Victoria Kirkham

Giulia Bigolina, *Urania and Giulia*, edited and translated by Valeria Finucci

Francesco Buoninsegni and Arcangela Tarabotti, *Menippean Satire: "Against Feminine Extravagance" and "Antisatire,"* edited and translated by Elissa Weaver

Rosalba Carriera, *Letters, Diaries, and Art,* edited and translated by Shearer West

Madame du Chatelet, *Selected Works,* edited by Judith Zinsser

Vittoria Colonna, *Sonnets for Michelangelo,* edited and translated by Abigail Brundin

Vittoria Colonna, Chiara Matraini, and Lucrezia Marinella, *Marian Writings,* edited and translated by Susan Haskins

Princess Elizabeth of Bohemia, *Correspondence with Descartes,* edited and translated by Lisa Shapiro

Isabella d'Este, *Selected Letters,* edited and translated by Deanna Shemek

Fairy-Tales by Seventeenth-Century French Women Writers, edited and translated by Lewis Seifert and Domna C. Stanton

Moderata Fonte, *Floridoro,* edited and translated by Valeria Finucci

Moderata Fonte and Lucrezia Marinella, *Religious Narratives,* edited and translated by Virginia Cox

Francisca de los Apostoles, *Visions on Trial: The Inquisitional Trial of Francisca de los Apostoles,* edited and translated by Gillian T. W. Ahlgren

Catharina Regina von Greiffenberg, *Meditations on the Life of Christ,* edited and translated by Lynne Tatlock

In Praise of Women: Italian Fifteenth-Century Defenses of Women, edited and translated by Daniel Bornstein

Louise Labé, *Complete Works,* edited and translated by Annie Finch and Deborah Baker

Madame de Maintenon, *Dialogues and Addresses,* edited and translated by John J. Conley, S.J.

Lucrezia Marinella, *L'Enrico, or Byzantium Conquered,* edited and translated by Virginia Cox

Lucrezia Marinella, *Happy Arcadia,* edited and translated by Susan Haskins and Letizia Panizza

Chiara Matraini, *Selected Poetry and Prose,* edited and translated by Elaine MacLachlan

Eleonora Petersen von Merlau, *Autobiography* (1718), edited and translated by Barbara Becker-Cantarino

Alessandro Piccolomini, *Rethinking Marriage in Sixteenth-Century Italy,* edited and translated by Letizia Panizza

Christine de Pizan et al., *Debate over "The Romance of the Rose,"* edited and translated by Tom Conley with Elisabeth Hodges

Christine de Pizan, *Life of Charles V,* edited and translated by Charity Cannon Willard

Christine de Pizan, *The Long Road of Learning,* edited and translated by Andrea Tarnowski

Madeleine and Catherine des Roches, *Selected Letters, Dialogues, and Poems,* edited and translated by Anne Larsen

Oliva Sabuco, *The New Philosophy: True Medicine,* edited and translated by Gianna Pomata

Margherita Sarrocchi, *La Scanderbeide,* edited and translated by Rinaldina Russell

Justine Siegemund, *The Court Midwife of the Electorate of Brandenburg* (1690), edited and translated by Lynne Tatlock

Gabrielle Suchon, *"On Philosophy" and "On Morality,"* edited and translated by Domna Stanton with Rebecca Wilkin

Sara Copio Sullam, *Sara Copio Sullam: Jewish Poet and Intellectual in Early Seventeenth-Century Venice,* edited and translated by Don Harrán

Arcangela Tarabotti, *Convent Life as Inferno: A Report,* introduction and notes by Francesca Medioli, translated by Letizia Panizza

Laura Terracina, *Works,* edited and translated by Michael Sherberg

Katharina Schütz Zell, *Selected Writings,* edited and translated by Elsie McKee

MADAME DE VILLEDIEU,
A WOMAN ON HER OWN

THE OTHER VOICE

Marie-Catherine Desjardins, known as Madame de Villedieu, was a prolific writer who not only played an important role in the evolution of the early modern novel in France, but also wrote poetry and plays. Her pseudo-autobiographical novel, *Memoirs of Henriette-Sylvie de Molière*, offers readers an unconventional and enterprising woman protagonist. The novel is innovative in its presentation of a love story that does not end with the marriage of hero and heroine. Through her protagonist's use of disguise, Villedieu explores gender roles, and in portraying a woman who is herself writing her life story, she calls into question the way in which women's writing was read in early modern Europe.

Villedieu was in many ways an innovator and pioneer. She was the first woman playwright in France to have one of her works produced by a professional theater company. As one of the small number of French women who lived by the pen, Villedieu practiced many genres, appealing to popular taste. Among her innovations are an early epistolary novel, the "gallant" tale, and the first-person, pseudo-autobiographical novel presented here.

In *Tender Geographies*, Joan DeJean describes the collective writing practice of many seventeenth-century French women authors. Villedieu, however, did not write in collaboration with others. She wrote alone, as did British women writers of the Restoration. Unlike a number of her better-known contemporaries, Villedieu was also "on her own" legally.[1] Like Delariver Manley or Aphra Behn, Villedieu was socially marginal, living on the fringes of fashionable and respectable society. Unprotected by a close-knit

---

1. For more on Villedieu's legal situation, see Joan DeJean, *Tender Geographies: Women and the Origins of the Novel in France* (New York: Columbia University Press), 130. On the issue of Villedieu's relationship to the female tradition and salon society, see ibid., 253, n. 3.

social alliance, Villedieu was the incarnation of that unnatural and transgressive creature, the "She-Author."[2]

VILLEDIEU'S LIFE AND WORKS

Any account of Villedieu's life and works must begin with the acknowledgment that the record of her life contains significant gaps.[3] Such an account must also begin with a word about names, since in that domain, as in so many others, Villedieu did not conform to societal norms. Until 1668–69 Villedieu's works appeared under her birth name, Marie-Catherine Desjardins. After that date, however, she adopted the name of her beloved, Antoine de Boësset, known after 1648 as the sieur de Villedieu, and published the rest of her works as Madame de Villedieu.[4]

Desjardins's parents were from the lower ranks of the provincial nobility. It is believed that she, the family's second daughter, was born in Alençon in 1640. Nothing is known about her childhood. In 1655, however, she met a cousin at a family baptism and secretly promised to marry him. When her father discovered this, he took legal action to invalidate the promise. Shortly after, Desjardins's mother legally separated from her husband. She moved to Paris with her two daughters and soon obtained control of her own financial assets. There is evidence to suggest that at about this time Desjardins made her first efforts as a writer. In Paris her mother renewed old acquaintances and alliances in an effort to obtain necessary protection, and in this way Desjardins made her first acquaintances among those who were to become her own friends and protectors. She remained well connected to members of both the nobility and the upper bourgeoisie during her entire career.

It was in about 1658 that Desjardins met Antoine de Boësset, sieur de Villedieu, a son of well-known court musicians. Antoine, whose father left him solid financial resources, was destined for a military career. It was love at

---

2. Laurie A. Finke, "The Satire of Women Writers in *The Female Wits*," *Restoration: Studies in English Literary Culture, 1600–1700* 8, no. 2 (1984): 69.

3. See Bruce Morrisette, *The Life and Works of Marie-Catherine Desjardins (Mme de Villedieu), 1632–1683*, Washington University Studies in Language and Literature, no. 17 (St. Louis: Washington University Press, 1947), and Micheline Cuénin, *Roman et société sous Louis XIV: Madame de Villedieu (Marie-Catherine Desjardins, 1640–1683)*, 2 vols. (Paris: Honoré Champion, 1979). There are also significant difficulties in establishing a fully reliable bibliography of first editions of Villedieu's works. Because of her popularity, spurious works were attributed to her both during her life and after her death. Cuénin's scholarship provides the most reliable guide to Villedieu's bibliography.

4. In what follows, I refer to the author as she referred to herself: as Desjardins until 1668–69 and as Villedieu thereafter. To avoid confusion, I refer to Desjardins's beloved, Antoine de Boësset, sieur de Villedieu, as Boësset throughout.

first sight for Desjardins, and her 1659 sonnet "Jouissance" ("Pleasure") has traditionally been thought to be a reflection of that passion. This sonnet, the initial source of Desjardins's literary fame, attracted as much criticism as it did praise because its erotic subject matter was considered unsuitable for a young woman. Although probably not her first work, "Pleasure," with its evocation of sexual enjoyment, was soon widely circulated in manuscript form and brought Desjardins a degree of literary success mixed with hints of notoriety. This sonnet, along with ten other poems that may or may not be by Villedieu, was published in a collection of fashionable poetry in 1660.[5]

At about the same time, Desjardins also came into the public eye because she wrote a summary of Molière's play *Les Précieuses ridicules*.[6] This secondhand account of the play was widely circulated and first published in an incorrect and unauthorized edition. In order to get a proper edition published, Desjardins entered into a professional relationship with Claude Barbin, the man who was to publish so much of the fashionable literature of the latter part of the seventeenth century. Their sometimes troubled collaboration would continue throughout Desjardins's career. The publication in 1660 of the authorized version of her play summary and of her poems in the collection mentioned above marked the beginning of Desjardins's success as a writer.[7]

At some point during these early years in Paris, Desjardins began living *sous sa bonne foi*, an expression that can be translated as "under her own responsibility" or "on her own" and means that although she was still a minor, she was considered independent of her parents and able to act on her own without their consent. This emancipation may well have been motivated by her family's financial difficulties and her intention to make her own way in Paris.

5. For editions of Villedieu's works, see the bibliography following this introduction. "Jouissance" appears in Charles de Sercy, ed., *Poésies choisies de MM. Corneille, Boisrobert, de Marigny, Desmarests, Gombault . . . et plusieurs autres. Cinquième partie* (Selected poems of MM. Corneille, Boisrobert, de Marigny, Desmarests, Gombault . . . and several others. Fifth part) (Paris: Charles de Sercy, 1660). It is also included in Villedieu, *Selected Writings of Madame de Villedieu*, ed. Nancy Deighton Klein (New York: Peter Lang, 1995).

6. Mademoiselle Desjardins, *Récit en prose et en vers de la farce des précieuses* (Prose and Verse Account of the Farce of the Precious Damsels) (Paris: Luyne, 1659; authorized edition, Paris: C. Barbin, 1660).

7. At the same time, Charles de Sercy included some of Desjardins's verbal portraits in a revised and expanded edition of the collection of portraits composed by Mademoiselle de Montpensier and her entourage: Mademoiselle Anne-Marie-Louise-Henriette d'Orléans de Montpensier et al., *Recüeil des portraits et éloges en vers et en prose dedié à Son Altesse Royale Mademoiselle* (Collection of portraits and praises in verse and prose dedicated to Her Royal Highness Mademoiselle), 2 vols. in 1. (Paris: Charles de Sercy and Claude Barbin, 1659), 265, 436, 444.

As her reaction to the unauthorized version of her play summary shows, Desjardins was already concerned with managing her literary reputation.[8] The first two volumes of a novel, *Alcidamie*, were published by Barbin in 1661, but the rest never appeared, either because the public was no longer interested in long novels or because the story alluded, indiscreetly, to well-placed members of society. The following year, Desjardins put together *Recueil de poésies* (*Collection of Poems*), including verses that had been published earlier as well as other pieces that had circulated in manuscript. The success of this volume led her to publish an augmented edition in 1664.

Known principally as a love poet at this point in her career, Desjardins turned her attention to the theater, and in 1662 one of the principal theatrical troupes in Paris produced her tragicomedy *Manlius*.[9] This production made Desjardins both the first woman playwright in France to have her work produced by a professional theater company and the first to have her work reviewed in the press. The play met with some success and attracted a good deal of attention both because of the sex of the author and because of the way in which Desjardins had modified the material she had taken from Roman history. That same year, seeking favor and protection, Desjardins published the *Le Carousel de Mgr le Daufin* (*The Dauphin's Carousel*), a fantasy in verse and in prose, which presented a flattering picture of the young Dauphin and of festivities sponsored by the king.[10] Here again the work was a success; Desjardins was invited to recite some of the verses in public, and Barbin published the text.

During the same period, the relationship between Desjardins and Boësset took its first important turn. The account of these events comes from the seventeenth-century writer Gédéon Tallemant des Réaux, who was very critical of Desjardins.[11] According to Tallemant, Boësset was locked out of his house after returning home late one night and sought refuge in Desjardins's room. She accorded it to him and went to sleep with her sister. The next day Boësset fell ill and was forced to remain in Desjardins's room. She cared for him during his illness, he promised marriage, and they lived together rather openly for three months. Boësset soon became unfaithful, however. Miche-

8. On Villedieu's concern with her literary reputation and success, see Myriam Maître, *Les Précieuses: Naissance des femmes de lettres en France au XVIIe siècle* (Paris: Champion, 1999), 372–74.

9. A tragicomedy is a play combining tragic and comic elements, usually a play about serious matters but with a happy ending. This was a popular theatrical genre in seventeenth-century France.

10. The dauphin is the title of the eldest son of the king of France.

11. Gédéon Tallemant des Réaux, *Historiettes*, edited by Antoine Adam (Paris: Gallimard, 1961), 2:900–909.

line Cuénin's study of relevant legal documents suggests that his behavior may have been partly motivated by the fact that Desjardins's family was having ever increasing financial difficulties: her parents' indebtedness made her a distinctly less desirable marriage partner. Intent on furthering his military career, Boësset in 1663 had Desjardins affirm that he had never promised to marry her.

Desjardins continued to devote attention to the theater, composing a second play, *Nitétis* (1663), with a subject taken not from Roman history but rather from the popular novel by another seventeenth-century woman novelist, Madeleine de Scudéry. This play, a failure, was put on by the same theatrical troupe as her first. For her third play Desjardins turned to Molière and his theater company. Rehearsals for the tragicomedy *Le Favory* (*The Favorite Minister*) began in early 1664. According to Tallemant, upon learning that Boësset had left for Paris to rejoin his regiment, Desjardins borrowed money from Molière in order to follow her beloved to the south of France. There, on June 21, 1664, Boësset made a second promise of marriage, this time in the presence of a notary. Boësset then sailed, and Desjardins apparently remained in Provence.

When Boësset returned, he put off the marriage, and Desjardins eventually returned to Paris, where she was again in contact with Molière. New rehearsals of *The Favorite Minister* began in the spring of 1665. Tallemant relates that when the play was to be advertised, Desjardins insisted that her name no longer be listed as Mademoiselle Desjardins, the name under which she had earned her literary reputation, but rather as Madame de Villedieu. Molière refused, saying that using Madame de Villedieu would cause confusion, but indicated that in everything save the advertisements for the play he would call her Madame de Villedieu as she wished. Molière's company performed *The Favorite Minister* on April 24, 1665, enjoying a modest success. Molière chose it for performance at Versailles on June 13, 1665, as part of one of the king's royal entertainments. *The Favorite Minister* was the first play by a woman to be used in a command performance before the king. Desjardins's own account of the performance appears in her 1669 collection *Nouveau recueil de pièces galantes* (*New Collection of Gallant Works*). Although her name would be regularly included in lists of playwrights in treatises on the theater up until the end of the seventeenth century, *The Favorite Minister* was Desjardins's final play, and she next turned her attention to the emerging genre of the novel, the domain in which she would make her most significant literary contributions.

On February 5, 1667, Boësset had Desjardins sign a document freeing him from his promises of marriage. In short succession, he then married another woman and left for battle in the recently declared War of Devolution. Despite the second renunciation, Desjardins used the name Madame de Villedieu during her travels in Holland and the Low Countries, a voyage beginning in March 1667. The ostensible motive for her trip was the need to settle some legal matters, but scholars speculate that her recent rupture with Boësset also motivated her departure. In Brussels the émigré community offered Villedieu a warm reception, and at The Hague she met the erudite Constantin Huygens. Her short fiction *Anaxandre* appeared in 1667. Villedieu continued to suffer from financial difficulties and apparently from health difficulties as well, spending some time at Spa in 1668.[12]

During a brief return visit to Paris to seek additional funding for his military activities, Boësset apparently gave or sold Villedieu's love letters to her publisher, Claude Barbin. Barbin was eager to publish them and finally reached Villedieu in Holland. Her refusal was categorical, but in the end all that she obtained was the removal of her name from the title page and a decrease in the number of copies printed. Villedieu never had the opportunity to avenge this betrayal of trust; Boësset was killed in 1668 at the siege of Lille, while Villedieu was at Spa. *Lettres et billets galants* (*Love Notes and Letters*) of 1668 chronicles Villedieu's unhappy love for Boësset. During this period, Villedieu remained outside of France, perhaps staying with the duchess of Nemours, to whom she had dedicated her pastoral novel *Carmente* (1668).[13]

She may also have composed her novel *Cléonice* at this time, although it did not appear until 1669. *Cléonice* was the first of her published works to carry the name Madame de Villedieu, although she had already been using that name in other contexts. She maintained excellent relations with the Boësset family after Antoine's death, and they made no known objections to her use of the name, or to her signing herself as Marie-Catherine Desjardins, widow of Villedieu. After Boësset's death in 1668, Villedieu used this name in her literary dealings as well as in other matters.

Upon her return to Paris, Villedieu faced severe financial difficulties. She continued to seek a royal pension and gave both *Cléonice* and her correspondence from Holland and the Low Countries to Barbin for publication.[14] Villedieu collected many of her earlier poems and a number of occasional

---

12. Spa is a village in Belgium reputed for the curative powers of its waters.

13. It is at this time that Villedieu probably wrote *Relation d'une reveue des Troupes de l'amour*, although there is some question about the attribution of this work. Mademoiselle Des Jardins, *Relation d'une reveue des troupes de l'amour* (*Relation of a Review of Love's Troops*) (Fribourg: P. Bontemps, 1668).

14. *Recueil de quelques lettres; ou, Relations galantes* (Paris: C. Barbin, 1668).

pieces, publishing *Nouveau recueil de pièces galantes* (*New Collection of Gallant Pieces*) with Barbin in 1668 as well. At the beginning of *Cléonice*, Villedieu underlines her creation of a new genre, the gallant tale, or *nouvelle galante*, with a new respect for verisimilitude that distinguishes it from the longer heroic works that had enjoyed great popularity earlier in the century.

From 1669 to 1672 Villedieu worked frenetically, producing one successful work after another, mainly novels. Her financial situation probably made the rapid pace of her writing necessary, and it may have been Barbin, encouraged by the success of *Carmente*, who pushed her toward the novel. It is also possible, as Faith Beasley has suggested, that Villedieu's move to the novel was motivated by her understanding of the increased power of the worldly, rather than academic public in cultural matters. Her position was thus a modernist one, allying her intellectually with those who would form one side of the Quarrel of the Ancients and the Moderns.[15]

In 1669 Barbin asked Villedieu to rewrite a manuscript he owned, called *Le Journal amoureux* (*Love's Journal*). She reworked the first and second parts of the text. However, there were difficulties with the original author, who subsequently published the third and fourth parts. Villedieu disavows these sections in her preface to a second edition (1671). This edition provides a clear demonstration of Villedieu's concern with the management of her public image as a writer. In it she not only dissociates herself from the lascivious third and fourth parts of *Love's Journal*, she also provides a catalog of her own works through 1671 in order to eliminate spurious attributions. The fifth and sixth parts, which Villedieu wrote, appeared in 1671 as well.

At the same time as he was having Villedieu rewrite *Love's Journal*, Barbin took out a privilege for a second series, called *Les Annales galantes* (*The Annals of Love*), and the four parts of this text appeared anonymously in 1670. This anonymity may well have been transparent and may have been motivated by the social criticism contained in the text. Both *The Annals of Love* and *Love's Journal* play an important role in the development of prose fiction, and Villedieu is credited by historian Pierre Bayle with the invention of the gal-

---

15. Faith E. Beasley, "Apprentices and Collaborators: Villedieu's Worldly Readers," in *A Labor of Love: Critical Reflections on the Writings of Marie-Catherine Desjardins (Madame de Villedieu)*, ed. Roxanne Decker Lalande (Madison, NJ: Fairleigh Dickinson University Press; London: Associated University Presses, 2000), 177–202. The Quarrel of the Ancients and Moderns was a literary and cultural dispute in seventeenth-century France, and in England as well. The Ancients advocated the supremacy of the literature of Greece and Rome as unsurpassable cultural models. The Moderns advocated the value of contemporary literature. The scientific discoveries of the time led the Moderns to assert that as it was possible to surpass the ancients in science, so should it be possible to surpass them in literary and cultural matters.

lant tale, which replaced the long sentimental novels that had been fashion-able.[16] French history provides the frame for the stories that make up the "days" of *Love's Journal*, but the characters are motivated almost solely by love, and it is in their passions that the reader finds the motivation for historical events.

In the preface to *The Annals of Love*, Villedieu gives readers a clear picture of her intentions. In her view, official history leaves out important aspects of the events it describes. By adding information, by creating speeches for the characters and by giving personal and often amorous motives for their public actions, Villedieu subverts official history and provides a critique of it, sug-gesting that great deeds are not motivated by principle or politics, but rather by emotion. In this way, Villedieu suggests that history is not one official story, but instead is made up of multiple, contingent tales. In so doing she creates a version of history in which women may play as important a role as men. The following year, Barbin published Villedieu's *Les amours des grands hommes* (*The Loves of Great Men*) and her continuation of *Love's Journal*.

In 1669, Villedieu had presented the king with an ornate manuscript of a work in verse, *Fables, ou, Histoires allégoriques* (*Fables, or, Allegorical Histories*). She gave the text to Barbin for publication in 1670—perhaps in order to remind the king of her gift. Barbin published it in order to profit from the recent suc-cess of La Fontaine's *Fables*. In quick succession, more of her important works followed. Parts 1 through 4 of *Les exilés de la cour d'Auguste* (*The Exiles of the Court of Augustus Caesar*) appeared in 1672, with parts 5 and 6 following in 1673. *The Exiles*, like *The Loves of Great Men*, continues Villedieu's rewriting of historical material.

The first four parts of the pseudo-autobiographical *Mémoires de la vie de Henriette-Sylvie de Molière* (*Memoirs of the Life of Henriette-Sylvie de Molière*) date from 1672, and the last two parts, from 1674. In 1673, both *Les Galanteries grenadines* (*Gallantries of Grenada*) and *Les Nouvelles afriquaines* (*African Tales*) came out. The sto-ries in *Gallantries* are set at the time of the fall of Grenada in the fifteenth century and exploit the seventeenth-century public interest in Spain and its past. The stories in *African Tales*, on the other hand, are set in another exotic location, but use contemporary historical events as their frame. Here again, Villedieu was re-sponding to a wave of public interest, this time in northern Africa.

Villedieu apparently spent time in a convent in 1672 but left in 1673 and thereafter lived a retired life. Her literary production slowed considerably. Her last works to appear in publication during her lifetime were *Œuvres mêlées* (*Selected works*), a collection that picked up a variety of earlier pieces but

---

16. Pierre Bayle, *Dictionnaire historique et critique*, 16 vols. (1820; reprint, Paris: AUPELF France-Expansion, 1973), 8:331–33.

also contained an important new work, the short epistolary novel *Le Portefeuille* (*The Letter Case*, 1674), and her collection of three short stories, *Les Désordres de l'amour* (*The Disorders of Love*, 1675). This last work is often thought to reveal Villedieu's new, and more sober, vision of love. It portrays the political disorder sown by passion and its manipulation. Critics also consider this text to be the one in which Villedieu brings her conception of historical fiction to its fullest fruition.

In 1676 Villedieu finally received the royal pension she had so long sought, one of only two women writers to receive royal support in the seventeenth century. In 1677 she married Claude-Nicolas de Chaste and in 1678 gave birth to a son, Louis de Chaste. The marriage remained secret, however, probably because her husband had to be released from the religious orders he had taken. That year Chaste was appointed Governor of the Invalides, but he died before he could take the position. Louis XIV gave both the position and a pension to the infant, and Villedieu, now Madame de Chaste, was also able to obtain her husband's inheritance from his father. She then retired with her son to a property at Clinchemore, where her mother, sister, and brother were living.[17] Villedieu remained there until her death in 1683.

Two of Villedieu's works appeared posthumously: *Le Portrait des faiblesses humaines* (*The Portrait of Human Weaknesses*, 1685) and *Les Annales galantes de Grèce* (*The Gallant Annals of Greece*, 1687). It is not known whether Villedieu had intended to publish these writings, or whether that decision was made solely by her publisher, Barbin, who gained possession of her manuscripts at the time of her death. The four tales that make up *The Portrait of Human Weaknesses* reflect an interest in moral instruction on the author's part, suggesting a date of composition at or after the 1675 *Disorders of Love*. The portraits of human weaknesses are intended as an admonition to those subject to the vices portrayed and an inducement to moral improvement. *The Gallant Annals of Greece*, on the other hand, are almost certainly intended to exploit the success of *The Annals of Love*. It is not known with certainty when the work was composed, or why Villedieu chose not to publish it, although some scholars speculate that its materials may have been incompatible with the more sober outlook of her later years.

MEMOIRES OF THE LIFE OF HENRIETTE-SYLVIE DE MOLIÈRE

Mémoires of the Life of Henriette-Sylvie de Molière is perhaps Villedieu's most striking work. The text, which has a number of picaresque elements, skillfully mixes

---

17. Clinchemore is west of Paris in the department of Sarthe.

real events from the author's life with fictional adventures, creating a first-person tale of an independent and enterprising woman. Its tropes of identity and disguise undermine conventional notions of gender and foreground the complexities of creating an authoritative female narrative voice in early modern France. The cultural conventions of the time, of course, enjoined silence and modesty on women, rather than the assumption of a public or published persona. The drama of seizing the pen, creating an authoritative narrative voice, is powerfully enacted in early modern autobiographical and pseudo-autobiographical texts like this one, where the distance between author and character is diminished.[18]

Appearing anonymously from 1672 to 1674, the memoirs comprise six long, first-person letters that the protagonist Sylvie addresses to a woman protector, at the latter's request. The letters tell the story of an abandoned infant of uncertain parentage who, as a young woman, is thrown out into the world on her own after her foster father attempts to rape her. Sylvie's trajectory includes encounters with libidinous and unreliable men and with both generous female protectors and ill-intentioned female enemies. Her life is marked by a grand passion for the young Count of Englesac. When their often-deferred and much-opposed union finally takes place, however, it turns out not to be what the audience might have expected—the end of the story—but rather the beginning of another series of troubles for the heroine.[19]

Sylvie's struggles are as much economic battles as amorous ones. Over and over again she seeks financial security, struggling with constant assaults on her reputation, which impede her in this effort. While at the end of her tale she is sufficiently disgusted with the world to retire from it, Sylvie shows a remarkable ability to fend for herself, whether in defending against her foster father's advances or in donning male disguise—and fighting duels and seducing women—to further her fortune. While her love for Englesac is great, it is not naive. Sylvie does not present herself as a paragon of traditionally defined virtue. Rather, she defines her innocence situationally. If she marries a rich elderly Spaniard, for example, it is because she believes she has lost Englesac forever and must survive economically.

The central issue raised by *Memoirs* is the question of how to read a woman writer's life. How does Villedieu—through her writing heroine Sylvie—adopt a viable narrative stance, one that permits her to resist the gendered reading to

18. See Jane Spencer, *The Rise of the Woman Novelist: From Aphra Behn to Jane Austen* (Oxford: Basil Blackwell, 1986), 41.

19. Cf. René Démoris, *Le Roman à la première personne* (Paris: A. Colin, 1975), 137.

which women writers were subjected, a reading that insistently conflated life and text?[20] The point of departure for *Memoirs* is the request from Sylvie's patroness for the story of her life. Villedieu's narrator explicitly intends her adventures as an agreeable diversion for her reader, not as a pathetic tale of woe or a treatise on economic or sexual oppression.[21] Sylvie is not just the writer of her own tale, however; she is also the subject of multiple readings. While the ostensible reason for telling her life story is her protector's request, Sylvie transforms herself into a textual commodity, a product designed to compete in the marketplace against the falsified versions of her life story. It is in crafting Sylvie's narrative stance that Villedieu offers us lessons on how to read a woman writer's life story.

Not only have false stories about the character Sylvie been circulated, her situation is all the more problematic precisely because her "real" life so resembles fiction.[22] It is in part by emphasizing this point—that her "true" adventures sound a bit too much like fiction—that Sylvie seeks the complicity of her readers, and thus corrects the false stories of her life. She is, nonetheless, well aware of the dangers of publication for a woman. In this context the verb *publier* has the full force of its double meaning, "to publish" and "to make public." The author of the fragmentary letter that precedes the novel—who may be taken as Villedieu, Sylvie, or both—makes this clear, noting that she will not be so foolish as to go to a city where she has been published.[23] To take back her authorial authority, her *auctoritas*, however, Sylvie presents herself as having no choice other than to publish, that is, to shape for herself a public persona of her own choosing.[24]

20. For a related but somewhat different discussion of Villedieu's positioning, see Nancy K. Miller, "Tender Economies: Mme de Villedieu and the Costs of Indifference," *Esprit Créateur*, 23, no. 2 (1983): 80–93. Margaret Wise looks at the cross-dressing episodes in the novel as giving us "an uncanny portrait of a (proto-)capitalist system and woman's place in it." Margaret Wise, "Cross-Dressing Capital: Villedieu's *Mémoires de la vie de Henriette-Sylvie de Molière*," *Romance Languages Annual* 7 (1995): 180.

21. Cf. Francis Assaf, "Madame de Villedieu et le picaresque au féminin: *Les Mémoires de la vie d'Henriette-Sylvie de Molière* (1641–74)," in *Actes de Wake Forest*, ed. Milorad R. Margitic and Byron R. Wells (Paris: PFSCL, 1987), 361–77; Démoris, *Roman*, 138–39.

22. "When one is born for adventures, no matter what one does, fate is too strong, and when one expects it the least, things happen which make the most simple and common matters turn into something worthy of a novel" (p. 159).

23. Cf. Jacques Chupeau, "Du *Roman comique* au récit enjoué: la gaîté dans les *Mémoires de Henriette-Sylvie de Moliére*," *Cahiers de Littérature du XVIIe Siècle* (Toulouse) 3 (1981): 94–95; Joan DeJean, *Ancients against Moderns: Culture Wars and the Making of the Fin de Siècle* (Chicago: University of Chicago Press), 34.

24. Cf. Debora B. Schwartz, "Writing Her Own Life: Villedieu, Henriette-Sylvie de Molière, and Feminine Empowerment," in *Women in French Literature*, ed. Michel Guggenheim (Saratoga, CA: Anma Libri, 1988), 85–87.

The most significant way in which Sylvie seeks to reassert her power over her own tale is by suggesting to the reader the appropriate interpretation of her text. From the beginning, Sylvie underlines the truthful character of her tale and seeks to win her reader's sympathy.[25] By showing her concern for her reader's pleasure, Sylvie creates complicity with her.[26] As Nicole Boursier has shown in her study of *Memoirs*, Sylvie, starting from her self-portrait, engages her reader in a game of flirtation and seduction. Her complicity with her reader is based on knowing not only how to live but also how to laugh.[27]

It is through the many passages that allude to the text's reception that Villedieu proposes a model of reading. We are to read *Memoirs* as Sylvie's correspondent does. We are to replace the false tales of Sylvie's life with these true memoirs. We must be able to smile and laugh at the narrator's adventures. But as Sylvie entertains us, her irony points up the dangers a woman faces, both in traditional society and on its margins.[28] By means of this ironic narration, Villedieu offers us the image of a woman who is not an object but a subject.[29] Through such a reading, Sylvie's initial wish will be realized:

> Not that I have any hope of being able to blot out of most people's minds the unjust images that slander has painted of my conduct. This age does not allow me to flatter myself with such a thought. But . . . a time will come when people will no longer be so liable to judge others to be as criminal as themselves, for their behavior will no longer be so corrupt or so criminal. Then people will perhaps give more credence to what I am going to write about the innocence of my actions than to what my enemies may have said about them. (p. 26)

25. "I will not hide anything, not even the most foolish adventures in which I have had some role, so that Your Highness can laugh at them while at the same time having compassion for me in other regards. Indeed it seems to me that even if you had not given me permission to amuse you, I should not fail to do so because without that, Madame, would I be worth the time you will spend reading a story as boring as that of my life?" (p. 26).

26. Cuénin, *Roman et société*, 1:646, 657.

27. Nicole Boursier, "Le Corps de Henriette-Sylvie," in *Le Corps au XVIIe siècle*, ed. Ronald W. Tobin, Biblio 17, 89 (Paris: PFSCL, 1995), 274. Cf. Chupeau, "Du *Roman comique*," 96.

28. Cf. DeJean, *Tender Geographies*, 133.

29. See DeJean, *Tender Geographies*, 133–34; Marie-Thérèse Hipp, *Mythes et réalités, enquête sur le roman et les mémoires, 1660–1700* (Paris: Klincksieck, 1976), 80–81. Josephine Donovan's conception of "a feminist critical irony" is particularly useful here. As Donovan notes, "The women's critical irony fractured the authoritative, monologic modes of earlier patriarchal forms, such as the epic and the romance, and established the dialogic, ironic mode characteristic of the novel." "Women and the Rise of the Novel: A Feminist-Marxist Theory," *Signs* 16 (1991): 462. Cf. Boursier, "Le Corps de Henriette-Sylvie," 276.

Memoirs is neither an autobiography, nor a novel, nor memoirs, nor an epistolary novel, but a text that has something of all these genres.[30] Through Sylvie, Villedieu proposes a text that consciously blurs the line between fiction and history.[31] The mixture of real incidents from Villedieu's life and fictional events creates a distance between Villedieu and her text.[32] She invites us to read her text and not her life. We can neither identify the author with her character nor deny that there are obvious parallels between them.[33] In *Memoirs,* the distance between life and text that Villedieu succeeds in maintaining is the space of creation and autonomy.[34]

In one telling incident, Sylvie republishes one of her own letters that had been previously circulated without her consent. For Villedieu, the publication of *Love Notes and Letters* in 1668 forcibly conflated private and public, author and text.[35] Villedieu recreates the breathing space between life and work through the publication of other letters, those of Sylvie to her patron. By making her text of both fact and fiction, she refuses to be pinned down and retains a degree of creative freedom.[36]

As a number of excellent studies of other women writers in early modern France have demonstrated in recent years, much of the fiction written by women in seventeenth-century France was an arena of experimentation, of play with alternative plots and possibilities for women.[37] Villedieu plays

---

30. Cf. Chupeau, "Du *Roman comique,*" 93–95.

31. Cf. DeJean, *Tender Geographies,* 134.

32. Critical opinion is quite divided on the extent to which *Mémoires* is autobiographical. I think the novel offers a mixture of fictional events, allusions to current events, and material taken from Villedieu's life. Cf. DeJean, *Tender Geographies,* 253, n. 3; Démoris, *Roman,* 312; Hipp, *Mythes,* 455; Assaf, "Madame de Villedieu," 364; Schwartz, "Writing Her Own Life," 78; Micheline Cuénin, introduction to *Les Mémoires de la vie de Henriette-Sylvie de Molière* by [Madame de Villedieu] (Tours: Editions de l'Université François Rabelais, 1977); Marie-Thérèse Hipp, "Fiction et réalité dans les *Mémoires de la vie de Henriette-Sylvie de Molière* de Madame de Villedieu," *Dix-Septième Siècle* 94–95 (1971): 96, 112–14.

33. Cf. Boursier, "Le Corps de Henriette-Sylvie," 278–79.

34. Cf. Chupeau, "Du *Roman comique,*" 104–5; Joan DeJean, "Lafayette's Ellipses: The Privileges of Anonymity," in *An Inimitable Example: The Case for The Princesse de Clèves,* ed. Patrick Henry (Washington: Catholic University of America Press, 1992), 39–70.

35. Katharine Ann Jensen, *Writing Love: Letters, Women, and the Novel in France, 1605–1776* (Carbondale: Southern Illinois University Press, 1995), 37.

36. This freedom is asserted through the kind of guide to resistant reading I have just described, as well as by Villedieu's use of the common seventeenth-century trope of disguise.

37. I am thinking especially of the work of Nicole Aronson, *Mademoiselle de Scudéry, ou, le voyage au pays de Tendre* (Paris: Fayard, 1986); Faith E. Beasley, *Revising Memory: Women's Fictions and Memoirs in Seventeenth-Century France* (New Brunswick: Rutgers University Press, 1990); DeJean, "Lafayette's Ellipses" and *Tender Geographies;* and Nancy K. Miller, "Emphasis Added: Plots and Plausibilities in Women's Fiction," in *An Inimitable Example: The Case for the Princesse de Clèves,* ed. Patrick Henry (Washington, DC: Catholic University of America Press, 1992), 15–38.

with and subverts a number of novelistic conventions. This play offers possibilities of play and pleasure to readers and helps Villedieu enact a viable narrative stance.

A number of critics, most notably Micheline Cuénin,[38] see in *Memoirs* a
kind of compensatory text in which Villedieu makes herself remarkably beautiful, gives herself the parents she never had, and marries her beloved. This
reading is invalidated by Villedieu's irony. Sylvie's magnetic beauty, which exercises its pull even when she is in male disguise, is the ironic counterpart of
the beauty of the romance heroine.[39] Villedieu skillfully manipulates Sylvie's
beauty so that it makes the heroine marketable to the reader of romance and at
the same time undermines the conventions of that trope. Likewise, the mother
figure, Mme de Séville, a fictive creature who lives by fictions, is surrounded
by gentle irony, as is the banal end of the marriage of hero and heroine.

I believe, as do Nicole Boursier and Debora Schwartz, that the text and
reading that Villedieu proposes in *Memoirs* are liberating ones.[40] Sylvie writes
her *memoirs* to respond to the *novels* that have been made of her life. Villedieu
offers us a *novel* that, by its guidance to readers, its play with novelistic convention, and its heterogeneous mixture of elements, explodes the traditional
categories for reading women's lives and their writing. Neither helpless virgin nor principle-free female rake, Sylvie asks to be judged in context.
Through her creation of a writing heroine, Villedieu takes for herself the
power to tell the stories about her life, which had become an appropriated
and falsified public commodity. The text and reading that Villedieu proposes
are coded as female—although they remain open to readers of either sex. To
the extent that she foregrounds a woman's experiences and sensibilities, her
text may be called feminist, as it may be called feminist by the bonding
among women that it enacts.[41] In *Memoirs* Villedieu uses materials from her
own life to assert woman's right to a writerly voice.

VILLEDIEU'S LITERARY FATE

Villedieu's success in her own time was considerable. She was widely known,
both praised for her skill as a writer and derided as an immoral woman whose

38. Micheline Cuénin, introduction to Villedieu, *Les Mémoires de la vie de Henriette-Sylvie de Molière*
(1722; facsimile, Tours: Editions de l'Université François Rabelais, 1977), vii–viii.

39. Cf. Ros Ballaster, *Seductive Forms: Women's Amatory Fiction from 1684 to 1740* (Oxford: Clarendon
Press; New York: Oxford University Press, 1992), 40.

40. Boursier, "Le Corps de Henriette-Sylvie," 280; Schwartz, "Writing Her Own Life," 85–87;
Hipp, *Mythes et réalités*, 316–17. Cf. Cuénin, "Introduction," ix–x.

41. Cf. Schwartz, "Writing Her Own Life," 83–84, 86–89.

work was of slight value. The publication of three editions of her collected works, augmented by a number of false attributions, between 1702 and 1741 indicates the degree of her popularity. Two pirated editions appeared during the same period. Many of her works were translated into English immediately after their publication. Like many of the women writers of the late seventeenth century, Villedieu continued to be read during the eighteenth century. However, as Joan DeJean has demonstrated in the final chapter of her *Tender Geographies,* the works of many women writers, including Villedieu, disappeared from view as the canon of French literature was formed after the Revolution. As a consequence, it was only in the latter part of the twentieth century that interest in Villedieu extended beyond the work of a few specialists. Until that time, scholars often read Villedieu's works almost exclusively as being unmediated reflections of her own life and experiences. This approach is particularly attractive in Villedieu's case, precisely because there are such gaps in our knowledge of her life. While this approach continues to be practiced, beginning in the 1980s a new generation of scholars has suggested that, while elements of Villedieu's experience are certainly reflected in her works, it is erroneous to assume that the works are merely a reflection of her life, when in fact their intentionally literary nature makes the relation between life and work a much more complex and subtle one. This approach has allowed scholars to foreground Villedieu's important and innovative role in the evolution of the novel during the early modern period.

THIS TRANSLATION

As indicated above, *Memoirs of the Life of Henriette-Sylvie de Molière* contains a mixture of real and fictional elements. A good number of the characters are real people, members of the minor nobility who would have been known to the seventeenth-century reading public. The presence of these characters both reinforces the story's verisimilitude and adds the spice of gossip to the reading of the novel. For twentieth-century readers, however, unless they want to use the text as the basis for historical studies, the flavor these characters add has faded. For this reason, only those characters whose identities help the reader understand the plot have been identified in the notes. On occasion, information is provided from Micheline Cuénin's annotations of the facsimile edition.[42] Because Cuénin's notes are intended for a French audience, the information has almost always been modified by the addition or deletion of details and explanations.

---

42. This edition is cited within the novel as MC, followed by the page number of the note.

Note: Stippled areas are those with provincial estates in 1661 and after.

Map 1 The French provinces in the seventeenth century. From David J. Sturdy, *Louis XIV,* 1998. St. Martin's Press reproduced with permission of Palgrave Macmillan.

Not only does Sylvie encounter a wide cast of characters over the course of her adventures, she also covers a good deal of territory. To facilitate an understanding of her travels, the principal places and cities she visits have been located in footnotes, and two maps are included, showing the French provinces (map 1) and the Low Countries (map 2) as they were in the seventeenth century.

Our modern use of certain words masks the sense they had in earlier times, and there are certain terms used in this translation that merit explanation at the outset. The terms *lover* and *mistress* are much more often used here to mean the person beloved than to designate a person with whom one has a sexual relationship. In the seventeenth century, the French word *honnête* conveyed a complex meaning. A man or woman who was *honnête* was both honest

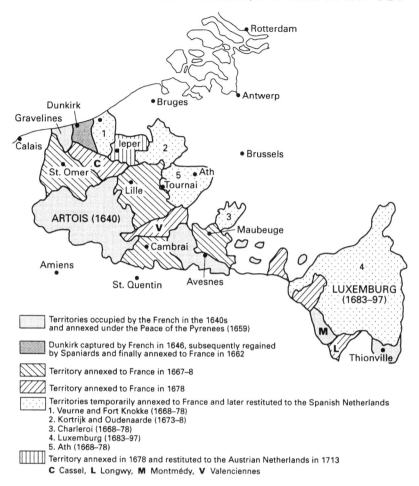

Map 2 Northern France and the Low Countries in the seventeenth century. From Jonathan Israel, *The Dutch Republic: Its Rise, Greatness and Fall, 1477–1806* (1995) by permission of Oxford University Press. © Jonathan Israel, 1995.

and honorable, possessed of social graces, and most often well born. In this edition, *honnête* has been translated as "honest" but should be understood to convey the web of meaning just described. Characters are often described also as "gallant." Unlike the contemporary resonance of this adjective, in this text a gallant man or woman is someone who has a penchant for love and who has made or wishes to make many conquests. In the course of her narrative, Sylvie uses a number of different terms (*star, fate, fatality, malign influence, fortune*) to indicate that fate has brought her into a particular situation. I have generally translated these terms as *fortune* since fortune may be either good or bad.

While noble titles have in the main been given in their English forms, *Chevalier* is used rather than *Knight* when it is associated with a proper name, as was often the case in seventeenth-century English. In addition I have preferred in proper names the French *Monsieur* and *Madame* to the English *Sir* or *Mister* and *Madam* and after these have naturally used the French *de* rather than the English *of.* Thus, for example, Sylvie's beloved Englesac is referred to both as the Count of Englesac and as Monsieur d'Englesac. For the sake of consistency, I have used *Monsieur* and *Madame* rather than *Mister* or *Madam* throughout as a form of address, even where these words are not followed by proper names.

VOLUME EDITOR'S BIBLIOGRAPHY

WORKS BY MARIE-CATHERINE DESJARDINS, MADAME DE VILLEDIEU

Alcidamie. Paris: Claude Barbin, 1661.

Les Amours des grands hommes. 4 vols. Paris: Claude Barbin, 1671.

Anaxandre. Paris: Claude Barbin, 1667.

Les Annales galantes. 4 bks. in 2 vols. Paris: Claude Barbin, 1670.

Les Annales galantes. Ed. René Godenne. 2 vols. 1670. Facsimile, Geneva: Slatkine Reprints, 1979.

Annales galantes de Grèce. 2 vols. Paris: C. Barbin, 1687.

Carmente. Paris: Claude Barbin, 1668.

Le Carousel de Mgr le Daufin. Paris: Mille de Beaujeu, 1662.

Cléonice; ou, Le roman galant. Paris: Claude Barbin, 1669.

Cléonice; ou, Le roman galant: nouvelle. Ed. René Godenne. Geneva: Slatkine, 1979.

Les Désordres de l'amour. Paris: Claude Barbin, 1675.

Les Désordres de l'amour. Ed. Micheline Cuénin. TLF, vol. 174. Geneva: Droz, 1970.

Les Désordres de l'amour. Ed. Arthur Flannigan. Washington, DC: University Press of America, 1982.

Les Exilés de la cour d'Auguste. 6 vols. Paris: Claude Barbin, 1672–73.

Fables; ou, Histoires allégoriques. Paris: Claude Barbin, 1670.

Le Favory. Paris: Louis Billaine, 1665.

Le Favori. In *Femmes dramaturges en France (1650–1750)*, ed. Perry Gethner. Paris: PFSCL, 1993.

Les Galanteries grenadines. 2 vols. Paris: Claude Barbin, 1673.

Le Journal amoureux. 6 vols. Paris: Claude Barbin, 1669–1671. [Parts 1, 2, 5, and 6 by Villedieu.]

Lettres et billets galants. Paris: Claude Barbin, 1668.

Lettres et billets galants. Ed. Micheline Cuénin. N.p.: Société d'étude du XVIIe siècle, 1975.

Lettres et billets galants. In *Lettres d'amour du XVIIe siècle*, ed. Jean Rohu. Paris: Seuil, 1994.

Lisandre. Paris: C. Barbin, 1663.

Manlius. Paris: C. Barbin, 1662.

Mémoires de la vie de Henriette-Sylvie de Molière. 6 vols. Paris: Claude Barbin, 1672–74.

Mémoires de la vie de Henriette-Sylvie de Molière. Ed. Micheline Cuénin. 1722. Facsimile, Tours: Editions de l'Université François Rabelais, 1977.

Mémoires de la vie de Henriette-Sylvie de Molière. Ed. René Démoris. Paris: Desjonquères, 2003.

Nitétis. Paris: Claude Barbin, 1664.

Nouveau recueil de pièces galantes. Paris: Jean Ribou, 1669.

Les Nouvelles afriquaines. Paris: Claude Barbin, 1673.

Œuvres complètes. 12 vols. Paris: Compagnie des Libraires, 1720–21.

Œuvres complètes. 3 vols. 1720-21. Facsimile, Geneva: Slatkine Reprints, 1971.

Œuvres de Mademoiselle des Jardins. Paris: G. Quinet, 1664. Augmented edition, 1664.

Œuvres mêlées. Rouen: Macherel, 1674.

Le Portefeuille. Ed. Jean-Paul Homand and Marie-Thérèse Hipp. Exeter: University of Exeter, 1979.

Portrait des foiblesses humaines. Paris: C. Barbin, 1685.

Recueil des poésies de Mademoiselle Desjardins. Paris: C. Barbin, 1662; augmented edition, 1664.

Recueil de quelques lettres; ou, Relations galantes. Paris: C. Barbin, 1668.

Récit en prose et en vers de la farce des précieuses. Paris: Luyne, 1659; authorized edition, Paris: C. Barbin, 1660.

Récit de la farce des précieuses. Geneva: Slatkine Reprints, 1969.

Récit de la farce des précieuses. In Molière, *Les Précieuses ridicules,* ed. Micheline Cuénin. Geneva: Droz; Paris: Minard, 1973.

Relation d'une reveue des troupes de l'amour. Fribourg: P. Bontemps, 1668.

Selected Writings of Madame de Villedieu. Ed. Nancy Deighton Klein. New York: Peter Lang, 1995. [Comprises "Jouissance," *Manilus, Lisandre, Fables; ou, Histoires allégoriques* (selections), *Les Amours des grands hommes* (selections).]

ENGLISH TRANSLATIONS OF VILLEDIEU'S WORKS

The Amours of Solon, Socrates, Julius Caesar, Cato of Vtica, d'Andelot, Bussy d'Amboyse. London: For H. Herringman and John Starkey, 1673.

The Annals of Love, Containing Select Histories of the Amours of Divers Princes Courts, Pleasantly Related. London: Printed for John Starkey, 1672.

The Disorders of Love: Truly expressed In the unfortunate Amours of Givry with Mademoiselle de Guise. London: Printed for James Magnes and Richard Bentley, 1677.

The Disorders of Love. Trans. and ann. Arthur Flannigan. Birmingham, AL: Summa Publications, 1995.

The Exiles of the Court of Augustus Cæsar. Being the history of the various amours of the celebrated Ovid, Horace, Virgil, Lentulus, Cornelius Gallus, Hortensius, and many other famous poets and heroes of that age. London: Printed for D. Browne, 1726.

The Exiles of the Court of Augustus Caesar: Being the secret history of the illustrious Ovid, Horace, Virgil, Lentulus, Cornelius Gallus, Hortensius, and many other famous personages of that age. In three parts. Dublin: Printed for William Williamson, bookseller, at Mecaenas'-Head in Bride-Street, 1754

The Favorite Minister. In *The Lunatic Lover and Other Plays by French Women of the 17th and 18th Centuries,* ed. and trans. Perry Gethner, 27–88. Portsmouth, NH: Heinemann, 1994.

Loves Journal, a Romance, Made of the Court of Henry the II of France. Printed with License at Paris, 1670. And now made English. London: Thomas Ratcliff and Mary Daniel, 1671.

The Loves of Sundry Philosophers and Other Great Men. [London] Savoy: Printed by T. N. for Henry Herringman . . . , and John Starkey, 1673.

The Loves of Sundry Philosophers and Other Great Men: A Translation of Madame de Villedieu's "Les amours des grands hommes." Ed. Nancy Deighton Klein. Studies in French Literature, vol. 17. Lewiston, ME: Edwin Mellen Press, 2000. [Comprises Solon, Socrates, Julius Caesar, and Cato of Utica. Transcription of the 1673 translation.]

The Memoires of the Life, and Rare Adventures of Henrietta Silvia Moliere. As they have been very lately Published in French. London: William Crook, 1672.

The Memoires of the Life and Rare Adventures of Henrietta Sylvia Moliere. Written in French by her Self. Being the II, III, IV, V, VI and last Parts. London: J. C. for W. Crooke, 1677.

Les Mémoires de la vie de Henriette-Sylvie de Molière (selections). Trans. Donna Kuizenga and Francis Assaf. In *Writings by Pre-Revolutionary French Women,* ed. Colette Winn and Anne Larson, 361–76. New York: Garland Press, 2000.

The unfortunate heroes, or, The adventures of ten famous men, viz., Ovid, Lentullus, Hortensius, Herennius, Cepion, Horace, Virgil, Cornelius Gallus, Crassus, Agrippa, banished from the court of Augustus Cæsar in ten novels. [London] In the Savoy: Printed by T. N. for Henry Herringman, 1679.

OTHER PRIMARY SOURCES

Bayle, Pierre. *Dictionnaire historique et critique.* 16 vols. 1820. Reprint, Paris: AUPELF France-Expansion, 1973. 8:331–33.

Montpensier, Mademoiselle Anne-Marie-Louise-Henriette d'Orléans de, et al. *Recüeil des portraits et éloges en vers et en prose dedié à Son Altesse Royale Mademoiselle.* 2 vols. in 1. Paris: Charles de Sercy and Claude Barbin, 1659. [Literary portraits by Villedieu, 265, 436, 444.]

Sercy, Charles de, ed. *Poésies choisies de MM. Corneille, Boisrobert, de Marigny, Desmarests, Gombault . . . et plusieurs autres. Cinquième partie.* Paris: Charles de Sercy, 1660. [Eleven poems by Villedieu including "Jouissance," 55–67.]

Tallemant des Réaux, Gédéon. *Historiettes.* 2 vols. Ed. Antoine Adam. Paris: Gallimard, 1960–61.

SECONDARY SOURCES

Aronson, Nicole. *Mademoiselle de Scudéry, ou Le voyage au pays de Tendre.* Paris: Fayard, 1986.

Assaf, Francis. "Madame de Villedieu et le picaresque au féminin: Les Mémoires de la vie d'Henriette-Sylvie de Molière (1671–1674)." In *Actes de Wake Forest: L'Image du souverain dans le théâtre de 1600 à 1650/Maximes/Madame de Villedieu,* ed. Milorad R. Margitic and Byron R. Wells, 361–77. Paris: PFSCL, 1987.

Ballaster, Ros. *Seductive Forms. Women's Amatory Fiction from 1684 to 1740.* Oxford: Clarendon Press; New York: Oxford University Press, 1992.

Beasley, Faith E. "Apprentices and Collaborators: Villedieu's Worldly Readers." In *A Labor of Love: Critical Reflections on the Writings of Marie-Catherine Desjardins (Madame de Villedieu),* ed. Roxanne Decker Lalande, 177–202. Madison, NJ: Fairleigh Dickinson University Press; London: Associated University Presses, 2000.

————. *Revising Memory: Women's Fictions and Memoirs in Seventeenth-Century France.* New Brunswick: Rutgers University Press, 1990.

Boursier, Nicole. "Le Corps de Henriette-Sylvie." In *Le Corps au XVIIe siècle,* ed. Ronald W. Tobin, 271–80. Biblio 17, 89. Paris: PFSCL, 1995.

Chupeau, Jacques. "Du *Roman comique* au récit enjoué: la gaîté dans les *Mémoires de Henriette-Sylvie de Molière." Cahiers de Littérature du XVIIe Siècle* (Toulouse). 3 (1981): 91–118.

Cotgrave, Randle. *A Dictionarie of the French and English Tongues.* 1611. Reprint, Hildesheim: Georg Olms Verlag, 1970.

Cuénin, Micheline. "Madame de Villedieu. Bibliographie." *Répertoire Annalytique de la Littérature Française* 2, no. 6 (January-February 1971): 7–26.

————. "Marie-Catherine Desjardins, Madame de Villedieu: mise au point biographique." *Répertoire Annalytique de la Littérature Française* 1, no. 5 (November-December 1970): 7–39.

————. *Roman et société sous Louis XIV: Madame de Villedieu (Marie-Catherine Desjardins 1640–1683).* 2 vols. Paris: Honoré Champion, 1979.

DeJean, Joan. *Ancients against Moderns: Culture Wars and the Making of a Fin de Siècle.* Chicago: University of Chicago Press, 1997.

————. "Lafayette's Ellipses: The Privileges of Anonymity." In *An Inimitable Example: The Case for "The Princesse de Clèves,"* ed. Patrick Henry, 39–70. Washington: Catholic University of America Press, 1992.

————. *Tender Geographies: Women and the Origins of the Novel in France.* New York: Columbia University Press, 1991.

Démoris, René. "Madame de Villedieu—Histoire de femme." In *Actes de Wake Forest: L'Image du souverain dans le théâtre de 1600 à 1650/Maximes/Madame de Villedieu,* ed. Milorad R. Margitic and Byron R. Wells, 286–319. Paris: PFSCL, 1987.

————. *Le Roman à la première personne.* Paris: A. Colin, 1975.

Dictionnaire de l'Académie Française. Paris: Chez la Veuve de Jean-Baptiste Coignard, 1694. http://www.lib.uchicago.edu/efts/ARTFL/projects/dicos/ACADEMIE/.

Donovan, Josephine. "Women and the Rise of the Novel: A Feminist-Marxist Theory." *Signs* 16 (1991): 441–62.

Finke, Laurie A. "The Satire of Women Writers in *The Female Wits." Restoration: Studies in English Literary Culture, 1660–1700* 8, no. 2 (1984): 64–71.

Furetière, Antoine. *Le Dictionnaire universel.* 3 vols. La Haye: A. and R. Leers, 1690. Facsimile, Paris: S.N.L.-Le Robert, 1978.

Goldsmith, Elizabeth C. "Publishing Passion: Madame de Villedieu's *Lettres et billets galants." In Actes de Wake Forest: L'Image du souverain dans le théâtre de 1600 à 1650/Maximes/ Madame de Villedieu,* ed. Milorad R. Margitic and Byron R. Wells, 439–49. Paris: PFSCL, 1987.

Hipp, Marie-Thérèse. "Fiction et réalité dans les *Mémoires de la vie de Henriette-Sylvie de Molière* de Madame de Villedieu." *Dix-Septième Siècle* 94–95 (1971): 93–117.

————. *Mythes et réalités, enquête sur le roman et les mémoires, 1660–1700.* Paris: Klincksieck, 1976.

Israel, Jonathan. *The Dutch Republic: Its Rise, Greatness, and Fall, 1477–1806.* Oxford: Clarendon Press, 1995.

Jensen, Katharine Ann. *Writing Love: Letters, Women, and the Novel in France, 1605–1776.* Carbondale: Southern Illinois University Press, 1995.

Klein, Nancy Deighton. "Madame de Villedieu's *Le Portefeuille*: Toward a New Esthetics of *La Coquette* and *La Prude.*" *Atlantis* 19, no.1 (Fall-Winter 1993): 92–99.

Kuizenga, Donna. "*Ce rusé d'amour*: les ruses des *Annales galantes.*" In *Écriture de la ruse*, ed. Elzbieta Grodek, 319–33. Amsterdam: Rodopi, 2000.

———. "Cherchez l'artiste: artistes et objets d'art dans l'oeuvre de Mme de Villedieu." In *SATOR: Actes du Dixième Colloque International (Johannesburg)*, ed. Denise Godwin, Thérèse Lassalle, and Michèle Weil, 9–19. Montpellier: Université Paul Valéry, 1999.

———. "'Fine veuve' ou 'veuve d'une haute vertu'? Portraits de la veuve chez Mme de Villedieu." *Cahiers du Dix-Septième* 7, no. 1 (1997): 227–39.

———. "La Généricité dans les *Mémoires de la vie de Henriette-Sylvie de Molière.*" In *Féminités et masculinités dans le texte narratif*, ed. Suzan van Dijk and Madeleine van Strien, 43–54. Louvain: Editions Peeters, 2002.

———. "'La Lecture d'une si ennuyeuse histoire': topoï de la lecture et du livre dans les *Mémoires de la vie de Henriette-Sylvie de Molière.*" In *L'Epreuve du lecteur: livres et lectures dans le roman d'Ancien Régime*, ed. Jan Herman and Paul Pelckmans, 120–28. Louvain-Paris: Editions Peeters, 1995.

———. "The Play of Pleasure and the Pleasure of Play in the *Mémoires de la vie de Henriette-Sylvie de Molière.*" In *A Labor of Love: Critical Reflections on the Writings of Marie-Catherine Desjardins (Madame de Villedieu)*, ed. Roxanne Decker Lalande, 147–61. Madison, NJ: Fairleigh Dickinson University Press; London: Associated University Presses, 2000.

———. "Playing to Win: Villedieu's Henriette-Sylvie de Molière as Actress." *Theatrum mundi: Studies in Honor of Ronald W. Tobin*, ed. Claire Carlin and Kathleen Wine, 113–21. Charlottesville, VA: Rookwood Press, 2003.

———. "Romancière à succès, succès de romancière: Mme de Villedieu et les topoï." In *Homo narrativus: recherches sur la topique romanesque dans les fictions de langue française avant 1800*, ed. Nathalie Ferrand and Michèle Weil, 285–99. Montpellier: Presses de l'Université Paul Valéry-Montpellier III, 2001.

———. "Les Ruses du roman épistolaire sous l'Ancien Régime." In *Écriture de la ruse*, ed. Elzbieta Grodek, 197–210. Amsterdam: Rodopi, 2000.

———. "Seizing the Pen: Narrative Power and Gender in Mme de Villedieu's *Mémoires de la vie de Henriette-Sylvie de Molière* and Delarivier Manley's *Adventures of Rivella.*" In *Women Writers in Pre-Revolutionary France*, ed. Colette Winn and Donna Kuizenga, 383–95. New York: Garland Publishing, 1997.

———. "Violences et silences dans l'oeuvre de Mme de Villedieu." In *Violence et fiction jusqu'à la Révolution*, ed. Martine Debaisieux and Gabrielle Verdier, 251–62. Tübingen: Gunter Narr, 1998.

———. "Writing in Drag: Strategic Rewriting in the Early Epistolary Novel." *Early Modern France* 8 (2002): 149–72.

Lalande, Roxanne Decker, ed. *A Labor of Love: Critical Reflections on the Writings of Marie-Catherine Desjardins (Madame de Villedieu)*. Madison, NJ: Fairleigh Dickinson University Press, London: Associated University Presses, 2000.

Lynn, John A. *The Wars of Louis XIV*. London: Longman, 1999.

Maître, Myriam. *Les Précieuses: naissance des femmes de lettres en France au XVIIe siècle*. Paris: Champion, 1999.

Margitic, Milorad R. and Byron R. Wells, eds. *Actes de Wake Forest: L'Image du souverain dans le théâtre de 1600 à 1650/Maximes/Madame de Villedieu*. Paris: PFSCL, 1987.

Miller, Nancy K. "Tender Economies: Mme de Villedieu and the Costs of Indifference." *Esprit Créateur* 23, no. 2 (1983): 80–93.

———. "Emphasis Added: Plots and Plausibilities in Women's Fiction." In *An Inimitable Example: The Case for "The Princesse de Clèves,"* ed. Patrick Henry, 15–38. Washington: Catholic University of America Press, 1992.

Morrisette, Bruce. *The Life and Works of Marie-Catherine Desjardins (Mme de Villedieu), 1632–1683.* Washington University Studies in Language and Literature, no. 17. St. Louis: Washington University Press, 1947.

Nicot, Jean. *Thrésor de la langue francoyse, tant Ancienne que Moderne.* Paris: Chez David Douceur, 1606. http://www.lib.uchicago.edu/efts/ARTFL/projects/dicos/TFL-NICOT/.

Oxford English Dictionary. Edited by J. A. Simpson and E. S. C. Weiner. 2nd ed. Oxford: Clarendon Press, 1989. *OED Online.* http://dictionary.oed.com/.

Schwartz, Debora B. "Writing Her Own Life: Villedieu, Henriette-Sylvie de Molière, and Feminine Empowerment." In *Women in French Literature,* ed. Michel Guggenheim, 77–89. Saratoga, CA: Anma Libri, 1988.

Spencer, Jane. *The Rise of the Woman Novelist: From Aphra Behn to Jane Austin.* Oxford: Basil Blackwell, 1986.

Stanton, Domna C. "The Demysification of History and Fiction in *Les Annales galantes.*" In *Actes de Wake Forest: L'Image du souverain dans le théâtre de 1600 à 1650/Maximes/Madame de Villedieu,* ed. Milorad Margitic and Byron R. Wells, 339–60. Paris: PFSCL, 1987.

Storer, Maud Elizabeth. "Bibliographical note on Mme de Villedieu (Mlle Desjardins)," *Modern Language Notes* 62 (1947): 413–18.

Verdier, Gabrielle. "Madame de Villedieu and the Critics: Toward a Brighter Future." In *Actes de Wake Forest, L'Image du souverain dans le théâtre de 1600 à 1650/Maximes/Madame de Villedieu,* ed. Milorad Margitic and Byron R. Wells, 323–38. Paris: PFSCL, 1987.

———. "Masculin/féminin: la réécriture de l'histoire dans la nouvelle historique." In *La Naissance du roman,* ed. David Trott and Nicole Boursier, 38–54. Biblio 17, 54. Paris: PFSCL, 1990.

Wise, Margaret. "Cross-Dressing Capital: Villedieu's *Mémoires de la vie de Henriette-Sylvie de Molière.*" *Romance Languages Annual* 7 (1995): 180–84.

Wolfgang, Aurora. "La Duplicité d'un roman par lettres: *Le Portefeuille* de Mme de Villedieu." *Cahiers du Dix-Septième* 7, no. 1 (1997): 241–53.

Zuerner, Adrienne. "(Re)constructing Gender: Cross-dressing in Seventeenth-Century French Literature." Ph.D. diss., University of Michigan, 1993.

MEMOIRS OF THE LIFE OF
HENRIETTE-SYLVIE DE MOLIÈRE:
A NOVEL

FRAGMENT OF A LETTER

. . . I'm bringing with me a lovely lady whom you know, and who threatens to make me take an even longer journey. She has this strange desire to see Paris again, but I doubt that she will be able to convince me to go there, and not only because my own business calls me back to Toulouse. I have no intention of going to a city where I was so foolish as to allow myself to be put into print. Since you are more prudent than I, I will let you be the judge of what still needs to be cut out. But let's change the subject. Your bookseller's request makes me quite uncomfortable; can't he do without what he asks for? What does he want me to say in a preface? I have nothing more to say to my readers; I have said everything I wanted to in giving them the wonderful story that you are printing. Furthermore, I don't think this book requires much justification. I couldn't avoid talking about some people who are still alive, but I don't think there is one of them who would not forgive me for the liberty I have taken. From this point of view, I will stand by this work in any eventuality.

I am very happy that you think the text needs to be corrected by skillful people; just make sure these skillful people are not too serious minded, otherwise they will find too many flaws. People say that you have to be of a playful temperament in order to read playful things, or at least that you have to read them playfully in order to take pleasure in them. I end here because I am expected back at the table to finish having my luncheon.

Farewell, sir. You are the most obliging man in the world, and if I had more time, I would end this letter with nothing but magnificent compliments on the good things you have done for me.

This fragmentary letter is best understood as Villedieu's ironic letter to her publisher, although some critics read it as having been penned by the novel's protagonist, Sylvie.

PART 1

It is no small comfort to me, Madame, in the midst of all the evil stories by which my reputation is slandered everywhere, to see that Your Highness wishes me to justify myself.[1] I feel all the gratitude that I should, and so as not to be ungrateful, I will willingly obey your command to entertain you with a faithful account of my innocent mistakes.

Not that I have any hope of being able to blot out of most people's minds the unjust images that slander has painted of my conduct. This age does not allow me to flatter myself with such a thought. But, if I may use Your Highness's own terms, a time will come when people will no longer be so liable to judge others to be as criminal as themselves, for their behavior will no longer be so corrupt or so criminal. Then people will perhaps give more credence to what I am going to write about the innocence of my actions than to what my enemies may have said about them.

I will not hide anything, not even the most foolish adventures in which I have had some role, so that Your Highness can laugh at them while at the same time having compassion for me in other regards. Indeed it seems to me that even if you had not given me permission to amuse you, I should not fail to do so because without that, Madame, would I be worth the time you will spend reading a story as boring as that of my life?

I believe I am all the more obliged to do so because surely no one would have suggested to Your Highness that you honor me with your letters if it were not in the hope of a response of this kind; and that is why I beg you to read me with good humor.

In the first place, I have never known with certainty who I am. All I know is that I am not a person who has an ordinary destiny. My birth, my education, and my marriages have been the products of extraordinary adventures, and if I wished to attribute to myself the glory of some fictional heroine, there would be people, as perhaps there are already, who would try to confirm such an account, making my story even more obscure than it already is.

I was named Henriette-Sylvie by order of my mother herself, according to what I have been told: Henriette, undoubtedly for some reason known to my mother alone, and Sylvie, apparently because I was born at the edge of a wood that was called Sylves.[2] I got the name of Molière, which I have kept out of habit, from the people who raised me and whose name it was.[3]

---

1. Like her character, Villedieu was the subject of gossip and scandalmongering. The most notable contemporary account in this vein are the *Historiettes* of Tallement de Réaux.

2. From the Latin *silva* meaning "wood" or "forest." Sylvia and Sylvie are common names for heroines of pastoral novels.

3. Molière was a common surname in parts of southern France in the seventeenth century. It is

Beyond this, I am tall and of good appearance; I have brilliant dark eyes, wide and well shaped, a sign of a good deal of wit. People can judge whether I have any. My mouth is large when I laugh, but quite small when I do not; unfortunately for my poor mouth, I laugh all the time. I have pretty teeth and a good nose; my breast is like my complexion, which is to say admirable. I would add, Madame, at the risk of seeming presumptuous, that one sees few women such as I. But I will spend no more time painting my portrait; it's easy to imagine that from head to foot I am a complete beauty. Those who have seen as much of me as I allow to be seen will testify that I do not use makeup. Those who have not seen me may believe that I am merely joking with them; they will nonetheless be more pleased with the idea of a beautiful person than an ugly one, or they are people who have no taste.[4] I always tell Your Highness the truth.

I hope I may be excused for not naming the family from which I come, after what I have said. Perhaps after reading the story of my life and finding me worthy of them, my parents will add to the good that charitable persons have already done me and will one day reveal the full story of my birth, which may then be added to the number of my adventures. Should that happen, I promise something illustrious because I know my own heart, and I cannot believe that an ordinary man would be the father of a woman such as me.[5]

Whatever the case may be, people assure me that I was born in a little village on the seacoast, situated two or three leagues from Montpellier.[6] Four men and two women brought the woman who gave birth to me to this spot in July 1647. They landed in a launch, which they burned on the beach after landing. Why they did this I do not know. They headed for the first house they saw. It was the home of a poor woman who was nursing her child. My mother, whoever she is, was there for hardly more than an hour before she gave birth. The peasant woman's baby was sent to a wet nurse, and I was left to the peasant woman, along with a sum of money. When night fell, the visitors all departed. The peasant woman, who had spent the night elsewhere, returned the next day to find that they had carried my mother off in the shadow of night. If you ask where they went, I do not know at all. I wish I did for my

---

uncertain whether Villedieu wanted to allude to the famous comic writer Molière. Micheline Cuénin has speculated that by using this name Villedieu is expressing solidarity with the playwright, who like herself was the target of criticism from pious people. Villedieu, *Mémoires de la vie de Henriette-Sylvie de Molière*, ed. Micheline Cuénin (1722; facsimile, Tours: Editions de l'Université François Rabelais, 1977), viii, 7 (cited hereafter as MC).

4. In this passage, Sylvie is parodying the seventeenth-century tradition of literary portraits. Portraits of the heroines of novels were usually filled with unmixed praise.

5. Not knowing one's parents is a frequent trope in early modern novels, and as is the case here, characters often infer from their sentiments and actions that they must be of noble lineage.

6. Montpellier is in south central France. A league is roughly three miles.

own satisfaction more than anyone else's, although I should take Your Highness's satisfaction into consideration first and foremost.

For the first five years of my life, I was raised in this village, and no one claimed me. Around this time the Duke of Candale[7] decided to go hunting in this area. He came into my nurse's cottage to get out of a storm. My little mannerisms pleased him, and he thought he saw in me qualities that were not those of a peasant.[8] He asked who I was, and was told my story. He turned with a smile to a gentleman who was with him and said, "What a cruel thing to abandon a child like that. One day, nonetheless, this little girl will be perfectly beautiful, and I want to take charge of having her raised, to see if I am right about this." And in fact, from that moment on until his death, he never let me lack for anything necessary for my upbringing. Indeed he did so much that when people found out about it, some started saying that I owed him my life, and some of them meant this maliciously. Nonetheless, I have been fully assured that he is not my father and that it was a hunting expedition that by chance brought him to the little village, where the storm made him seek out my nurse's house from among all the others, although this house was not the closest, given the direction from which he came. I will not claim otherwise, and I will not say that I am a relative of his heirs if they do not wish it. But enough on this subject.

The first thing this generous duke did was to take me from the peasant woman and give me to someone who could raise me with more care. At Pézenas there was a financier whose wife was one of the duke's friends, and this man owed the duke all his good fortune.[9] This couple had a daughter my age, who was being cared for at one of their tenant farms. This child was so sick that the doctors had given up on her, and every day news of her death was expected. It was not difficult to substitute me for her when she died and to make people believe that, by having her cared for by someone else, good remedies had cured her. (Consider, Madame, how Fortune pushed me toward adventures.) The exchange was skillfully made, and the financier did everything very well. In this way, I became the younger sister of his son, and

---

7. Louis de Noraget, Duke of Candale, was well known as a gallant member of the court. His name was often used in gallant tales and scandal chronicles in seventeenth-century France (MC 11).

8. In the early modern period, it was believed that noble birth and noble character went hand in hand. It is thus a common trope that, when a character is disguised as a member of a lower class, or has been mistakenly considered to be a member of a lower class, his or her intrinsically superior nature will be revealed by appearance or behavior, or both.

9. Pézenas is a town on the river Hérault in the province of Languedoc, about twenty miles from Sète and the Mediterranean coast. A financier was a financial officer who was part of the royal bureaucracy.

the considerable sum that the duke gave the financier at that time inspired in him all the tenderness required to pretend a fatherly affection for me.

At the risk of boring your Highness, I will begin my story with the things that made my childhood as surprising as the rest of my life. I had an innate charm that made it plausible that this gentleman was my father—I was intelligent, vain, and brave, and my ability with languages was so good that I was able to learn them with great ease from the financier's son's tutors. Even German! I was also a passionate hunter, and from the time I was ten years old, I despised all girlish amusements, to an extent rarely seen, and preferred riding horses, shooting pistols, and other similar activities. It is not impossible that such inclinations were the cause of some rather charming little adventures, if I cared to recall them. However, my plan is to talk only of those matters of which the wider public is aware, and at that time only unimportant people witnessed my doings.

I will only say that I knew no father or mother other than the people to whom I was given, and that I was not enlightened until quite late, by a rather unusual adventure.

The wife of the financier, Madame de Molière, was an attractive woman and had a good deal of wit. The Marquis de Birague was a man of noble lineage, gifted with many good qualities. In a word (though I could not then consider him in the same way because he was a married man), he is such that I would be very happy to be served by such a gentleman, now that he is a widower. This gallant man, I say, often visited Madame de Molière. At a time when the two believed her husband to be away taking care of responsibilities, Monsieur de Molière found them asleep next to each other in a small wood at one of his houses. I don't know how the lady cleared herself, but a few days later I realized that her husband had decided to avenge himself and that, in his heart of hearts, he had decided to make me a part of his vengeance. The details of how he came to make me understand this would be boring. I was playful and full of caresses for those I thought I was related to, although I was the most standoffish of little girls for everyone else. Thus, when Monsieur de Molière showed me affection, I responded in kind. After this had gone on for some time, I ended up pleasing him so much by these caresses, which I gave in all innocence, that, without realizing it, I made him the most amorous of men, and he decided to pursue the matter further.

He took me hunting; that was my passion.[10] Having skillfully separated me from his wife and the Marquis de Birague, who perhaps were also looking

10. It was not uncommon for women to participate in hunts during the early modern period, although they often did not participate in the kill. Sylvie's passion for hunting and her willingness to defend herself are not, however, stereotypical female behavior at this time.

for the opportunity to go off on their own, he managed things so well that we found ourselves alone deep in the forest. The spot was inviting, perfect for two people of like mind. The trees formed a sort of bower; a spring gurgled nearby. In a word, Madame, Monsieur de Molière was clever, and the place was not badly chosen for the plan he had in mind. I dismounted at his request and, seeing him stretch out to rest, I did likewise next to him, without any suspicion of what was about to happen to me. My so-called father then came a bit nearer and, embracing me tenderly, began to reveal a secret to me that I would never have imagined. He told me the story of my birth. Then he detailed all that I owed him because of his willingness to continue passing as my father, by which I was assured of inheriting his whole estate (which had been freed up by the recent death of his son). He said many other things to commend his love to me, and his constant refrain was that I should respond to his passion in order to avoid the vice of ingratitude. He said that he would always love me with the greatest secrecy and that our relationship would not prevent him from soon finding me a suitable husband.

Your Highness can judge how surprised and confused I was on learning these things. I was in an even more difficult situation because, after having finished his speech, this man began to go beyond his usual gestures of affection, and my resistance only inflamed him more. He threw himself at my feet and did a thousand extravagant things. Although I told him that only the remnants of respect and tenderness that habit had left in my heart prevented me from avenging his insolent behavior, he did not stop and indeed was on the point of using force. It was then that I became furious. I tore myself from his arms, ran to my horse, took a pistol from the saddle, and threatened to kill him if he did not leave me alone. He did not obey. On the contrary, his advances turned into rage. I saw him coming at me like a satyr,[11] swearing that he would satisfy his desire. I fired the pistol, wounding him with two bullets in the body. Here, Madame, is the first example of my cruelties.

This was, however, a very awkward situation for a girl my age, to find myself alone in the woods, having shot a man down, needing to escape, and not remembering the path we had taken to get there. I was thus so frightened that I almost fell to the ground like that unlucky man. But this agitation did not last, and necessity called back my reason. I got back onto my horse. The wounded man, more touched with my predicament than I was with his, told me to go to the left, and I set my horse running along this path and was soon far away. But I was about to encounter Monsieur de Birague and Madame de Molière, who had been off somewhere else conversing with each other with-

---

11. A satyr is a part-human, part-beast companion of Bacchus and is associated with lust.

out almost killing each other as the financier and I had done. They were coming to join us, guided by the noise of the shots. Good Lord! How afflicted I was when to my present predicament was added the danger posed by a wild boar fleeing the hunt, which dashed across the path, almost running into my horse. As I recall, despite my surprise, I did not fail to seize the pistol, which I still had, as though to shoot this animal, and I must add in passing that it is in such a circumstance that I sometimes recognize the courageous lineage from which I might well come.[12]

Monsieur de Birague, who saw what I had done from a distance and who thought I was riding at full speed in order to catch up with the boar, cried out against my bravado. He galloped up to me and asked me if Monsieur de Molière was out of his mind to expose me to such danger. But since he was so far from imagining what had really happened, and since I had no time to lose, I told him, without taking the time to explain anything, that I knew him to be a good gentleman, and that I had important secrets to tell him. I said that while I was talking to him, he should tell Madame de Molière to go find her husband, who was a little farther in the wood and seriously wounded. I had hardly finished these words when she joined us. When she heard what I said, she immediately had two of the forest keepers take her to her husband.[13] I took this occasion to tell my gentleman that I was the one who had fired the shot, and I begged him to take me someplace where I would be safe. His surprise and the fact that he believed the wounded man to be my father caused him to reproach me, showing how astonished he was. But since I wanted to avoid anything that was useless to my cause, I replied with sadness: "He is not my father, and this is not the place to explain this mystery to you. If you plan to help me, put me in some place where I will be safe," I said to him again, "and I will answer all the questions you want to ask." As I was saying this he saw his man, who came riding up behind him at a gallop. He ordered the man to take me to his wife at the chateau of Sersac. He then followed his mistress.

She had arrived at the fatal spot. I don't know whether what people today say is true, that a woman can have a lover and still love her husband just as much, but I have been told that no one has ever seen grief to compare with that lady's, when she saw her husband lying on the ground in his own blood. She leaned over to embrace him, and it was almost impossible to separate her from him. The tendency to slander, which does not spare even the holiest of

---

12. Heroes in early modern novels often prove their prowess by confronting an enraged wild boar. Here, Sylvie passes this test of male heroism.

13. Forest keepers were employed by noble or royal houses to maintain their lands, in particular to keep them filled with game for hunting and to keep poachers out.

actions, led people to doubt her extreme love and to suppose that she was clinging to him in order to impede others from stopping his bleeding, for he had already lost a lot of blood and perhaps would not survive. But whatever persecution this lady has caused me to suffer, and although her actions could indeed have caused her husband's death, I want to do her the justice of believing that she acted in good faith.

With a great deal of difficulty, the injured man was picked up and carried to the closest village in order to put some initial dressings on his wound. Then they tried a number of times to get him to name the person who had wounded him, but it was in vain—he always answered that it was three masked men who had wanted to kidnap me. Even Monsieur de Birague, to whom I had already told the essence of the story and who hoped to learn more about it, could never get anything else out of him. The upshot was that they gave up on trying to make him talk and concentrated on getting him into town.

However, Madame, the unfortunate man's discretion, whether it was the effect of shame or of some remaining love for me, would have saved me in the eyes of all those to whom I had confessed nothing, if I had had the courage to appear after what I had done. The Marquis of Birague came and told me that everyone thought my flight was caused by my fear of my alleged kidnapers and that he believed this too. His hypothesis was that I could have wounded the financier when trying to fire on the kidnapers. However, another misfortune occurred, which let the truth out, and I will recount this by Your Highness's order.

I had been placed in the care of the Marquise de Birague at the chateau of Sersac. The marquis came to see me there after having taken the time to calm Madame de Molière. I will admit to you that I was touched by the discretion the wounded man had shown, and although I did not repent at all of having saved my honor at the price of his life, I could not help shedding a few tears at having been forced to this extremity. I lamented the situation in which I found myself, and then I recounted in detail what the financier had done—which very much surprised the marquis. Like me and everyone else, he had believed that I was this man's daughter. Madame de Molière had never entrusted him with this secret, although she often entrusted him with herself.

As for the rest, the novelty of my adventure won the gentleman over entirely, and he greatly praised my action, instead of criticizing me for it, and promised me a hundred times that he would serve me. In sum, Madame, he talked to me as would a man who found me beautiful and who was beginning to understand that I was not the daughter of his mistress. I say this without criticizing him.

I understood all this at the first moment, but the necessity of finding someone to help me made me reluctant to commit a second murder to nip in the bud the hopes he had perhaps conceived, which were not to my advantage. Far from that, I thanked him for his generosity and was as agreeable to him as I could honorably be. I would dare to say that this was the only situation that could ever have made me listen to a declaration of love without becoming angry, so much was I a mortal enemy of that passion.

I stayed at his chateau for two days, learning news from town only by what information he sent me through one of his gentlemen. Until that moment there was no danger for me; indeed the belief that I had fallen into the hands of the masked men increased the mourning in the Molière household. But things changed the next day when, before dying, fever made the unhappy man speak in his sleep. He had let almost everything out and, thinking that his wife was me, for whom he asked continually, he criticized her for the pistol shot. Thanks to some other partially coherent things he said, people understood that he was speaking of me. The family was totally alarmed, and they stopped pitying me and started blaming me. Their blame was all the more violent because the son, whose sister they thought I was, had died, as I already said, and they saw me as the only obstacle preventing them from inheriting a considerable fortune. For several reasons, including a fondness for me in memory of the duke,[14] whom she had not hated, Madame de Molière herself thought that decency no longer permitted her to let me pass for her daughter. And perhaps, from another point of view, she thought that as a widow she would have an easier time remarrying if people knew she had no children.[15] In sum, she had already made up her mind to abandon me, and there was nothing easier than ruining my reputation.

Monsieur de Candale[16] had been dead since 1657, and the gallant duke, who undoubtedly liked to keep his generous actions secret, had not said anything of me to anyone other than the financier and his wife, for fear, I believe, that people might discover his charity in treating me as though he were my father. In any case my good fortune had not yet abandoned me. Monsieur de Birague, who wanted me to feel obligated to him, helped me greatly in this matter for several months, and in another matter which happened a bit later; thus there was enough time for the same accident of fate as had once brought the Duke of Candale to the hut of my nurse to bring now out of the depths of

14. Sylvie is alluding to the Duke of Candale, who placed her in the Molières's care, and here implies that perhaps he had been Madame de Molière's lover at some earlier time.

15. If she had no children, her entire estate would pass to any children she had in a second marriage.

16. The duke's father.

Flanders to France a powerful woman to take care of me as though she were my mother.

When suspicion first fell on me, things were going very badly. But the marquis prevented the storm from forming. He suggested to Madame de Molière that it would be a thousand times more to her advantage, for reasons of her own self-interest and honor, to protect me rather than to destroy me. Even if these reasons were not very good, the notable charms of the marquis's person persuaded the beautiful widow. Thus, after a few more days, and some invented incidents to explain both my absence and my return, Monsieur de Birague came to announce to me that I could leave the chateau of Sersac, which I did, going to hide myself in a convent about a league from there.[17]

He found a thousand excuses to come and visit me there frequently, without alerting the suspicions of his beloved widow. The story of all this would not be disagreeable if I told it. As I already said, he put great stock in having me feel more and more obligated to him as time went by. He lost no chance to tell me that the only reason he continued to profess love to Madame de Molière was in order to be able to use her affection to prevent all the things that I had to fear and thus merit my love. He even wrote me very amusing letters on this subject when he couldn't find a pretext to visit me. I had struck up a close friendship with the abbess of this convent, and she shared with me the most pleasant amusement in the world in reading these letters, especially when he wrote that the sadness that he felt at my indifference had drawn from the widow many a tender caress, since she thought his sadness was due to an increase in his love for her. But it is time to move on and say only that I was responsible for my own perdition because I was weak enough to agree to the playful abbess's idea that I should write a letter in response. I don't know how it happened, but my letter fell into the hands of the beautiful widow. In reading it, she understood that she had consoled a sadness of which she had not been the cause. This knowledge made her furious, and her jealousy dictated my destruction. She decided to punish her unfaithful lover by stirring up my story, which she had helped quiet down. He tried unsuccessfully to find reasons to appease her and to get the idea that he loved me out of her head. She was strong enough to hide her displeasure until she was able to get her hands on his answer—which was even worse than my letter had been. In it he mocked her savagely and treated her as an amusing dupe. All her love turned into an extremely impatient desire to avenge her-

17. Convents played a number of different and often contradictory roles in the early modern period. They were at times places of refuge for women and at times places used to imprison them. Young women were often put in convents to be raised until their families wanted them to marry. Adult women who were not nuns often stayed in convents for various periods of time.

self. To manage this she began to make public the story of my birth and to let it be known that I was not her daughter or her husband's. The novelty of the story meant that the news traveled quickly through the town, and her husband's relatives soon got together to discuss the best ways to ruin me. All Monsieur de Birague could do for me in the middle of all this tumult was to jump on his horse and carry me off before they had had time to think of imprisoning me. He hid me only half a league from the convent, in a fortified house that belonged to the Countess of Englesac, sister of my friend the abbess.

Madame d'Englesac was a widow of great virtue and very devout, although she liked to live luxuriously and to enjoy all sorts of harmless pleasures with her friends. At that time two of her daughters were living with her, as well as a son, who was the most accomplished young gentleman in the kingdom. Beautiful eyes, a lovely mouth, a noble air, tall, erect, majestic, graceful in all his actions, a gallant spirit, the soul of a prince and the courage of a hero are the smallest praises that I can give to this gentleman. Forgive me, Your Highness; he was dear enough to me that I could become even more carried away. He is the person who will play the greatest role in what I will talk about in the rest of this tale.

In this household I received all kinds of help and good treatment during the most extreme persecution by my enemies, and everyone in this family made it a point of honor to protect me in my extraordinary disgrace, which they considered to be a heroic action rather than a cowardly murder, as Madame de Molière called it everywhere. And finally, thanks to the court being then in Provence, they were able to obtain my pardon from the king[18] along with several benefits useful against my enemies.

Fortune, however, had no intention of leaving me without problems for very long, wanting once again to have the pleasure of raising me up from my difficulties. Birague, who had really set his mind on me, was a friend of Madame d'Englesac's son. He talked to him so often about me, and about how wonderful it would be to be loved by me, that the young cavalier believed him and began to look at me for himself. His eyes spoke to me, and I was not insensitive to them; I admit this without shame since I shall be justified in this by what happens later. Birague saw what was going on and became jealous—so jealous that there were no limits to his desire to punish me for preferring this other gentleman. I excuse him for this; a lover who loses is not obliged to act any more civilly than he did. He surreptitiously let the count-

18. The king is Louis XIV. He and his court often traveled to various parts of the kingdom for political reasons.

ess know about her son's love and the dangerous consequences it could have.[19] The lady, who was ambitious, and rightly so since their family was one of the richest and most noble in the kingdom, wasted no time in giving her orders. She called me into her chambers one day to talk with me, and after chiding me very gently she told me she thought I was too well-behaved to ever commit the slightest fault, and also too grateful to be willing to profit from the foolish love of her son. She asked me to give him no hope so that he would give up on the plans she knew he had.

"Don't be vexed if I speak to you frankly," she said, seeing that her words had made me blush. "I love you infinitely, and I would be inconsolable if, because I had failed to warn you, you became enmeshed in something that would cause me to send you away from me and make me unhappy with you."

A secret sorrow, which followed my blushes, made me keep my eyes lowered until she had finished speaking. And although I foresaw that I would have great difficulty in doing all she asked, I nonetheless promised her that I would so that she would not send me away. My obeying her caused great sorrow to the cavalier, who could not guess the cause of the change in my behavior. A hundred times he wanted to ask me what it was, but I was always so closely watched either by Birague or by his mother that I never dared to speak to him about it, however much I wanted to. He took this for disdain and was in such despair about it that he became dangerously sick.

It is at this point, Madame, that I would willingly dispense with the rule I have made for myself (to say many things in few words), so that I could develop at some length the story of this love, which is still dear to my memory. But I fear that I might be offering to Your Highness something that, while intended to give you pleasure, can give pleasure only to me because I am still touched by it. How out of her senses is a woman who loves! Or how unhappy is she when she is both virtuous and in love! How I suffered during those few days when my beloved was in his bed, and I was not allowed to visit him! How he suffered not to see me! I think it was only his vexation at not seeing me that cured him because of his desire to reproach me with my hard-heartedness as soon as possible. I can remember the very words he said to me one day out of this vexation, which seemed to him to be perfectly well justified. Madame d'Englesac was busy receiving the Duke of Villars and the Bishop of Agde, who had both come to visit her at the same time. The Chevalier des Essars, a gentleman of merit and the handsomest of his region, had accompanied them. As I have already said, the Count of Englesac had two sisters; the chevalier was

19. The young Englesac's love could make him resist whatever marriage plans his mother might have for him. At this time, marriage was viewed as an alliance between families and fortunes rather than as a mode of finding personal satisfaction.

in love with the older one. I think that the only motive for the Duke of Villars's visit was to find a way to make the marriage possible, and I don't know what prevented this from happening. But in any case, while the mother was talking with him in one room, the bishop had induced the others to go into the gallery, where everyone sat down on long benches. My young count came and sat next to me, and after giving a great sigh because I would not look at him (I did not dare to because the youngest of his sisters was on the other side and was playfully leaning against my shoulder), he said to me very quietly but in a vexed tone, "Cruel one, you want me to die, I can easily see that, and it's easy to understand that I would have pleased you if I had succeeded in dying from my malady during these last few days. But I will perhaps live long enough to reproach you with your inconstancy more than you might wish."

I didn't answer him at all. On the contrary, for fear that his sister might hear what he was saying, I turned my shoulder to him and pretended to joke with her while he was talking, which irritated him more and more. He continued to reproach me, so much that I had a very hard time keeping my tears from showing and refraining from answering. I put my fan in front of my face, and taking advantage of a moment when the Chevalier des Essars got the young Mademoiselle d'Englesac to turn towards him, I said to my beloved, while glancing at him from the side, "Be quiet and don't afflict me any more; I do what I do because I am forced and constrained to, and I am the most unhappy young woman in the world. I wish I had never seen you." Thereupon, I got up and took his sister along with me to end this conversation that could have been damaging to us.

It would be difficult to describe the confusion in which this amorous gentleman found himself after I gave this answer. He knew perfectly well that I was sincere and that I would have to have very important reasons for doing what I did if I had spoken to him thus. But I had not told him enough to satisfy him. A conversation was necessary to make things clearer. What didn't he do to make it possible?

Well, Madame, what he did is incredible, but worthy of me, who was destined to see and to cause extraordinary things. Not seeing any other way to get rid of all those who seemed to be paid to annoy me other than by obliging them to fear something worse than our conversations, he set fire to the chateau.

By reading this story, Madame d'Englesac will perhaps be surprised to learn the cause of this accident, something that she would never have known otherwise. But in the end such was her son's passion for me; and she spoke more truly than she realized when, in accusing me of having brought trouble into the house, she said that I had "brought fire" into it.

I have never been more surprised than when I saw my beloved, very agitated, enter my chambers and throw himself at my feet, while the others all ran out in little more than their nightclothes, for it was nighttime. As he stopped me from following them, he confessed that he had purposely caused this disorder.

"Fear nothing," he said to me. "There is a trench between us and the fire. You can remain safely in this room. Don't refuse to listen to me now—I have sacrificed so much for a chance to talk to you."

I did as he wished and listened to him as I finished dressing, having no doubt that a man who would burn a house for the purpose must have a great need of talking to me. I explained to him the reasons behind my coldness and my feigned disdain. I told him of the things his mother had said and the promises I felt obliged to make to her, for fear that she would separate us. This clarification did him all the good in the world. Finally, Madame, after we had consulted briefly on what means we would use in the future to fool those who watched us, I saw my man so happy that he was far from regretting having burned such a beautiful building.

The fire, however, had spread alarm in all the neighboring villages. The Marquis of Birague, who was only a league and a half away, was far from the last to realize that it was our chateau that was burning. He had ten horses saddled and came there in haste. Not finding me with the other women, who had retreated to the grounds, he ran in every direction to get news of me. He even took it upon himself to come up to my room, so that he almost surprised the Count of Englesac there. Since the marquis (in whose debt I really was at that time) was calling out to me everywhere with a great deal of noise, the count had plenty of time to hide. This worked so well that I got out of the situation by pretending to have fainted, which gave me an excuse for remaining in the house. I had to endure a few kisses the marquis gave me in exchange for the trouble he took in carrying me out of there in his arms, kisses that I pretended to suffer without regaining consciousness until we were some distance from my room.

From that time on the Count of Englesac and I lived very discreetly, and in order to better hide our love, we pretended to be mortal enemies. We managed this pretense well enough, and we provided for it the most plausible reasons we could. Birague was so happy about this hatred that he was the first to be fooled by it. Englesac's mother was so taken in that she even reproached her son for it and sought to console me with a thousand new proofs of her friendship and her protection. In sum, we would have been happy if we had limited ourselves to this precaution. But a man of quality from the area fell in love with me during a visit he made to Madame d'Englesac. The count wanted me to pretend that I was agreeable to his affections, and this was too clever by half. The man really fell in love with me and wrote to me often. The count, with the imprudence of a young man, decided to write an answer for me. Looking for amusement, he made me speak somewhat amorously in the answer. The rival, being indiscreet, as almost all men are when they think they are favored by a lady, and even when they think they are not, showed this answer to a friend, who told another about it, who told Birague, who believed I had written the response. He came to me and complained greatly, and I in turn complained to the count, seeing the wrong this did me. The count recognized his error and thought he could make up for it with an even greater one: he admitted that he was the author of the letters and that he had written them to make fun of his rival. In conclusion, a great misfortune came from these follies.

The Chevalier des Essars gave a ball for the eldest daughter of the Countess of Englesac, and a distinguished group attended, people whom the nearness of the court had drawn to the home of the Marquise d'Ampus. Both of the rivals were there, and I don't know how, but they managed to quarrel and agreed to a duel the next day near Villeneuve. The combat was bloody; two of the seconds were killed, and the count's adversary was badly injured. This produced two very negative effects. The first was that since the king had renewed his edicts against duels, there was no safety for my poor beloved in France.[20] The other was that, from the explanations of the causes of this duel, the Lady Englesac realized that the hatred between her son and myself was nothing but a show we had concocted together.

Nothing worse could have happened to me. Since by my disobedience I was the apparent cause of all this disorder, she had me shut up in a cloister the very next day, and she forbade me to have any contact with anyone until I agreed to take religious orders. What I found even more upsetting about this was that it wasn't even the same convent where her sister was the abbess and where I could at least have hoped for some company. It was a convent— good God what a convent!—that was more like a horrible prison than anything else. I spent two months there while my dear Count of Englesac fled through Piedmont,[21] where the majority of ladies, who spared no effort to make him love them, justified the tender inclination I had for him.

At the end of these two months, the king came to Avignon on his way back from Marseilles and spent several days there because of the citadel of

---

20. Both the church and the monarchy opposed duels. Royal edicts banned the practice. Nobles, however, were frequently pardoned for participating in duels and for killing their adversaries.

21. Piedmont is a region in northwestern Italy and includes the city of Turin.

Orange, which he did not want to see fortified in the middle of his kingdom.[22] This meant that all the gallant men of the court spread out through
the area, and that the inhabitants of the convents found their parlors inun-
dated with a large share of these courtiers.[23] This was a period of universal
enjoyment for our little religious community; the women were all pleased to
admire the gallantry of so many charming cavaliers and to honor their king
by honoring these gentlemen. Hence I was not so severely restricted and, although Madame d'Englesac had not consented to it, I was sometimes allowed
to come into the parlor, so that I would have no grounds for criticizing the
others for being there.

I will always remember this stay of the court in Avignon. It gave so much
joy to the youngest of these poor nuns that, every time they heard that the
governor of Orange was going to surrender as a compromise, they cursed the
man's cowardess a thousand times and thought him worthy of the worst tor-
tures because he did not—by courageous resistence—make the king stay in
Avignon for an entire year.

Birague, who had not forgotten me, used this occasion to continue to offer me his services. A little later, thanks to a gentleman to whom the Count of
Englesac had entrusted letters for me, I received assurances that I was still
loved. On that very same day, one of the nuns, as though to add another
cause for joy, predicted that Love would soon free me from captivity. It is true
that I took a long time to figure out how this could happen, since it seemed to
me I was so well guarded that, unless my beloved came and set fire to the
cloister as he had done to his chateau, it would not be easy to escape without
notice. It was possible to get over the wall of the little garden, but the mother
superior always kept the garden keys, and it was impossible to go in there
without her permission. This is what I told the nun who had made the prediction, but she did not say anything except that things would happen as she
had said if only I would be patient.

Three days later, Monsieur de Lorraine, for whom a treaty had been
made at Saint-Jean-de-Luz, came to join the king in Avignon.[24] This prince
was always more gallant than unfortunate and adored women's beauty
whether behind a veil or not. After making his first round of visits, he came to
join the ranks of the suitors in our parlor. The now-deceased Duke of Guise

22. Louis XIV went to Marseilles on March 9, 1660, to complete the surrender of the city. He
went to Avignon on March 24 and remained there until April 1 (MC 39).

23. Convents had parlors in which, under varying degrees of restriction, the nuns and other
women housed there could receive visitors. The restrictions depended on the order and on the
particular convent.

24. The Treaty of the Pyrenees restored his former states to Charles IV, Duke of Lorraine (MC 40).

followed him there and paid more attention to me than to any of the others, which made me think that the prediction was talking about him and that it would be by this means that I would get my freedom. For, Madame, from the first day on, he did not fail to pay court to me in the most agreeable way imaginable and to give me hope of my freedom and of a great fortune, if I would be so good as to hear his suit. I even believed that I saw the first consequence of his offers soon afterwards, in the care he took to talk to the queen mother[25] about my situation. But the Countess of Englesac, who had found out about things thanks to her spies, had already influenced this good princess. She had painted for her an evil picture of my conduct, accusing me of causing all her son's problems. The Marquise des Essars and even the Marquise d'Ampus had added to this, saying that the best thing to do was to leave me shut up. All this was enough to set the queen herself against me. Thus the Duke of Guise obtained nothing; Her Majesty refused him kindly, saying that he was too gallant an advocate and that it would not be right to put me in the position of being so in his debt. The duke tried again the next day, with the help of Monsieur de Lorraine and a princess who, in order to be obliging, offered to be responsible for me, but the queen did not want to change her mind. At this point a charitable group advocating my case formed itself, saying that if I wished to leave the convent, it would have to be to marry the old Cabrières who had made an offer to Madame d'Englesac to marry me.

The Duke of Guise chose to be the bearer of this news, foreseeing that if I heard it from anyone other than him, my reaction would make useless all that he had done for me. And in truth, he was right about that, for I had a very hard time hearing it even from him. When he—in all seriousness—tried to make me understand what an advantage it was for a beautiful woman to have a husband whom she didn't have to love, my fun-loving temperament made me laugh, even though I saw all my hopes for his negotiations go up in smoke. Still laughing, I answered that he must be joking and that I would prefer to hear him make his own suit rather than make the case for the elderly husband he offered me. He began to laugh, too, finding in my foolishness a charm that made him even more attracted to me. The matter remained thus, and the nun's prediction did not come true by this means.

This nun, to whom I confided everything that happened, saw clearly the erroneous impression her words had given me. She had not meant, when she had said that love would free me, that it would be the love of this prince. But, being prudent, she thought it wiser not to reveal anything more specific to

---

25. Anne of Austria, wife of Louis XIII and mother of Louis XIV.

me until everything had been put in place to make her prediction come true. Only when she thought it was time did she reveal things to me.

The moments of freedom that the nuns had allowed themselves to take in the parlor since the king's entrance into the city were, as I have already said, contrary to the rules of the order—an extraordinary gesture intended to honor this monarch. During one of these moments Fouquet, a very witty young gentleman, made friends with the nun who had made the prediction. She was the daughter of the deceased Baron of Fontaine, who had followed the principle of the majority of the nobility and sacrificed his daughter to the convent in order to make his son richer.[26] This victim had protested many times against her vows; her brother had died in the interim, and it enraged her to see the fortune she could have inherited pass into the hands of two aunts. Fouquet, as I said, found her charming, supported her in her resentment against the cruelty of her situation, and had promised to serve her. Their love became more intense from hour to hour because the bars of a convent stood in its way, and Birague fanned the flames, since this affair was not going on without his knowledge. Finally the gentleman decided to carry the lady off. The arrangements were made, the key to the garden stolen and a copy made, and a *tourière*[27] brought into the plot, for nothing is impossible for a woman in love when she wants to escape from a convent and hopes to obtain release from her religious vows. That evening the nun told me the whole story and asked if I, too, would like Fouquet to carry me off, away from those who persecuted me in the same manner. At first I was taken aback by this proposal; it seemed to me that there was something questionable about this conduct. However, when I had reflected on my situation, which might last a long time if I did not seize this chance to free myself, I agreed to go into the garden with her at midnight. We managed to do so quite subtly, and we had been waiting only a few minutes when we heard Fouquet's signal. After we responded, he began to climb over the wall and down along a trellis of the espalier, which was not very strong and made noise as it broke. I was seized with fear, and I must say I was ten times as afraid as the nun, although I ran less of a risk. Fouquet saw this and reassured me. To gain time, he began to help his beautiful veiled lady escape.

I don't know if I will be able to recount to Your Highness the amusing

---

26. In order to consolidate inheritances, families married off their eldest sons, while younger brothers and sisters were often put into religious orders.

27. The *tourière* was the nun charged with relations between the convent and the external world, or a servant who did errands in the outside world and received visitors to the convent. In novels of the early modern period these nuns or servants are often key figures in plots involving lovers separated by convent walls. There is no English equivalent of this word.

way he managed to get us up on the wall. Since having us use the already broken trellis would have been too dangerous, he bent over, bracing his two hands on the wall, and had us climb, one after the other, onto his back. When he had us on his back, he straightened up little by little, and we stood on his shoulders. While we held ourselves in this position thanks to some pieces of iron affixed to the wall to hold the trellis, he climbed on a big rock that was at his feet. After this we stood on his head, and from there we could sit on the top of the wall, from which someone (presumably a servant), who did not have so high to reach from the other side because the ground was higher there, helped us down onto horseback. He then gave us hats and great capes that covered all of our skirts, and in this garb we cheerfully rode out of the town, the gates of which were no longer closed after the arrival of the king.[28]

We went along for some distance without my being able to see where I was being taken, and I thought many things, some pleasant, some disturbing, as I considered the consequences that this kidnaping could have. Birague, whom I knew to be clever at intrigue, was not the least of my worries. When Fouquet and his pretty companion began to talk maliciously about him to me, I told them, "You will see that he will make it a point to find out where we are, and he will ruin all our plans." "Why, why?" asked the nun. "I think Monsieur de Birague a more gallant man than you say, and I would be perfectly willing to trust him." Fouquet, who betrayed me as she did, added that in fact Birague was an honorable cavalier, more suited to serving a lady than displeasing her. "Yes," I replied, "if his own self-interest were not so involved, and if he did not want to be recompensed for the most minor obligations one might have to him. I have never seen a more tiresome man or one more insistent on what he wanted than this one."

And thus we continued on our journey. They said a thousand good things about this gentleman, and I made no secret of how he displeased me, which made them laugh and laugh as they looked toward their serving man, who pretended to be asleep. You can judge, Madame, if they were not right to be amused, since this serving man was Monsieur de Birague himself, who had secretly made an agreement with Fouquet and who was taking me to one of his houses. I think I will never forgive them for this deceit. When we arrived, the nun, who was less fearful of men than I was, cried out, "Noble Valet, get down from your horse and help this lovely woman get off her horse." I made a great cry, which could be heard from some distance, when I recognized the face of Birague, and they had a terrible time getting me to

28. In the seventeenth century towns were still customarily surrounded by walls with gates that were closed at night.

calm down. "What!" said this poor gentleman, who was saddened by my reaction. "In good faith, would you prefer still to be in the convent, exposed to all the vengeance that Madame d'Englesac might be capable of exercising against you, rather than to know that you have me to thank for your freedom?" Fouquet and his lady helped him to persuade me to be a little less frightened and not to resent him so much. Then we all thought about what measures we needed to take to prevent ourselves from suffering ill consequences from this escapade. The nun and I went to bed, and the two gentleman thought it prudent to return to Avignon before dawn in order to show themselves there the next day and to hear the news of the town. This is what they did, returning to the town by another gate.

Daylight had barely come when the convent became alarmed and the news began to spread. One of the nun's aunts, who was at court at the time, made great complaints against the nuns, whom she accused of having agreed to her niece's escape. Madame d'Englesac, out of concern for her son (whose pardon she still hoped for) and for fear that I would go and marry him outside of France, made even louder complaints and asked the queen mother for justice. His Majesty suspected the Duke of Guise of having been part of the plot and was cross with him all day long. The duke, who was innocent of this intrigue, protested that he had nothing to do with it and, wanting to end the king's suspicions, dispatched people to follow us, resulting in a very difficult situation for us. There was no other solution than to let things calm down with time and to wait until the king had taken Orange. While we waited, we amused ourselves as best we could in Birague's house.

People do not believe that these two gentlemen were as good as Capuchin monks, preferring to believe that they availed themselves of the opportunity that Fortune had given them, but I will do them this justice: never did two men show more respect or modesty. In the state in which I found myself, and timid as I was, I did not expect such behavior; therefore I began to have more respect for the Marquis of Birague than I had had before. People will judge this fairly, if they wish.

We didn't stay in this house very long, however, because in a few days the king obtained everything he wanted, and, having set some prisoners to work tearing down the citadel in Orange, he traveled across all of Languedoc, en route to the Isle of Pheasants, where the Spanish infanta was due to arrive.[29] Fouquet, who lacked neither a devious mind nor friends, thought it

29. Languedoc is a French province on the Mediterranean coast, between Provence and Roussillon. The Isle of the Pheasants is located in the Bidassoa, a small river in the Basque region of Spain. It was there that the Treaty (or Peace) of the Pyrenees was signed in November 1659, whereby Spain ceded to France the province of Roussillon and part of Cerdagne (a region in the

would be a good idea to make use of the confusion occasioned by the passing of the small army of people who normally follow the court to allow us to get farther away from this dangerous area without arousing suspicion. He put us on baggage carts and disguised us as the wives of merchants following the court. Word was given that the convoy should turn right on the other side of Carcassonne, but Fouquet took us to Toulouse instead, under the pretense of going there to provide provisions for Monsieur, the king's only brother.[30]

The Présidente[31] of —— (I don't remember her name), a good elderly widow who was a cousin of the nun and who had never approved of the family's forcing her cousin to take vows, took us into her house. Taking up her relative's case, she began to promote her cause in the parlement,[32] from whom she requested protection and freedom for her niece so that she could request the dissolution of her vows. With time and much effort she succeeded. Fouquet, who had himself gone to so much trouble, was not the one who got the fruits of his labors, however. But I will not say any more about the circumstances of this story, which no longer has any elements in common with my own.

Having arrived at the *présidente's* home, I scarcely thought myself to be safer there than in Birague's house. On the contrary, Reputation, that monster that grows bigger the farther it travels, had carried news of my affairs to Toulouse and depicted me in an even worse light than the Marquise d'Ampus and the Countess of Englesac had used to ruin me in the queen mother's eyes. Without knowing who I was, people every day told me stories, or rather fables, about my life, and I was quite chagrined. Beyond this the *présidente* seemed to suspect something. Although I was passed off as a serving woman to the nun, her cousin, she was unhappy at my presence in her house. The situation only worsened when her cousin tried to help me out by telling her the true story. Birague's attentions to me displeased her, and the suspicions that Birague's wife, the marquise, now made public only aggravated things. The Countess of Englesac's efforts to find me were the last straw. The poor old woman feared that people would come to ask the nun about me, especially as

---

eastern Pyrenees) in southern France as well as some fortresses in Flanders and Artois, and whereby it was agreed that Louis XIV would marry the Infanta Maria Teresa, daughter of Philip IV of Spain. They were married in June 1660.

30. The oldest brother of the king was given the title "Monsieur," and his wife, the title "Madame." Here "Monsieur" refers to Philippe, Duke of Orleans.

31. A president was a magistrate who presided over a parlement or similar body; his wife had the title of *présidente*. There is no English equivalent for this word.

32. In France, a parlement was a body of judges to which one could appeal a decision of a lower court. Parlements also registered and sometimes commented on royal edicts. The French spelling is retained to distinguish this body from the English concept of parliament.

she no longer kept her whereabouts secret, and it was with her I was said to have escaped. All this together prompted the *présidente* to advise me to leave Languedoc as soon as I could, under the pretty pretense of looking only after my interests. I understood what she meant and considered myself ordered to go. I found myself reduced to a strange state of perplexity, not knowing where to go unless I entrusted myself to Birague. He had, in truth, offered to take me to Paris and never abandon me, but I feared his passion, and his company was questionable. What was I going to do? As usual, my good fortune took care of things.

After the Lady Molière spoke out against me in order to avenge her husband, news of it spread everywhere, and a curious article about the story of my birth appeared in some of the gazettes.[33] A certain Duke of Candale (whom we encountered above) noticed the matter, since the news had crossed the most distant borders of the kingdom. And the Marquis de Saint-Etienne, captain under Monsieur le Prince,[34] who was still in Brussels, told the story to a charming lady of that country who loved to hear of wonderful adventures, and this was a step toward my salvation.

The Marquise de Seville (that was the name of this lady whose salon was always full of the most gallant people in the Low Countries)[35] was a very well-formed woman who had once been very young and very beautiful, and people thought she resembled certain princesses. She had, to an extraordinary degree, that witty and intelligent turn of mind that was so well received in France, before it became fashionable to be less clever, and nothing pleased her more than witty stories and plots. Princes, marquis, counts, and barons pleased her thus, including the brother of the secretary of commands under the Prince of Condé.[36] There are few fashionable people whom she

33. Gazettes were flyers containing interesting bits of news. They were unreliable and often filled with gossip and scandalmongering.

34. Monsieur le Prince (the Duke of Enghien, Prince of Condé, also known as the Great Condé) and the Marquis de Saint-Etienne were important figures in the Fronde. The Fronde was a tax revolt which led to civil war in France, 1648–53. The Frondeurs objected especially to payments imposed on public officials by the king and his agents. Leading figures changed sides in the course of the struggle, including Monsieur le Prince, who originally sided with the king but then led the rebel army. After the defeat of the Frondeurs Condé offered his services to the Spanish king and led their forces against the French. The Spanish army under him was defeated by by the forces of Louis XIV in 1658. The repatriation of Condé was one of the issues settled by the Treaty of the Pyrenees: he was required to write a letter of apology to Louis and to beg his forgiveness. His future rights and status were left up to Louis XIV to determine. The Marquis de Saint-Etienne followed Condé into exile.

35. Ladies customarily received guests, often on a fixed day of the week. Women received them while reclining on a kind of daybed, and the guests sat around it in a space called a *ruelle*.

36. The title *secretary of commands* designates the king's four secretaries of state as well as the principal secretaries in the houses of princes such as Condé.

did not involve in some kind of intrigue worthy of her wit. Your Highness will consider what I say here criminal when you learn in the rest of this story that this lady has done me a great deal of good. But how could one fail to share with one's friends such a rare portrait? It would rather be criminal to take it out, especially when the person portrayed would herself be grateful rather than angry, if she were still alive. I will therefore add that the Duke of Candale, young and handsome, was her first hero, when she traveled through Paris on her way to join her husband in Catalonia. Six or seven years later, when this lord was a lieutenant general in the army, she still wanted to involve him in gallant intrigues and adventures, even when he was in arms. Not a day went by when she did not send him news of herself, enhanced of course by her subtle wit. She often disguised herself to go join him in his tent, and one time she had herself taken there in the guise of a captured spy. The duke, who had not been dissatisfied with her previously, in the year 1645 or 1646, was not ungrateful for these new proofs of such a special esteem, and he responded with all the kindnesses she could have expected. Those who want to find reasons for everything even say that it was not hunting and chance that brought the duke to my nurse in 1652, but that he came at the request of this marquise. People may have told her stories of my extrordinary birth, and, pitying me, she perhaps persuaded this charitable lord to do something for me. But that is enough of this digression; I need to return to my subject.

The Marquis of Saint-Etienne, therefore, recounted the story of my adventures to this lady, and since she had a heart easily touched by beautiful misfortunes, she immediately came up with a generous plan to come and help me. Whether this was a continuation of the compassion that people say she had for me in 1652 or a purely fortuitous pity for a famous person unknown to her, I remain always grateful to her for it. To carry out her plan, she suddenly felt a great desire, which she would not otherwise have had, to be present at the meeting of the two kings at the river Bidassoa and to see the marriage ceremony of the infanta and Louis Auguste.[37] She crossed all of France and, to get news of me in the Comtat Venaissin,[38] she pretended to go there to join the court. It was at this same moment that Fouquet and Birague carried us out of the convent. The marquise arrived in Avignon the day after this adventure, which gave her an even greater desire to meet me. Noble of

---

37. One of the appellations of Louis XIV, emphasizing his role as peacemaker (MC 55). Auguste alludes to Augustus Caesar, whose reign was considered a golden age for Rome, as Louis's was supposed to be a golden age for France.

38. Comtat Venaissin is a region of southeastern France, consisting of the territory around Avignon. In 1274 King Philip III gave it to Pope Gregory X. It remained in papal hands until 1791, despite efforts of several French kings to regain it.

heart, she esteemed others according to the degree to which their adventures made them interesting to her.

My kidnaping, nonetheless, mixed much sadness with the joy she had had in finding me because, thanks to this latest adventure, I was all the more worthy of her attachment. It was really too bad that she had come so far to see me and now did not know where to find me. She made herself acquainted with those who were the closest to the affair, in the hope of getting whatever information they had. She made friends with the Marquise d'Ampus for the same reason and renewed her friendship with the Duke of Guise, whom she had known in the Low Countries, when he was making amorous conquests there. She hoped to get him to reveal to her what he did not know himself. Indeed she drove this poor prince quite crazy. But all this effort gained her little, and the court moved on without her having any idea what route we had taken. The lady followed the court to the Isle of Pheasants and didn't learn anything more. The marriage of the king was not the end of a novel in which all the heroic characters find themselves reunited.[39] On the contrary, it was the reason why she did not think of coming to look for me in Toulouse, for as a result of attending this marriage she was not in the region of Toulouse when the news of the nun's flight circulated, along with the suspicion that I was with her.

In the end she traveled back distressed and dissatisfied, telling everyone she encountered about my grim story and the failure of her trip; she sometimes had her squire do this while she rested, so as to keep up appearances. Then finally a new adventure gave her all kinds of satisfaction. The Countess of Englesac had not failed to send agents to Toulouse, just as the old *présidente* had foreseen. Her agent showed an order from the queen mother whereby I would be shut up somewhere if they could capture me. Hence there was no more time for me to hesitate between Birague's offers and this disgrace. I accepted his offer and went to await him at Bordeaux under the tutelage of Madame du Prat, one of his relatives, who had business there. After that, I was to entrust myself to his good faith to take me to Paris, where I wanted to shut myself up the very day after I got there. What happened? Madame du Prat and I went to stay in Bordeaux, at the very same place where Madame de Seville had arrived the day before. Something that I cannot explain moved both of us when we saw each other. Whether this was caused by the natural sympathy between someone like me, who was the subject of adventures, and someone like her, who had adventures as her goal, or whether some more hidden sentiment moved us, from that very moment we felt a mutual admiration and desire to see each other. Madame du Prat thought that there was also

---

39. In novels of this period, all the principal characters are usually reunited at the end.

a resemblance between us. Our desire to become acquainted resulted in a visit, and the lady, who was accustomed, as I have said, to relating her story to all those who appeared to be illustrious strangers like us, left her squire with us in the evening to tell it.

You can judge, Madame, what my surprise must have been when I heard myself mixed into the tale and when this squire added that the marquise had purposely come from Brussels to adopt me and to take me to Flanders and that she had offered to give half of her fortune to whoever could give her news of me.

At first it seemed to me that I had been caught, and I could not understand why anyone was spending time coolly telling me my own story, unless it was to make fun of me before my arrest. For, since I did not yet know this lady's character, I saw nothing natural about this encounter, and I spent the worst night I ever had. Whatever assurances Madame du Prat, who saw things more clearly than I did, tried to give me, I could not help trembling and fearing the agents of Madame d'Englesac until dawn broke.

In truth, all this agitation dissipated the next day during the marquise's second visit, which she made as soon as she was dressed. Madame du Prat, who is very witty, began to understand the talents of such an extraordinary woman. After many questions, she decided to repay her story with another and revealed to her that I was the one for whom she had such generous compassion. Madame du Prat had imagined, as might very well be the case, that the story of my misfortunes, told by the Marquis de Saint-Etienne, had inspired in that tender marquise a maternal love for me.

Indeed, no one has ever felt as much joy as she did when she learned my name, and finding me in this way made me even dearer to her. I thought she would suffocate me in hugging me. Two days later I resolved to profit from this adventure without waiting for the Marquis de Birague, who, because of his anger over this, soon forgot all my charms and reunited with his lady, Madame de Molière. I don't blame him; he is not the only man who is (or thinks he is) very amorous to act like this sometimes. I was grateful to heaven for the new help that had been sent to me in such a critical moment, and I left Bordeaux with more happiness and less fear than I had had coming there. Along the way the marquise fussed over me and praised me, and she showed a tenderness for me so intense that at this point I looked at her as though she were my real mother. But she did not want me to use that word because, although her heart acknowledged me, her face could not accept it. Indeed, for twenty-five years her face had retained a youth that was incompatible with being my mother. Thus, I had to limit myself to calling her my sister, with which I said I was happy and very honored.

At last we arrived in Paris. We stayed there until after Their Majesties' magnificent entrance, which had attracted to the city spectators from all parts of Europe.[40] In such an amount of time and with such a sister, Your Highness can imagine that still more curious things could happen, but what happened had nothing to do with me and much to do with Madame de Seville. I had asked her to let me be seen by as few people as possible until we got to Brussels. One person I did see was a friend of Monsieur de Guise, who was in disguise and who offered to make me a sovereign if I wished. The next day I refused his offer of very valuable earrings and preferred to listen to the unfortunate love of Englesac, who was still in exile, rather than that of a man who offered me nothing but beautiful things. Beyond this nothing extraordinary happened to me. I am not going to name this suitor, Madame. Your Highness knows who I am talking about and that he chose to avenge my lack of interest by choosing a young lady who was not as disdainful as I had been.

A month after I saw the walls of Brussels, my new sister led me there in triumph, and I stayed there for more than fifteen days. I was the subject of a hundred tales of adventure, told by the lady in carefully chosen terms, and this made all the accommodating people at court prize the reasons she gave for my adoption. Some of them even exaggerated our physical resemblance to provide an additional justification, but I do not know if this pleased her as much as the rest.

In conclusion, Madame, I spent two years there in the midst of both Spanish and Flemish courtship and gallantry.[41] But for fear of bothering Your Highness with too long a reading, and to give myself a little time to breathe, I will not undertake the tale of the remarkable things that happened to me there, nor the rest of my adventures, until the next chance I get to write to Your Highness. I beg you with great humility to consider me your very humble servant,

H. S. D. M.

PART 2

The first visits I received in Brussels were those of the Prince of Aremberg and the Duke of Arscot, princes certainly worthy of the greatest esteem and whose finest qualities would have shone at the court of France. The Duke of

---

40. August 26, 1660 (MC 60). It was customary for kings and queens to make triumphal entries into cities on various special occasions, accompanied by elaborate decorations and ceremonies.

41. At this time Brussels was ruled by the Spanish Hapsburgs.

Croülly came next; the Prince of Ligne, the good Don Antoine of Cordova, and a thousand others imitated them. Finally the governor himself came and, despite his grave majesty, was the most smitten of all.[1] I cannot refrain from telling a rather unusual thing that his passion made him do.

Since he loved me a great deal and believed that his being older made it necessary to show himself to be generous in order to touch my heart, he resolved to use this means and began to behave like a perfect gallant. I had taken a great deal of pleasure in a new carriage I had seen, which seemed to me like a new and very charming invention. He came to see me the next day, and since I talked about it again in his presence, he said, "Would you like to wager something against it with me?"[2] "I would," I answered, "but what would I wager against Your Excellency that would be of such value?" He answered that all he wanted was a bit of my esteem. Since I had an inexhaustible supply of esteem for all honorable people, joking with my usual gay humor, I took him at his word, and I gambled for the carriage. He lost it, and I also won the horses, the coachman, the footmen and their upkeep, even down to the straw in the stable, for a period of three years. He insisted on gambling the next day, so that I would lose everything I wagered, and indeed I lost. That very evening he asked for his payment in a note written in Castilian Spanish, which explained his wishes quite clearly. When he realized that the word *esteem* did not mean the same thing in my French as in his Spanish expectation, he convinced me to gamble again in order to avenge himself. He won back the carriage, the horses, the coachman, the footmen and the straw, and I saw no more of him.

This did not stop others of that nation from visiting me, and they did not admire me any the less. Among them was the old Don Francisco Gonzales de Menez, a witty nobleman, who was twice widowed and looking to marry for the third time. He was the one who made the most persistent efforts to conquer me and who in the end succeeded. He was from that illustrious family of Menez, which is spoken of in such fine terms in the histories of Spain and Portugal. His desire to serve his prince in the Low Countries had prompted him to move there with all his fortune, as had the love of his first wife, whom he had married for love, something that contributed to his choice as much as the other considerations.[3]

As for me, I found myself without family, at least any that I was permit-

---

1. All of these characters are real people who would have been in Brussels around this time.

2. Gambling was a popular pastime in aristocratic circles during the early modern period.

3. Marriage was considered a way of making alliances of power and wealth, and it was unusual to marry for love, as Menez is described as having done here.

ted to recognize; I had not had any news at all of the Count of Englesac for three years, although I had written a number of letters to the man who had given me letters from him when I was in the convent in Avignon. In addition, while marrying another lover seemed to her to break the rules of heroic adventures, Madame de Seville backed away from this point of view and advised me not to let this old Spaniard get away. What can I say? His fifty thousand pounds of income and his jewels helped persuade me that Englesac had completely forgotten me. I accepted the proposal he made to marry me; everything was worked out, and the ceremony was held in less than ten days. The good man immediately set me up like a princess. Most of my servants were French, and he neglected nothing that would make me happy, or so it appeared.

But, Madame, could I have such good fortune without a mixture of problems? No, undoubtedly that would have been contrary to the ends for which it seems I was born. In the midst of all this happiness, which made some people jealous and others happy, something very displeasing happened, which spoiled things for a long time to come.

Englesac, whom I had thought unfaithful, or in fact dead, came to Brussels three or four months after my marriage. This poor gentleman (whose love still endured in all its intensity, although, because of his mother's trickery, he had not received any news of me for three years) had visited all the princely courts. He had gone from Savoy to Switzerland; he had traveled into Germany and had stayed for some months at the imperial court. He traveled back through —— and saw you there, Madame, and received a thousand proofs of goodness from the princes of your illustrious house.[4] In the end, filled with hopes that people gave him from time to time of his pardon, he moved closer to Paris through the Low Countries, in order to be nearer his friends who championed his case at court. What was the very first thing he saw when he had barely gotten off his horse? His mistress married off! Good God, what a spectacle for him! Struck as though by a thunderbolt by this sight, and after having found out the details of his disgrace, out of grief he wanted to throw himself on his sword, and he would have done so if his valet had not been quick enough to stop him. This faithful and loving servant held him back, interrupting the flow of his first violent emotions. Having found out the next day that the Marquis de Menez needed additional French servants, the valet rallied his master by giving him the hope of being able to come and reproach me with my inconstancy. Thus Englesac got it

---

4. The place is not named in order to preserve the anonymity of the lady to whom Sylvie addresses her memoirs.

into his head to use this opportunity to be close to me. Listening only to his anger, the amorous count disguised himself sufficiently to make him look suitable for such a position in a place where no one knew him. The Marquis de Menez, who wanted only attractive people in his service, found him to his taste and employed him. I have never been so surprised in my life as when, wanting to get a look at the new steward[5] who was serving us, I saw that it was the unfortunate Englesac!

Alas, Madame, I still tremble merely at the memory of this. That secret power, which binds hearts and always ties them to what they love despite all the tricks that fortune often uses to separate them, made me blush and turn pale twenty times in a single instant. This secret power treated me with such cruelty that, unable to resist its violence, I lay unconscious in the arms of old Gonsales. I was lucky to be married, and that my husband could attribute my fainting to something that averted suspicion and turned to his advantage,[6] because it is absolutely certain that otherwise it would have produced the worst impression in the world. I came to, but did not want to remain a minute longer in the sight of that imprudent man, who was in almost as bad a state as I was. Having asked the marquis to have me put to bed, I stayed there all the rest of the day, suffering the greatest worries that could afflict a mind like mine.

I had been virtuous, and still was, whatever contrary slanders this corrupt century and the rage of my enemies may have published. Thus this unexpected encounter with a man whom I had loved and still could not hate left me cruelly divided between different courses of action and tore at my soul. I wished that he had not come to Brussels, yet I was nonetheless glad to have found him again. Sometimes I was angry with him because he had exposed me to such evident dangers, and sometimes I was angry with him because he was low enough to accept such a position. It seemed to me that he had a thousand other ways to see me and to speak to me. But, then, I wanted to see in this action indubitable proofs of the strength of his passion, and I was amazed by what love is capable of making us do.

I remained in this state of mind until the Marquise de Seville distracted me from it. Having heard that I was indisposed, she came to visit me, which meant that I did not think about the situation again until that night. I asked the Marquis de Menez to leave me alone under the pretext of needing to take some kind of medicine. It was, in reality, to have the time to confide every-

5. A steward is "an official who controls the domestic affairs of a household, supervising the service of his master's table, directing the domestics, and regulating household expenditure." *Oxford English Dictionary*, s.v. "steward."

6. That is, that Sylvie is pregnant.

thing to a French maid who had served me for two years and from whom I hid nothing. I asked her opinion, and she was as confounded as I was. We agreed, however, that I should talk to the count as soon as I could, for fear that if I were unkind to him, his excessive sorrow might reveal his identity, which it was absolutely essential to hide from the old marquis. His Spanish temperament was to be feared, should he suspect the very least part of the truth.[7] Merinville (that was the name of this maid) took care of this message, and the very next day, pretending she had some orders from me to give to this new steward, she told him that I had indeed recognized him. She reproached him for the danger he had put me in and added that he should be very careful not to do anything that would give any suspicions to Menez. She said that I would find a time to accord him a secret meeting as soon as I possibly could. If ever a lover, believing he had lost everything, passed from great melancholy to great joy, it was the poor count, who read into my promise all the meaning and all the hopes he wanted to. He seemed twice as handsome during the two days I needed to find a way to talk to him in private. But after I talked to him for a moment, both his face and his state of mind changed when he understood that I was urging him to decide to leave the Low Countries and that I was asking him to leave as a final proof of the love he said he had for me. As luck would have it, at that moment the Marquis de Menez was busy gambling with the Marquis de Castel-Rodrigue.[8] If that had not been the case, I do not know how we would have been able to avoid being found out, since my old husband could not live a moment without seeing me. The count spent an hour in a dead faint on my bed after I made my intentions clear. "Add to this, add to this, Madame," he said to me a moment before fainting, "that I am going to give myself up in Paris, and that in order to spare you the regrets occasioned by an infidelity of which I would not have thought a soul like yours capable, I am going to erase the memory of this with my blood."[9]

These words pierced my heart, and I was even more upset when I saw him faint. Merinville left my room and pretended that I was resting in order to make sure that no one came in, which was a successful strategy. As for me,

7. Stereotypes about national temperaments and characters were common in the early modern period. The French considered Spanish men to be especially subject to jealousy, a notion based in part on the different social roles French and Spanish women played. The French considered themselves more sophisticated in this area because French women, at least in high society, had greater freedom than did Spanish women.

8. The Marquis de Castel-Rodrigue was the governor of Spanish Netherlands and led the defense of Antwerp against the French in 1646.

9. Englesac had not been pardoned for his participation in the duel and risked punishment, perhaps execution, if he returned to Paris.

as soon as I saw that this overly amorous man was coming back to his senses, I hid him in a little room whose door was at the side of my bed until we saw that we could get him out of my rooms without danger.

We were just in time, for I had scarcely shut the door when the Marquise de Seville arrived and wanted to come in despite Merinville's efforts, saying that it was not right to let me get used to sleeping during the day. She said she had something urgent to communicate to me, the telling of which would be good for my health, and that this rest I was taking was not appropriate. She wanted to tell me about a new adventure in which she had involved a Frenchman named the Chevalier de la Frette. She wrote to him every day under the name of the Invisible Lady, and he responded to her without knowing her.

I listened to her distractedly and with much impatience. I was all the more in ill humor because my little lap dog, which, without thinking, I had shut up in the little room with the count, was barking his head off at him, which put me in a state of mortal fear. It is not that this lady would not perhaps have been more delighted than scandalized to find that I had such a faithful lover; she probably would even have envied my good fortune rather than have found anything to criticize. But I had everything to fear from the indiscretion that is typical of heroic minds, having seen in novels that they tell everything they know to the first person they encounter, without any precautions; and I feared that among the people to whom she would be tempted to tell my story, there would be someone who knew who I was.

In the end, I avoided the difficulty and, being given my dressing gown, I found an excuse to take this dangerous marquise into another room in order to give Merinville a chance to get Englesac out of the room he was in, which she succeeded in doing.

But it was in vain that we took all this trouble, and in vain that we took still other steps to prevent the marquis from finding out anything during the month that this dangerous steward insisted on staying with us. Unfortunately for us, Sir ———, who had retired to Brussels after the disgrace of Monsieur Fouquet, Superintendent of Finances,[10] came to dine with the marquis, along with a great number of Frenchmen. Sir ——— was a man of merit and was quite good company: he knew and was known by all the fine people in

10. Fouquet was a rich financier and an ally of Louis XIV's prime minister, Mazarin. When Mazarin lay dying, another financier, Colbert, accused Fouquet of misappropriating Louis's funds. Louis welcomed the charge since he was jealous of Fouquet's wealth. A trial resulted, but Fouquet defended himself well, even sometimes against forged evidence. After three years the court, much to Louis's disappointment, found Fouquet guilty of only mismanagement and banished him. Louis, however, ordered him imprisoned for life. Thereafter Louis decided to be his own prime minister. There is no relation between this historical figure and the young man named Fouquet who helped Sylvie and the nun escape from the convent in part 1.

France. He had even spent time with Englesac during a trip they had made from Bordeaux to Paris. He no sooner saw Englesac enter the dining room where he had come to preside over the service than, mistaking him for one of the guests, he cried out: "Ah! Monsieur the Count of Englesac, are you in this country too? Oh! What good fortune brings one of my best friends back to me?" And in saying this he rushed up to embrace him.

I had not arrived yet, and that was a good thing, because this was even worse than when I recognized the count in his livery. He disengaged himself from ——'s arms, blushing nonetheless, and pretending to think that —— had greeted him thus as a joke, he continued to set the table as though he were not the person for whom —— took him. —— did not know what to think of this reaction—or perhaps of the extremely marked resemblance between the Count of Englesac and this steward—because his behavior had begun to give him doubts. All during dinner the conversation was about nothing else, and each of the guests asked the steward a number of questions. As for me, I had had enough time to be aware of the situation and to compose myself before coming to the table. I questioned him like the others so that, apparently, everything went well, and we thought there would be no bad consequences.

But it was not so easy to fool a Spaniard who had often been told the story of my life and who knew of the love that someone named the Count of Englesac had had for me. As part of his strategy, Menez hid his feelings until everyone was gone and, when he saw that he was alone, he reproached me a thousand times and threatened me a thousand times, telling me I was unworthy of a man of his rank and birth who had done me the honor of marrying me. He said a hundred things that were even more terrible, making it clear to me that he did not intend to stop with threats. I saw that I was in a situation where I not only had to fear for myself but also for that unfortunate gentleman who, for fear of giving everything away, was less willing than ever to depart. I knew, however, that he would suffer cruel vengeance if his identity as the Count of Englesac could be confirmed.

He always insistently denied it and offered to demonstrate who his parents were, and then did it, and urged the marquis to check on it himself. He added that this had been a trick of ——'s in order to get him fired. In the end, he made such a fuss that one would have believed he was telling the truth, so industrious was his insane love in trying to save the reputation of his beloved.

It was impossible, however, for my reputation ever to recover from the mortal blow that it had received on this occasion and, although the count skillfuly managed to get out of Brussels a few days later, from that time on my husband treated me so badly that people began to think I deserved it. The sarcastic comments of ——, who was annoyed with Englesac for refusing to confide in him, convinced my husband even more. In addition, some people who have nothing better to do than to hurt others snooped around and found out where the count had stayed after his arrival; this of course ruined everything.

It is from this source, Madame, that have come all the cruel falsehoods with which people have since then sought to tarnish my innocence and the purity of my behavior. No one could believe that I had no part in the actions of a crazed lover who had risked everything to give expression to his jealousy and anger. On these grounds, the world has taken it upon itself to condemn what this great misfortune forced me to do in order to avoid catastrophe. People have even drawn conclusions about the past and say that the Countess of Englesac had good reasons for persecuting me. In sum, my name was held in contempt by honorable people, I was the subject of gossip in all the courts of Europe—to the extent that things were published about me, and novels were written about my life, not one of which contained a word of truth. But that's enough of my defense of myself. Let us return to the story.

Englesac made such a fuss that Menez was almost persuaded, or he pretended to be in order to save his honor. But he did not keep him in his service very long, and he ordered him not only to leave his house but to leave the city. Englesac obeyed, more out of consideration for me than for that jealous man, and he subsequently went to Holland, as I have already said. I received nothing but bad treatment from my husband, and I lived under this tyranny until the month of Janaury of the year 1664. Then, having learned with certainty of his ill will and that he planned to carry me off to one of his houses, where he would imprison me, I resolved not to wait around for this outrage. The frost made the roads passable,[11] so I took all my jewels, which were worth almost a hundred thousand crowns, and I left Brussels, going five leagues from there with Merinville, both of us dressed as men. When night fell, we took a post coach[12] and got to Nancy by crossing Luxembourg.

Immediately all kinds of rumors flew about my escape, and people looked for me for a long time in places where I was not because our disguises and the nighttime had prevented anyone from finding out our route. My husband did not believe that this escape had been contrived without Englesac's participation and went all the way to The Hague to reproach and threaten him, although for more than eight months Englesac had been in no state to

11. Mud made travel on unpaved roads difficult. The frozen roads facilitated travel.

12. The post was a system of horses or carriages posted at regular distances to facilitate rapid travel.

participate in such an undertaking because of a quartan fever.[13] His fever almost doubled because the poor man had no news of me. I will explain, in the appropriate place, the effects this produced.

Having arrived in Lorraine, I thought it was not a good idea to allow myself to be seen much since His Highness[14] knew my face. Because we also did not yet know how to play our roles that well (at least that was the case for Merinville), a fun-loving prince like His Highness might easily have penetrated some part of our secrets. I contented myself with staying there for a little while in secret, boarding at the home of Cavigny, a man of unknown temperament who, for our money, took us for what we said we were. He had a beautiful daughter with whom we amused ourselves sometimes, and if I am not mistaken, it was my handsome face that taught her how to fall in love with a man.

After that, when we thought Menez's efforts had slowed down, we decided to enter France by going through Champagne.[15] I pretended to be a young German who had come to see the wonders of the kingdom, and Merinville was a Frenchman who served me. Nothing was easier for us than to fool everyone this way. I had known German since my childhood, and I did an admirable job of speaking in a broken French when I had to talk. No one doubted that I was the young Prince of Salmes, whose name I usurped, knowing that there was someone of that name who was traveling through Europe. Having arrived at the court, I was not at all afraid to go and salute Their Majesties in this disguise, as well as all the ladies and the majority of the lords. I very quickly got the reputation of being a most gallant German and quite dangerous to the beautiful sex. I will need to talk about this at some length because the rumors of my amorous talents caused me to be involved in many great and horrible affairs, and my goal is to amuse Your Highness. But before doing so, I need to recount some other details that are part of the rest of my story.

The first encounter worthy of us, which we made in Champagne, took place early in the morning, and it was an adventure that was at least as extraordinary as any of my other ones. Leaving Troyes[16] and passing Mon-

---

13. A quartan fever recurs every fourth day, counting inclusively; that is, there are two days of relief between attacks. *Oxford English Dictionary*, s.v. "quartan."

14. Charles IV, the Duke of Lorraine (1604–75) (MC 79). Lorraine is a province in northeastern France, between Alsace and Champagne, that shares borders with Germany, Luxembourg, and Belgium.

15. Champagne is a French province, east of the Ile de France (the region around Paris) and west of Lorraine.

16. Troyes is a city in Champagne.

sieur de Vilacerf's superb house at Saint-Sepulchre, we had only gone a league or two when we saw in the distance a horseman on a promontory. At first it seemed as though he was doing dressage exercises with his horse, but after a moment he stopped what he was doing and came riding toward us at full gallop. "Be careful, Madame," Merinville immediately cried out. "It's a thief, and the proof is that he is riding straight across the fields in order to catch up with us faster." I had reason to be afraid because of my jewels, and I must admit that although I pretended to believe that a man alone would not attack what appeared to be two others, I did not fail to find myself in a difficult position. My consternation doubled when, after Merinville had shown me the road to take to the house of Monsieur de Vilacerf, I realized that this horseman was still following us. The poor girl thought she would be killed, and I, that I would be robbed indeed, especially when, by an excess of ill fortune, a little river blocked our route and gave the person we feared time to catch up with us.

Who was this fearful horseman, Madame? A woman disguised as a man, like us, but more embarrassed than we. She excused herself and asked for our mercy as she approached, and her horse threw her out of the saddle as he halted behind our horses. When she had seemed to be doing dressage, she had had trouble managing the horse; when she took off across the fields, it was because her marvelous horse had seen ours and, being used to galloping across fields, it took the bridle in its mouth and set out to join our horses, in keeping with its habits.

Merinville and I looked at each other and, after our fear was replaced by a charity suitable for a woman so like us, we smiled and joked about this adventure, which had ended in such an amusing way. We were getting out of this situation rather happily when Merinville, by calling me Madame, brought on us another, much more unpleasant, adventure. It almost would have been better for us if this adventuress had been who we thought she was.

Jealousy, as we soon understood, had caused her to disguise herself, and some plan had brought her near to Saint-Sepulchre (the people she was angry with lived in that area). As soon as she found out my sex, her wounded imagination made her forget the pain of her fall. She thought I was the rival who had robbed her of her peace and her fortune. Suddenly altering her manner toward me, she said, turning pale, "They told me that my unfaithful one had abandoned me for another and that she looked more like a man than a woman, and it seems to be true." I was afraid I would not be able to clarify things soon enough, but Fortune did more than I, and it was perhaps not without design that she offered me such a wonderful opportunity. "Let's go," she added, getting up filled with fury and pulling out her sword rather clumsily. "Either you will have my life with Monsieur So-and-So, or both of you are going to die." She named Monsieur So-and-So quite distinctly, but I was so attentive to the rest that I could never later remember his name.

Your Highness can judge how surprised I was. Initially I thought the encounter admirable rather than frightening and, regarding it as a joke in my soul, I even wished that the Marquise of Seville had been there to witness this last marvel. For I indeed considered myself innocent, and I thought I would quickly be able to persuade this crazed woman that she had taken me for someone else by continuing to speak German and my broken French. But this was precisely what made her think she was not wrong. In the end, I was obliged to defend myself to save my life, which she did not intend to spare, and this is what gave rise to the story which circulated at court around that time, that two women in male dress had fought a duel over a lover. The thing was true, and only the details were wrong. But I must end the tale of this combat.

We were trying to wound each other. Rather than helping me disarm her, which would have been very easy, Merinville decided, in absolutely the wrong situation, to begin crying out. La Roche, squire of Monsieur de Vilacerf, was on horseback on the other side of the water, and he hurried up to the bank. Seeing that his call out to Merinville to separate us was to no effect, he galloped off to find a place to ford the river. Some gentlemen came up and followed him. It was necessary to get done quickly to avoid any unfortunate discoveries. This necessity doubled my courage and, pressing my enemy, who was retreating, I finally gave her a sword thrust in the middle of her body, which knocked her over. I have found out, however, that she did not die of it. After that I got on my horse quickly and got far enough away before those gentlemen found a place to cross the river.[17]

All that I was able to find out about this adventure—and I found this out only a long time afterward and by chance—was that the lady was the daughter of a very fine man who had once been the governor of La Bassée.[18] Her mother had taken her to court with one of her sisters, and their beauty had attracted the homages of the most gallant men. This woman had not shown herself ungrateful for the services of a very accomplished cavalier. She had heard that he had fallen in love with a Dutch woman who had recently arrived in France and that he was with her at one of his properties, where he kept her dressed as a man. The violence of her jealousy suggested to her that she go and surprise them in the same disguise. The wife of an officer in Troyes

---

17. Duels between women were not rare, and they were the subject of comment in the gazettes (MC 87).

18. La Bassée is close to Lille in northern France.

helped her and provided her with the outfit. I have told the rest. My German, which she did not understand, persuaded her all the more that I was her Dutch rival.

After this we came within ten or twelve leagues of Paris, where Merinville had a relative named Saint-Canal, whom she wanted to convince to accompany us in the role of my tutor. He was an old soldier without much money and not in very good physical shape. Merinville was so good at cajoling him that he agreed to everything we wanted, and eight days later we took him to Paris. There, since he was not imprudent, he first had us put up in a proper middle-class home where he was known. This was intended to allow us time to decide our plans for the future and to lessen the chances of our running into troublesome people, something that would be almost impossible to avoid in a rooming house.

But prudence can do nothing in the face of fate. The first person I encountered when going out to eat was Madame the Abbess, sister of the Countess of Englesac, with whom I had laughed so much long ago over the letters of the Marquis of Birague. An important matter, which had to be pleaded at court, had temporarily brought her out of her cloister, and her character and concern for propriety had led her to the same house where we were staying for other reasons. She did not recognize me, however, although the old sympathy she had felt for me reappeared, and she was kindly disposed toward me in my German disguise. It would have been easy for me to let her return home without ever seeing through my disguise, if I had not been so foolish as to want to amuse myself with her by playing upon her foibles and her fondness for me. For, Madame, I was loved by her, indeed a great deal, and if I wanted to tell everything that happened between us during these few days, there would be nothing boring in it. But why not tell it? Your Highness will perhaps wish to be amused by it, and it will not do any great harm to Madame the Abbess.

At the beginning, therefore, I was quite surprised to see her, and I blushed. But the lady, who is attractive, was gracious enough to see in this change of color something more agreeable than its real cause. Attributing it to her lovely eyes and her quite pretty mouth, she said in order to reassure me a bit, "Ah! What a handsome gentleman! Come, sir, come. I think that Madame de Modane is the luckiest woman in the world to have a guest like you." Then she took me by the hand to lead me to the table, and after that she made me bolder and bolder as much as she could. For my part, I was curious to see how far this excess of esteem and friendship could lead a person of her profession, and beginning the very next day, I profited from her goodness. I visited her, and she offered to teach me to speak French well. To accomplish this, she made me promise to answer a little note that she would send me every morning from her room to mine. Nothing could have been as gallant as these notes. Mine, while badly written, seemed to her to be filled with good sense. In the end, Madame, we were so charmed with each other that, one night, when I was reading *The Bores*[19] with her, I don't know what got her to cry out, "Oh, Monsieur the Cavalier, the most annoying of all annoying people is a third party who comes and disturbs two good friends who want always to be alone together." And another time, in relation to some subject or another, she said that many rules of conduct were not made for clever people, and that one only had to know the secret of violating them without it being known, and then there would be no punishment for us. The only difficulty was to put this secret into practice.

Of course, I am only giving these details as a sample of all her wit, without suggesting that any negative conclusions should be drawn. Frivolously thinking that all I would have to do to find yet other weaknesses in her was to put her under pressure, I discovered on the contrary that no one was more solidly virtuous. She allowed herself a great deal of that wonderful freedom to say and to love whatever she pleased, a freedom that is, so to speak, accorded to ladies who are very witty. She was, however, the mortal enemy of the potentially dangerous consequences of these actions. And once, having pretended to take advantage of the opportunities she seemed to be purposely offering me, I almost lost all her esteem. All I had to do to obtain her forgiveness for my insolent behavior was to laugh like a fool and let her know that I was only a woman.

That she was still resentful of the fact that I had put her virtue and constancy to the test (and only for a woman), I would not dare to deny, for she was very disconcerted when I told her my name. In the end, however, she quickly recovered her good humor well enough to answer my playful comments with other even more playful ones. We renewed our old friendship. I told her in detail what had happened to me since I had had the honor of seeing her. She pitied my tribulations and promised to keep secret everything that needed to be hidden. Because she was generous, she offered me the chance of retiring again to her abbey until I was able to work things out with my husband. I, however, did not dare return under the skies of her region, which had been so dark for me during my younger years, and I still feared anything that would bring me any nearer to the Countess of Englesac.

---

19. Molière's *Les Fâcheux* (*The Bores*) was one of the plays performed at *Les Plaisirs de l'île enchantée* (*The Pleasures of the Enchanted Island*), the royal entertainment described later in part 2. The play's title might also be translated as *The Annoying People*, and the rest of the sentence plays on the word *annoying*.

That is the whole history of what happened to me in that middle-class house, where I kept her company some time longer without anything new happening to me. I said that my story would not be boring, and I do not think that I have bored Your Highness.

Finally, the abbess went home. Being satisfied with my male disguise, which fooled even ladies' hearts and in which I had confronted emissaries from my husband, I wanted no other asylum. I thought I would be safer in the midst of Paris than if I decided to take refuge elsewhere dressed in a way suitable to my sex. It was at this time that I decided to pass for the Prince of Salmes.

Good Saint-Canal's hair stood straight up on his head when I told him of this plan, and that I had already falsely confided this identity to my hostess and her daughter. "You want to ruin us all," he said, frightened, "and you do not realize that this will be a source of new adventures and new complications that you will not be able to get out of by yourself. What did not seem obvious to two or three or six individuals, will not go unnoticed in the presence of all the people in society whom you will have to see. And where will you be if the real Prince of Salmes happens to be here at the same time as you?" He used a thousand other reasons to argue against my plan, reasons suggested as much by his fear as by his concern for me. But his efforts were useless, as were his threats to go back home if I went any farther. I was charmed by the hope of hiding myself all the better, and what was even more important, by the possibility of amusing myself in this way.

I calmed him down and convinced him to run the risk with me. He rented a house for me, which I had furnished. He hired servants, and all this created an effect. I made visits and was visited. I set myself up as a man of good fortune, imitating any number of light-headed young men at court, who are sometimes not at all what they appear. I even went to court and was well received. At the Marquise of Seville's I had learned enough secrets about the family I pretended to come from that I made no mistakes.

But soon enough I had to pay for the pleasure I took in all this recklessness in the form of the troubles that Saint-Canal had predicted. The first of these, however, was annoying only because it was so gallant; it is worth recounting in full, for it was caused by the love I inspired, and I promised Your Highness that I would tell all about that subject.

The king, wanting to fete the queens and the ladies of the court with some festivals worthy of his riches and his gallantry, invited them to come to his enchanted palace at Versailles.[20] He had ordered the witty Duke of Saint-

20. Villedieu was not in Paris when the week-long festivities described here took place in May 1664. Her description is drawn from contemporary accounts (MC 95). The chateau at Versailles

Agnan, who was at that time the first gentleman of his chamber, to create the design of a ballet or, better, of all the festivities together. This lord chose as a subject the palace of Alcina, hence the festivities were called the *Pleasures of the Enchanted Island*.[21] I was invited, both as a foreign prince and as a young gallant.

The festivities began with a course at the ring, and I will willingly describe this in passing.[22] There was a round, open space decorated with four gateways made of shrubbery and a thousand other beautiful things. Four spacious paths, with high palisades on each side, led to this space. Nothing so magnificent or superb has ever been seen. After all the members of the court had taken their places, the king, costumed as Ariosto's Roger, appeared around six in the evening, followed by the ten knights who were to compete.[23] His arms were in the Greek style, his cuirass made of thin plates of silver, ornamented with embroidery in gold and diamonds, his helmet covered with plumes the color of fire. In this dress he rode one of the most beautiful horses in the world. Its harness was also of gold with precious stones. The duke, who played the role of Roland, came next and rode alone. After this Apollo appeared in a chariot quite beyond description. At his feet were depicted the four ages of man.[24] Time, as we see him portrayed in paintings,

---

was far from complete at this time; there was no town nearby and hence no place for the more than six hundred guests to sleep. But Louis spared no expense on the celebrations themselves, which were dedicated to his mistress, Louise de La Vallière. Notably, Lully composed and conducted the music. Two plays by Molière were performed for the first time: *La Princesse d'Elide* (*The Princess of Elide*) and an early version of *Tartuffe*. Molière's *Les Fâcheux* (*The Bores*) and *Le Mariage forcé* (*The Forced Marriage*) were also performed.

21. Alcina, as well as Roger and Roland, mentioned below, are figures from Carolingian mythology. Alcina is an evil and powerful enchantress, like Circe and Calypso in Homer's *Odyssey*. She lives on a distant enchanted isle and can turn her victims into plants or animals. Roger (Rogero or Ruggiero), originally a Muslim and the head of the Saracen army, converts to Christianity and marries Bradamante, Charlemagne's Amazon-like niece. Roger comes under Alcina's power but is rescued by the magician Melissa with the help of Bradamante's ring. Roland (or Orlando), the hero of the French epic *La Chanson de Roland* (*The Song of Roland*) and of Ariosto's *Orlando furioso* (*The Frenzy of Orlando*), is Charlemagne's nephew and main supporter. Ariosto's text was popular in seventeenth-century France, and the work read in the original or translated into French was a frequent influence on artistic production.

22. In this competition, a metal ring is suspended from a post, and competitors, galloping on horseback, attempt to carry the ring off on the tips of their lances. This exercise and riding at heads, below, had replaced more dangerous forms of ritualized combat inherited from the Middle Ages and were practiced both in academies where dressage was taught and at noble tournaments.

23. The festivities included a fanfare in which French nobles, dressed and armed in imitation of famous knights, paraded by on horseback. The tournament was won by the Marquis de La Vallière, the brother of Louis's mistress Louise. Louis himself declined to participate.

24. This refers to childhood, youth, prime or middle age, and old age.

drove the chariot, and four horses, whose hair seemed to be a pale gold and which were admirably built and covered with great footcloths[25] fastened with golden suns, pulled this invention. A long train followed it. Then came the knight's pages with the lances and their coats of arms. Then came a troop of shepherds carrying the various parts of the barrier that was set up for the contest. The contest lasted until evening.

When night fell and after a prodigious number of torches of white wax with more than four thousand candles had lit the site, we heard a pleasant concert, while people costumed as the four seasons served delicious dishes to the table of Their Majesties. The Sun and all its attendants danced a lovely *entrée de ballet* in the round space. Then Spring entered, and it was poor du Parc who played this role.[26] She rode as skillfully as a knight on a magnificent Spanish horse. Summer on an elephant, Autumn on a camel, and Winter riding a bear followed her with a troupe made up of an infinite number of people, who carried on their heads great basins containing the food for the meal. The first course was served covered with flowers woven together like the baskets and carried by gardeners; there followed other courses brought in by reapers, those of Autumn by vintagers,[27] and the last were ices covered by other ices, which chilly old men brought to cool the drinks.[28] To the accompaniment of flutes and small bagpipes, Diana and Pan brought us all kinds of exquisite meats; his came from his menagerie, hers from hunting.[29] They were on an amazing device that looked like a rock shaded with many trees. It seemed like a veritable enchantment because it appeared to float in the air without anyone being able to see the mechanisms that moved it. The controllers general,[30] representing Abundance, Joy, Prosperity, and Good Eating, suddenly covered with all these things a table of a newly invented style. All this was done by officers costumed as Pleasures, Games, Laughter, and Delights. Was this not truly royal, Madame, and did Your Highness not enjoy this description? But this is not all, and now I need to tell how such a beautiful spectacle was able to cause me trouble.

25. A footcloth is "a large richly ornamented cloth laid over the back of a horse and hanging down to the ground on each side. It was considered as a mark of dignity and state. Obs." *Oxford English Dictionary*, s.v. "footcloth."

26. The actress Marie-Thérèse du Parc (1633–68) was part of Molière's troupe. She then joined the troupe of Jean Racine and created the role of Andromaque.

27. Laborers who work in the grape harvest.

28. The four season theme is common in seventeenth-century art.

29. Diana and Pan were played by the dramatist Molière and his wife.

30. Officers of the royal household responsible for overseeing areas such as finances, the king's household, building projects, and so forth.

What I have just described was the entertainment of just one day, and festivities continued from May 7 until May 13, becoming ever more gallant. You can judge, Madame, what this entailed: comedies, concerts, new feasts, lotteries, more courses at the ring and riding at heads,[31] fireworks. Nothing was left out, including the last grand ballet that represented the destruction of the palace of Alcina, which was performed on islands floating in the artificial lake and which was, to my taste, the most beautiful part of it all and an undertaking most worthy of a great monarch.

On the second day, when the play *The Princess of Elide* was being performed, I found myself placed between two beautiful women, one of whom was a very great lady, proud and serious. The other was playful, or in fact very forward, and said a thousand foolish things to me and tried to get me to say the same to her. If I were not ashamed to say how forward she was, I would add that she tried to get me to do foolish things too. But I have started to tell this, and these things are too important a part of my story to be suppressed. Your Highness will take them as they should be taken, and I will write them that way as well, if I can.

After I had really flirted with her and asked for favors that I did not believe she would accord me, this foolish woman took me by the hand at the end of the play and, leaning toward my ear, she said, "Come on, take me home, you are too handsome for me to refuse you anything." This good fortune, which would have made another happy, made me tremble. I answered very clumsily, and how could I have done better? I only managed to avoid this difficulty by leaving her immediately, as though I thought she was just joking, and by saying to her that, even though I was a German, I saw that she was making fun of me and that I would find more sincere beauties elsewhere.

In order to avenge herself and mock me for my cowardice, the lady decided the next day to have the most ridiculous mock truths in the world sung about me.[32] People took them for the truth. They portrayed me as the most dangerous gallant in the court. Again, the next day, on the occasion of a great challenge in a course at the ring that the Duke of Saint-Agnan had won from the Monsieur de ——, and on the subject of which he had composed some verses addressed to ladies, some joker said that the duke had done nothing in beating Monsieur de —— if he had not yet defeated me. There were many other allusions and insinuations as well. Thus, within a few days I had the

---

31. Riding at heads involves lancing paper or cardboard heads, as well as using other weapons such as a sword against them.

32. As Micheline Cuénin explains, a mock truth is a minor literary genre, in verse, wherein gossip and slander are expressed by saying the opposite of what one means (MC 99).

reputation of being both dangerous and a great flirt. (Let us say, Madame, that it is a shame if all those who have this same reputation do not deserve it more than me.) People had such a good opinion of me that, not only did rumors reach the relatives of the real prince, but I had to respond to offers from a hundred curious beauties. My necessary ingratitude made them into troublesome enemies.

But the newest and most terrible adventure was that the other of the two ladies, who I said had appeared so serious and proud, had a heart that was touched nonetheless. After a few tender conversations that we had in the queen's apartments, she tried, more determinedly than any of the others, to find out whether what was said about my gallantry was not a false rumor. She made me understand the esteem she had for me, at first by her offers of help in every situation that presented itself, then by the notes she wrote, which even the least enlightened German could understand, and finally in a message she sent one of her serving women to tell me. This deprived me of any chance of pretending I did not understand.

I must not lie; I thought I was lost. This was not a lady whom I could treat as I had many silly coquettes. After all the advances she had made to me, there was peril in not responding clearly and promptly to her desires, and her confidant had tried, as much as she could, to make this clear to me in her message. I also did not dare reveal my sex to her. That would have been imprudent. My secret could pass into the wrong hands, and the lady's own secret disappointment might moreover push her into doing me an evil turn. Another thing alarmed me a good deal. Although she had found out, I know not how, that I was not the real Prince of Salmes, she had not revealed this because of her love. What did I finally make up my mind to do? To pretend to accept the great honor that she did me and to be impatient to profit from it, and then to get out of the kingdom as quickly as possible, before the three days she had given me to prepare myself ran out. I consulted Saint-Canal, who, initially even more frightened than I, told me that I should not hesitate. I would have acted the very next day had my unexpected encounter with the Count of Englesac, who had finally obtained his pardon and returned to Paris, given me the opportunity to change all my plans. I must tell the circumstances of this encounter, as well as some other things.

I was in the habit of paying court every day to Madame,[33] and people said I came there because of the beautiful Madame du Ludres.[34] Others

33. As the oldest brother of the king was called "Monsieur," so his wife was called "Madame." "Madame" here is Henrietta of England, wife of Louis XIV's brother Philippe, daughter of Charles I of England, and granddaughter of Henry IV of France.

34. One of the ladies in waiting of Madame, who later became a mistress of Louis XIV (MC 101).

thought it was because of the charming Mademoiselle de Fiennes. But this is not really relevant to what I want to tell.

Since I went there the very evening I had received the message, for fear of anyone seeing anything out of the ordinary, I immediately ran into the young Count of Englesac, who was with the Chevalier de Lorraine, the Marquis de Villeroy, the Prince of Monaco, the gallant Benserade,[35] whom Your Highness likes so much, and some others. Englesac was very different from the way he had been in Brussels: he laughed, sang, and was not in love—or if he was in love, it was no longer with me.

While nothing obliged him to kill himself from melancholy in my absence, as up until then I had not done in his absence, and perhaps indeed he would have tormented himself uselessly in remaining faithful to me, I could not help but be very surprised to see him so lighthearted, and this surprise meant that I did not greet the ladies with my usual grace. Englesac, who had been brought there, almost with the dust of the road still on him, so that he could see the man with such a great reputation, did not seem any less surprised when he looked at my face, and he almost ruined everything by a ridiculous idea he got into his head. Later he confessed to me that he had thought they had purposely put me in this disguise to surprise him in this way, knowing how much he loved me. Consider how unlikely that was, especially where we were.

What confused him even more was that he had bragged of knowing the Prince of Salmes personally in Germany, which was true. Having agreed to come there that night only in order to congratulate him on the news of his conquests, he did not know to whom to address himself. The situation was delicate. He would put me in danger if he believed it was me, not recognizing me as the Prince of Salmes, and I would betray myself if my distress continued in his presence. We nonetheless managed to get out of this difficulty by both doing our duty. I can still hear the amusing compliment he paid me, embracing me as though I were that Prince. He was so transported with joy that, to prevent something from going wrong, I was obliged to tell him more than I wanted and to let him know in a few words how important it was that he play his part well.

He climbed into my carriage to accompany me home. Your Highness will excuse me from having to tell you what joy made this ecstatic lover say, who was not so disengaged from me as I had believed. I never in my life saw a happier man or one who was more in love. Tears, sighs, laments, expres-

---

35. Isaac Benserade (1613–91) was a Norman poet and gallant, who was a favorite at the court of Louis XIV.

sions of joy, confusion, fainting—all of these were present and prevented me from doubting that any greater happiness could happen to him than finding me again. He would have continued these follies until the next day if I had allowed him to do so.

His follies did not make me forget my resolution to get out of Paris as soon as possible to avoid the misfortune that threatened me, and I interrupted him in order to confide this to him. "What do you think, and what do you advise me to do?" "I really do not know," he answered, "and I see as much problem in fleeing as in staying. If you flee, this marquise will know that you're not the Prince of Salmes. She has many secret contacts and needs but to express her will for harm to come to you before you are out of the kingdom or, for that matter, wherever you go. On the other hand, if you stay, I can well imagine your being exposed to great perils. She passes herself off as virtuous, and these virtuous women, having risked their secret and placed their trust in the wrong person, sometimes stop at nothing to preserve it. At the very least, you'll have to reveal your sex to her to ward off any secret ambushes. Once you have revealed it, one of two things will happen: it may remain secret or it may be divulged. If it is revealed, Menez will find out at once and will dispatch his men to carry you off, without anyone being able to defend you against the apparent justifications of his complaints. If the lady remains silent, I will still be deprived of the opportunity to enjoy your presence here and of the happiness it affords me as much as I would like. We shall be hindered by reasons of propriety." (You may judge from that, Madame, what pretensions the count entertained.) "In the end," added this foolish man, whose recent joy prevented him from being saddened by my difficulties, "all of that is really cruel, and, were I not afraid of being unfaithful to you, I would almost prefer to go and save your honor by fulfilling the lady's desires under your name and in your stead, until we had time to adopt other measures."

His idea made me laugh, for, in truth, that was the best expedient. Besides, he had added that he feared committing an infidelity to me. I think that it would indeed have been one to a person more jealous than I and that such a person would have been angry at him. Perhaps people may accuse me, in what is to come, of lacking in refinement, but frankly I've never been able to accept some forms of jealousy: those that seem to me too centered on the physical. The assurance of an undivided heart has always been enough for me, and always will be. Everyone has his or her own way of loving; I believe myself to be more refined, by loving in such a way, than those who profess refinement.

"An infidelity!" I replied quickly. "I cannot really say that you can be unfaithful to me as long as I have my husband. I want nothing from you, and you are free to give away all you have to whomever you please!" As long as our mood and opportunities for jesting lasted, we pushed our conversation to extravagances. In the end, the conclusion was that, in spite of the remonstrance and oaths of Saint-Canal, who returned home out of great fear, I would consent to this useful deception of the marquise. In truth, Madame, now that I am a little wiser than I was then, I am amazed at the foolish courage I had.

The count was handsome, of a height close to mine, and could pass for me if need be in the room of a lady who was cautious enough always to cover her pleasures in darkness and who didn't have all the time she would have liked to spend in pleasing her lovers. I informed him in minute detail of everything that had happened to me since I had appeared at the court, so that he would not make any mistakes. He in turn would tell me all that had transpired between them. (How impudent I am, to recount all that to Your Highness!) This sharing of information of the secrets of days and nights continued for some time, until eventually the lady's husband, having found, I know not how, some of her letters with replies I had written in my own hand, became extremely jealous and gave orders to spy on us. Madame, we are approaching the dreadful ending of all the comedies I had acted out.

This jealousy had gone on for about two weeks without the marquis being able to gather enough evidence to convict his wife when the king wanted to present some new entertainment to the ladies, whom he took to the plain of Trévers dressed in *amazones*.[36] My marquise, who disliked these showy amusements, returned to Paris. Thinking that her husband would remain at the king's side, as he had said he would, she wrote to me, saying that she was alone and inviting me to come and play with her.[37] I went there trembling, not out of fear of the husband, because I foresaw nothing from him, but for fear that she would propose a certain game that I could not play well with her. And my fear was not unfounded: I would have been in a horrible fix if the husband had not come into the room as the lady was vigorously urging me to take advantage of our solitude, and I could not defend myself, save by weak arguments. I do not know whether his sudden arrival caused me more relief or dismay.

With the help of a servant, he had hidden himself in a place where he could hear us. Having become only too well convinced of our relationship by our conversations, and losing patience, he came to sacrifice us both to his

---

36. Trévers is a village near Fontainebleau, where the king passed the members of his household in review. (MC107). An *amazone* was a riding costume worn by women in the early modern period. Its name derives from the women warriors of Greek mythology.

37. As will be seen below, there is a double entendre here. The verb may allude to a game in which one gambles or to amorous pastimes.

honor. The marquise, who heard him first as he crossed the room, gave a loud cry and ran out to the garden through a door leading there from her rooms. She left me alone, exposed to her husband's rage, while she took refuge in a convent facing one of the garden's gates. I thought my days were over; that man, all the more furious because his wife had escaped him, came at me with sword raised and, his eyes flashing with anger, said, "Ah, traitor! You must die!" All I could do was to parry his blows as best I could for as much time as it took him to abandon his plan to kill me on the spot in favor of the idea of inflicting on me a slower and more cruel death. He disarmed me, and then, calling his footmen, he commanded them to strip me naked in order to treat me in a more humiliating way. The order was unusual; people can think what they like. A husband who does not kill right away sometimes takes strange forms of revenge.

Consider, Madame, how shameful it was for me when, in spite of my resistance, tears, and protests to inform that jealous man that I had never been capable of wronging him in the way he believed, these tormentors began to rip my clothing away, and my bosom was exposed. I had to endure this, nonetheless, and was quite lucky they could see I was only a woman.

Never could the marquis have been more astonished than he seemed at that moment. Passing from anger to a deep sorrow for having so mistreated, as he said, such a lovely thing, he cried, "Ah! Madame, for what purpose, and why have you forced me to become such a criminal?" He begged my forgiveness on bended knees. He dismissed all his servants, and he came and held my hands, which he kissed a thousand times, begging me to forget what he had just done. As for me, having been so frightened and embarrassed, I hardly knew where I was while this went on. In the end, Madame, he added a thousand fine protestations that he would repair any displeasure he could have caused me if I would only tell him who I was. He told me he believed himself to be noble enough for that. In short, he became so tender that, in whatever mortal danger I had believed myself to be just moments before (I must again tell Your Highness of this foolishness), the greatest danger I ran that day was not that of being killed.

But the best part of the adventure was when the marquis, reassured by all this of his wife's fidelity, thought he had to beg her forgiveness and laugh with her about his folly. The poor lady did not know how to interpret the account he gave her; she thought he had concocted it to protect his honor from the incident caused by his injudicious outburst. After all, she well knew that it was not a girl who had enraptured her every night. The oaths by which the marquis sought to persuade the nuns that he was telling the truth seemed to her to be so many traps he was setting. When a number of the servants told her about the incident and recounted what they had seen, she seemed dumb-founded. The husband, in turn, could not make sense of his wife's stubborn-ness and terror, and both were on the verge of losing their minds.

From then on, however, farewell my secret! Whatever promises the mar-quis had made to me about keeping it quiet, too many people had found out for it to remain hidden much longer. The rumor spread throughout the court and occasioned many jokes and considerable surprise, especially among the ladies who had taken me for a very different person. I had to dress like a woman again, for I was not bold enough to remain dressed as a man. Indeed, I had to use all my wit to invent tales that would satisfy the curious and pre-vent my real story from coming to light. I passed myself off as the beautiful Marquise de Castellane, who has since come to such a tragic end, and claimed to have fled persecution at the hands of my husband's brothers, who were searching for me high and low, seeking to murder me.[38]

All my artifice, nonetheless, could not long shelter me from these latest blows that Fortune struck against me. For everyone gradually recalled the search for his wife that my elderly husband had launched in France this past January, and they suspected right away that I was the Marquise de Menez rather than of Castellane, whom many had failed to recognize in my features.

The Count of Englesac's attachment for me, the memory of what had happened between us when we met at the Palais-Royal, in the quarters of the ladies-in-waiting, and what had been learned of his amorous adventures and duel—all that served to confirm the suspicion. Eventually, many other cir-cumstances brought wind of my misadventure to old Menez, who was dying of sorrow and illness in Brussels. He wrote immediately to the queen mother, begging her to send me back to Flanders.

I had taken refuge at the Guise mansion. The Count of Englesac, having decided that I could not be safe in any cloister, had preferred entrusting me to the duke's magnanimity. The duke had recognized me and offered me every sort of secrecy and protection. It is also true that he gave me every rea-son to be happy with his kind treatment and, if he did mix with that some ef-fort to persuade me to thank him by some means other than words, he left me nonetheless quite free not to do so. I was very surprised to see that prince en-ter my apartment one morning earlier than usual and say to me, with tears in his eyes, "It is with a heavy heart, Madame, that I come here to disturb your rest, but a higher power orders me to put you in a carriage and hand you over to three ladies, who are to take you to the queen mother, who wishes to speak

---

38. This is an allusion to a real contemporary event, in which a widow was murdered by her two brothers-in-law, after she remarried (MC 111).

to you. Do not harbor false hopes, Madame," he continued, seeing that I had received that news with a kind of indifferent indignation, as if I had guessed the essence of the matter that he was hiding from me, "I believe it's to bring you back to Brussels, to your husband. Would to God that the traitors who revealed your place of refuge find themselves in the deepest abyss, or that I myself had died before this betrayal." He crowned those tender words with more tears, which I think this gallant prince could produce at will. I said to him, "Your Highness is joking; I have more strength than you; I do not deserve the sorrow you inflict upon yourself over something to which I am indifferent. I tried to avoid a misfortune but couldn't. My fate has more tricks than I do cunning. Well, sir!" I added, "I must please the queen, and wait for my destiny to improve. It is not the most constant in the world as far as I am concerned, and, while it never bestows any lasting good on me, it does me no lasting evil either."

He led me by the hand to the carriage, which I saw was escorted by thirty Flemish horsemen. I thought the poor Count of Englesac was ready to lose all hope in the room where he stood and from which he dared to follow me only with his eyes. But I, whether from strength of mind or secretly foreseeing that such a disgrace would not last long, appeared not to be upset. Smiling, I bade farewell to all those present as I boarded the carriage and took my seat along with my ever-faithful maid, Merinville. I was taken on the road to Flanders, but we didn't go far beyond Péronne[39] when I began to glimpse from two quarters strong indications that I would soon get out of that new fix, as had been my premonition. One was that Englesac, determined to free me or die trying, had assembled many young gentlemen and descended, masked and bold as a lion, on my mounted escort, forcing them to flee and let me go free, which fortunately they did. That poor count, having then hoisted me behind him onto the back of his horse so as to separate me as fast as possible from my enemies, carried me off to the castle of one of these gentlemen. The other thing was that, having secretly lived in that castle for two weeks, I saw, when looking out the window, a retinue and believed I recognized the servants' livery. Indeed, it was that of the Marquise de Seville, who was coming to Paris by relays,[40] trying to find me and apprise me of the Marquis de Menez's death, which that latest bit of news[41] had hastened.

The count mounted his horse to go out and meet her. I cannot express to

39. Péronne is a town in northwestern France, about thirty miles east of Amiens and about fifty miles south of the Belgian border.

40. A relay is "a set of fresh horses obtained, or kept ready, at various stages along a route to expedite travel." *Oxford English Dictionary*, s.v. "relay."

41. The news of Sylvie's rescue by Englesac.

Your Highness the joy he felt when that lady informed him of the reason for such a hasty journey. He scarcely took the time to let her know I was in that castle and to invite her to go there before he came back to announce to me what he had been told. He was greatly agitated, waving his hat at me as he rode at full tilt, and shouting with all his strength, "Joy, Madame, Joy! Your travails are over; the jealous man is dead!" The Marquise de Seville, who arrived a moment later, confirmed it. On that very day, the Count of Englesac, embracing the marquise's knees, begged her in these terms: "Ah! Madame," he said, "help me regain my dear mistress, whom so many misfortunes have taken away from me for so long!" That outburst could not have seemed more appropriate, and they struck the marquise in her weak spot. She wept—we all wept—and the conclusion was that, after the mourning period was over,[42] she would bestow upon me a large portion of her wealth so that the Countess of Englesac might console herself more readily upon her son's marrying me.

There, Madame, is part of the story, which, as you wished, I have taken the liberty to relate to you. The fear I have of tiring Your Highness out by too lengthy a reading prompts me to postpone to a later occasion the tale of what befell me after I became the count's wife.

I most humbly beg Your Highness, however, to believe that I have said to you nothing that is not utterly true, that I shall always be ready to confess to you my most secret follies, and that, however my enemies may have chosen to interpret them, appearances, which often deceive, are all that was ever criminal in my conduct.

H. S. D. M.

PART 3

Madame, it seemed that after Madame de Seville's generosity we were going to be at peace, and I must tell Your Highness that thinking this we were already experiencing that kind of great joy that follows long suffering. We even considered celebrating this happy marriage before the end of the mourning period.[1] We chose the date, as if everything depended only on us.

But we had failed to take Fortune, who was far from our friend, into consideration. She had sworn that the Count of Englesac would have a number

---

42. Traditionally widows wore mourning for two years. In the seventeenth century this period was reduced to one year and six weeks.

1. See note 42 above.

of adventures worthy of my own before he could be happy, and for her taste he had not had enough strange ones yet. She wanted him to merit being my hero by an infinite number of additional difficulties, and this situation caused me to fall into new extravagances. I believe the story of them will amuse Your Highness no less than what you have already read, all the more so since my fate has always been careful to mistreat me only in amusing ways.

First of all, Madame, at the same time we were making such lovely plans, we once again had to put more than two hundred leagues between us. This is not the best thing that can happen to lovers.

The count's friends said that it was necessary for him to travel to Languedoc to distract his mother, who had not seen him since his return to France, while I should go to Brussels with Madame de Seville to seek my dowry[2] and to justify as best I could my past conduct. There were still other reasons that justified this course of action, and it would have been no way to profit from the death of a jealous man, who seemed to have left this world on purpose to get us out of a delicate situation, for Englesac to let himself be considered guilty of my kidnapping, just for the sake of a little more time together— time which would profit us nothing. He broke into tears and took his farewell; we separated from each other on that very day, each taking a different road; and so we went to begin the third part of our tale.

As for me, I did not have as much trouble as I had expected in obtaining the favor of people in Brussels. They remembered my spirit, playful but exempt from malice. They could well judge that I might innocently have suffered the presence of the false steward in my husband's house, since he had not entered that house with my consent. Even better for me, they imagined what an aged Spaniard, convinced of the infidelity of a sixteen- or seventeen-year-old wife, might do to her, and no one thought it strange that I might try to escape from a long period of suffering.

In short, my male disguise was attributed to my need to hide from my husband, who was a powerful lord and who had a long reach. As for my adventures, people said that I had not sought them out. They did not think it was a small thing that, in grappling with Fortune, who was toying with me, I should get out of it suspected of so little. I say "so little," Madame, because they indeed thought the need to keep my identity hidden had, as much as my virtue, obliged me to behave well, and that, at most, this need had let me lead some other women from the path of virtue.

Thus the majority of Flemish women, and I mean the most strict, did not

---

2. In this case the dowry is the money, property, or both given to the wife by the husband as her inheritance after his death.

think badly of me. When they spoke of me it was only to pity me. Indeed, I think that by doing such a good job of justifying myself, I gave someone the idea of imitating me, for the Countess of Cardonnoy did just that five or six days after my arrival. Dressed as a man, she fled the house of her husband, who treated her inhumanely. You may know all the particulars of this story since the lady took refuge in Your Highness's country.

I did not get my dowry without a lawsuit, however. The suit came from one of my husband's heirs, a nephew who was named Menez like him. This was another bizarre story, involving love, and it would have taken me a long time to succeed if a brother of this Menez, who was the governor of several places in the West Indies under the king of Spain, had not been audacious enough to declare himself king. This news, along with orders to take all the relatives of this new monarch into custody, came just at the right time to the Marquis de Castel-Rodrigue.[3] My man was arrested, and that helped my side, or at least sped up this pretty business, which was the only such business I had in that country.

As for the Count of Englesac, he was not so fortunate in Languedoc. The Marquis de Birague, who could not make up his mind to give up on his hopes, had been careful to keep up with all the news. There was nothing about my good or bad fortunes that he did not know. He knew about my kidnapping and suspected who was responsible for it. He had learned of my husband's death. I don't know who told him that the count and I had promised to marry each other (perhaps it was through his friend Monsieur de la Frette, who had heard this in Brussels), but in order to prevent this from happening, as soon as he saw Englesac arrive, he convinced Englesac's mother to marry him off to a cousin he had, named Birague like himself.

It was an illustrious match, as the name Birague attests. The great fortune (for she was an heiress), the great wit, and the even greater beauty of the young lady made her not only a worthy wife for the count but for a prince; and so I did not have a weak rival.

The count understood the ruse, which was all the more refined because the marquis avenged himself on him by showing him every outward sign of great respect, and because, in fact, this marriage would have been a kind of good fortune for him, if this faithful lover could have considered anything other than possessing me to be good fortune.

In any case, as filled with passion as he was, the count did not lack the ability to conduct himself skillfully, and he only fought off this storm by dissimulating. Unlike many others, he did not believe that because one was in

3. See part 2, note 8.

love with one woman, one could not pretend to behave gallantly toward others, nor that it was necessary to brutally offend all other women to prove his fidelity. Even less was he a man to insult a young and beautiful woman in public by a refusal, and besides he could not have done so without making Madame his mother extremely angry, for she was a force to be dealt with. What did he finally decide to do? To see his new mistress and to talk of love to her. He behaved like many honorable people who do not think it a crime to lie to ladies, even if in doing so they put these women in danger by making them fall in love. And he did all this while waiting for an opportunity to break off with her easily. Thinking that it was unnecessary to make me unhappy by telling me that he was obliged to engage in this deception, he wrote nothing to me about it; this omission caused a great deal of disorder.

Birague was the world's most skillful lover and most annoying rival; one must no more deny him these two qualities than that he was also a brave and accomplished cavalier. For he is truly what I say, and he alone has more cleverness than all the demons taken together. He is one of the most charming men in the world when he is not unhappy in love. I would not be unhappy for him to learn that I am giving him his due by publishing his fine qualities, so that he will be more likely to excuse the complaints I will make about him in what follows. Birague, as I was saying, who knew that in Brussels Monsieur de la Frette kept up a lively correspondence with some ladies in Montpellier and with others in his environs, and he did not fail to make sure that these ladies wrote to this gentleman about the marriage that was being planned. La Frette, who often came to visit the Marquise de Seville (who was good enough to think that she was the cause of his visits), told her this news. Then he skillfully told it to me, and he did this with particular malice because he knew that this would cause me pain, and in this way he could avenge himself for my rejection of him. I speak in this way, Madame, because he was yet another one of my suitors, and because my evil Star had persuaded him, as it had persuaded many others, that no one could see me without loving me, or at least without saying he was in love.

You can imagine fairly well what happened to me when I heard this news, having no reason to doubt the ladies of Montpellier, and in fact it was not an invention. At the beginning, however, I had trouble persuading myself that it was true. In the end, however, my capricious nature in combination with my unhappiness made me so angry with the count that, without taking anything else into consideration, I suddenly stopped writing to him. The Marquise de Seville, who foolishly told all her secrets to her dear Monsieur de la Frette, went so far, to really finish me off, as to confide in him this consequence of my anger. He thought this was the perfect occasion to replace the count in my thoughts, if he could increase the reasons I had to distrust him. He intercepted and destroyed several letters that the count had sent me, which might have enlightened me and in which the count said that my silence was killing him. Believing that in fact he did not care about writing to me any more, I fell into a pathetic disordered state, and I was subject to a passion that I had great difficulty in hiding, I wanted to leave and go tell this perfidious lover everything I thought, right in front of his new mistress. All the reasons the marquise and Merinville gave me to persuade me not to do this only served to put my departure off a few days. All I needed was a pretext to make this trip appropriately and, having found it, I left with all my anger, or, if you prefer, with all my jealousy, because indeed I think that is what it was. I have to tell you what my pretext was.

I have spoken elsewhere of the kindnesses of the gallant Duke of Candale, and I have said that in asking the financier, Monsieur de Molière, to adopt me he inspired in this man a paternal tenderness due to financial incentives. The pretext came from this.

I had always viewed this money as lost and considered it foolhardy to ask his heirs for its restitution, not thinking that the duke would have been prudent enough to take any precautions. But the marquise, who was always a great help to me and who understood the situation I was in, searched her memory and finally recalled that there had been some kind of document written then. She said that the duke himself had put it into the hands of a monk belonging to the Chartreuse de Villeneuve who had been at that time the procurator of the monastery and that this Carthusian monk had promised to give it to me if it happened that my father the financier did not make the best use of it.[4]

This discovery made me feel all the joy imaginable, less for the money that could come to me by it than because it was my passport to Languedoc. I thanked the marquise, embracing her a thousand times. And to show her my gratitude even more, I did not amuse myself by embarrassing her with questions about why it was she who had then been so well informed about these things, and why she had not said anything to me about them when we met at Bordeaux.

I set off, accompanied as always by my faithful Merinville and an old man who was my squire. What happens to us, Madame, when we are possessed by some passion? I never got to any of my stopping-places soon enough; I would

---

4. The Chartreuse de Villeneuve is a Carthusian monastery at Avignon in Provence. The Carthusians follow the rules of Saint Bruno: they live in a community, but each passes most of his time in his own cell, where he prays, works, eats, and sleeps. The procurator is the monk charged with dealing with the temporal matters of his order or monastery.

have wished that my coach was a flying chariot or that I myself had wings in order to get more quickly to Montpellier, where I wanted to be.

However, I got there, and I would have been satisfied if my haste had not been useless. I learned that the Count of Englesac was no longer in the region. His sorrow from no longer receiving any letters from me and the rumor that Birague had purposely spread that I was engaging in some new love affairs, his jealousy, his annoyance, and his anger against me, which were no greater than mine against him—all this taken together had caused him to leave his mother and his mistress abruptly, without saying good-bye. He had taken the post to go and reproach me in Flanders at the same moment that I came to Languedoc to reproach him. He had told those close to him nothing, other than to give some intimations about a new duel, which drew tears from the eyes of those who cared for him.

Can you imagine my surprise, Madame, upon arriving? Not that I then knew all these details, because I only learned them afterward, when the count explained things upon his return. Then I only heard that no one knew what had become of him.

To increase my misfortune, the Marquis de Birague was in Montpellier that day, and during a visit he made to me he let me think that the pretext of a duel was something Englesac had used only when he heard that I was coming because he did not want to have to explain why he was not going to marry me. This falsehood shocked me; I believed it, although if I had reflected on it a bit, I would have soon figured out that what he told me could not be true.

My affliction was great, but I am not going to talk about it in order to turn my thoughts again to the Marquis de Birague's malice. Madame, when I think of the way he tried to persuade me to believe him, I cannot help but cry out that the greatest misfortune that can strike a lady is to be saddled with a second lover like him, and to be unable to love two men at the same time.

However, he did not profit, as he had hoped, from raising my anger against the count to an extreme state. That only served to augment my aversion for Birague, whom I accused of all my troubles.

I cried out sadly, "Alas! I am fated always to suffer!"—despite the resolution I had made to pretend that I had not come there because of the count. Then, looking at the marquis with menacing eyes, and in tears, I said to him, "Go away, get out of my presence. Your betrayals and cowardly acts are the sole reason why I have lost Monsieur d'Englesac, if it is true that I have lost him. And you still have the effrontery to come and annoy me with your visits after having ruined my life and made me everyone's laughingstock."

He was very surprised; he had not expected this outburst. He blushed, and he turned pale because of several other things I said to him. He did not know how to answer me and was embarrassed, for which I ask his pardon now that nothing any longer obliges me to be his enemy.

Afterward, I got over my violent emotion, which fortunately only he saw and which he did not divulge. He did not want to shock me, not having given up on his hope of one day bringing me around. I left the next day to go to the Chartreuse to get my document. It was indeed there, and they gave it to me; I then went and gave it to the people in the court, to begin the first steps in the lawsuit. The suit astounded a number of people, who never expected such a thing. The interested parties visited me, flattered me, threatened me. A settlement was proposed. Proceedings then began, were broken off, started up again, and in the end I won out over my debtors thanks to the passage of time. But this is too unrelated to my subject, so I am going to leave off here.

I put my old squire in charge of these minor interests. My sorrow made me dislike staying in the city, so I left it to go join the Abbess of Englesac in her convent. I was so fortunate to find her still of good will toward me, and to have in her someone to whom I could talk sometimes about my unhappy love, for she was my confidante and I was hers. She had never been able to blame her nephew for the esteem in which he held me.

Nonetheless, I was there for four or five days, unable to be consoled about what I believed to be his unfaithfulness to me. I even had the displeasure of seeing my rival come there, to feel my heart tremble on seeing her and to find her, in my opinion, much too worthy of love. She had seized on the opportunity to come and visit the Abbess in the company of Madame d'Englesac, who was the abbess's sister. Perhaps she came out of curiosity, to see if I was as beautiful as people said, and out of a desire to triumph over me.

It is true that I had reason to believe that she was as afraid as I, because she appeared to be just as embarrassed as I. She scarcely opened her mouth to answer the things that Madame the Abbess said to her. We took turns looking each other over disdainfully from head to foot, so much had our reciprocal anger (at finding in the other someone to fear) silenced us and made us jealous. For a long time, I will remember this encounter, which was as bad as all the pains I had already suffered. If one can say such a thing, she did well to die of smallpox soon afterward to escape the revenge that I could have taken, since I could not forgive her for having enough beauty to be capable of making my beloved hesitate.

The death of my rival was another incident worthy of me, Madame. A little while after her visit, she felt the symptoms of smallpox and was very upset about this misfortune so feared by beautiful women. She had gotten through the ninth day of her illness without great danger, and it would have been easy to cure her. But she made someone give her a mirror, and seeing herself ugly and marked, she said to everyone, "What shall I do, since I am no longer beautiful?" She did not want to make any effort to save her life. She insisted that she wanted to die and did so several days later, like a heroine.

She did not do me this kindness without my having to purchase it at the price of many difficulties. For while she was still alive, I learned that the Count of Englesac had come back, very upset about her illness and resolved to marry her right away. If Your Highness is surprised by this change, I will explain the enigma and give the reasons he thought he had to return like that.

The officious Marquis de Birague came to tell me this news, for he was the messenger of all my misfortunes. I thought I would die when the tale was confirmed by a man whom I had sent to find out and who reported to me that the count, knowing that he was one of my servants, did not even want to see him. I almost lost my mind over this. To the great surprise of everyone, I went not just to the house but to the very room of the sick woman, where the count was. I behaved like a madwoman. To tell you the truth, that did nothing to help the improvement of my reputation, for this is not how one makes a good impression, although sometimes one can get away with even worse things, provided one knows how to pretend to be prim and proper at the right time.

What pain I felt, Madame, to say the least, when I saw him on his knees beside the bed, behaving like a man dying of love for my rival, when I saw him take her hands and kiss them through the sheets and beg her to live while he shed hot tears. He shed tears even more abundantly seeing that I was present, swearing to her that even if smallpox had turned her into the most deformed person on earth, he would always love her more than the most beautiful of women. I think that I would have killed them both if I had had the strength to do so and if, from the moment I entered the room, I had not fallen, outraged, onto the first seat that presented itself.

The sick woman, who immediately saw what a miserable state I was in (and perhaps she had pity for it) looked at me as if she had something to say to me. Seeing that I looked fixedly at her, too, she raised her voice as much as she could in order to talk to me. "Do not be afflicted," she said to me, "I return to you with all my heart what my life and my parents almost took from you." Then, gently pushing the Count of Englesac away from her and closer to me, as if she wanted to make him turn toward me, she said to him, "Go, sir, go. This is too much pretending; it's cruel of you to treat like this someone who loves you so much. Marry her and let me die in peace."

Madame d'Englesac was highly scandalized by her last words, "Marry her." I do not know what she would have said had she not had some remnants of circumspection and had her son not led her away without so much as looking at me, in order to demonstrate to her how much he disdained me. He left the chateau, and I did too after him, being taken quite far away by the marquis, who never missed an opportunity to persecute me, but who spoke to me then without my paying any attention to him.

I say nothing about what I did from that day until the day of my reconciliation with the count, which took place no later than eight days after the death of Mademoiselle de Birague, because all I did was cry. But here is the reason for the terrible anger that made him want to punish me by marrying this relation of the marquis.

He had taken the post coach to go and reproach me in Brussels. Having stopped one night in Paris to rest, by chance he ran into the real young Prince of Salmes, who had recently arrived in France and was lodged in the home of Brissac. He had just gotten there. This was the prince whose name I had usurped the year before, and the same man that Englesac thought he was going to greet when he was brought to me at the Palais Royal,[5] in the chambers of Madame's gentlewomen, for, as I have said elsewhere, they had met in Germany.

They wanted to get reacquainted and ate together that evening. And among the dishes that were served, we ladies, who are talked about everywhere, were served up as entertainment during the meal. The young German had studied the spirit and the manners of the gossipmongers of the court, thinking that they were the most gallant of men. He would not have considered that he had really profited from his trip if at every moment he did not talk about the good fortune he had had and make people believe that he knew all the ladies whose reputations were scandalous. For my misfortune, he had heard my name mentioned among those who were part of the scandalous tales. In Paris, he also had learned what had been done under his name, and in Brussels, too, everything people knew—the story and circumstances of my lawsuit, my departure for Languedoc, where I was also going to bring suit, and other little secrets, which could give the impression that he

5. The Palais Royal, originally Palais Cardinal, is adjacent to the Louvre and was built by Cardinal Richelieu, the prime minister of Louis XIII. He built the magnificent buildings, garden, and theater (now home of the Comédie Française) that made up his "palace" so that he could be close to the king who lived in the Louvre. After Richelieu's death in 1642 the Palais Cardinal became the Palais Royal because Louis XIV and his mother moved into it. She found it more comfortable than the Louvre. When Louis moved permanently to Versailles in 1678, the Louvre was used to house members of the court and also for office and storage space. It also became the home of the French Academy. The Louvre was turned into a museum in 1793—by the leaders of the French Revolution.

had had an intimate relationship with me. And since he remembered that the count had been involved in the affair, I was the first woman he talked about in order to make an impression. He said, with a laugh, that he had known me as well as the count and that I had shown a very gallant gratitude for the good things his name had done for me while I was in disguise.

What an adventure, Madame! What strange news for a tired and jealous man who had just arrived in Paris that night to get a little sleep! Are you not amazed at the propensity of the majority of young men to tear up our reputations in this way, when normally they do not even know what color hair we have? For I swear to you, Madame, that this Prince of Salmes had never seen me, and that I did not meet him until fifteen months later through an adventure I had in the Place Royale.[6]

The count had not yet been able to suspect me of a betrayal. But hearing a very coherent story (for it was coherent), told by a young prince from Germany, the most faithful and sincere of nations, and the most truthful on earth, and remembering also the tales of my amorous adventures, which had even reached Languedoc, he no longer doubted but that I was guilty. The indifference he thought I had shown for his letters (for I had not responded to many) was the final element in convincing him.

He hid the displeasure he felt at hearing this news and, when the evening ended, he went to bed, where he spent the whole night in a terrible fury against me and the German. He later confessed to me that he was tempted more than a hundred times to go and stab the indiscreet man in his room and thus to have spared the Marquis de Tréchâteau the trouble of killing him two or three years later in a duel, as he did in Nancy. But in the end, considering me the more guilty and more deserving of the first fruits of his anger, he decided to return to his home in order to punish me by his marriage to Mademoiselle de Birague while waiting for the opportunity for an even greater revenge. He left without saying good-bye to the German prince.

I cried a great deal when he explained these unfortunate things to me, which clarified everything. I swore that I would never forgive him for the outrage he had done me by suspecting me. But how can one resist someone one loves who is repentant and who is as handsome as the Count of Englesac?

He came back to the convent often to ask my forgiveness and to find ways to prevent another similar misfortune. What can I say? In the end, he won me over, and despite Fate, to whom I had resolved to give other opportunities to create talk about my fortunes if that was what it took, I agreed to

---

6. The Place Royale is known today as the Place des Vosges (MC 138).

an engagement. The priest of Nice helped us in this,[7] and the very next day I took leave of my abbess to go and await my fiancé in Paris, where we planned to be married secretly by the archpriest of the Magdelaine.

Our plan would have succeeded, Madame, if that demon Birague had not turned up again where he was not wanted. I do not know how, but he found out that the priest of Nice had engaged a young gentleman and a beautiful woman. He let the Countess of Englesac know that her son was still trying to fool her by pretending to despise me while waiting for news of me so he could join me. In her usual way, the lady exploded into horrible anger and threats to make us break everything off. I, who was too proud to conclude the marriage until everything was worked out, did not want to allow the count to go any farther, although he had come hastily by post coach for precisely that purpose. I was content to try the strength of my enemies in seeing what they would do about an engagement. Here I promise more adventures. Your Highness will have pity for me, and may also laugh while having pity.

The Countess of Englesac lost no time in getting to Paris, where she arrived in a fury, threatening to ruin any priest who would be audacious enough to contemplate marrying us. I would never finish if I tried to tell in detail all the rages of this turbulent woman and all the insults she gave me. Let it suffice to say that her first effort was to circulate everywhere those novels that I said in the second part of my memoirs people had written about my life. This cast me in a bad light in the minds of the people I could have had on my side if they had not been prejudiced by this. It was something worse (if possible) than that famous satire where the too beautiful Madame d'Olonne is unworthily disparaged by false stories for having, without doubt, pleased someone who did not please her. To my first misfortunes and innocent intrigues, which were portrayed God knows how, were added other adventures of which Monsieur the Count of Soissons, and Messieurs d'Armagnac, de Sault, and de Louvigny were the heroes. I call them to testify, however, if they have ever met me. Monsieur the Duke of Beaufort and the Duke of Nevers were said to have strolled with me in their turn, one at Bouteux's in Ville l'Evêque[8] and the other I don't know where.[9] Even the General Hospital,[10] where I never set foot, allegedly complained of my profanations and, when my identity was found out, would only let me stay three days. What a horrible lie! In

---

7. A promise of marriage made in this way has legal status (MC 140).

8. This may be the name of a merchant who allowed some rooms of his shop to be used for gallant intrigues (MC 144).

9. These men are all real personages, famous gallants of their time (MC 143).

10. The Hôpital Général was an institution where, among others, women considered to be of incorrigible morals were shut up (MC 144).

sum, Madame, everywhere there were lies like this or praises made as poisonous as possible. The reading of all these lies did all the more damage to my reputation since defamatory stories tend to please and to be believed; the part of these stories that was true seemed to vouch for the truth of all the rest.

Following this, all the old complaints to the queen mother were renewed, and she, who was in the end tired of having spent six years of hearing about nothing but my outrageous behavior, became really angry with me, at least as much as a good princess might permit herself, and she permitted herself to do so only when virtue was at stake. And as a result of this there came secret orders to find out where I was hidden. (For the count and I had hidden in these early days, in order to see how things would go.) A second order came to seize me if I could be found and to take me I know not where. Finally this brought about the detention of the count who, having heard about this scandal, could not stop himself, in his sadness, from throwing himself at the queen's feet, where he foolishly tried to justify me and found out that there was also an order to seize him.

He was arrested and, when almost immediately thereafter I learned the news, I had the additional displeasure of fearing that it was not because of me alone that he was arrested, since other rumors were flying at this time. And what did I do, Madame, when this was told to me again?

I understood that it was really in earnest that they wanted to ruin me; all I had to do was stay in my hiding place, which was safe, to avoid falling into the hands of my enemies. No one had thought of looking for me there, a place that I will not name, if you do not mind (for I promised not to) and that Your Highness will never guess. It is enough to say that it was in a monastery and that I was there in appropriate dress. I might even have done many things there, because there was no lack of idle people who were ready to serve me in whatever I wished.

But it would have been unworthy of a person of my character to have had the prudence to think about her own safety when her lover was being persecuted, even when my safety would have been useful to both of us. A person with an ordinary mind, someone who had not begun her life as I had and who was not suspected of being somehow related to the Marquise de Seville, might have agreed to such low conduct. But I, Madame, I wanted no rest until I was assured of that of my dear Count of Englesac. I decided to present myself in turn at the Louvre,[11] to be lost with him or to save him. I sought out the queen mother at Val-de-Grâce[12] (it is true that I did well to commit this

11. On the Louvre, see above, note 5.
12. Val-de-Grâce was a Benedictine convent located on the Left Bank (MC 144).

piece of folly) in order to ask her for my death or the freedom of my beloved, and to say a thousand other tender and touching things to her.

"Madame," I said to her, throwing myself at her feet, covered in tears and telling her my name to the great satisfaction of a number of curious people, "you do not see me here to beg you to have a better opinion of me. At some other time I could demonstrate the innocence I have maintained in the midst of my troubles, if Your Majesty would permit me. I would use in my defense the example of the women of your court whose reputations have been destroyed by mere appearances or out of mere vengeance, and the number of these women is only too great. I would say that most often all that is necessary is to have a few extraordinary qualities but no good fortune, and that is reason enough for imprudence to attack our reputation without scruples; in such a corrupt time scandalmongering spares no one. One of Madame d'Englesac's friends, for example, who does not dare to take my side here in front of Your Majesty, may not know what people are saying about her. At the moment when she flatters herself to be considered virtuous everywhere, a bold stranger who knows only her name is turning her into the scandalous heroine of his imagined love intrigues that he recounts two hundred leagues away from where she is. I have had this happen to me once in my life. In sum, Madame, I would not lack for justifications, but something else makes me audacious enough to present myself before the sight of an outraged queen. They are persecuting, and have seized, the Count of Englesac. This unfortunate gentleman's only crime is not to have doubted my virtue and to have seen things more clearly than others. I come to offer myself up to whatever you would like to do with me, to sacrifice my freedom for his, for he has undoubtedly been deprived of his only because I was still free. I am come to give him up forever, if necessary, to agree that the slanders are true, and to make myself a prisoner, if only Your Majesty will have pity on him and will order that he be left alone."

I accompanied this noble speech with many other ornaments, which I will not mention; they had the charm of novelty and produced a good result, for the queen was amused by it. Smiling, she said to all her retinue that this was the action of a tender and faithful lover. This encouraged some of her waiting women to say a few words in my favor and inclined Her Majesty herself to kindly pardon me. She indicated that she would not be disappointed if a person such as I were innocent; she said she could not free my beloved but that she would leave me free so that I could defend myself. With a very kind nod of her head, she even added a sort of request that I justify myself if it were in my power.

Only God knows how much grief this news gave to the Countess of Englesac, who had already thought she was free of having to make more efforts in order to destroy me. She was in despair about it and would willingly have made more trouble, but all her malice did her no good. In addition, whatever it is in my face that speaks for me had already almost won over the queen mother, because the good, virtuous Madame —— was still on my side. She said she passionately loved beautiful women and that her desire for the ruby of my lips had caused her to be one of my friends, so that she might sometimes get drunk on my kisses. (What will Your Highness say about this effect of my beauty?) Since this desire, as I was saying, obtained for me such a protectress, it was impossible for the Countess of Englesac to have any further success in her original plans, and she had to make up her mind to attack me in the usual way, with lawsuits, which she did.

Thus began between us, Madame, a great and lengthy legal battle, but much less dangerous than the troubles caused me by stealthy calumny, for I could at least explain my reasons. First I was called before some judges (I can't remember which), then the parlement[13] got wind of the affair. The council took it up in turn, and in one of these two chambers, I even had a court reporter[14] fall in love with me. I will have something to say about this later.

Madame the Marquise de Seville, who had come to Paris at the beginning of the storm, defended me in a manner worthy of her. Madame the Countess of Bossut, who had stopped there on her way back from Rome, added the force of her rank and reputation (the latter acquired through several adventures in France). I received the recommendations of several other influential people as well. In the end each side conspired together. Mesdames de Ville-Savin, de Bercy, and d'Escures, two other ladies who were *présidentes*, and a great number of virtuous ladies of every rank, in whose eyes calumny had ruined me, were supporters of the Countess of Englesac, at least that is what I was told. On my side I had all the ladies who felt sorry for me because of their own situations and who very much wished to show, in taking my side, that everything people had said about them could be just as false as what was said about me. The beautiful marchioness, among others, helped me as much as anyone.

And I would have beaten my enemy, Madame, since the fine ladies pleading for me were superior to hers, if what they did for me had not failed through my own fault, or rather the fault of my usual fate.

13. On the parlement, see part 1, note 32. The council is a group charged with the regulation of judges and also with judging cases.

14. At this time a court reporter was the person who would summarize the arguments in a case after they had been made and before the court made a judgment. The reporter could influence the outcome of a case by the way he made his summary.

At the time when everything was for the best, and when people were beginning to criticize the virtuous ladies and say that they were too inclined to persecute the innocent—in sum when, for sheer lack of evidence people were beginning to give me the benefit of the doubt—my evil fate involved me in some ridiculous adventures, which blew all the stories out of proportion and almost ruined everything. The court reporter whom I mentioned and who was in love with me participated in some of these adventures, and Monsieur the Count of ——, in others. I will recount them right away and in few words in order to get on with the story. I begin with my court reporter.

He was a dark-haired man, about thirty-four or thirty-five years old, fairly handsome, and someone who did not think that nature had created him solely to look handsome while sitting in parlement. He was among those judges whose looks persuade them that it is not a crime, counter to the duties of their positions, to make ladies buy with their favors, I will not say justice because that would be disreputable, but the speeding up of their lawsuits.

Given this situation, I naturally was not among the fortunate female plaintives from whom he did not want a favor. It was not his intention to let me off without payment; he was just giving me credit. The extravagant acts of this foolish young man could fill a book, and the following was the most amusing of all. He thought that I would never love him enough if I did not consider him courageous and, under this illusion, one night when we were supposed to go to a ball, he arranged for three men to attack our carriage and to flee as soon as he began to defend himself. This plan succeeded, and far beyond his expectations, for before the false thieves could come and test his courage, three others, who had not promised to flee, robbed us. He threw himself on them with all the courage of a man who does not realize what he is doing, and the result was that he was beaten, and mercilessly at that. But what did it matter, for at least his courage, which I believed to be authentic, had fooled me and this good result consoled him for the blows he had received. But here, Madame, I come to the cruel outcome of all this, which ruined our fine hopes and both of our reputations.

I became convinced that this court reporter was an Amadis[15] disguised in the robe of a judge when I saw him fight off the other men whom he easily made flee, but the Watch was set up in all of Paris and they seized his false thieves. They mistook them for some real thieves, who had just stopped the carriage of the daughter of the Dutch ambassador, now the wife of the handsome Marquis de Rossan. The men were dragged off to prison, and these

15. Amadis is the hero of the Spanish chivalric novel *Amadis de Gaule*. Written at the beginning of the sixteenth century, the novel was translated into all the European languages and enjoyed immense popularity.

poor things were forced to admit the truth in order to clear themselves. For my misfortune, everyone believed them. Satirical gossips soon made of it what they could, and this had a negative effect on my suit and on the judge. In the end, Madame, this gave Madame d'Englesac the chance to have the judge recused and then to use the incident to give more credibility and power to her calumnies, just when people were losing interest in them. Has Your Highness ever heard of anything more laughable? And yet it was a great misfortune for me.

But the affair in which the Count of —— was involved was even more bizarre and cruel. I don't even know if it will seem believable to you, although there has never been anything more true.

Two beautiful ladies, whom I will not name—well, I will name them to give you additional pleasure, for Your Highness has sometimes heard about them elsewhere—it was Madame the Baroness of Saint-de-Fer and Madame Feronne. These two beauties were tired of the long disgrace of the man about whom you asked in your last letter.[16] Whether it was gratitude or simple human weakness that interested them in his misfortune, they had decided to try to bring an end to it and to begin by praying (and I think that this would have surely been the fastest way), and if that did not work to take a completely opposite tack and use charms. I do not mean the charms of their beauty as you might imagine; I mean, Madame, the charms of black magic.

I will not put anyone in danger by revealing the secret of these admirable magicians: it was to take something or other that they had been led to believe a colt has on its forehead when born and to prepare this by means of some ceremonies. In their view, this would become a marvelous and foolproof potion. This potion was to be given surreptitiously to soldiers and even to their captain. And right away these soldiers and their captain would run through the streets offering to do whatever they were asked. Gates and towers were, I dare say, supposed to fall down of their own accord and liberate the person whom these ladies wanted to help. I will not dally by asking you to have compassion for this simplemindedness or by telling you that these ladies appeared to be intelligent, for fear of slowing down my tale.

To accomplish this a mare was needed, and this is how the young Count of —— becomes involved in this mysterious story. The mare they used belonged to him and, in order to earn ten or twenty pistoles,[17] one of his grooms had taken her out of the stables and thought he would get out of the affair by pretending to have found her a few days later.

---

16. This may be an allusion to Fouquet (MC 152). On Fouquet, see part 2, note 10.

17. A pistole was a Spanish gold coin or any of a number of other European gold coins.

The stage on which this comedy was played was a stable belonging to a carter[18] from the port on a little street near the Pont-Marie. The two beauties had gone there in the evening in great secrecy and without any servants. They had dragged me along dishonestly, hiding their real plan. We had already spent the night like ridiculous sentinels watching over the mare, which frightened me and made me think that my friends were mad. We were supposed to continue this extravagant ceremony until the precious animal was born, for some reason I can no longer remember. They were preparing me to see other new things, when to our great misfortune the Count of —— was told that his mare, which he was very unhappy to have lost, had been taken to this carter. He came there right away, accompanied by the Marquis de Plumartin and the Count of Signac, who out of friendship were as worked up as he was. (It is true that this anger did not last very long matched against the new passions aroused by an encounter with three ladies like us.) They caught us in the middle of our fine ceremony, which seemed to them to be a true enchantment in every sense of the word. And in the end the inevitable consequences followed. The story got out. If it did not get out because of the indiscretion of these young lords who had become our gallants—and this is what I must not forget: the Count of —— was subsequently in love with the Baroness of Saint-de-Fer, the Marquis de Plumartin with Madame Feronne, and I got the Count of Signac, who in his turn will help to make this story longer. At the least, I will be bothered by him as much as by the Marquis de Birague—if, as I say, it did not get out because of the indiscretion of these young lords, then it was because of the indiscretion of some of their servants. At the same time, although I had only the smallest part in it, as you have seen, that did not stop people from generously making me responsible for the whole thing and adding to my other well-known qualities that of being an honorable sorceress.[19] Please excuse me for using this shocking and disagreeable word that I could not avoid.

You can judge, Madame, all the wrong that this matter could still do to me, especially when taken up by the Countess of Englesac, for she was not concerned about sacrificing the honor of the other two ladies along with my own in order to achieve her ends. If you believed the enhancements she added to the story, I could be accused of more than magic, and Monsieur the Count of —— and his two friends were said to have immediately avenged our innocent theft of the mare with some other thefts that amorous gallants likewise term "innocent." These gentlemen, who were always the most hon-

18. A carter is someone who drives a cart or wagon. *Oxford English Dictionary*, s.v. "carter."

19. Sorcery was a serious crime in the seventeenth century and the penalties for it extreme.

orable and best-behaved of the court, would have stopped being that in regard to us alone. And our faces, which normally command respect even while inspiring desire, would have done us no good at all in the stable. She even said worse things than this, which I do not dare repeat. It would have meant little that this misfortune ruined all my business in Paris, if it had not caused the cruelest quarrel in the world between me and my beloved, as you will presently see.

Although the Countess of Englesac had the place that served as the count's prison closely watched, he nonetheless was faithfully informed of everything that happened. In addition, his mother did not fail to bring him this bad news right away. It was confirmed by the people who gave him information from time to time. People he knew who sometimes visited him, and of whom Madame d'Englesac was not suspicious, perhaps presented the story in such a way as to make it believable to him. Then something happened that I thought would not happen again once we cleared up the last ruses of Birague and the vain bragging of the Prince of Salmes. The count doubted my conduct. What can I say? Such was my misfortune on this dismal occasion, and jealousy must have produced strange changes in the poor count's mind, for he no longer doubted that his love for me had always made him blind. Thanks to the anger this caused in his heart and which Madame d'Englesac believed to be permanent, he signed every document she wanted. He asked her to free him so that he could flee me and distance himself from me with the same haste as he would have sought me out, had it not been for my crime. She let him go. At that time there was a war between the United Provinces[20] and England, and many illustrious cavaliers had decided to join the Dutch army. He went with them. I found out about it the same day. Because of my pain, it was almost the last day of my life.

What worries! What anger at those wonderful court reporters who wanted to pretend to be brave! What hatred for the Baroness of Saint-de-Fer and for Madame Feronne! How many imprecations against their ridiculous magic! How much rage against the owner of the mare and his two friends! I would tell you the consequences of all this, if I did not have more interesting things to tell you. For, Madame, this disgrace was not the only one, and to really do me in, Madame de Seville decided, at her age, to fall in love with a young man seventeen or eighteen years old and wanted to ask his parents'

---

20. The United Provinces, as the Netherlands were known at this time, was a federation of the seven northern provinces of the Low Countries. It was created 1579 and lasted until 1795. The United Provinces were an ally of France until the 1660s, for the French aided the Dutch in their battles against the Spanish and English.

permission to marry him. I had no success in telling her that if she could not do without love, she should choose other remedies and that she should remember that God forgave everything and men nothing. (In truth, that was a little crazy, but what else could I say to a crazy woman?) I had no success in making her see that in terms of proper behavior, in my interest and in her own interest, she was going to make an irreparable mistake. I could not influence her at all. It was not her fault that the effort failed. Everything I had done to dissuade her only succeeded in making me quarrel with her, my only ally. This quarrel might well have been irreconcilable had there not been between us, as I have often suspected, a tie stronger than friendship and a liking for each other.

Madame, what can you say about these latest caprices of my misfortune? In quarrel with almost all those whom I knew and who could help me—with my court reporter, with the ladies who pleaded in my favor, for a long time with Birague, with Signac almost from the moment I met him (for he did not have the patience to wait until he was loved; I had gotten rid of him, at the risk of making out of him a great enemy). Finally, I was mistreated by the man whom I loved and, so to speak, by a mother, since it was by Madame de Seville. Could I fear any new disgrace except death? Indeed I could, and I soon had the cruel experience of it.

I had sent a man to the Count of Englesac with letters providing justifications of everything that had happened and, when he came back, he told me that there had been a bloody naval battle between Holland and England and that my dear beloved had been swallowed up by the waves. This battle was the one that took place in the month of June, 1666. He had gotten onto the same boat as the Prince of Monaco and the Count of Guiche. In the end, after dreadful exploits (for that is the proper word for them) and after having supported like a lion those two illustrious volunteers, whom glory mixed with something else made fight, as did he, like men who were more than men, he died saving the life of the first of them.

The prince, taken by surprise by a fire on the boat where he had remained too long in the heat of combat, jumped into the water, thinking that he could reach a launch. He was drowning among the broken masts and ropes that prevented him from swimming. The Count of Englesac, who had always admired his courage and that of the Count of Guiche, jumped off the boat into another launch to help him. He did in fact save him, for it was he who made it possible for some of the prince's men to get hold of their master and pull him out of the sea. (This account may surprise some grateful minds, who never knew to whom they should be thankful for playing the most significant role in the prince's rescue.) In sum, he gloriously crowned his actions by this last one. But at the same moment, his launch broke apart. It sank with him in it. Since other boats came and sailed on the spot where he had sunk, no one doubted that he was lost without hope.

This, however, was not the case, and it would be unjust and contrary to literary convention for the hero of a story that must resemble a good work of fiction if he were really to die before having completed all his adventures. We are going to resuscitate him, by your leave, at the appropriate time. It will turn out that the waves had merely carried him around on the sea until, by the mercy of a fate worthy of a novel, which made him its plaything as much as me, he was saved by a frigate belonging to the enemy itself.

But, Madame, what terrible news it was for me when they came to tell me that he had died in this way. Your Highness cannot be the judge of the pain I suffered because at some time you would have to have loved a man as passionately as I loved the Count of Englesac, and you are too wise to do that. You can nonetheless imagine a part of my pain based on the sincere admission that I make to you that if this gentleman had always been dear to me, at that moment I adored him despite the injustice he had done me. This only made me more mad with grief because I had wanted to be reconciled with him. I became furious—this term alone expresses the state I was in. I was almost going to avenge the son on the mother, and to make every effort to tear her apart. It is true that she was said to be in such affliction that she was in almost the same state of despair. Thus, rather than smothering the seeds of our disagreements with the death of the person who had caused them, this misfortune only made us more eager to go after each other. The Countess of Englesac wanted to put the finishing touches on the proof of my scandalous life and find her vengeance in having me punished for it. I wanted to find mine in making her retract her words about me in public. We both stuck to these plans, not having other ways to hurt each other. We persisted despite our lawyers, who thought this would lead to nothing and who in good faith discouraged us. (It was the same Jurandon and Graffet whom Your Highness subsequently chose to take care of your interests in France and with whom I believe you will be quite pleased.) In the end, we astounded the whole courthouse with our quarrels, and it was a lawsuit unlike any other.

However, I may be spending too much time on a matter that is not amusing and, to provide amusement, I must return to the funny adventures that were subsequently not in short supply. The belief that the Count of Englesac's death was certain was a new source of them. This belief attracted new lovers and brought back the old ones. The Marquis de Birague and the young Count of Signac, among others, began again to make their suits more insistently than ever. Even my court reporter came to see me to say that, although

I was defamed, his passion was such that he would marry me secretly if I wanted.

As you can believe, I thanked him with the civility that I thought such a passionate compliment deserved. I said that in this matter I wanted to praise his rare prudence because, if by chance I became able to love him after having lost what was dearest to me, I would no longer be able to marry him any way except in secret since the episode of the fake thieves had dishonored him no less as a man than it dishonored me as a woman. You can judge, Madame, whether that pleased him very much. The poor man left so embarrassed and so outraged with anger that I do not doubt that he hoped with all his heart to be able to be my judge again so he could make me lose my lawsuit.

But this was nothing in comparison with what happened to me because of Birague's jealousy of the young Signac; it was to my mind a ruse worthy of a witty man, and quite a comedy. They say that in fact it was because Birague had made the most of his reading of *Astrea*,[21] where there is a very similar dirty trick, but wherever he got the idea, it was a very funny and clever thing.

I admit that I had a more familiar relationship with the Count of Signac than with that marquis, perhaps because he had more merit, but that is not for me to say. Perhaps he was more amusing or younger, and this last quality is often very important. In sum, either because he did not give me the same reasons to feel aversion for him as did Monsieur de Birague or because I feared him less, I was quite willing to have him visit me. His turbulent little passions did not displease me and did not seem to be very important. In the melancholy humor that my loss, which I considered irreparable, had put me, I was not unhappy that he came from time to time to steal a few hours away from my cruel reverie.

Birague feared that this familiarity and my cooperation might be followed by my marriage, which he wanted for himself. For, Madame, judging that it would be impossible to win me over another way, he had in the end resolved to lead me to the altar. And you will soon see a great proof of this: he would not even have asked for a secret marriage like Monsieur the court reporter, if I had been able to resign myself to making him happy. And if what I say here surprises you because Madame the Marquise was still alive, I will tell you that she had been sick for a long time with a disease from which she could not recover, and the poor marquis counted on the fact that I would no sooner have made up my mind to marry him than he would find himself a widower—at just the right moment.

21. *L'Astrée*, by Honoré d'Urfé, is a pastoral novel that appeared in the early seventeenth century and, like the *Amadis de Gaule*, was very popular and widely read. Villedieu's tale ironically undermines the assumptions of the perfect fidelity of perfect lovers that is enacted in these texts.

As I was saying, Birague, who would have been in despair if Monsieur de Signac had taken me away from him after he had suffered for six long years everything one can suffer in not being loved, moved heaven and earth to take the place of this dangerous rival. I was supposed to go with the count to visit a fortune-teller (or astrologer, as they called her) and a knowledgeable woman (according to what people said) named Dame Voisin.[22] All the unfortunate beautiful women of the court and some gallants as well consulted her. For everyone has this weakness; others may well have it, since I had it myself. As I said, all the beautiful women of the court who were in love made no scruple in going and asking her for some consolation (for this strange urge to know the past or the future rarely strikes anyone other than lovers). Having found out about this visit from a spy he had in my entourage, Birague thought he had found the real secret for obtaining his ends.

He went to this woman a day before we did and persuaded her that she would do no harm to her profession if she consulted him alone about the answer that she would give me. He gave her a good description of me, so that she would not make any mistakes. He told her about the past and indicated what she ought to say and to predict: among other things, that I should distrust and get rid of Signac and that I would marry a widower whom I would be able to identify by certain signs. You can see where all that was leading. And this was in fact what this woman told me when we were at her home, after having questioned me in her way in a small room that she called the Chamber of Oracles.

I confess to you, Madame, that this stratagem had been well set up and that it would have fooled me entirely if the memory of the Count of Englesac, to which I wanted to remain faithful, had permitted me to think of marriage after his death. For, believing these predictions with a gullibility that still makes me blush, I began from that very moment to distrust the Count of Signac, as I had been told to do, to not spend time with him as I had before and to look for reasons to get rid of him. Soon afterward I did in fact get rid of him, to his great regret because he was already in the pleasant habit of loving me dearly.

But the best part was that one of the principal signs by which I was to know the one who would marry me was that he would take refuge in my house from people attacking him. I was not a little surprised when I saw that it was Birague to whom this happened a few days later. He had taken it on himself to fulfil the prophecies and had not failed in his plan. Perhaps he had

22. Catherine Deshayes, known as Dame Voisin, was a midwife who became well known as a fortune-teller. Later implicated in a series of poisonings, she was executed in 1680.

remembered from the adventure of my court reporter the trick of setting up people to attack him. What a trick it was, now that I think of it—one that I never questioned!

I do remember that when they began to draw swords against the tricky marquis, I was at my window, from whose corner I was amusing myself by contemplating the admirable Madame de Castelnau, whose carriage was stopped across from my door. I was satisfying an old curiosity I had about this lady, whom people had always described as being very accomplished. Merinville was also in my room doing something.

"Good Heavens," I cried at the sight of those swords, and turning quickly toward Merinville, I said, "It is all over for me; I am lost. Here is the outcome of what the fortune-teller told me, and worst of all it is Birague, whom I do not love at all, who is being attacked and who is going to take refuge here. Will I be so unfortunate," I continued, "as to be one day the wife of Birague! You wretches," I cried to my footmen, who were in the street, "do not let anyone enter my house; rather let them go ahead and kill each other."

Judge, Madame, what passersby must have thought, hearing me pronounce these cruel words at such a bad time. That would have been enough to make me be taken for an accomplice of the murder if there had been a real one. Merinville came and pulled me away from the window and, more embarrassed than I by my extravagant behavior, asked me if I were not dreaming in thinking that Birague, whom I knew to be married, was the widower of the prophecy. This calmed me down a bit and got me to agree to let him take refuge. It was too late, however; I had already done enough to injure my reputation severely and to give ample material to gossips and to my enemies so that they could put the final horrible touches to my portrait.

It is true that I could almost be excused because of the strong aversion I then had for the marquis, more the result of a bad habit and perhaps of caprice than of any good reason. But, Madame, this is not yet the whole story. It is necessary to take it up in regard to what this dangerous man said to me after he had entered my house and what I said myself when, among other things, he told me—and it was only too true—that his wife was dying and might already be dead. "What!" I cried like a madwoman. He would have been quite amused in reflecting on my distress if he had not been both in love and mistreated, but an unhappy lover is incapable of laughing. "What," I said to him, "is it really possible that you will become a widower or already are one? Come now, Monsieur," I added, "as soon as you possibly can, get out of my sight. Flee from here. And if you are capable of any gratitude, never think of me again." I think I also told him that I regretted saving his life.

But perhaps I should keep silent about these last circumstances, since they scarcely do me any honor and hardly seem believable, for unless a woman is judged worthy of being shut up in an asylum, it is almost unheard of for her to go to such extremes. I have not, however, told you anything that did not happen, and my fate was the cause of it. I will bravely add that I did not stop there and that, given time, I would have committed other great extravagances if the Count of Englesac, over whom I had wept as a dead man for more than ten months, had not returned at just the right moment to put an end to the bizarre effects of two contrary passions. Madame, I have to tell you the unusual circumstances of this very unexpected return.

First of all, it was Signac who, although he was his rival, brought the count back to me, more in love with me than ever and more convinced than ever that I was virtuous. On that subject Signac himself had taken care to enlighten the count. Has anyone ever seen more honorable behavior? They had run into each other on the avenues of Champlâtreux,[23] where the one was getting some air when the other passed by on his way back to Paris.

Second, the way Signac brought the count back to me was quite singular. He did it this way in order to surprise me all the more agreeably (or, to put it better, all the more dangerously because it almost killed me). This young gentleman wanted to make me change from anger to joy. To manage this, he sent me a bold letter—rather than the submissive and modest complaints that he had been accustomed to write to me since I had banished him, he wrote that he was tired of his exile, that I should be ready to receive him into my bedroom at midnight, that he had found the secret for making me fall in love and for making me grateful for his visit, and that, if I did not go along with this, I would regret it.

What could I think of these insolent terms? I was far from understanding them, and who could? But this was nothing, and I was very surprised that my man turned up at my house at the hour he had said and came to the door of my room with no consideration or respect. (It is true that he was very sure of his excuse since he was accompanied by the Count of Englesac.) I was, as I said, filled with surprise when I heard him call out, "Madame, open up, open your door. I come to give you joy and love, and a repose that will be more agreeable to you than what I now interrupt."

I cannot express how well he had succeeded in making me angry by this disrespectful behavior, so far removed from the gentility with which he had always treated me. Merinville had not gone to bed, and I told her to speak through the door to tell this indiscreet man that he should leave and that I was deeply offended by the liberty he had taken. But he answered that he

23. Champlâtreux is an estate near Saint-Denis, outside of Paris (MC 174).

would not go away until the door was opened and that he would enter by force rather than to fail to make peace with me that night as he had planned. He added so many other things capable of offending me, although he said them in a way that corresponded to his good intentions, that I decided in the end to open the door. But this was after I had seized a sword in order to give him the sort of reception that I thought this insolence deserved. "Oh! Open the door to him," I cried, "and let's see what his plan is." Frankly, in my anger I do not think I would have spared him.

Alas, Madame, how quickly my weapon fell from my hand at the sight of the Count of Englesac, who had agreed to this deception. I cried out, but that was all because I fainted almost immediately. I was very fortunate that the different joys that came together all at once in my heart did not kill me on the spot, for they say that women die in this way. When I came to, only my tears spoke. Running to the embraces of that dear object, I felt indeed that Signac had brought love and joy back to me.

As for the Count of Englesac, since he was prepared to see me before he was brought to me, he perhaps did not suffer from such violent passions, although in remaining mute and, like me, in only using the language of tears he revealed the depths of his soul sufficiently. Almost an hour passed like this. Afterward, having thanked the generous Signac a thousand times, and after my beloved and I had clarified things and promised never again to doubt each other's fidelity, we separated, agreeing to meet the next day at a certain place. For the Countess of Englesac was unaware that her son was alive and had returned, and he did not want to present himself to her until he had taken the necessary steps to marry me despite all the obstacles. He wanted to be sure of at least this happiness before putting himself in the hands of Fortune, which had been so hostile to us.

Here, Madame, is the third part of my tale. In the fourth part, I will recount to Your Highness all the things we had to endure before this marriage could be happily accomplished, and this will be no less curious than the rest. I will also tell you on what part of the earth my count had been so rigorously detained, or rather in what distant place he had spent the time during which he was thought to be dead and had been unable to give any news of himself to anyone. I beg Your Highness, however, to do me the honor of believing that it is out of respect for your commands that I continue to tell you things that it might be better to leave forgotten, and that I remain your very humble and very obedient servant,

H. S. D. M.

PART 4

Here I was at last, Madame. I had arrived at that part of my life so long awaited and so ardently wished for. The Count of Englesac told me what had happened to him since his jealousy had torn him away from me. I found nothing in this tale unworthy of a man who was my beloved. We made the protestations and the reproaches that one makes in such a situation, and with the help of some friends whom we had to let in on the secret, we were married without the knowledge of the Countess of Englesac and with no ceremony.[1]

What a joy, Madame, if only it had lasted a full day, but that would have been too much. When this poor lover thought that he was the happiest of men, when he thought that he had finally outwitted Fortune, by whom he had been fooled so many times, he discovered that he had (in his view) fallen into the most appalling disgrace that could befall him. I am at a loss as to how to express myself on this matter. What I mean to say, Madame, is that he discovered that he was married to no purpose and that a cruel spell had been put on us by one of our enemies.[2]

How foolish men are to think that they are contemptible on this score. I said a thousand things to him but to no avail. If I repeated them here, it would perhaps create a favorable impression of my sagacity in those who would do me the honor of taking me at my word. My speeches did not persuade him; he had regrets that, while arousing in me much pity, did not fail at times to make me burst out laughing also. Suspecting his mother of having something to do with his misfortune, he went and revealed to her by his reproaches the marriage that we had hidden from her with so much care.

Madame, please imagine the rage of this woman when she saw her son come back to life to give her such a great displeasure. She insulted him a thousand ways, threatened him a thousand ways, and, not satisfied with words, she resorted to legal proceedings, as was her habit. This new trial brought my court reporter back to me. He thought the situation was one that promised to make him look good, and he had not forgotten my charms, nor had my other suitors, whose hopes were rekindled by the Count of Englesac's misfortune. For the imprudent Madame d'Englesac told everyone about it and called it a result of divine justice.

---

1. A clandestine marriage like this one, not done in the proper forms, was condemned by both Church and State law (MC 179).

2. Impotence was commonly attributed to spells. In the seventeenth century the dominant Christian culture associated Jews with magical practices. For this reason, later in the novel, Englesac believes himself to be cured by a Jew.

The Marquis de Birague was among the first to come and drive me crazy. With his wife on the edge of death, he hoped soon to be able to marry me, and he had not been discouraged by either my disdain or my adventures. He tried all kinds of ways of making me break off my marriage. He had always maintained good relations with Madame d'Englesac, and he advised her to try to win me over through self-interest. The old Cabrières came from the depths of Languedoc to increase my persecution; he offered me thirty thousand pounds on the countess's behalf if I would put a stop to all the proceedings.

Even Madame de Seville entered into this conspiracy, letting me know that she would revoke the gifts she had given to me if I persisted in remaining the wife of the Count of Englesac. I think I know who made her talk that way; at that time she was very taken with the Marquis de Sainte-Fère, and I was warned that he had ties to my enemies.

But none of this can compare with what I am about to tell you. The Count of Englesac was moved by Madame de Seville's threats and advised me to do everything she wanted, provided that she not demand back her gifts. I want to believe that he was only acting in my interests, as he said he was. But I offered another motive for his advice: I accused him of loving me too little. We quarreled, and we often found ourselves in the same place without looking at each other. Signac noticed this. He had not been successful in his plan to be just a friend to me, and so he came back to me, more in love than ever, to see if he could profit from this alienation between the count and me. The Marquis de Birague was afraid of this rival and could not see his return without feeling a great deal of jealousy.

I will tell Your Highness a pleasant effect of this. One day, Birague was more tired than usual of Signac's presence, and he called him a liar in my chamber. It was over a trivial thing he had just said himself—that is Signac's story. Signac did not want to react to this insult in my home and in that showed great respect for me since he did not do this for lack of bravery. I notified Monsieur the Marshal of Estrées, who lived near me, and had guards put on them.[3] The Marquis de Birague could never say why he had called Signac a liar, and I think that, even if Signac had said that I was beautiful, Birague would have nonetheless told him he was lying.

Madame d'Englesac found out about this quarrel and did not fail to turn it into new material for her calumnies. But I at least had the consolation of being freed of these annoying men for some time, for Birague was sent for three

---

3. This was a way of trying to calm the quarreling parties and avoid a duel (MC 182).

months to Fort-l'Evêque,[4] and I got Signac to agree not to come to my house so as not to compromise me in the old countess's gossip.

This poor young man fell ill from unhappiness, and this was worse than coming to see me because I could not refuse to visit him. I think that demon Birague had some malignant spirit at his command. In prison, he found out about the visit I had made to the sick man and let the Count of Englesac know about it.

Jealousy is a great remedy for cold lovers. The Count of Englesac wrote to me to obtain a reconciliation and asked me for so much forgiveness in that letter that my heart could not refuse him. I pretended the contrary, however, for I wanted to break his habit of quarreling with me. I was difficult in order to make him behave better the next time. He took my pretense as evidence of Signac's progress and became so jealous he almost went insane. He had me followed by people unknown to me. He bribed my footmen and had me so well spied upon that he caught me in a secret conversation with Signac in the Labyrinth of the Jardin des Simples.[5]

For, Madame, I held Signac in great esteem, and I pitied him because he nourished vain hopes. I had met with him so as to order him once and for all to get this passion out of his head. "No, Signac," I said to him, "I cannot accept your love. Try to overcome it; it makes you unhappy, and I am not so indifferent to you that I can see your suffering without displeasure. What more do you want me to do? I love the Count of Englesac and our quarrel is about to end, and when it does, we will be more in love than ever." "But, Madame," Signac interrupted, "the count cannot be happy, and this reconciliation about which you speak, which would make any other man happy, will only increase his despair. Have you never imagined the rage of a man in love who has his mistress under his power, who is ardently loved by her, and who could legitimately possess her but does not possess her?" What Signac said touched me with such pity for the Count of Englesac that I could not hold back my tears. Signac interpreted this to his own advantage, fell to his knees, and said such convincing things that I do not know how I resisted them. "Allow yourself to be touched by my sighs, my beautiful countess," he said to me, "and do not kill a miserable man whose love and persistence are worthy of a better fate. If the Count of Englesac could profit from your constancy, I would die rather than fight against it, and you know that I brought him back

---

4. Fort-l'Evêque was a prison belonging to the bishop of Paris (MC 185).

5. This garden, located on the Left Bank in Paris, belonged to the king. Today it is known as the Jardin des Plantes.

to you a while ago. But your fidelity is fatal to him. While you let me perish in order to remain faithful to him, you inflict on him a death no less cruel than that which I am suffering. Take pity on us both and on yourself. You do not know what it is for a beautiful woman to have a husband who, for a good reason, has a low opinion of himself. You will be the most unhappy of all women, and that is what drives me to despair." "It doesn't matter," I replied in tears. "No amount of suffering is too great; I will suffer anything whatever in order to recompense the love that the poor count has always shown me. I will love him all my life, and whatever happens, I will be only too happy to spend the rest of my days with him under any conditions whatsoever." The Count of Englesac, who heard these words through a hedge, was so touched by them that he could not hide any longer. He came and threw himself at my feet, and the sight of him surprised us so much that Signac cried out, and I thought I was going to faint. "Fear nothing," the count said to his rival. "I have not come to reproach you for your efforts to seduce her. You are more worthy of her than I, and I am a wretched man who has nothing left to do but die." He thought he would indeed die in saying those last words. Turning his gaze on me in pathetic fashion, he said, "No, my dear Sylvie," for this was what he always called me, "I will not make bad use of your resolution, for it will make you unhappy. Marry Signac. I give my consent. I more than consent—I beg you to do this." After this plea, he left the Jardin in a state of despair and took the post to Flanders, where troops were beginning to march.[6]

Signac hoped to profit from this departure and from the consent given in his favor, but he was far from getting what he wanted. I reproached him a thousand times for my husband's having abandoned me. Accusing him alone of this misfortune, I swore to him that I would hate him more than death itself unless he brought the count back to me. Consider if you will, Madame, the nature of this man's love for me. He ran after the count, and I found out subsequently that he omitted nothing in trying to make him come back. But this is enough talk about serious matters, and some diversity is needed in this story. To amuse you a bit after having perhaps afflicted you, I must tell Your Highness what my court reporter did to seek my good graces.

He made constant visits, and I was obliged to accept this, for when one does not cooperate with these men, one has trouble in the courts. One day he came and said he had found an admirable way for me to win my lawsuit and drive the Countess of Englesac crazy. I naively thought that he had found some articles of law that justified my winning the case. Forgive me,

6. In May 1667 Louis XIV invaded the Spanish Low Countries. This was the beginning of the War of Devolution.

Madame, that is not what it was. He wanted to persuade me that a skillful woman never dies without an heir. What do you think of such a legal opinion? I did not even deign to get angry because that would have meant taking the matter seriously, and beyond that I had other concerns.

The cunning Madame d'Englesac had sent to me a young lord named the Marquis de Villars, whose mother she knew, so I have been told. He was one of the handsomest men at the court. He had been asked to play the role of my suitor, in the hope, I think, that he would succeed in making me love him. Then, after he had succeeded in getting me to annul my marriage, he would leave me, without a husband, to be everyone's laughingstock. Things went otherwise, however. This amiable young man fell in love with me instead and revealed to me Madame d'Englesac's designs, which still make me tremble in thinking about them. The poor man! His frankness should have spared him the musket shot that killed him at Dermonde.[7] They had planned to use force to put me back in that convent in Avignon from which I had escaped. Madame de Vendôme, whose goodness had been deceived by the things she was told about me, was supposed to persuade the Cardinal of Vendôme to back this plan. She might have succeeded if she had been able to find me, for the zeal of good souls is impetuous. I had never been more worried, and more at a loss as to what to do. Every noise I heard seemed to be a carriage come to carry me off, and I was in a house, the Hotel of Holland, where I often had this kind of fear.[8] Monsieur the Abbot of Villeserin lived across the street, and already at this time the salon of witty people, held at his home, was in the planning stages. All I ever saw were people with severe expressions stopping at his door and passing in my street, and I thought they were all people sent by the devout ladies.

No longer daring to remain in Paris, I put an agent in charge of my lawsuit, and with Merinville alone I went to seek the Count of Englesac so that he could protect me from his mother's undertakings. But, Madame, to what dangers is one exposed when one travels about in this world! In passing through the forest of Senlis, the chaise that I had rented from Blavet broke, and I was left sitting at the base of a tree while someone went to get workers from a nearby village to fix it.[9] They took such a long time to come that I lost patience, and I sent Merinville after them to hurry them up. I was no sooner

7. Dermonde, in southwestern Belgium, was the site of one of the first defeats of the campaign of 1667 (MC 189).

8. This rooming house contrasts with the proper middle-class house in which Sylvie stayed when she came to Paris disguised as the Prince of Salmes, under the tutelage of Saint-Canal.

9. Senlis is about forty miles north of Paris. A chaise is a light open carriage for one or two people. Blavet was a merchant who rented coaches and chaises (MC 190).

alone than a horseman passed near me and, after great exclamations, descended and spoke to me. He was, from what I could understand, the illegitimate son of the King of Portugal, usually called the Prince of Portugal; he had visited all the courts of Europe under that name.

He claimed that that same Voisin who had previously given me such a fright about having to marry Birague had shown him, in a glass of water, the image of a person who resembled me and had predicted great misfortunes if he failed to make this person love him. I laughed very hard when he told me this, and I, in turn, made some terrible predictions about him. But this did not stop him because Voisin had predicted this as well, saying that I would respond to him as I had, and that he should push his efforts even further. He would have done so had not the Marquis de Sainte-Fère, who was going to join the army, passed by this same road. He did not think that I was happy to see him, as in fact I was. On the contrary, finding me alone in the forest with a rather handsome man, he thought he had interrupted me at a bad time and made a thousand excuses. I could not undeceive him, for a carriage passed in which I recognized Madame de Seville. She called out to stop the carriage and, jumping down, made I cannot say how many amorous reproaches to the Marquis de Sainte-Fère. At first he answered politely, but, seeing that the more reasonable he was, the angrier she became, he ran off, and Madame de Seville remained in my arms half fainting with pain.

From what I could understand of their conversation, Sainte-Fère had only pretended to love the Marquise de Seville during a period when he was quarreling with another mistress. This quarrel had come to an end, as there is hardly ever an eternal one between people who have really loved each other, and Madame de Seville, finding herself without a lover, followed him everywhere to reproach him with his infidelity. I consoled her as best I could, and she was so grateful for my consolation that she forgot all the differences that had been between us. She promised not to abandon me until she had put me back in the arms of the Count of Englesac.

As for our Portuguese prince, I do not know what became of him. I think he feared some punishment for his audacity when he saw that I knew a well-connected gentleman and a woman with a fine coach. I distracted the marquise from her sorrow in recounting this adventure to her and, when Merinville got back to us, we took the road to Avesnes together.[10]

The queen was there at that time, and the king had come to see her, followed by a number of noble volunteers, among whom I immediately recog-

10. Avesnes-sur-Helpe is southeast of Lille, about ten miles from the Belgian border. It was given to France in the Treaty of the Pyrenees. On this treaty, see part 1, notes 29 and 34.

nized Signac. He thought he would die of joy when he saw me. You will see that he was right to be happy. He still loved me and carried with him a letter from the Count of Englesac, in which, far from saying he would come back to me, as Signac assured me he had asked him to do, he once again told me to marry his rival.

"Make happy the person whom I love most in all the world," he wrote in this letter, speaking of me, "and allow me to contribute to this happiness by my consent, since I can contribute to it in no other way. I ask your agreement as a last proof of your love." The poor count gave me a great proof of his love when he wrote to me in these terms. But when one is in love, one is not wise; I did not take his letter in this way. I cannot tell you how much his insistence on giving me up angered me.

The king returned to the head of his troops. It is a pity that it is not someone who understands war who writes this account. Your Highness would see in it fine examples of courage and fitting praises of our august monarch. We followed the queen as she visited the places conquered, and I acquired a lover who amused us very much by the way he courted me. Up to that point I had known only submissive lovers and, in my playful moods, I used to say that, because they are so rare, once in my life I would like to find a proud lover.

The man about whom I am speaking was the right one to fulfill this wish. When he was in my chambers, one would have thought he was going into the trenches; he always spoke in the language of war, and he spoke to me of his intentions with such confidence in his own value that he made me fall over laughing. Two or three times he almost got angry, seeing me laugh so, but I told him this was my nature and that he should be patient.

Signac, however, continued to press me. It was the time of the siege of Douai,[11] where the Marquise de Seville lost her Sainte-Fère, over whom she wept as if she had a good reason to do so. Signac accomplished many marvels during this siege, and he did not fail to come and see me from time to time in Tournay, where we were and where he said the most tender things in the world to me. The marquise was touched by them and, since I must tell you all, Madame, I was also very touched. In addition, I had no news of the Count of Englesac. He had left the camp as soon as he learned of my arrival, not daring to face me, I think. For he still believed he had made me unhappy, no matter how I swore the contrary to him. The marquise kept reminding me that the Count of Englesac fled my presence, while Signac loved me more than

---

11. This siege took place in July 1667 (MC 194). Douai, like Lille and Valenciennes mentioned below, is in Flanders, a northern French province on the Belgian border.

life itself. In sum, Madame, I do not know what would have happened if the Count of Englesac had not returned, transported with joy to tell me that the spell had been broken.

He had decided to retire near Your Highness, and on the way there he had found a Jew who promised to cure him and who in fact did not lie about that. I don't believe in these superstitions, but experience is a great teacher.

Englesac's return (and his return to good health) was a fatal blow for poor Signac. I never saw him again. I have no doubt that his despair contributed to his throwing himself into the perils that caused his death at the siege of Lille.[12]

I wept tenderly for this noble young man; it was the least I could do to honor all the love and respect he had had for me. My gallant sought to comfort me for this loss. In his usual way, he offered to replace, alone, all of my lovers. I was not in the mood for his speeches and did not laugh as I had in the beginning. I asked him, seriously, to leave me in peace, and I saw that the time had now come when I would make a hard test of his gallantry. He no longer honored me with his attentions, and his resentment freed me of him, as the end of the campaign freed me from following the army. For, Madame, I could not get the Count of Englesac to leave the army. He was present at the defeat of General Marcin[13] before I could get him to return to Paris. The Marquise de Seville took us back there, and I brought visible evidence that the Jew had broken the charm.

This circumstance of my return almost made the Countess of Englesac die of rage. She made incredible efforts to persuade her son that the child I was carrying was not his. She had found out about my encounter with the Prince of Portugal. She described it to her son as Sainte-Fère had understood it—for he had undoubtedly gossiped about it. I think she claimed that I had followed this adventurer when he was in the army, although he may never have been in the army, and I suspect she may have claimed that I entertained some of the leading officers of the encampment.

I will say this in favor of the Marquis de Birague—he did not support the Countess of Englesac's plan to ruin me as he had her plan to annul my marriage. He defended my virtue before all those who attacked it. His efforts were useless, however, and the defamatory story had made the rounds.

I do not know whether these false stories cooled off the Count of Englesac or if marriage alone caused this change, but he became tired of me, as is

12. Lille is in northern France. The city fell in August 1667. Antoine de Boësset, sieur de Villedieu, was killed during this siege (MC 195).

13. This is an allusion to the fall of Lille.

usual. As soon as I pleased him less, many other women began to please him more.

The Marquise de Seville was the first to see this and to call my attention to it. She always had to have several love affairs on her mind, and since by chance she found her heart unoccupied with any of her own, she busied herself with figuring out those of the Count of Englesac.

She found out every visit he made; he did not make a single amorous plan without her being aware of it and telling me about it. I made an amusing use of her information, and if I dared to tell Your Highness about it, you would find it funny, but at the same time you would think me mad. It doesn't matter; I will have to make you guess what I do not have the confidence to tell you.

One day I deceived the desires of the Count of Englesac, mostly out of playfulness and to see if he would recognize me rather than for any other reason. He was so far from recognizing me that he gave me a diamond hair ornament, thinking he was giving it to his mistress. I wore it the next day. The poor man! He had never been so certain that he would not be his wife's only husband, for he had promised part of his good fortune to one of his friends. It was by the greatest good luck in the world that I was no longer to be found where the count had sent him. He might have fooled me, for he had the password, and it was nighttime. My Lord! When I think about it, how worried my husband was. How much pleasure his friend gave him when, by accusing him of breaking his word, he let him know that misfortune had been avoided. Are you not surprised by the mania of husbands for being so jealous of those whom they seem to despise?

But that's not everything. The Marquise de Seville told me about an assignation that the count had in the Place Royale with a lady whose merit and manners were familiar to me. She was one of those fancy women who, without ever really taking anything, ruin a lover through expenses. One day someone told me that she once indicated to a man who loved her that she would love to have flame-colored ribbon for a masquerade at the Louvre, and he was crazy enough to send to London to get some. She did not want to accept it without paying what it cost, but the gentleman had spent two hundred pounds in sending to get it, and those were little costs she didn't bother about.

This thought or, if you prefer, a bit of jealousy (for I was not exempt from it) made me try to break off this assignation. I used a trick to keep the Count of Englesac longer than he wanted in a house where he had dined. Finding myself at the meeting place, I gave the signal that I knew he was supposed to give and the door was opened for me. Old Saint-Canal, whom I had asked to

accompany me, helped me. His man's face fooled the maid who was supposed to open the door for the count. When Saint-Canal got through the
door, he held it open so that I could enter. Here, Madame, you may note a
most amusing aspect of this story. The maid had not been ordered by her
mistress to do what she did. Her mistress tolerated the Count of Englesac,
and perhaps even loved him a little, but he was not on such terms with her as
to obtain a nighttime assignation. He was being let in without permission,
and he hoped that his love and his merit would allow him to make peace for
himself and the maid once he was alone with the lady.

This produced two amusing effects. The first was that the maid was so
seized with fear that I got all the way to the bed of her mistress without her
being able to make a sound. And the other was that, having learned from that
lady of her innocence and my error, I found my rival to be so beautiful that we
formed a close friendship. I told her, smiling, that I forgave the Count of Englesac the infidelities she was making him commit. She gallantly responded
that she would not forgive him for them. What can I say, Madame? We had
the world's most agreeable and unusual conversation.

I was not the only person out on the streets that night. Under the gal-
leries of the Place Royal, I came upon a man who was undoubtedly awaiting
some good fortune in love. It was, as I guessed from his speech, the same
Prince of Salmes whose name I had formerly taken and who, by his subse-
quent bragging, had caused a falling-out between me and the Count of Englesac. As soon as I spoke, he knew I was not the one whom he expected, but
I seemed pretty enough to him to be able to replace her. He asked me to take
a turn or two around the gallery, and I agreed to do so. I had hoped for a long
time to meet this prince and to reproach him with what he had said about me.
I brought up this adventure at a good moment and, without saying who I was,
asked him for details. I expected him, at the least, to be taken aback and to
struggle for an answer. But, Madame, what are we poor women exposed to?
My German prince told me details of my affair with him that almost persuaded me, for they seemed so true. I was ready to speak out and would certainly have done so had not Monsieur the Duke of Richelieu, who was
coming from the home of Monsieur the Marshal of Albret, interrupted us.
His servants carried torches. The Prince of Salmes did not, I think, dare let
himself be seen there without his retinue, and I was not pleased about being
seen alone with him. We separated quickly.

I do not know if what I said to him about myself had recalled my name to
his memory, or if chance alone brought him to my home. But he came to dine
there with the Count of Englesac a few days later. They had run into each

other at the home of the Grand Prior,[14] and the count liked to treat his friends regally. The prince did not recognize me as the lady he had spoken with at the Place Royale. I told him the story as if I had heard it from another source, and I asked him what he thought about it. I embarrassed him terribly, and he would have amused me for a long time had not the Count of Englesac, who was in despair over the trick I had played on him, revealed that I was the person of whom I was speaking. The Prince of Salmes undoubtedly remembered other things he had said to me. I saw him turn red, and I understood that he was more touched by embarrassment than by scruples. This would have been a sufficient intrigue with him, if Fortune had listened to me, but she did not consult me. As far as I can tell, this prince wanted to be telling the truth when in the future he would brag of a liaison with me. From that day forward, he spoke passionate discourses to me. I heard some more after he found me on the balcony of Madame de Montausier, where I had been allowed to come to see the ambassador of Moscovie.[15] He told me in an amorous tone that I was more beautiful than all the ladies of the court. He exaggerated a great deal. But I must have been looking beautiful that day, for the Count of Englesac noticed and deigned to tell me so. He did more than that. He pointed me out to the Marquis de Castelan, Major of the Regiment of Guards, who was strolling with him in the courtyard. By this little moment of emotion, he increased the number of unwelcome suitors by whom, it is written in the heavens, I will troubled all my life. For, Madame, this marquis fell in love with me and, as the ultimate sorrow, Madame de Seville fell in love with him.

This is how I found out. The marquise's love affairs were all fictions; never has any woman had so many intrigues and so few denouements. Every morning she sent verses or gallant notes to Castelan, without his knowing where these gallant things came from. He dropped one of these notes in my chamber and did everything in his power to persuade me that it was a favor from a lady of importance. I recognized the writing and burst into peals of laughter at the vanity of this gentleman. The marquise came in while I was laughing and was very resentful of my joking.

But this was not the greatest evil that his vanity caused me. The marquise had had a magnificent scarf made for Castelan, and she timed its deleevery to

14. This is the Grand Prior of Malta, i.e., the head of the lay religious order known as the Knights of Malta.

15. In the fall of 1668 the ambassador of Moscovie visited Paris (MC 200). Moscovie is the name that the French used at this time for the principality of Moscow, and by extension, for the state of Russia.

him to coincide with the day when the king presented a revue of troops for the Prince of Florence, who was visiting the court incognito. She used one of my servants to deliver the gift and, although he was disguised as a courier who had come from far away, Castelan recognized him. He unfolded the scarf and admired it and showed it to everyone around him. There were some people who were malicious enough to say he had given himself the present. He wanted to justify himself and could not do so without naming me. I was totally surprised to hear myself linked in *vaudevilles*[16] with Castelan. I cannot tell you, Madame, how many troubles this caused me. Two or three ladies who deserved to be in these rhymes more than I did, believing that I was their rival, attacked me. These songs came to the ears of the Count of Englesac and found him disposed to believe them. He said a thousand unpleasant things to me, and if the lady from the Place Royale had not made an effort to calm him down, I would have been in danger of never seeing him again for the rest of my life.

This was not all. He was secretly annoyed that I got on so well with the person he loved. He thought, perhaps, that our friendship would slow down his progress, and I foresaw the time when I would ask this lady to be more cooperative so that the Count of Englesac would be in a better mood. The Marquise de Seville completed my unhappiness. At first she thought she was helping me by making it known that it was she who had sent the scarf to Castelan. He refused to cooperate, not finding the lady young enough to do him honor, I think. She and I quarreled again, and the Count of Englesac, following the practice of husbands who have lost interest in their wives by making everything the grounds for a quarrel, was angry with me because the marquise complained about me.

This disgrace was followed by another, even worse one, which had even more far-reaching consequences. The Prince of Salmes continued to behave as my suitor and was annoyed that he got no advantage from his love other than the freedom to visit me. He confided his unhappiness to some woman or other, whose name I have forgotten. (And should I remember it, I do not know if I would dare say it to Your Highness.) This woman made fun of him for having made so many unsuccessful efforts and assured him that she knew a shorter road to my heart. For all I know, she may even have said to him that this road had been tried before and that with her help some other lovers had traveled it. The German prince believed her and promised her immense sums of money if she could seduce me. She pretended to be working on this, por-

---

16. A *vaudeville* is a song written to an easy tune, whose words evoke and sometimes satirize a contemporary event.

traying me sometimes as cruel and sometimes as ready to give in, according to what suited her purposes. Finally, she portrayed me as having made up my mind to do whatever the Prince of Salmes wanted. I had been promised and, according to the lady, I know not how, I had been delivered. Are you not horrified by this imprudent behavior, Madame, which you would find unbelievable were it not recounted to you by the person to whom it happened?

I do not know what was done to deceive the Prince of Salmes, whether darkness alone sufficed or if magic was used. But he was so well deceived that, thanks to seeing me wear a bracelet that he thought he had given me, he understood that he had gotten the full satisfaction of his desires. This deception made him think that he had the right to be very familiar with me, and he wanted to make use of this privilege. The first time he found me alone, he started out with some private caresses. I will let Your Highness judge how much they surprised me, I who had always found him to be very respectful and who had done nothing to weaken that respect.

I asked him if he had dined in town, trying to excuse him by only accusing him of having drunk too much. He burst out laughing, and as you see, he was right to do so. On my arm I was wearing the very bracelet he thought he had given me. The person who had actually received it needed money more than jewels. She gave it to someone to sell, who by chance brought it to me and offered it at such a low price that I could not stop myself from buying it. Imagine the roles we both played, Madame. The more the Prince of Salmes laughed, the more offended I became. To his mind, my anger was a form of dissimulation. We said hard things to each other. Without giving him a chance to explain himself better, I threw him out of my house.

As you can judge, a lover who thinks himself happy and sees himself treated in such a way considers that he is no longer obliged to be discreet. The Prince of Salmes made the story public, as he understood it, and it was in this way that the Count of Englesac heard it.

Madame, I cannot tell you how irritated he was. He made outrageous reproaches to me, without being willing to hear any explanations. He said he never wanted to see me again and withdrew to his mother's. I ran to find the Prince of Salmes and said to him everything a perfectly justified resentment would make one say. He did not know what to say, but in the end he acknowledged the trick that had been played on us. I set him straight about what happened. I have no doubt that the traitress who played this vile trick on me told him the truth herself, for the Prince of Salmes himself made the truth public, accompanied by signs of sincere regret for the trouble he had caused me. His speeches and his repentance were useless, however. The Count of Englesac did not believe them; on the contrary, he thought that I had bought the prince's testimony thanks to new favors. Becoming angrier from day to day, he agreed to break off our marriage.

The lawsuit that the Countess of Englesac had let die down, waiting for a better time to pursue it and counting perhaps on her son's becoming disgusted, started up again. The Count of Englesac was not of legal age[17] when I married him, and the marriage had not been made with all the required formalities. Is this not a sad outcome of such a violent passion, and are not women crazy to fall in love, seeing this example?

I did what I could to see the Count of Englesac and to make one last effort to use the power I once had over him. But he took pains to avoid me, and this cruelty drove me to despair.

One day I was sadly daydreaming in the Luxembourg gardens. A man of quality, whose name I will keep secret because his repentance merits this consideration, came and sat on the bench where I was resting. Dispassionately, we exchanged our opinions about of the beauty of the young Mademoiselle Stroup and of Madame de la Mailleraye, who were formerly ladies in waiting to Madame the Princess of Carignan and were walking along the same path where we sat. The man of whom I speak enjoyed conversing with me and said to me, after several comments on brunettes and blondes, that the case for the former would always be the stronger if made by me.

I was not in the mood to respond to this gallant remark, but I knew this man had good connections with the legal world and, in my state, I needed whatever help I could get. We had a rather long and rather witty conversation. He asked for the liberty to come and continue it at my home, and I gave him permission for the same reason that had obliged me to talk to him.

I do not know whether my free and playful manner gave him hopes of which I had had no thought, or if it was his custom to be very forward, but he didn't make many visits without expressing to me his awful intentions.

I made it very clear to him that they displeased me and that he should desist. He did not reform his behavior, however, and went so far as to leave a purse full of money on my dressing table. I sent it back to him and gave instructions to my servants so that, at whatever hour he tried to see me, I was never home.

His disappointment got the best of him. He made the incident of the purse public, without mentioning that it had been sent back. This calumny attracted two or three other annoying propositions, which Madame d'Englesac found out about, and she did not fail to draw malicious conclusions.

Her reaction did not surprise me since I was used to her injustices, but

---

17. The age of majority for marriage without parental consent was twenty-five (MC 207).

her son began to believe her and worked so hard for my ruin that his mother could not be said to have worked harder.

The lawsuit started up again with unparalleled ferocity. Madame d'Englesac took up the information she had formerly gotten against me and claimed that the baby I had had, who had died, was not the Count of Englesac's child.

The Marquis de Birague insisted that this was not true. He would have liked to have seen my marriage broken, for his wife had died and he still held to his plan to marry me, but he wanted Madame d'Englesac to base her claim of invalidity on procedural matters, not on bad morals. This perseverance in defending my reputation touched me, and although his generous behavior was not without self-interest, we did not fail to reconcile. The Marquise de Seville also came to my aid. She angered easily but had an admirable nature and offered me much solace if I should lose my suit.

But I was beyond solace. The Count of Englesac's disdain, which he exhibited to my face and not while fleeing from me as he usually did, put me in despair.

"Why are you using the law against me," I said to him one day when we met in one of our judges' chambers. "Have you not always been the master of my fate? Previously, you wanted it to be my fate to spend the rest of my days with you, and I agreed—and not without sufficient proof that this desire was sincere. Today you want to break off that union. Very well, I consent. I only wanted your heart, and since your heart no longer belongs to me, nothing remains. But please attribute my submission to my love. Say to me: I ask you for the freedom that our marriage took away from me; give it back to me, and I will take it from your hand as a mark of your passion. After that, ingrate, I will sign anything you want. Go ahead and use your authority, and nothing will be impossible for you, but don't use the authority of the law, for if I must give you up to something other than yourself, I will fight you until my last breath."

The Count of Englesac responded to this speech with only disdainful looks. Thinking that he was being kind to me by not reproaching me with what he called my infidelities, he reproached me with them all the more cruelly by his silence than he would have with the most outrageous words.

I do not know if Madame d'Englesac feared the pity I inspired in the judges—for, Madame, my speech touched them with true compassion—or if she simply wanted to get the case out of Paris. In any case, she stirred up one of the heirs of Monsieur de Molière with whom I was still at odds about Monsieur de Candale's money, and he joined her in the suit. On the pretext of obligations that caused him to remain in Toulouse, he asked that the case be referred to that parlement.

I strongly opposed this plan, for I knew that Monsieur the President of —— and numerous other presidents and counselors in the parlement of Toulouse were relatives of Madame d'Englesac.[18] I did such a good job of demonstrating the wrong she intended to do me that, although I was unable to keep the case in Paris because of her legal tricks, I was able to have it moved to Grenoble.

My lover with the purse was helpful to me in this situation. He felt real remorse over what he had done, and tried to make up for it with all his power. I even think that this remorse contributed to his pious retirement from the world a few months later, for he never seemed consoled about the wrong he had done to my reputation.

He gave me letters of recommendation for Monsieur de la Berchère, chief president of Grenoble, and for some of his other friends. Before arriving in this town, I must, if you will, have Your Highness stop for a little while in Bourbon,[19] where I stayed a while when passing through. For my sorrow had left me so ill that I thought I needed the cure.

There was a fine company there that year: Madame de Fontevrault, worthy daughter of Henri IV, Monsieur the Marshal of la Ferté, Monsieur and Madame de Sully, Madame de Guitaut, Madame the Marquise de la Trousse, and many other French people and foreigners, all taking the baths and the waters. Only a Swede seemed to me to have come there for pleasure rather than by necessity.

He was called Wakmestre, a Swedish title, which we used instead of his name. He spoke French fairly well and was lodging in the same place as I was. We soon became acquainted. We shared our opinions on the people at Bourbon and, without going so far as to be malicious, we allowed ourselves some innocent fun at their expense. It seemed to me that I was not displeasing to this foreigner, and I was not the only one who held this opinion, as Your Highness will see.

One day I was coming back from the Priory of Saint George, near Bourbon, where I had gone to hear a good singer. In going down into a valley that has the town at its end, one of Wakmestre's pages came and threw himself at my feet. I fled because this young man, while very handsome, had a dreadful look in his eye, and Madame de la Trousse, who was with me, had a hard time convincing me to listen to him as the page requested.

I have never heard anything as touching as the page's speech. He was, in

18. On president, see part 1, note 31.

19. Bourbon-l'Archambault was a fashionable place to take the waters reputed to have curative powers (MC 212). It is about 120 miles north of Lyon.

truth, a young lady of quality from Germany whom Wakmestre had seduced and who hid herself in this disguise. Believing that I had become her rival, she begged me, sobbing, to kill her or to leave her beloved to her.

I felt great pity for the suffering of this young woman, and I greatly reproached Wakmestre with the fact that, after having torn her from the arms of her parents, he treated her so badly. He listened to my reproaches and reconciled with his mistress in good faith. How I envy them, and how grateful I would have been to someone who could have thus reconciled me with the Count of Englesac!

From that day on, Wakmestre's page and I were inseparable, and Wakmestre was inseparable from his page. This produced two amusing effects. A young woman from Provence, whose name I have forgotten, was in love with the page, taking him for what he appeared to be, and a count from Piedmont, whose name it is not necessary to know, fell in love with me. He thought that Wakmestre was his rival, and the page's lover thought I was her rival. The man from Piedmont tried to win over the page, so that he could spy on us, and the young lady from Provence tried to influence Wakmestre, so that he would oppose the liaison of which she suspected me.

Wakmestre only laughed at what this foolish woman said, but he was displeased by the attention the man from Piedmont was paying the page. They quarreled and fought, and people did me the honor of saying that it was because of me.

This false rumor made me hate Bourbon. I said good-bye to Madame de Guitault and Madame de la Trousse and some other worthy people (with whom I had become friendly) and, followed only by Merinville, I left for Grenoble, where my lawsuit awaited me and where I found that the news of the duel had arrived before I did.

As was her habit, Madame d'Englesac made the most of this news, and her son used it as grounds to hate me more. We ran into each other everywhere—in the Grenette,[20] in the Saulsaye, at the entrance to the law chambers—for people run into each other more frequently in Grenoble than in Paris. The Count of Englesac acted as if he had never seen me before. At first I thought I would die of sorrow. I said things to him that would have moved a tiger if it had heard them. But in the end I stopped playing such a foolish role and pretended, in my turn, to have totally gotten over the passion I had felt for him. This pretense brought him around. We began to speak the way polite people do when they first become acquainted, and we talked of our common business as though we were talking about the business of others. He

20. Locations in Grenoble. The Place Grenette was the marketplace.

agreed that, for the sake of honor, I needed to insist on my marriage, and I said to him, although it was not true, that I was pleased that he had tried to break it off, that his temperament and mine were becoming incompatible, and that sensible people should separate in this way when they were tired of each other.

You would not be able to stop laughing, Madame, if you had been witness to our conversations. One day I betrayed myself, and the Count of Englesac noticed that I was still looking at him tenderly. He told me, taking the tone of a disinterested person giving advice, that, to avoid a relapse, I should find some amusement for my heart, that he knew me, and that I would have a hard time getting over him without the aid of another. He disingenuously named to me men he knew whom he considered the best suited to obtain my love. This conversation seemed very unusual. I argued with him over the lovers he proposed: one seemed too cool, another too passionate; one did not know how to please me, and I feared the inconstancy of another. I hoped to make him understand in this way that he alone suited me, but he did not understand me, or turned a deaf ear.

I took up my feigned indifference and exchanged with him pieces of advice, although it enraged me to do so. He had had two or three passions that made me ashamed, if such relationships can be called passions. I told him that I deserved more illustrious rivals and proposed some to him. "Choose Madame ———," I continued. "She is beautiful enough to please you, she is witty, and if she were to fall in love, I believe she would love a great deal. That is just the kind of mistress you need."

The Count of Englesac took this advice. The lady of whom I spoke was in Grenoble, and he began to court her. So that my pride should not be injured, a nephew of the Bishop of Valence, who had come to Grenoble on business, undertook to try to make me forget the Count of Englesac. He could have pleased me a great deal, and I willingly consented to let him try. I will even admit that the speeches of this young man, who had a good deal of merit, provided me with some relief from my legal efforts.

For, Madame, the conversations between the Count of Englesac and me did not diminish the intensity of our legal proceedings and sometimes, after leaving each other politely, we went to have summonses served on each other. I have been told that the Abbot of Montreuil, who perhaps got news of me through my lover from Dauphiné,[21] told fine tales about this manner of

---

21. Dauphiné is a region in southeastern France comprising the present day departments of Isère, Hautes-Alpes, and Drôme.

pursuing a lawsuit, and that the lovely Madame de la Mothe in Valence was often amused by the comedy I was acting out in Grenoble.

This comedy was beginning to amuse me, too. I had pushed my love very far. There is no heart so constant that it cannot in the end be put off by persistent disdain and, to hide nothing from Your Highness, I was becoming quite indifferent to the Count of Englesac.

I do not know whether he noticed this or whether, following the normal behavior of men, he felt my loss after he thought it certain, but he interrupted me when he found me in conversation with the Bishop of Valence's nephew.

This brusque behavior rather amused me. The young gentleman, for whose sake it was done, noticed it and said gallantly that he was going to serve me at his own expense. He neglected nothing to make the Count of Englesac jealous. He did so much that he succeeded. One day, quite troubled, the count asked me if this was the lover whom I had chosen. "I don't know yet," I said to him. "He has merit, and he does not displease me, but I have decided henceforth to treat my lovers like my servants, that is to say, to keep changing them until I find one who suits me." "Do you want to be a coquette?" the count asked me. "Why not?" I replied. "It is the manner of loving that is the easiest for ladies." "Ah Sylvie!" continued the count, "you have really changed or you would never love in that way."

That he said Sylvie seemed to me to be a good sign, and I had hopes of avenging the disdain I had suffered. For I would swear, Madame, that if the Count of Englesac had loved me again, I would have made him the most unhappy of all the people who have ever loved. I was already nourishing a thousand cruel ideas, and I think that is why I still felt the desire to please him. My God! How little we know ourselves!

One day I was in the garden of Monsieur the Duke of Lesdiguières, governor of Dauphiné, for all people of quality are welcome to walk there, and the Count of Englesac was there also. I will remember that day for a long time. I was as gay as I had been before my troubles. I laughed, I joked, I said amusing things. The Count of Englesac came up to me and criticized my gaiety as something unsuitable for someone who had lawsuits in progress.

"Why shouldn't I be gay?" I replied. "My heart has been freed from captivity. Isn't it natural to be joyful when one has gotten freedom back after a long period of slavery?" "Then you are really free, my Sylvie?" responded the count, squeezing my hand. I was planning to say yes and to say other disdainful things, but unfortunately I looked at the Count of Englesac and saw so much love in his eyes that I couldn't stop myself from feeling a little love too. I was troubled and did not say anything other than that I was as he wished me to be.

The people who were with us were considerate, and they moved away when they saw that we were talking to each other. "And if I wished you to be otherwise," said the count, "would I find you as I wished?" I answered only with tears. The Count of Englesac was on the point of shedding tears himself and, had it not been for the annoying Madame d'Englesac, who had come to walk in the garden with the Marquise de Fargue and some other ladies, we might have been reconciled forever.

The Count of Englesac left me when he saw this company. He seemed to be ashamed to have been seen alone with me, and this was not without justification. After all he had done to ruin me, where would he find now the effrontery to admit that he had only a minor quarrel with me?

I think it was this view that made him leave Grenoble, for he departed without saying good-bye to anyone. It was only in a letter that he assured me of his repentance and the return of his passion.

Ah! Madame, what a letter! How much love was expressed in it, and how hardhearted one would have to be to read it without being touched!

He told me that he was writing in the same spirit to his mother, to ask her to leave me alone. I wanted to see if the countess was as touched by her letter as I was by mine, and I ran to her home in tears.

She was with her friend and relative Monsieur de ——, a man of great virtue, who is presently retired in the Grande-Chartreuse.[22] Since our arrival in Grenoble, he had made efforts to settle matters between us. The countess held in her hands the letter that her son had written. "Ah! Cruel woman," she cried when she saw me, "is it possible that once again you deprive me of my son? You have destroyed his wealth, his reputation, and his intelligence. Your flattery, your infidelities, or the shame of having been so long their plaything, have torn my son from my arms four times. Unhappy woman, what have I done to you? Is this the reward I should receive for saving you from Madame de Molière's resentment and for welcoming you so tenderly into my house?"

I answered these reproaches only with my tears. What could I have said? It was the Count of Englesac's mother who said these things.

"Do and say against me everything you wish," I said to her, "for you will never be able to do as much evil to me as you have done good in bringing the Count of Englesac into the world. I will never forget what I owe you and,

---

22. The motherhouse of the Carthusian order, in a valley of the Alps fourteen miles north of Grenoble.

were you to kill me with your own hands, you would not wipe this good deed from my memory."

These words so greatly moved the countess that one could call the effect they produced a miracle. Her face softened and compassion visibly replaced fury. The pious witness to our conversation seconded this feeling of pity, and I have never heard anyone speak with such power and such charity as this devout personage. I found out subsequently that before his departure the Count of Englesac had asked him to play this role. What can I say, Madame? I left there thinking our disagreements were over.

In fact, a few days later we signed an agreement by which the Countess of Englesac gave up all further prosecution. She excused herself to me; I asked her forgiveness; and we thought of nothing but getting the count to return.

But, alas, that was the problem. In leaving Grenoble, he had run into a gentleman from the court of Savoy whom he had known in Thurin and who was going off to Crete.[23] This man took the Count of Englesac along with him, and we did not know of this decision until after they had set sail.

I thought I would die of grief when I heard this news. The Countess of Englesac was very affected by it also, and without the exhortations of the man of whom I have spoken, who consoled us as best he could, I do not know, for my part, what I would have done. I only know that the least of my resolutions was to sail from Toulon[24] and follow my husband to Crete. Our common friend calmed me and persuaded Madame d'Englesac to take me to Languedoc with her.

It was very surprising to see this same person, who formerly had worked so hard for my ruin, lead me by the hand to the Count of Englesac's relatives, ask them to recognize me as his wife, and praise my constancy and my virtue to them, about which she had in truth received good reports.

For the Marquis de Birague, who still wanted to marry me and whom Madame de Seville had strengthened in this resolution by a thousand promises, had made it his duty to reestablish my reputation. He clarified the adventures that people had attributed to me; he publicly attested to the innocence of these adventures and had this attestation circulated about. Undoubtedly he did not think that my reconciliation with the Count of Englesac would be the result of all his trouble; otherwise I think he would have waited to act until after I had lost my lawsuit, but I am nonetheless grateful to him.

23. The Venetians fought the Turks in Crete from 1645 to 1669.
24. Toulon is a French city on the Mediterranean coast, about fifty miles east of Marseilles.

These justifications, in combination with the efforts I made to please Madame d'Englesac, brought back little by little the esteem she had formerly had for me. I think that in time I would have seen great proofs of this, had death not overtaken her. But it seems that the poor woman had nothing more to do in the world after her just action, and she died in completing it.

I wept for her sincerely, so much had the friendship she was beginning to show me wiped out the memory of the evils she had done me. I subsequently found new reasons to weep for her, for I found myself in new difficulties that I might not have had, had she lived.

First of all, the people who had some claims on the inheritance of the Count of Englesac, whom they saw engaged in a dangerous war, did not want to recognize the agreement the countess had signed. They said she was near death when she had committed this folly and that she was not fully competent. They had a guardian named to watch over the Count of Englesac's assets until his return. When I wanted to oppose this formality as the wife of the absent count, they took up the lawsuit again with as much enthusiasm as Madame d'Englesac had had when she brought it in the first place. They had the same reasons as she had had, for it had never been in my husband's name that I had been sued, but rather in his mother's name. If she had not given up the suit, the Count of Englesac's guardian would indeed have had the right to continue it after the countess's death.

To this sorrow another was added. I remained under the tutelage of an old aunt of the Count of Englesac, who was the most bizarre woman I ever encountered. One had no idea how to keep her satisfied. What pleased her one day displeased her the next, and because she had once been beautiful but had not been the subject of gossip, it seemed that the whole human race was subject to her criticism.

I had left Languedoc after the death of Madame d'Englesac, and I was with this woman in a house she had near Marseilles. The same Castelan who had already caused me problems in Paris, as I told Your Highness, thought he would do the same in Provence. He had come there in order to sail for Crete and, having learned that I was in the region, he came to see me.

He said nothing that the finest sense of propriety would not approve, and for a man who did not like to restrain himself and who was naturally a great flirt, I admired the good manners he showed the elderly aunt.

But, Madame, even if he had preached penitence to me, or the most austere virtue, this woman would still have found things to criticize in what he said. Why come and visit me? she asked. Why did married women receive such visits? What an age! What behavior! In her time, people did not behave this way. I saw the moment coming when she would shove Castelan out of her door by the shoulders.

You can judge, Madame, whether she was right. I charged him to convey a thousand tender things to the Count of Englesac. I conjured him, with tears in my eyes, to send him back to me or to get his permission for me to go and join him. Castelan smiled when I gave him this errand and asked me if I had forgotten that he had been my suitor and could be so again. I in turn smiled at this comment, and we would have said amusing things about it if the murmurs of the old woman had not made me ask him to leave.

This visit was not the only thing about which the Count of Englesac's aunt thought she had found reason to object. My suitor from Grenoble was not happy with me. He had helped make the Count of Englesac jealous. This jealousy had been useful to me, and I had left Grenoble without thanking him. He wrote me a letter to complain; it was filled with witty remarks but was no love letter.

But our old lady took everything negatively. Unfortunately this letter fell into her hands, and no matter what I said in my defense, she made so many tedious reprimands and so many ill-founded reproaches that I could not endure them any longer. I withdrew, using the pretext that I had business still pending before the parlement of Grenoble, which required my presence in that city.

The old woman has never forgiven me for my departure. For, Madame, though she was such as I depict her, she thought she knew how to live well and could not understand how I could complain about her temperament. Her anger did me a good deal of harm, as Your Highness will find out.

In Grenoble I found my former suitor, the nephew of the Bishop of Valence. The business that had brought him there was finished, but he was kept there by new matters. He was once again in love, not the playful kind of love he had had for me, but a very solid and very violent passion.

He had great esteem for me, and although he was no longer my suitor, I had always had respect for him. We became friends, and I became his confidant. I could play this role without any scruples, for his love was a legitimate one. I therefore happily used my wit and my skill to help it succeed. But who were we dealing with, Madame?

The woman whom my new friend loved had herself fallen for the Marquis de ———; she could not marry him, however, because of the difference in their social stations. My friend, showing a sense of honor rare in a twenty-four-year-old man (that was his age then), did everything he could to stop this young woman from becoming more passionate about the marquis.

The marquis avoided seeing her and talking to her, and when politeness forced him to be alone with her, he said such wise things to her that one cannot esteem him enough for it. We did not yet know this yet, and we thought that the young marquis was profiting from his good fortune. The young woman's whole family was alarmed, and I was asked by one of her relatives, who was a friend of mine, to explain to her the error of her ways.

I have never been more eloquent, for I had more than one purpose. By serving the relative who had asked for my help, I also advanced the cause of the nephew of the Bishop of Valence. Madame, I thought I had convinced her of everything I had wished. The young woman pretended to give in to my persuasion and asked me to say the same things to the Marquis de ——. I willingly took on this errand, being unaware, as I have said, that the marquis did not need to hear these exhortations. But I wanted a letter of confidence, that is, a note saying that I was not speaking without her consent. Guess what kind of letter I carried, Madame? A new protestation of tenderness and a request not to believe anything that was said to the contrary.

I myself had dictated the letter I thought I was carrying. I watched the young lady as she wrote it and folded it up, but she had another letter all ready in her pocket and was awaiting the first opportunity to send it off. She tricked me, and while I lit a candle and she pretended to look for some ribbon,[25] she fooled me so skillfully that I ended up carrying a love letter rather than a letter of farewell.

Madame, don't you admire what love is capable of doing? The person of whom I am speaking was only eighteen; she had never been to the court, where people are usually more subtle in matters of gallantry than in the provinces. I am not without wit, and since my destiny has dictated it so, I have only too much experience. I was, however, the dupe of the young woman from Dauphiné.

The Marquis de —— began to laugh when I read this letter, and he understood by what I said to him how little relation it had to my errand.

But I tell this little story not only in passing and to amuse you, for it is related to my own, as Your Highness will learn. The young woman—to whom I made a thousand reproaches for her trickery (which I had first suspected and which the marquis, as wise and discreet as he was, could not but admit)— this young woman, I say, embarrassed to see her trick uncovered and angry, I believe, to have failed so badly, spread the rumor in Grenoble that I was in love with the Marquis de —— and that it was out of jealousy that I had undertaken to give her advice.

25. It was common practice to seal letters with ribbon and wax seals.

This misrepresentation was carried from Dauphiné to Provence, where the old aunt still was, and she took the story to Languedoc. The people who hoped to profit from my ruin circulated this calumny about, so much so that it even reached the Count of Englesac.

He should have been cured of his gullibility, but one rarely can correct faults in one's nature. He combined the news of my affair with the Marquis de —— with the stories his aunt had sent him, for she had not failed to take this revenge on me. He was distressed and was angrier with me than ever, and, driven by the jealousy that had been so fatal to us, he sent a power of attorney to his relatives to break off my marriage.

What a setback for a poor and innocent woman who believed herself beyond the reach of malicious gossip and who, knowing in her heart that she had not deserved this gossip, waited only for the return of the Count of Englesac in order to enjoy a peace that she had earned through so much suffering.

I was so transported with pain and anger that I almost lost my reason. Boats often sailed from Toulon, taking supplies to the French in Crete. I resolved to get on one of them, and, without considering the dangers to which I would have exposed myself, I would have gone to Crete in person to reproach the Count of Englesac with his frivolity, had I not been stopped by new adventures.

I will tell Your Highness about them in sequence, and you will not find them less singular than the adventures I have already recounted to you.

But, Madame, I must give you a little repose; you must be tired of reading for such a long time, as I am of having written so much. I ask of Your Highness a bit of freedom to think about what I still have to say and request that you take into account the obedience I show in thus telling you my follies. You are the only person in the world who could have caused me to make these admissions, as there is no one of whom I am with so much zeal and so much respect the very humble and very obedient servant,

H. S. D. M.

PART 5

You must have found me very foolish in the fourth part of this tale, and so I was. Not only did I want to go to Crete, as I have admitted to Your Highness, but when I learned from some people coming back from there that the Count of Englesac was dead, I wept for him as if he had been the most faithful man in the world.

I no longer remembered all his ingratitude; I thought only of our past love. I leave you to judge, Madame, if I was right to remember him in this way, for in Crete the Count of Englesac had been unfaithful to me a thousand more times. I will tell Your Highness about them in due time, but first I must tell how my business in Grenoble was progressing.

The Count of Englesac's heirs persecuted me extensively. I was laying claim to a great deal of the goods he had left them, and they could not bring themselves to leave it to me without a fight. They brought lawsuits without end. They depleted my purse and my patience and continued to tear my reputation to shreds.

Fortune, who on the one hand has oppressed me but on the other hand has done even more to support me, happily allowed me to find a protector. I will not tell his name to Your Highness, for you do not know him, but he was a fine man, very influential in the parlement. I can say that he is the only man I have seen take up the interests of a beautiful woman without any motive other than generosity. Through him I hoped to overcome my enemies, but I did not have this hope for long, and you are going to learn what destroyed it.

The Chevalier de Montchevreuil came to Grenoble for some business. I had met him in Paris, where we had been good friends, and as soon as he found out that I was in Grenoble, he did not fail to come and visit me. He happily spent time with me, and although he was more in love with gambling than with women, he amused himself sometimes by saying to me that my widow's clothes suited me well.

This banter never turned into flirtation. When he had spent a whole evening with me, I told the chevalier, laughing, that he owed me all the money he had not lost. He replied, laughing too, that he had made more than one gain and that he hoped to be rewarded for having prevented me from thinking about the Count of Englesac during that time. I put on a severe expression, and forbade him, very seriously, to speak of my husband. He laughed at my scruples and said I was not wise to be so careful of such an inconstant husband. "You are one of my friends," he added. "I want to cure you of this weakness, and I am going to try to make you love me, if only to get that ingrate out of your memory."

You can judge, Your Highness, whether that could be called a commitment. We made no secret of it and were the first to joke publicly about our way of behaving. When evil spirits want to poison things, however, they can make a crime out of anything.

Your Highness may remember that despite myself I stole the heart of the Marquis de —— from a young lady of Grenoble. She still resented me because of this theft and, knowing that my protector was a man of great virtue, she did such a good job of persuading the marquis that the Chevalier de

Montchevreuil's visits were more criminal than they appeared that he wanted nothing more to do with my affairs.

I do not know how such a wise man could be misled so easily, nor how our innocent playfulness could be interpreted in such an evil way. But, in the final analysis, that is how they were interpreted, and people said things about the two of us that make me blush when I think of them. The people of quality on whom he depended were critical of his gambling. And indeed he should never have gambled, for he had no luck. He could not do without it, however, and shut himself up at night with other players to be able to gamble in freedom. I was considered responsible for these nights, and the pious man was made to believe that every time someone looked for Montchevreuil and could not find him, he was enjoying my favors.

My adversaries gave credence to this false rumor through their authority and their testimony, and for all I know they may have used some trick to make it appear true, for they talked about a man who left my house at daybreak, covered with a great coat. They also invented I do not know what other equally unbelievable details. What can I say, Madame? My protector was ashamed of having played that role, and no matter what I wrote to him to justify myself (for he refused to see me), he remained inexorable.

His change brought about such a great alteration in my affairs that I had no doubts about losing my case, and I resolved to go and throw myself at the feet of the king, to ask him for a different parlement or for commissioners.[1]

To this purpose I left Grenoble. At least I gained one advantage from all my difficulties: they made all men seem to me insufferable. One of the greatest drawbacks for me in going to Paris was that I would be obliged to listen to some of them, for I realized that when one who is somewhat pretty undertakes a solicitation at the court, she is often exposed to the flirtations of the courtiers.

More than once this thought almost made me turn around, and I do not know what I would have done without Merinville's exhortations. She asked me if I wanted to live without resources and without a name. When I was not sufficiently moved by this consideration, she got angry and said that I was losing my good sense and that she would wish that I had ten lovers, provided that one of them could get me out of trouble.

She did not have much occasion to say such foolish things to me, for when I arrived in Lyon, I learned that the king had left for Lille, where he had decided to spend more than two months.[2]

I was greatly afflicted by this delay. I had no doubt that my departure

---

1. This refers to a commission named to judge special cases (MC 240).
2. In 1670 the court visited cities that had been conquered (MC 240).

from Grenoble had cost me my few remaining friends there. Seeing myself deprived of the prompt help for which I had hoped, I repented of having managed things so poorly. But I had to be patient—what else could I do? The king did not want to deal with business until his return. Even if I had been able to touch his compassion, how could I have caught up with him, since he covers so much ground in a day and was a hundred leagues ahead of me?

I consoled myself as best I could and resolved to spend in Lyon the time the king spent in Flanders. I thought it would be easier for me to live in solitude there than in Paris. I had formerly had a friend in Languedoc who was at this time staying in the Abbey of Saint Pierre. I expected great consolation from her. She had hardly any more reason to praise men that I did, and we spent whole days strengthening the hatred we had for them.

A nun who was among her friends and who was very witty and very charming sometimes joined our conversations and always made them more gay, for she had a playful nature. She told me and my friend that we were crazy to flee men because they had done us harm. "It is not by fleeing them that one punishes them," she added. "On the contrary, you must see them, try to please them, and then drive them crazy."

"But when they are enraged, they destroy women's reputations," I replied, "and when men are honorable enough not to do so, the general public does it without their help. Men's discretion is considered a great merit, and people manipulate it in whatever way they can imagine." "Add to that," said my friend, "that usually when you want to reduce a lover to despair, you end up falling in love, and you will find, at your own expense, that you should not play with love."

One day we were talking like this when the Count of Tavanes, who was in Lyon and who knew the nun of whom I speak, came and asked to see her. A *tourière*[3] sent him to the parlor where we were, and although I withdrew from his sight, I was nonetheless very distressed by this encounter. The next day I told my friend that if her parlor became open to everyone in this way, she would rarely see me there. She calmed me down as best she could and assured me that I had nothing to fear from the man I had encountered.

In fact, Madame, she had already seen the Count of Tavanes many times, and he had persuaded her that he hated our sex as much as I hated his. At first I did not believe this hatred was real. I told my friend that there was some mystery hidden in it and that she was being duped. But she and the nun told me so many things to eliminate this suspicion that in the end they persuaded me, and I myself wanted to see such a rare man.

---

3. See part 1, note 27.

It wasn't difficult. I went to the Abbey of Saint Pierre every day, and hardly a day went by when he did not go there too. We met as we had the first time, and I admit that everything I had been told about him was confirmed.

He pointed out the difference between my friend and other women. "She is more than a little obliging," he added, "and a man must really esteem women, if he understands your sex and does not flee from you." I am naturally flirtatious, and by chance that day I was in a joking mood. Smiling, I told the count that he was very brave to make such a declaration before three women such as ourselves, that he deserved to be punished, and that, during my playful days, I would not have failed to make him repent of it.

He took this threat with an indifference that resembled disdain and continued to behave in the same way during the rest of the conversation. I remained so convinced of his hatred for us that little by little I stopped avoiding him, as I avoided all other men. For, Madame, it was not men themselves I hated, but rather their mania for attaching themselves to me and then unfailingly entangling me in some troublesome adventure.

Since I did not think that the Count of Tavanes was of such a temperament, I got used to seeing him as the fourth party in our conversations. He very graciously offered me the help of his friends at court, and I was very obliged to him for it. One day when it was raining and I was without my carriage, I allowed him to take me back home in his.

He only took me to my room and departed as soon as we got there. The next day the nun teased him about not using this opportunity to pay me a visit. He defended himself on the grounds that he wanted to have little to do with women. Although he spoke of me very politely, he nonetheless did so with such little interest in knowing me better that I was pleased to see his friend criticizing him, and I did not oppose her advice that he should come and repair his fault.

Thus he came, Madame, and as if he wanted to clear up any suspicion that this visit might have any consequences, he recounted to me the reasons he said he had for hating all women. This story has nothing to do with me, and I could do without telling it to you, but why shouldn't I tell it? It increased my confidence in him, and will perhaps amuse Your Highness.

THE STORY OF THE COUNT OF TAVANES

"I was born to love," he said to me, "and although I am not that old, I have had five or six amorous adventures. I have reasons to be dissatisfied with all of them. I have always found cruel or inconstant women, or capricious or flighty ones. In sum my reasons for changing have been only too good. The most painful of my relationships, however, and the one that made me determined never to have another, is the one I am going to tell you about.

"I had stopped off in Dijon on my return from the campaign in Franche-Comté.[4] As you perhaps know, I am from Burgundy and my land is in that region. In Dijon there was a beautiful woman pursuing a lawsuit; I will not name her, for an honorable man owes it to himself to be discreet in this way. She pleased me, and I began to court her. I found in her nothing but that degree of cruelty necessary to make her favors more desirable.

"I was helpful to her in her lawsuit, and when she had some free time, I introduced her to all the diversions that this provincial area could offer. She accepted both my attentions and my help as though she would remember them all her life. But ladies do not have very good memories, and you are going to learn how she acknowledged her obligations to me.

"The Marquis de Castelnau had received a deep bruise at Besançon,[5] and an abcess that had formed had been closed too hastily. It flared up again as he passed through Dijon, and it forced him to remain there for some time. My lady was taken with his good looks. I can accept that, since a woman is not always mistress of the feelings of her heart, but what was singular is that this devious woman pretended that she had a kind of natural aversion for the marquis.

"He was one of my great friends, and only capriciousness could make someone hate him without any reason. I blamed my deceitful lady for this, and after telling her that she must overcome this hatred, I myself brought Castelnau to her, so that by his merit he could finish the reconciliation I thought I had started.

"As you can imagine, he did not have great difficulty doing this. This visit was followed by many others, and if what I have been told is true, my unfaithful mistress made all the advances in this affair.

"The marquis was not cruel, and the lady had many charms; they soon began a relationship, and what made this particularly spicy for my friend was that I continued to be their dupe. They had agreed that they would interpret as signs of passion all the hateful things she would say to him in front of me, so that when I was made sad by his professions of love, she would say the cruelest things in the world to Castelnau in return.

"I was sincerely chagrined; I made excuses to him and asked him naively

4. This was in 1668. Franche-Comté is a mountainous province in east central France on the Swiss border, south of Alsace.

5. This refers to the siege that took place in 1668 (MC 247). Besançon is the capital of Franche-Comté.

whether it was possible that he had met this woman only in Dijon, and whether the hatred she showed him indeed had no legitimate basis.

"He smiled at my simplicity and told me, jokingly, that he had to bear this misfortune like other tricks of Fortune and that the injustice that surprised me was not the only kind women were capable of.

"He continued this pretense all the time we were in Dijon, but one day after our return, when we were strolling in the little Versailles park[6] and we came to talk about this woman, remorse overtook him, and asking forgiveness for his betrayal, he told me all that I have told you.

"I did not want to believe him, and I think I would still be doubtful about the truth had he not persuaded me with twenty letters, each more convincing than the others. There were letters in which she delighted over this deception as one of love's most agreeable mysteries. In others, she recommended this course to him as a strategy that was necessary for her to win her lawsuit, telling him of the influence I had in our parlement.

"In faith, Madame," added the count in looking at me, "do you think that I am right to hate women? After the betrayal that I have recounted to you, do I not show moderation in not doing them harm?"

I was truly touched with compassion for the trick they had played on him, and, feeling very obliged by his confidences, I felt that I needed to respond in recounting, in my turn, some of the Count of Englesac's ungrateful behavior. Your Highness does not know about the last part of this, and it seems to me that this is the place to tell you about it.

In Crete, this inconstant man fell in love with a Greek woman, and finding her to be virtuous, whether in truth or in appearance, he told everyone he was going to marry her. He wouldn't have done it—he couldn't have. And if he could have, I cannot believe that he would have behaved in such bad faith. Nonetheless this story ruined my reputation, especially since people would rather believe bad things than good, and because he was not secretive about it. When he died, the whole army was persuaded that I was not his wife.

What ingratitude, Madame! Alas, previously he had done so much in order to become my husband and was so grateful to me for pledging my faith to him. But this is not all. He lived for nine or ten days after being wounded and used almost all this time to show his love for my rival. He said he regretted losing his life only because he was dying without being able to marry her. If the army chaplains had not considered such ideas dangerous for a dying man

---

6. "The park of the chateau of the Condé, on the banks of the river Ouche, today known as the park of La Colombière" (MC 248). The Ouche is a river in Burgundy.

and had not forced the Greek away from his bedside, the perfidious man would have given up the ghost speaking in this way.

"In your opinion," I said to the Count of Tavanes, "are the injuries you have received more bloody than those I have received, and is your hatred better justified than mine?" "Let's join together, Madame," he replied, "and give ourselves the pleasure of hating the whole human race."

This way of speaking made me smile, and I replied playfully that any sort of union with a man was suspicious in my eyes. However, since he had a great deal of merit and seemed to hate intrigues as much as I did, he saw me when he wished, and I loved him as if he had been my brother.

A certain Chevalier de la Mothe had the bad timing to come and disturb this innocent society. He was the captain of a galley[7] who was going to Marseilles to set sail. Each year, on his way, he spent twelve or fifteen days in Lyon, where he added to the number of admirers of Madame Carle.[8]

Unfortunately for me, this year, Madame Carle was not the only reason he stopped there. He had seen me in the garden of Ainay,[9] which is a rather pretty spot where the ladies of Lyon normally go walking. I went there only at times when they were not there, and I sought out the most solitary places. I do not know by what chance the Chevalier de la Mothe sought out the same places as I, but he saw me there, and from that moment on, no matter where I went, he was there.

He followed me to every church. He was constantly on my route to the abbey, and when, vexed at meeting this man everywhere, I stayed in my room, I found he frequented a neighboring house from which he saw me through my windows as well as if he had been in my house.

All this displeased me a great deal, and one day I said to the Count of Tavanes that if the Chevalier de la Mothe continued bothering me like that, I would leave Lyon and go await the king's return in Paris.

I do not know if the count feared this threat or if he simply wanted to oblige me, but he went to find the chevalier, whom he knew, and asked him not to pursue me so. "This woman has reasons to want not to be noticed," he said, "and you are making her be noticed because of your insistence on following her. Please do not follow her anymore, Chevalier, I beg of you. An honorable man should never vex a pretty woman."

The chevalier smiled at Tavanes's remonstrance and told him mali-

---

7. A galley was a war or merchant ship that was rowed (usually by convicts) but might also be equipped with sails. They were used in the Mediterranean but not generally on the ocean.

8. Madame Carle was well known in Lyon society for her romantic intrigues (MC 252).

9. Ainay is an area of Lyon, most famous for the church of Saint-Martin d'Ainay.

ciously that he had advanced his suit more than a little, since his pursuit had been noticed and was feared. "My God," I said to the count when he repeated this conversation to me, "let him do what he wants. I don't want you to talk to him about me again." And in fact, Madame, to prevent the chevalier from thinking that I feared him, I pretended not to notice him.

I do not know whether this made him more daring or if he was trying to push my patience to the end, but one day when I was at the abbey for the investiture of a nun, which I had to attend, he found a way to have a seat near mine. Without any respect for the holiness of the place, he talked to me of love.

You can judge, Madame, how well he chose his moment, and if my soul was well disposed to hear this declaration. I looked at him with a proud air and told him imperiously that he should find someone else to address his gallantries to, which he did not dare continue. He remained embarrassed and left before the end of the ceremony.

Alas! I would have done better to hide my anger and allow him to remain near me. For, Madame, he went to console himself in that same garden of Ainay where he had seen me for the first time. You are about to learn the new unpleasantness that Fortune had prepared for me.

The Count of Tavanes was walking there alone, dreaming, and the Chevalier de la Mothe, having seen from a distance a packet of papers fall from his pocket, picked it up. Ah Madame! What papers were these? Eight or ten letters that I had written when I was in love with the Count of Englesac. They did not have an address on them, for I always use two envelopes. When one is very much in love and not as wise as Your Highness, one willingly writes mad things to one's lover. This crazy Chevalier de la Mothe imagined that these letters were addressed to the Count of Tavanes. Since by chance I had signed some of the letters, he viewed the Count of Tavanes as his rival, and in his soul considered him responsible for all the bad treatment he had received.

This was not so, alas, for I had never written to him! The mere fact that people believed I had a relationship with him obliged me never to see him again. I told him this very directly, and he was touched by it. He had a great quarrel with the Chevalier de la Mothe, and they almost fought. Some of their common friends sought to reconcile them and took their proposals for an accommodation. I do not know if, in the process of reaching a settlement, someone figured out the real nature of these letters or if the Count of Englesac was recognizable in some of them, but they began to be properly attributed.

I became more innocent because of this, but I was no less embarrassed.

One of these letters found its way to me, and Your Highness will perhaps not be unhappy to see how one writes when one is very much in love and when, because this love has only a legitimate goal, one does not constrain the desires of one's heart. Here is a copy of the letter of which I speak:

How cruel you are, with your reproaches and your suspicions! Have you found no other way of making me say that I love you than to accuse me of not loving you? Alas! Look in my eyes. Everyone sees my passion there. Are you the only person who cannot see it? That would be a terrible thing, for there is no passion there for anyone in the world other than you. No, no, my dear count, it is only the sight of you that gives me these transports of joy, which I cannot control. It is only your absence that has the power to make me sad. You alone can charm my heart, and all my actions assure you of this. I try to hide this to other, indifferent people but they do not fail to see it. I admit all this to you, and you still doubt that you are ardently loved by your,

Sylvie

How mad one is when one has such ideas in one's head! I only found out much later that this letter was circulated in all the salons of Lyon. The Count of Tavanes had not bothered to tell me, for other than the fact he had his reasons for not intervening, he had left angry over our quarrel, and I did not know what had become of him. I got the idea that it was the Count of Englesac himself who had lost my letters, that he was not dead, and that I would once again see him come back to me as he had after the naval battle with the Dutch.

This thought made me imagine a thousand crazy things, and if I must admit all my weaknesses to you, I think even the slightest repentance on the part of this unfaithful one would have made him dearer to me than ever. But his death was all too certain, and in addition, Madame, even if I had been able to delude myself into doubting it, I hardly had time to think about all this, as I am going to tell Your Highness.

My legal adversaries had profited from my absence and had gotten an order permitting them to hold me until the trial was ended. You can see, Madame, what strong measures they used against me. I was the Count of Englesac's widow, and both that title and my inheritance were called into question. They wanted to deprive me of the freedom to defend my claims. Because I was absent, they got everything they wanted. This order, to look at it in a good light, was advantageous to me because it gave me a new way to solicit the king's justice.

I hastened to get to Paris where Their Majesties were expected within a few days. And because I feared some surprise, I made my journey incognito. I pretended that I had obtained permission to enter the Abbey of Saint Pierre. My servants thought that is where I was, and I left them in Lyon to fool people all the better. I brought only Merinville with me and took the passage boat.[10]

This conveyance brought tears to my eyes. It hardly suited the widow of the Marquis de Menez and the Count of Englesac. However, in addition to the fact that it is not in my temperament to be afflicted too long, I had an encounter on this boat that distracted me from my sad reflections.

The person I encountered was the famous des Barreaux, who planned to spend the winter in Provence.[11] This year he had come too early and, finding that it was still too warm, he was going to a place near Châlons[12] to spend the rest of the harvest season with one of his friends.

I had heard a great deal about this man, and I was dying to meet him. I sat next to him and did everything in my power to get him talking. That was not hard, and if one provided him with an audience, he was not stingy with the stories he knew.

He told several in which it seemed to me that he spoke without restraint of people of the greatest quality, and going from one adventure to another he came, I know not how, to my own. He had never seen me, and I did not reveal my name. He thought I was from the Abbey of Saint Pierre. He spoke of me as of someone who was not there, which is to say he spared me almost nothing.

He was fair to me in some matters, and there is no doubt that he had not learned all that he knew from the public. However, Madame, something that surprised me very much, and that should surprise you, too, was that when he talked about my stay in Lyon, he said that the Count of Tavanes had been my lover there. I almost revealed my identity by the way in which I told him that that rumor was known to be false and that the Count of Tavanes had certainly never loved the Countess of Englesac.

"To whom do you think you are speaking?" he asked me with a smile. "It is from the Count of Tavanes himself that I learned about this whole affair. I just left him in Forez[13] at the home of the Marquis de ———, where we were together for ten or twelve days." And then he told me, Madame, that the

10. Passage boats regularly transported people from one city to another.

11. Jacques Vallée, sieur des Barreaux, was a well-known free thinker, who converted to Christianity on his deathbed (MC 259).

12. Châlons, known today as Châlon-sur-Sâone, is in Burgundy.

13. Forez is a mountain range and plateau in south central France, between the valleys of the Loire and the Dore.

Count of Tavanes had seen me in Grenoble, that he had fallen in love with me. He had followed me to Lyon, where he saw that I often went to the Abbey of Saint Pierre. He told his wishes to the nun of whom I have spoken, who was an old friend of his, and who undoubtedly thought his designs were legitimate, since she undertook to help him.

They agreed together that, for him to gain entry to my home, he would pretend to hate women and to want to have nothing to do with them. First they had deceived my friend, and, to get right to the point for Your Highness, I was fooled by appearances: what I thought happened by chance was the result of a plan.

This information surprised me so much that I could not hide it. I kept asking more questions of Monsieur des Barreaux, and they were not in vain, for never in my life have I seen such a well-informed confidant. He knew even the smallest things I had said to the count; he told me everything this lover thought and everything he thought I thought. When it came to the matter of my letters, he told me what had happened as if he had seen it himself. Your Highness only knows part of the story. I am going to tell you the rest.

The Count of Englesac had a valet whom I did not trust because he had been given to him by his mother, the countess. I had told him and I had often written to him that he should not trust this man, and, given where he had come from, I was suspicious of everything about him. However, I had never been able to make the count fire him because he liked him and thought I was prejudiced against him without reason.

This valet was still with him when he died, and having found in his master's papers some letters in which I spoke very badly of him, this man did not come and ask me for recompense but made the best use of them he could.

By chance he had become the valet of the Count of Tavanes, and this just at the time when the count was in love with me. As Your Highness can imagine, he did not fail to question his new servant. He found out that the valet had some of my letters and, having taken them, he had them with him in Lyon, when he lost them and the Chevalier de la Mothe found them.

I had no way of figuring all this out, for, to avoid making me suspicious, the Count of Tavanes had sent the valet to Toulon, where the rest of his retinue already was and from which he sailed a bit later, to take more reinforcements to Crete.

Monsieur des Barreaux recounted all this to me innocently and put me in a state of extreme vexation at having been so foully tricked. The Count of Tavanes did not profit a great deal by this trickery. I only thought of him as one of my friends, and my behavior remained within the limits of the most innocent friendship. But do I know if I would always have behaved so? He was a handsome lover with an agreeable personality, whom I had allowed to see me for more than two months, without thinking about it. Who can say if, little by little, I might have become so used to seeing him that, whatever I later found out, I would not have had the strength to banish him?

This thought made me forgive the Chevalier de la Mothe for all the annoyance I had received from him. In fact, if he had not gotten it into his head to be in love with me, the incident with the letters might not have happened, and I would still be seeing the Count of Tavanes very familiarly. But since the chevalier had not done any of this out of good intentions, I did not hate his sex any less and said all the bad things about them that I could.

Monsieur des Barreaux pretended to say the same of our sex and was in no mood to spare us. He recalled his past adventures and found a thousand reasons to consider women more perfidious than men. I did not want to agree, and we sometimes had disputes that resembled great quarrels, for this man did not argue like others. He defended his opinions with as much conviction as if they had concerned him personally. When anyone persisted in contradicting him, he became furious with them, and this fury made him behave outrageously.

Perhaps I am tiring Your Highness in speaking at such length of my anger toward men. I must amuse you with a little story that made me laugh a great deal and will undoubtedly make you laugh also.

In our boat there was a man who, although he had but one servant, nonetheless seemed to be a man of quality. By chance he sat beside me, and we often chatted together. Somehow or other, we came to talk of different cities in Languedoc and this man said, rather indiscreetly, that the women of Montpellier were not too cruel.

This was said in front of a man from that city, who had a rather pretty wife of whom he was very jealous. He was scandalized by this comment, and he asked the man who had spoken first if he had personal experience with the kindness of the women of Montpellier or if he knew them only by what was said about them.

"I spent a whole winter with them," the man responded coolly, "and I became acquainted with one of the most important and most gallant of these women, from whom I learned about the adventures of many others." "Dare I ask you her name, Monsieur?" the jealous husband responded right away.

I do not know whether the man knew him and whether he wanted to punish him for his jealousy, or whether it was chance that was responsible, but the man named the other's very own wife. "You are wrong," the husband interrupted. "The person you name does not have the temperament you describe, so you must be mistaking her for someone else."

This dispute made me curious, and I wanted to push it further. Maliciously I asked the man who had spoken first what the lady in question looked like.

"She is tall," he said, "and if she were more buxom, she would have a very good figure. She has lovely eyes. Her mouth is a bit big, but she has admirable teeth, a smooth complexion, and sings very beautifully."

Madame, you would have died laughing if you had seen the poor husband listening to the man draw the portrait of his wife. He changed color two or three times and, turning to a friend who was near him, he said, louder than he imagined, "They are talking about my wife. You can see that it resembles her in every detail."

"She loves balls," continued the other man, "and there are often balls at her home. A certain man," he added, mentioning I cannot remember what name, "gave five or six lovely ones for her while he was in love with her."

"That does not sound like her at all," continued the husband, talking to his friend, "the man they are talking about never entered my home. I was in Paris when he was in Montpellier, but I receive reliable information on everything that happens in my absence, and I can see that they are taking some other woman for my wife."

"She has a lovely country home, where she spends all her summers, and it was there that I saw her for the first time. All strangers go to see this house out of curiosity because it is much nicer than provincial homes ordinarily are. There is a room full of ancient weapons that is one of the rarest things one can see."

"Ah! That resembles my wife more than all the rest," cried the desperate husband, "and she is undoubtedly the coquette they are talking about."

We all burst out laughing so hard that the poor man was deeply embarrassed and went to hide in another part of the boat, where I imagine he made terrible resolutions. But they did not give him time to make them stronger. They went and swore to him that everything they had said was intended to give him a hard time, that the story was false from the beginning to the end.

And perhaps it was, for who can believe what men say? But now I return to tell you about new ruses and new lies, and I beg Your Highness to pardon me for not being able to refrain from telling you in passing the story of the husband from Montpellier.

Chatting and joking in this way we gradually arrived in Paris, where I had an encounter that gave me both joy and chagrin together.

My encounter was with a footman of the Marquise de Seville, who was looking for a means of bringing to me in Grenoble, where he believed I still was, a small chest that his mistress had sent. He was an old servant who had been found to be very trustworthy, and you will see, Madame, whether they knew his character well. In this little chest were a good number of beautiful jewels. The footman did not know this perhaps; in any case, he did not look inside and faithfully brought them to me.

I must admit, Madame, that they gave me great joy and that, after having undergone so many lawsuits and undertaken so many trips, these jewels were a great help to me. In receiving them, however, I also received the news that this poor marquise had died.

Even in her death, there was an admixture of adventure. It was claimed that she had drunk some kind of beverage (and that a man had drunk it too) that was supposed to give them eternal love for each other. Perhaps the drug had been badly prepared, or perhaps the marquise's time had come. She died rather suddenly, and the claim was that the beverage had greatly contributed to her death.

The poor woman! In her will she had left me everything she could leave me, and, while dying, sent me all her jewels. Alas! She did not have to accomplish this final generous gesture to make me cherish her memory. She had her little manias, which were not to everyone's taste, and we had had a number of quarrels, but under it all she was a good and generous person, and I had significant obligations to her. I wept for her as if she had been my mother, and I believe Your Highness is sensitive enough to share in my affliction at this point.

I kept her footman with me, and I rewarded him as I should have for having so faithfully carried out his mistress's last orders. This man was intelligent and knew many people in Paris. He found me a lodging, where I was safe until a stay of proceedings could be obtained from the council.[14] I do not know how my affairs got to the Privy Council. I had been involved in many lawsuits. I do not know much about legal chicanery, and if I did I would not go on about it to Your Highness, because I do not think it is very amusing. However it happened, I found myself free and in a situation to make my adversaries travel the same road I had traveled.

I sent for my coach, which I had left in Lyon, and by luck a man from Dauphiné, who had become ill along the road and could not ride his horse, asked my servants for a place in my coach, which they were polite enough not to refuse.

---

14. The privy council was a body to which decisions of a parlement could be appealed (MC 271).

I say by luck, Madame, for this man was a close friend of Monsieur de Lionne,[15] and when he got to Paris he introduced me to him. This generous minister saw something in my face that pleased him. He wanted to know all my business. I had a stroke of luck: the most stubborn of all of the Count of Englesac's relatives had a great matter before the court that was under the jurisdiction of Monsieur de Lionne's ministry.

Very obligingly, he promised to make the most of this favorable circumstance. And, in fact, he did such a good job in manipulating this man's mind that he started him down the road toward a settlement, and he extracted promises from him and from my other adversaries that were inviolable assurances for me.

I cannot remember spending a more peaceful period than the one I am speaking of. Each day I awaited my adversaries, who promised to do what Monsieur de Lionne wanted, and I was persuaded that he would not prefer their interests to my own. Madame de Seville's jewels had gotten me out of all kinds of difficulties. The gift she had given me was disputed in Flanders, but I had consulted skillful lawyers who had assured me that this claim would not hold up. What pleased me more than all the rest was that I did not have any annoying men bothering me, but I did not have this latter pleasure for long, and it is undoubtedly written in the stars that, despite what I wish, suitors will make problems for me all my life.

I was in an area where people gambled a great deal, and I gambled like the others, but principally to make the acquaintance of some ladies rather than because I particularly liked gambling. A man of great quality who was at the court was often part of our games, and following my destiny's caprice, he took it into his fantasy to make me love him.

He was not well suited for this. Honors and magnificence scarcely touch me, and to arrive at my heart it is necessary to please my eyes. Since he had a great deal of influence and since I did not need to make such powerful enemies, I defended myself more politely with him than I had with the Chevalier de la Mothe.

Without lying, when I think about it, the beginnings of this acquaintanceship gave me a good deal of pleasure. The man of whom I am speaking is intelligent in his way, but his mind is easily confused, and if he tries to present a line of reasoning, he soon falls into nonsense. I maliciously asked him questions when he started to get confused, and praising his eloquence when it was the least praiseworthy, I led him into a confusion that made me die from laughing.

15. Hugues de Lionne, secretary of foreign affairs, was a protector and personal friend of Madame de Villedieu (MC 271).

I do not know if he realized I was making fun of him, or if, through malice, someone else realized it, but he showed himself to be very angry with me and threatened me with nothing less than a memorable revenge.

I did not fear him, for I could be convicted of nothing. It is true that in my own mind I made great fun of him, but I always maintained the kind of external appearances he would have wished, and if I failed in some aspects of this, I do not think that one should take revenge over this on a woman like me.

Rather than being frightened, then, by the warnings people gave me, I became only more mocking. One day when I was in a playful humor, I said on this subject that he was ungrateful and that he should remember that I had sometimes understood him.

I admit that remark was very sharp for a man who was mocked for saying nonsense, but it seemed so amusing to me that I could not help but say it. What usually happens to people who are too eager to make a witty remark did not fail to happen to me, for not only did this great lord find out about it and never forgive me for it, as Your Highness will soon find out, but it brought me yet other problems.

I had made my remark in front of the Chevalier du Buisson, who by chance was in the house where I often gambled. You have met this chevalier, Madame, and you know how fond he is of clever witticisms. He was taken with this one, and wanting to get to know me better, he asked the young Count Deschapelles, who was one of my good friends, to bring him to my home.

Deschapelles asked my permission, and I willingly gave it. Look at what a concatenation of things this is. The now-deceased Madame d'Englesac had told me that she had some pretensions to the inheritance of Monsieur Deslandes-Payen, who was the uncle of the chevalier. By chance, I had in my hands the documents relevant to this matter. I got them somehow or other after the death of Madame d'Englesac, and I had been looking for someone who knew about Monsieur Deslandes's affairs, to see if I could possibly get something from his heirs.

It seemed to me that the Chevalier du Buisson was suited for this. I told the Count Deschapelles that I would be happy to see him and that he could bring him when he wished. He brought him, and by misfortune for me, Madame, I pleased him as I had pleased so many others.

He told it to the young count in confidence, from whom I later learned it, and he made him to understand that he was going to do everything in his power to get into my good graces.

I have told Your Highness that the Count Deschapelles was one of my close friends, and you may recall that we had had plans to come and see you around the time when he died. This poor young man, who knew I was sincere and to whom I had often insisted that the thing I most detested were lovers, did what he could to rid me of this one.

"Don't play with this woman," he told him. "She will give you too much trouble. She is put off by love and has no reason to be happy about it. She does not want any adventures and would give a man who sincerely loved her a very hard time."

Du Buisson only laughed at this advice. Beyond the fact that he did not believe in the cruelty of women, he judged my heart by the intrigues attributed to me. You can judge, Madame, that by that standard one would not think me too severe. He asked the Count Deschapelles, in an annoyed tone, who had taught him so much of the world. Their conversation became heated, and they bet, the one that he would make me love him within two months and the other that he would never succeed.

Perhaps the Count Deschapelles was fair enough to me to believe that I would cause him to win without his needing to ask, or perhaps he had given his word that he would say nothing to me of the bet. He remained faithful to the Chevalier du Buisson, and I knew nothing about what had passed between them. I accepted the cooperation and services of this new lover very politely.

He was not able to make any progress in the matter of his uncle, for that was impossible and my papers were not in good form, but it seemed to me that he had done everything he could, and for me that was as good as if he had succeeded. He provided me with some new diversion every day, and he knew so well how to manage things that I always believed he was providing them for someone else's sake, and the others knew he was providing them for my sake.

This was not all. He acted like a happy lover. He acted mysterious and played at being discreet. He got out of my presence as soon as someone noticed that he was with me. People kept coming upon him as he was reading some letter, which he would hide as soon as he saw he had been observed.

All this gave the impression of something, but he could not persuade the Count Deschapelles that he had lost. He wanted to hear me say that I loved du Buisson, and that was not something that was going to happen. For how could I have said that? The Chevalier du Buisson had not yet told me that he loved me, and I said such terrible things about love and lovers in front of him that he did not dare declare himself. He did want to win his bet. He undoubtedly thought his honor was involved, or perhaps he was like some other people who are almost as happy that people think they are loved, as they would be if they really were loved.

What did this tricky young man do? He had letters written in a hand that resembled mine, letters that were filled with tenderness. He made the Count Deschapelles believe that I had written them. He used some other illusion to make me appear with him in the Tuileries[16] at suspicious times. What can I tell you, Madame? He played his role so well that the poor count was duped and agreed that he had lost.

Du Buisson must have been very clever to fool him in this way, for in addition to having a very penetrating mind, the count was not a novice in terms of the airs that the Chevalier du Buisson took on, and if what people say is true, he could have given lessons in deception to others. But in this case he found his superior, and he has never been better persuaded of anything than of my secret relationship with the Chevalier du Buisson.

He had had to make great promises to be discreet, and I think that they may have returned to him the money he had bet on that condition. But how could a man who was so close to me, and who saw his confidence in me deceived, be silent? He was not silent, Madame, and the first time we found ourselves in conversation alone, he criticized me sharply for my duplicity and told me all that I have just recounted to you.

At first I did not believe he was telling me the truth. He was a natural joker, and he put on that air when he reproached me, probably in order to that I would take it better. I started to laugh and told him I was not so easily fooled, but since what he told me was only too true and since in the end we distinguished what was true from what was mere joking, I began to believe him and was never more astonished or more angry in my life.

I did not know how to reproach the Chevalier du Buisson. I did not want to compromise the Count Deschapelles, and I also knew that gentlemen of good fortune take pride in great quarrels and that I would oblige the Chevalier du Buisson more than I would punish him if I had such a quarrel with him. I thus resolved to embarrass him in public. Here is how I did it.

One day I was in the Jardin du Roy[17] with a lady of quality from the provinces who was staying in the same place as I and who had dragged me along on this walk. Many people of our acquaintance were there as well, among others the two men of whom I have been speaking. Both of them came up to us, and as soon as I saw the Chevalier du Buissson near me, I stopped short.

"By the way, Monsieur le Chevalier," I said to him, "remind me when I will be at home to tell you that I love you. I have put this declaration off for

---

16. The Tuileries was a fashionable promenade during this period.
17. The Jardin du Roy is another name for the Jardin des Simples.

too long, and I would have spared you many lies if I had thought of making it sooner."

This remark made people laugh, for it had no context. The chevalier appeared very embarrassed, and in order to embarrass him more I continued, looking at him tenderly: "Are you going to be cruel? Ah! Monsieur le Chevalier, do not decide to be so. It would kill me. It is enough that I love you; but do not let my love be futile. Believe me, cruelty does not suit your sex, and I love you so much that you cannot (without being ungrateful) refuse to love me a little."

I said this with such a malicious tone that the chevalier was quite taken aback. He wanted to regain his control and asked me seriously what the basis of my mockery was. But unfortunately for him the Count Deschapelles was looking at him at that moment, and he saw something so mocking in his eyes that he was completely taken aback and withdrew, full of embarrassment.

Your Highness can imagine that he was not spared by the people who remained there. He was of a joking nature, and either because they were charitable to him or because the rumors circulating about him were true, they said that I was not the first woman whose lover he had falsely claimed to be. People are always delighted to see someone like that tricked, and there was no sort of mockery they did not make of him. He found out about most of what people were saying and used a rather amusing strategy to quash these rumors.

He pretended to take my words literally and said to the people talking to me that he and I were not getting on because he had not been able to love me. "I admit that she is attractive," he added, "and that she has a very amusing personality, but everyone has his own things to do, and it is not possible to love everyone. A man would need a great stock of love if he were to love everyone who merits it."

I only laughed at this speech, and those who knew the truth laughed as I did. Everyone did not know the truth, however, and there were some people so simpleminded as to spread the story that I was insanely in love with the Chevalier du Buisson and that I couldn't make him love me. I think they may also have claimed that I committed some desperate act because of this, for the death of a lovely lady the previous spring had made desperate acts fashionable, and perhaps people did me the honor of believing that I was dying because of that ingrate.

These stories reached the ears of a lady who, as Your Highness will learn, did not hear them with indifference. She was a false prude who had deceived some good friends, and since pious people willingly judge others as they do themselves, they thought her to be a very good woman and had liberally contributed to her reputation.

She was very proud of this and in her circle one only heard about the severe reprimands she made to all women. She honored me with some, and you can judge, Madame, whether she picked a good time to do this. I had just found out about a love affair she had had for more than a year with the Chevalier du Buisson.

The coincidence made me smile and, wanting to amuse myself, I said to her, "For such a charitable and virtuous woman, it seems to me that you have a great penchant for judging your neighbor harshly. I have treated you with more charity, for whatever anyone has said about you and the Chevalier du Buisson, I have never been willing to believe a word of it."

You would have laughed heartily, Madame, if you had seen this woman's distress when I mentioned the name of her lover. She did not know what to say and was embarrassed, but it did not take her a long time to recover. Assuming her prudish manner she said that people knew her well, that she had no fear of these calumnies, and that they would fall back on the people who had invented them.

The people who had told me this story were very accurate, and I saw no reason to hide this. I forgot no detail and I made my false prude so extremely angry that she could not hide it.

She called me ill-bred and a gossip and I don't know how many other names. Leaving my house in a fury, she swore that I would regret having offended her.

I only laughed at her threats, and I made Monsieur de Lionne laugh too when I told him about the conversation. I was a fool, however, to take this matter so lightly. One should never play around with people of that type, and very soon I learned at my expense that a quarrel with them is no subject for laughter.

I told Your Highness that this person passed for a woman of great virtue. This was inaccurate, as you can see, but the people who were fooled by her were powerful and blindly supported her interests. She persuaded them that I was leading a dissolute life and that she was right to reproach me with it. She accused me of having insulted her, something that I had never thought of doing, and she undoubtedly mixed in some suggestion of irreverence toward that which merits our respect.[18] She fired them up so much that, despite their good intentions, they became the instruments of her revenge.

All the evidence that the deceased Madame d'Englesac had put together

18. This refers to a lack of respect toward religion.

to destroy me was brought out of the files. All the slander our lawsuits had been full of was circulated about again. The last order of the parlement of Grenoble was not forgotten, nor the orders that had formerly been obtained from the queen mother, which were found somehow or other. I was very surprised when the Chevalier du Buisson came to tell me that they were trying to get a new order to have me put in a convent and that they were on the verge of getting it.

"You can judge, Madame," said the Chevalier du Buisson in giving me this information, "that I have no part in the evil they want to do you. I was a bit angry with you, and if I think about it I am still angry, but not to the extent that they have acted against you. I did what I could to prevent it, but I was not able to succeed, and they have so little deference for my pleadings that they have freed me from any restraint. Here is what I can do for you. I know of a good means to avenge you, and if you wish we can have an order given against your enemy just like the one given against you."

I did not accept his offer, as Your Highness would expect. I had enough trouble without thinking of attacking anyone. I was, however, grateful to him for his good will, and that made me forget the reasons I had to complain about him.

However, they were making great efforts to get the order, and the great lord of whom I have spoken did me as much disservice as he could. I do not know how my false prude found out that he was an enemy of mine, but in the end she got him to work for her, and I was well informed that he struck great blows against me.

My only hope lay in Monsieur de Lionne, and my hope was not in vain. He would have defended me generously, for those whom he loved, he loved strongly and let no cowardly considerations restrain him in regard to those who did not make good use of their influence. He was at Fontainebleau,[19] where the court was at that time, and as I was getting ready to go find him, I learned that he had returned to Paris, sick.

At first his illness was only a tertian fever,[20] and his physicians laughed at me when I asked if his life were not in some danger, but they were wrong to do so, for something foretold me my coming misfortune, and as soon as I saw Monsieur de Lionne sick, I would have sworn that he was on his deathbed.

Ah! Madame, what a loss for me! What a generous and powerful protector I had in this worthy minister! I was not alone in weeping for him, for

19. Fontainebleau is a forested area about forty miles southeast of Paris. French kings had a chateau there.

20. A tertian fever is "characterized by the occurrence of a paroxysm every third (i.e., every alternate) day." *Oxford English Dictionary*, s.v. "tertian."

everyone regretted his loss, and everyone said with a common voice that people of merit should never die. There are so few of them, however, that it is not worth it to make a special rule for them.

As soon as his death was known in Languedoc, the Count of Englesac's relatives did not want to keep any of the promises they had made to him. They had agreed in their letters that they would recognize my marriage and that they would provide me with a reasonable income for life. I agreed to settle for six thousand pounds a year, and they thought that was reasonable. When Monsieur de Lionne had died, however, they no longer thought they owed me anything. I was not, they said, the widow of the Count of Englesac, and they again began their persecutions and their calumnies.

I no longer dared to address myself to the king as I had decided to do upon leaving Grenoble, for I feared that my new enemies had blackened me in His Majesty's mind. Perhaps I was wrong to have these apprehensions, and people scarcely talk to the king about such trivial matters, but I was apprehensive and I did not want to put myself in danger of unhappy consequences.

I decided to go and see if I could not be more fortunate in obtaining the inheritance of Madame de Seville than I had been in trying to get my inheritance from the Count of Englesac. I found myself in Paris without means of support or allies. The Chevalier du Buisson assured me that some people in that city were about to do me an evil turn, and Madame de Seville's heirs were profiting from my absence from Brussels. What better could I do than go there? I got myself ready to travel, Madame, and although many unfortunate things had happened to me in Paris, I will confess to Your Highness that I did not leave it without some sighs.

It is a comfortable and charming place to live. You can find palaces and walks and other similar things in other places as well, but only in Paris can you find the free lifestyle that is practiced there, and it is, in my opinion, the most precious thing in the world.

I wanted to pass through the region of Artois[21] in order to see a man who had managed the business affairs of Madame de Seville, for I knew he had retired there after her death. I hoped to gain a number of clarifications from him. This almost brought me more troubles and did attract new enemies.

My hostess found out from my servants that I was taking the road to Artois and asked me to offer a place in my carriage to a person who she said was the relative of one of her friends and who wanted to go and see her husband, who was garrisoned at Artois.

I do not know whether this hostess had been bribed or if she had simply

21. Artois is a province in northwest France, on the coast south of Flanders.

been fooled, but, Madame, the person she had put in my charge was Mademoiselle de ———, who, after having hidden in Paris for two or three months, fled incognito and was going to meet the Duke of ——— in Flanders.

You know her story, Madame. She has caused too much talk for nothing of it to have reached you. Imagine, please, the difficulty in which I would have found myself if the relatives of this young woman had discovered me taking her secretly out of Paris. They would never have forgiven me, and they are not people who spare those whom they do not like.

It is true that I was not in this dangerous situation for a long time. The Duke of ——— joined us in our second day of travel and took Mademoiselle ——— to one of his castles outside of the French borders.

I do not know how these two people came to know each other. Perhaps the people who hid her in Paris did not hide her from everyone, and he saw her during the trip he made there a little while ago. However it happened, they seemed to me to be quite good friends, and according to what I could judge, without realizing it, I had taken a mistress to her lover.

When I found out, I only laughed about it, my good intentions relieving me of any scruples. Besides, Madame, I had many other things to think about, for the Duke of ——— had warned me not to cross the lands of the King of Spain[22] and that in Brussels there was a warrant for my arrest.

Your Highness is undoubtedly surprised to hear talk of a warrant. I was very surprised too, and I did not think I had done anything that would bring me before the courts. One cannot be sure of anything, however, and you are about to learn of a legal maneuver that you would never have guessed.

Madame de Seville's heirs had undoubtedly thought about their affairs, as had I. It is probable that they had been told that the inheritance had been left to me in a proper way and that if they tried to dispute it with me, they would be obliged to pay the expenses. They came up with a strange strategy to prevent me from having the enjoyment of it.

I told you that Madame de Seville had charged her footman with bringing me the little chest in which I found some jewels, and that he had brought it to me. That had been done without any formalities. His mistress had confidently put the little chest in his hands, and I had received it from him. Somehow or other, the heirs had found out about this gift, either because the marquise had told someone that she had sent me her jewels or because I myself, who had made no secret of this present, had spoken of it in front of people who corresponded with Brussels. It had been presented as a theft, and thus they said they were perfectly justified in pursuing me. For in the case of

22. The Spanish Hapsburgs controlled the Low Countries at this time.

bequests or other similar things that one receives from someone who has died, it is necessary to make a declaration or the items must be included in the will.

I had done nothing at all, for I did not know I needed to, and I have to believe that the marquise did not know this any better than I did. They made a great crime out of my ignorance and brought decrees against the poor footman as though he were a thief. They had obtained a judgment in absentia in which I was also included.

I have never been so astounded as when the Duke of —— explained to me that all of this was criminal. I had never heard talk of such a thing, and either they had bribed the people who handled my business in Flanders or had taken them unawares, for these people had never told me anything about these legal requirements.

Madame, I must confess that my patience almost abandoned me and that when I saw myself persecuted in Languedoc, in danger of being arrested in Paris, and in even greater danger in Brussels, I muttered things against my fate that were stronger than anything I had ever said.

The Duke of —— did what he could to console me. He offered me his influence and that of his friends, and told me that if I wanted to be in a safe place, he could offer me one in a castle that was on the lands of the Empire[23] and that belonged to one of his relatives.

I did not accept this offer. I did not want to shut myself up thus in a land that was unknown to me, and I simply asked him to talk to the marquise's heirs to see if there were not some way to make them be a bit reasonable. He promised to do everything possible, and we agreed that he would let me know what happened in Liege,[24] where I had resolved to go.

You know, Madame, that the State of Liege is a neutral land and that this neutrality is well respected. However, I did not dare trust this completely, for it is near Brussels, my adversaries had influence, and I feared betrayal by some magistrate. Thus I did not want to say who I was. I went to Spa.[25] It was the season to take the waters, and I pretended to be a French woman to whom this cure had been recommended.

In truth, when I think about it, this plan to hide my identity elicited a great deal of curiosity, and people form strange ideas about you when you create some mystery about who you are. There was a very fine group of peo-

---

23. The Holy Roman Empire, including territories now part of Germany and Austria.

24. Liege is in Belgium, about fifty miles east of Brussels and about twenty miles from the German border. At the time of the novel, the prince-bishopric of Liege was independent of the Spanish Netherlands.

25. Spa is a village in Belgium reputed for the curative powers of its waters.

ple in Spa that year. Monsieur the Count of Marsin was there.[26] He recognized me but was faithful to me in not revealing my identity to anyone. The Prince and Princess of Nassau were there, as were I know not how many foreign lords and an abbess from a convent in Cologne who was from a great German family and who had with her two very pretty nuns.

Everyone decided to guess who I was. I cannot tell you, Madame, how many outrageous judgments that occasioned.

There was a Frenchman who pretended that I was Madame ——, that he knew me well, and that he had formerly seen me in Paris. Someone else pretended that I was her mother, without thinking that if I were the one, it was impossible that I could look like the other. The Frenchman and she bet on it and came to me innocently, asking me to tell them which one had won.

Madame, you can judge if they were reasonable to ask me this question, and supposing I was who they said I was, do you think I would have said so? I only laughed at their folly, telling them that after the season for taking the waters I would settle their question. I sent them away angry over my silence.

An English lord, who was taking the waters and of whom Madame —— was a relative, found out about the bet. He came to find me and, after having strongly encouraged me to have full confidence in him and not to hide my name from him as I had from people of no account, he explained to me the particulars of our feigned relationship and offered me a safe retreat in England.

His generosity touched me. I treated him more civilly than the bettors of whom I have spoken. I told him in good faith that I did not even know the ladies of whom he spoke. He did not want to believe me. I do not know what it was he saw in me that made him hope I would go to England, but he insisted that I was his relative and from that time on kept tormenting me to make me agree that I was.

I laughed at his obstinacy and for two or three days it rather amused me, but in the end it annoyed me. I became angry and I told this English lord that he should learn to know me better, that I was not capable of the actions of which that person was accused, and that I had never been involved in any business like hers.

I believe he thought that the honor of being his relative wiped out any other considerations. He was surprised that in this circumstance I did not want to become Madame —— and, to make me want to do so, he outlined his genealogy.

---

26. Marsin was one of Condé's military captains. After the Fronde he joined the Spanish troops in the Low Countries. He was unable to keep the French from taking Lille (MC 195).

I do not know if it was illustrious or not, for I am not familiar with the great houses of England. Listening to him, however, all the lords in his lineage were heroes, and he forced me to hear the praises of every one of them.

That evening, in the meadow where all the water drinkers met, I told the story. People found it very amusing and got the Englishman to talk about his ancestors. He told their history again, and since each person who arrived asked him to start over, they made him say the same thing more than ten times.

This gave us yet another amusement. In Spa there was a rich bourgeois from Liege who would not have changed his title for that of an ancient baron and who believed that there was no finer title than that of citizen.[27] He made fun of the lord and said that his rank was inferior to that of a bourgeois. They quarreled and said a thousand outrageous things to each other about the way of life and the customs of their countries, as if each were the incarnation of his whole nation.

I really laughed at this quarrel in the company of Monsieur de Marsin and the abbess from Cologne, for this person and I became inseparable, Madame. She showed me extreme tenderness. I loved her with all my heart, and we could not refrain from confiding in each other all the secrets of our lives.

Some day I will tell you her story. I think she will give me permission to do so, for there is nothing in it that will not be to her advantage. What a reasonable and charming person! Your Highness would absolutely love her if you knew her, and I am dying to introduce her to you.

However, I received letters from the Duke of —— informing me that Madame de Seville's heirs were inexorable. They wanted the jewels, and they wanted me to renounce what she had left me. I could have satisfied this latter desire, but it was no longer in my power to satisfy the former. I had sold some of these jewels, and even if all of them had been in my hands, I would never allow myself to be held responsible for having them taken. Giving them back would have been like admitting the theft, and I was not going to make this mistake. I would have held on to the jewels no matter what happened.

Never in my life had I been more worried and more at a loss as to what to do. The season for taking the waters was coming to an end, and I was afraid I would reveal my presence to my enemies if I remained in Liege without some justification. Monsieur de Marsin offered me the use of his beautiful castle of

---

27. In France, while the bourgeoisie had some privileges, any suggestion that their status was as good as that of the nobility was comic. Hence the man from Liege makes himself ridiculous by this assertion (MC 296).

Mondave,[28] where I had no doubt that I would be completely safe, for Monsieur de Marsin was too well respected in the Low Countries for there to be any fear that anything could happen to people in his home.

Thus I went there, Madame, and he was good enough to take me there himself. My dear abbess from Cologne was willing to come and spend some time with me. She was waiting for a carriage to take her home. It had not come yet, and she thought she could wait for it at Mondave just as well as at Spa.

This house is one of the most charming and magnificent that can be seen. For some days I forgot all my troubles there. It is true that I had received a great consolation, for Monsieur the Count of Marsin had promised to defend my interests, and I knew that in Brussels there were few things that his influence could not accomplish.

But, Madame, he came up against the stubbornness of my bad fortune. The first letter I received from him told me that I should expect no more help from him. Here is the reason he gave me.

Madame de Seville's principal heir had just married a young woman who was related to the Count of Montmorency, Governor of the Low Countries. This relationship made him so important that attacking him would have been like attacking the governor.

Monsieur de Marsin excused himself a great deal, and the way in which his letter was written made it appear to me that he was genuinely distressed that he could not help me and that he had really had the intention of doing so.

To get me to take my new misfortune with patience, it was necessary for my friend to help me with her advice and her exhortations. She showed that she was as distressed by them as I myself, and enjoined me, with tears in her eyes, to choose a more tranquil kind of life than the one in which I had languished for so long.

"Are you not tired of fighting against Fortune?" she said to me, "and do you think you have more patience than she has malice? You are in error if you think that. When Fortune decides to persecute someone, there is no amount of strength she cannot conquer."

She then gave me I do not know how many examples that touched me a great deal, among others that of the king who after losing his freedom, his wife, and his children without shedding a tear, wept piteously over the death of one of his slaves.[29] "Why do you think that happened?" my friend

---

28. This was a chateau near Huy in the region of Liege (MC 299).

29. This example is modeled loosely on the story of the Egyptian King Psammenitus. Herodotus *History* 3.14–15.

continued. "It was not because his slave was dearer to his master than everything he had lost but that his endurance was at its end, and he only had patience up to that limit. The same thing will happen to you one of these days. You have been quite strong until now, and your temperament has overcome everything, but in the end it will weaken. You will see that a misfortune will occur that will reduce you to despair. Do not wait for this extremity. Retire with me to my solitude, and shelter yourself from the storms that threaten you. Reflect on all the events of your life, see how many difficulties you have had since you killed Monsieur de Molière. There is enough material for a long novel. Do you not want finally to allow yourself a little repose, and to put yourself in a situation where Fortune and your enemies cannot injure you?"

I wept when she said all this to me. We embraced tenderly and I understood that she was giving me good advice, but I was not yet in a mood to follow it. It seemed to me shameful to leave the world because I was unhappy in it. I wanted my retreat to be a choice dictated by my heart and not by necessity.

She criticized my reasoning and told me it was a false pretext for continuing to run around the world. She said that one would hardly leave the world if one could live happily in it, and that if by some event that she could not predict I could settle my affairs, I would have only less desire to retire to a convent.

It seems to me that she was telling me the truth, Madame, and that really taking everything into consideration, I would have preferred the goods Madame de Seville had left me to a retirement from the world. These goods were becoming quite uncertain, however, and the asylum she offered me was a present resource. I accepted it, therefore, with the intention of leaving if Fortune became more favorable to me.

The abbess's carriage arrived as she had hoped, and we got into it together to take the road to Cologne, for, Madame, I had given up my coach and retinue as soon as I had decided to go with her, and I kept only Merinville with me. We did not take the shortest route. The abbess had friends in several communities of canonesses[30] whom she wanted to see as she passed through and who awaited her impatiently. We stopped there for a while, and Your Highness would no doubt be pleased to know what we did there. I have resolved to tell you, Madame, but this account requires that I catch my

---

30. A canoness is "a member of a college or community of women living under a rule, but not under a perpetual vow; hence, a woman holding a prebend or canonry in a female chapter." *Oxford English Dictionary*, s.v. "canoness."

breath. I beg you to allow me to do so. I have already been writing for a long time, and I would fear abusing the attention that Your Highness gives me if I were to tire you with a very long narration.

PART 6

Madame, are you not tired of hearing my complaints against Fortune? I am tired of it myself, and it seems to me that I was not in the habit of according them so much attention.

But one must admit, Madame, that she has treated me very cruelly, and that no one could be more beaten down than I was at Mondave when I received Monsieur the Count of Marsin's letter.

I saw that all my hopes had been dashed. The alliance of my enemies with the Governor of the Low Countries made me afraid of some violence from that quarter, and if I must admit all my weaknesses to you, I still looked at the necessity of retiring to a convent as a misfortune.

It was not that I did not really love my abbess, and that in any place other than a cloister I would not have considered myself happy to spend my days with her, but the word *cloister* frightened me. I still remembered the sorrows I had had in my old convent, and I imagined I would have as many in all the other convents where I might find myself.

I was mad to imagine these things. Fortune treated me more favorably than I realized, and I admit that I never did a better thing than to follow the abbess's advice. I must however tell you things in order, Madame, and begin, as I promised, with the incidents of our trip.

First of all it was much longer than we had expected, for we were only at Maubeuge,[1] where the abbess had gone to see some friends, when she got news of the troubles in Cologne. Your Highness is not unaware of them, and you undoubtedly know that the citizens of that city refused to open their gates to their Elector, who is also the Prince of Liege. He relied on the authority of the King of France, who had promised him help, and resolved to open the gates by force.[2]

This caused a war in the area around Cologne and made approaching

---

1. Maubeuge is southeast of Valenciennes in northeastern France, very close to the Belgian border.

2. His expansionist ambitions to the north blocked by the Triple Alliance, Louis XIV sought allies to the east. He encouraged the Elector of Cologne in the latter's efforts to take control of the free city of Cologne. The city was completely surrounded by the Elector's territory. The Dutch Republic backed the city in order to counter French influence. Jonathan Israel, *The Dutch Republic: Its Rise, Greatness, and Fall, 1477–1806* (Oxford: Clarendon Press, 1995), 783–84.

the city dangerous for people like us, so the abbess decided to remain at Maubeuge until the troubles died down.

She was very distressed by this delay, and although I said everything I could to convince her that one should always stretch out one's reasons for traveling as long as possible, she answered that she had much business at home and that nothing more distressing could happen to her than to be away for such a long time.

I loved her enough to share in her sorrows like a good friend, but as for this sorrow, Madame, I admit to you that I only shared it partially, for, as I have said to Your Highness, I was going to Cologne regretfully, and the stay in Maubeuge was beginning to seem very amusing to me.

You know the reputation of the communities of Flanders, Madame, and you undoubtedly know that the canonesses who inhabit them, having taken no vows against marriage, keep up honorable gallant relationships as though they were in the most gallant court in the world.

Men write them notes and love verses, and they answer when it suits them. They are visited as if they were in their own homes, and they receive visits in rooms and in gardens, where they are observed only by ladies who are as sociable as they are virtuous.

In truth, all of this takes place with the goal of marriage, and eligibility for marriage is considered to be a man's best quality. But since many of the proposed matches are never completed, there are many legitimate suits that in the end become simple flirtations and are different from love affairs only because of an intention that everyone interprets as he or she pleases.

One of the ladies of Maubeurge had had such an adventure, and when we arrived there no one talked of anything else. I am going to tell you the story because I think it will amuse you. Fortune, moreover, gave me such a role in it that I could not tell you the story of my life without saying a word about it at least in passing.

Your Highness has no doubt heard of a man named Don Antoine of Cordova, who was a commander of the troops that the King of Spain kept in Flanders and who had been taken prisoner of war in the campaign of Lille. He had been very much in love with the canoness of whom I am speaking, and the articles of their marriage had been drawn up at the moment when war broke out between France and Spain.[3]

I do not know whether the Marquis de Castel-Rodrigue, who governed Flanders at that time, thought that celebrations were inappropriate in time of war and that a married man would be less likely to risk his life than a man not

3. The War of Devolution, 1667–68.

yet married or whether he had some other thing in mind that the lovers did not know about, but he made it clear to Don Antoine that he would be pleased if he delayed his marriage until the end of the campaign. This request was made in terms that permitted no resistance. This delay was painful for the fiancés, who loved each other very much and had for a long time hoped to marry. They had to be patient, however, for the governors of Flanders have almost as much authority as kings. And since, in the case of marriages, obstacles never occur alone, not only was Don Antoine made a prisoner of war, as I told Your Highness, but after the peace he was sent to Madrid, where he was in great danger of losing his head.

I have never really known what he was accused of, but it seems that he was too involved in Don Juan's interests.[4] Whatever the case, he was made prisoner, and he needed all his friends to avoid death on this occasion.

There was even a rumor in Brussels that he had died. People recounted all the circumstances of his death, and the canoness, who thought them true, wept for him as if she had really lost him.

She loved him enough to have preferred him to all those who would have wished to marry her, but this love was not so extreme that she wanted to remain unmarried all her life. She soon thought of finding a suitor, and since she was beautiful and from one of the finest families in Hainault,[5] she did not lack for volunteers to fill the empty spot.

People talked of two or three possible marriages as if they were at the point of being concluded. This talk came to the ears of a man named Don Pedro of Larra, who was the best friend Don Antoine had in the world. This Don Pedro had been the confidant of the love of his friend and the canoness. He believed that Don Antoine would die of sorrow if he returned and found his mistress married.

Don Pedro quickly came to Maubeuge and, after having criticized this young woman for her ingratitude, he assured her that he had received news of her lover, that he was on his way back, and that she would soon see him returned to favor and more in love than ever.

She did not have great faith in his assurances. She wanted to see a letter from Don Antoine, and that is what no one could show her. He was a prisoner of state, and such persons are not permitted to exchange letters with their friends. The canoness continued on her way, and the officious Don Pedro, who did not know what to do to spare Don Antoine the misfortune that threatened him, came up with a rather amusing ruse.

---

4. Don Juan of Austria was involved in intrigues in Spain that sought to undermine the monarchy (MC 308).

5. Hainault (or Hainaut) is a province of Belgium, south of Brussels on the French border.

Don Pedro, who was wellborn and quite wealthy, pretended to be one of the suitors, and when he was accepted, he was so good at creating obstacles to concluding the marriage (for this is not difficult for anyone who has the will to do it) that the canoness was still unmarried when Don Antoine returned to the Low Countries.

I still laugh, Madame, when I think of the outcome of this poor man's good intentions. Subsequently he has said that he had to do himself terrible violence to play the role of the young woman's suitor, and that because of a caprice he could not explain, he had a natural aversion for her. However, Madame, he was so assiduous and seemed to be such a passionate lover that he was taken for a true suitor. Upon Don Antoine's return, he expected to be praised for his efforts and liberated from such a painful constraint, but instead he found that his friend's feelings had changed and that he did not want his mistress back.

It is probable that the canoness's flightiness had put Don Antoine off; he did not want as a wife a woman who was so easily consoled for his death. But this was not the reason he gave, and either because he still mistrusted himself sufficiently to fear explanations or because he wanted to behave respectfully toward the girl's parents, who were very powerful people, he pretended to think that Don Pedro was really in love. Saying that he wanted to show himself the most generous of men, he added that he would give up his place to his friend without regret and that he was pleased to make this sacrifice for him.

You would have really laughed, Madame, if you could have heard the compliments they made to each other on this occasion. They were at this point when we arrived in Maubeuge, and I never found anything so amusing in my life as this dispute, for they fell over themselves saying good things about the canoness. They said that it was because they were such good friends that neither wanted to take her from the other, and with these fine speeches they both got out of the affair, and the poor girl was in great danger of never being married.

I told Your Highness that she had very powerful parents. They were tired of seeing her toyed with in this way and absolutely wanted one of the two of them to marry her. Things went so far that the Count of Monterey was obliged to become involved and to try to reach a settlement.

To do this, he sent frequent messages to Maubeuge, and I was always a witness to all the messages that were sent, for I had found this story so droll that I had insinuated myself into it for amusement. I had done such a good job of winning the canoness's friendship that she did nothing she did not confide to me.

This produced a rather pleasant effect, for, Madame, it was the heir of Madame de Seville who was charged with coming to find out what the young woman's sentiments were. Since the canoness and I were always together, he saw me, and it was apparent that he found a good deal of pleasure in doing so. I did not know who he was, for he bore the name of a marquisate that he had recently bought, and he did not know me as Madame d'Englesac, for I was passing as the abbess's niece and using her family's name.

Somehow or other, we began to joke about Don Pedro's problem and Don Antoine's deference. I said some rather good things about it, and in the end I said such funny things that the marquis became taken with my conversation and decided to visit me on my own account.

I did not want to receive these visits. I feared attracting other people who would recognize me, and two or three times I had him told that I was not well. Since he persisted in asking for me, and since it would have been insulting to him to keep telling him the same thing, my abbess was the first to send me to receive this man's visit, telling me that I did not need to make new enemies.

Initially, for my part, the visit was kept rather serious, and I think it would not have left much desire in him for another visit if I had continued in that vein. However, the subject of the Count of Monterey came up, and the marquis convinced me that he had total control over the count's thinking, such that I thought him able to help me, and I hoped to use him as a counterweight to balance against the favor in which my enemies were held.

Madame, you can judge whether this idea of mine was a good one, and whether I was not really comic in thinking I could make this man act against himself. Since then I have often laughed in my own mind about it, and it would have been quite something if I had been so mistaken as to confide in him about my business and ask him for his protection. I was all ready to do so, and would have done so if he had not spoken first and told me to whom I was speaking, before I had made up my mind what to tell him.

I told Your Highness that I was not so cold at the end of the first visit as I had been at the beginning. I had become a bit more sociable, and if I did not treat him like a man who was one of my best friends, I at least let him think that he might become one in time. Without any difficulty, I gave him permission to visit me when he wished.

He did not fail to profit from this, for, Madame, it is certain that he found me much to his liking, and his error produced even more amusing effects on him than mine had produced on me. He took on all the obligations that could require him to stay in Maubeuge. There was always some new business, sometimes from the canoness whose affairs he complicated a good deal, sometimes for some kind of settlement for two or three gentlemen in the area. He did such a good job that without there seeming to be anything out of the ordinary in his conduct, he spent fifteen days with us, leaving us only during those times when he could not see us.

But his conduct did have a certain something about it, and I do not know how I managed not to notice. For this man always had his eyes fixed on me, his looks were very passionate, he praised me with enthusiasm, and when an opportunity occurred to talk about his wealth and his possessions, he always said that he had a wife who was near death and that he would soon be in a position to make the fortune of an unmarried woman.

But, Madame, I did not apply any of this to myself, and either because I had so completely forgotten about lovers that I no longer remembered how they acted or because, since I no longer wanted to give love, I flattered myself with the thought that I did not inspire any, and so it never occurred to me that this man was in love with me.

He was, however, very violently in love, as he showed later on, and could not remain any longer without letting me know something about it. This conversation was very amusing and is worth recounting precisely to Your Highness.

I do not know whether on that day I really looked particularly becoming or whether our Flemish marquis found that to be so, but initially he exclaimed how well I looked, saying it was the consequence of my tranquility. Sighing, he went on to say that he did not have similar tranquility and that for about a month he had been unable to sleep.

"Are you in love?" I asked, without believing it was true. He answered that I had guessed very accurately, and that in fact he was the one man in the world most tormented by love. He began expatiating on the beauty and the merit of the person he loved. He said so many things that seemed to be addressed to me that it opened my eyes, and I realized that I might be the object of his tenderness.

This suspicion caused me a great deal of pain, for, as I have told you, Madame, I thought this man could help me, and I was very distressed to see that love was going to come and confuse this matter, too, as it had confused so many others.

Thus I said everything I could to this new lover to persuade him that when one is married, one should not get love affairs into one's head. He agreed with what I said, for in that land they hold to the maxim that one should be faithful to one's wife.[6] He did not think he owed much to his, however, for he swore that he had never loved her, and that he had only married

6. The French nobility's attitudes toward conjugal fidelity contrasted sharply with this perspective.

her to ally himself with the influence of His Excellency in some business matters he had, of which my affair was one.

Imagine, Madame, how astounded I was to hear him say these things. I made him repeat it several times, and when through these repetitions I was persuaded that I was speaking to my enemy, I was so surprised, as I still am, that he did not realize it.

But he had other things on his mind. He thought only of his love and never imagined that the confidences he made to me were made to the Countess of Englesac. I found this adventure so amusing that I could not help but laugh, and despite all the trouble I saw in it, I had to begin by having fun with it. He would have wished that I had taken things more seriously, and he said many things critical of my playfulness. But the more he talked, the more he gave me reasons to laugh. Since he could not deal with my laughter and since I could not stop laughing, he left me, very distressed, I think, that I cared so little about his sorrows.

I went to find my abbess to tell her what had happened. I found her scarcely in a state to enjoy my tale. She had received news from Cologne that had touched her to the quick, and here is the place, Madame, where I must tell you something of her story. I promised it to you at the end of the previous part. I have reassured her so much that she could be confident of your goodness and your discretion that she has given me permission to send to you whatever information about her I judge to be relevant.

One must admit, Madame, that love is a universal passion, and that if it were only necessary to have company to be consoled for one's love affairs, I would not have lacked this consolation. But I do not know how to comfort myself in this way, and women unfortunate in love are a new source of affliction to me.

The abbess of whom I speak was one of this unfortunate number. She is German and women of this climate are not considered to take love too much to heart, but she had a more lively temperament than ordinary German women, and she had greatly loved a lord from her region who from childhood had been chosen to be her husband.

For, Madame, in praise of this person it must be said that no one could be more reasonable than she. If her parents' wishes had not authorized her feelings, she would surely have overcome them, but since everyone approved them and since she foresaw no obstacle, she fully gave her heart to them. The young lover had done no less for her. They loved each other ardently and at first everything seemed to favor them. The only thing that prevented the marriage from taking place was that they were awaiting the arrival of one of her uncles, who wanted to be present at the ceremony but was off negotiating some kind of business or other at the Emperor's[7] court.

But, Madame, when one is born for adventures, no matter what one does, Fate is too strong, and when one expects it the least, things happen that turn the most simple and common matters into something worthy of a novel.

First, the young woman's father fell ill while they were waiting for the uncle. He died of this illness, and when he had died, his widow, who was still rather young and mistress of a great fortune, made known a secret passion that she had long had for her future son-in-law.

At first she hid it under other pretexts. She said that since the death of her husband she had a better understanding of her financial holdings than she had had before and that this match did not suit her daughter. She said she had another man in mind who was richer and who would be much more suitable. However, seeing that this reason was not considered strong enough to break off a marriage that had been planned for so long, and since the most powerful relatives of the dead man said they intended this matter be concluded and that it must be done, she decided to take another route.

The uncle for whom they had waited so long and so discontentedly was a very stingy man; he could be made to do anything for money. He had great influence in the family, for he was the only brother of the dead man. The mother won him over with presents and promises, and when she saw him fully on her side they conspired together on one of the greatest deceptions that has ever been wrought, of which Your Highness undoubtedly will be much surprised to learn.

In his second marriage the old man had married a widow who had a very docile son from her first marriage, a son whom the old man loved a great deal. This young man was not rich, and his stepfather wanted to see him have wealth without having to give him anything. They decided to substitute him for the fiancé, and here, Madame, is the way they went about doing it.

They had tried exhortations and threats to the young lady with no effect. She wanted to keep the word that her father had given, and the amorous mother was constantly afraid that she had already kept it. The bribed uncle was the first to advise her to do what she wanted, but to do it secretly. He promised her his protection and his help. Her mother, he said, was carrying off a good deal of the inheritance; she could remarry and take that wealth to another family. It would be a mistake to irritate her by public disobedience. It would be better to bring her to agreement by degrees and not let her know

---

7. The Holy Roman Emperor Leopold I (1658–1705).

that the situation was without remedy until she had been prepared for it by a thousand other things that should precede this admission.

The poor girl, who was incapable of any malice and believed that everyone else was incapable of it too, received her uncle's advice with great thanks and gave herself over to his guidance. He took her to his country house and impressed her with the difficulties he had had in getting permission from her mother to take her there. He made sure a priest and a lawyer were there, and he assured her that her fiancé had been told to be there at the appointed time. He had made her understand that it was necessary to hide everything from the servants, for fear that her mother might get wind of what was happening. For this reason they had chosen nighttime, and the chapel where this was done was kept very dark. What can I say, Madame? The poor girl married the stepson of her uncle rather than the man she thought she was marrying. As chance never does anything halfway, they did look somewhat alike, and the resemblance of their voices was very strong.

This exchange seems so extraordinary that it will seem like fiction to anyone who does not know the original story, as I do, or who, unlike Your Highness, has little confidence in my words. However, Madame, nothing is more true than the story I am telling you. But why am I trying so hard to make myself believed? You knew personally a famous abbess in France to whom the same thing happened. In truth, the abbess of whom I speak told me that the deception was not pushed as far in her case as in that of the French lady, for she recognized the substitute husband when leaving the chapel, and nothing more passed between them. But too much had already happened for a virtuous person who by her very nature feared adventures like death itself.

I cannot tell you all the regrets and all the lamentations of this unfortunate lover when she realized the trick that had been played on her. A thousand times she called her uncle a deceiver and a trickster. She criticized her own naïveté. She called her fate unjust, and most of all she was afflicted by the suspicions that her beloved might conceive about her fidelity.

She wanted to prevent this by telling him the truth of the situation, but she was not given the freedom to do so. Perhaps they hoped that with time she would come around, and so that nothing would dampen this hope, they did not allow her to communicate with anyone.

You can imagine, Madame, that her secret rival was not asleep. She found people mean enough to assure the lover that his beloved had given her full consent to the marriage, that they had been witnesses to it, and that she lived with her husband like the most tender and passionate woman in the world. These false reports produced the expected effect. The poor man was in despair, and the amorous mother, trying to take advantage of this opportunity, did not fail to make proposals to him.

She gave them the best appearance she could invent. She told him she was horrified by the flightiness of her daughter, and that it was to make up for it in some way that she offered this betrayed lover her self and her fortune. Everyone knew she had been openly opposed to him, and she could not deny it, but she said that in the end she had given in to the perseverance of the two lovers, that she was already vacillating at the moment when her daughter left, and that she was displeased that she had not been allowed to make up her mind.

What she said and did was no use, Madame; the lover was still in love with his mistress. If he was in despair over being betrayed, it was a tender and delicate despair, and not a brutal and vindictive resentment.

Two full months passed in this way, during which our new bride (who was not, however, a wife) knew how to make clear to her husband the kind of remorse that an honorable man feels when he does violence to the feelings of his wife and the fact that he was abusing a power he did not legitimately possess. She did this so well that he himself became horrified by the action he had committed and resolved to make up for it in every way he could.

He was, as I told Your Highness, a docile type of young man, who had a fundamentally good nature and who was more obedient than malicious in everything that had happened. His stepfather had proposed this deception to him, and he had accomplished it without understanding the consequences it might have. When he saw, however, that it was a matter of making someone extremely unhappy and of passing his life with a wife from whom he could hear only reproaches and lamentations, he voluntarily contributed to breaking off the marriage. He took his wife to a convent where one of his aunts was the abbess, and of which she herself has since become the abbess, and they parted on the friendliest of terms.

This departure caused an enormous fuss in the whole province in which this affair had occurred. Its cause was found out, and the lover ran as quickly as possible to confirm the truth. He no sooner discovered the innocence of his mistress than he thought he would take her with him and finally conclude the marriage that had been subject to so many obstacles.

He found, however, that she had an unconquerable revulsion for having two living husbands. It was no use for him to tell her that he did not consider her the wife of the first husband and that he would only think of this adventure in order to esteem her all the more. She said that the world would not judge her as he did. She remained firm in her resolution to become a nun, and they converted their love into such a tender and pure friendship that one cannot admire it enough.

One time they wanted to marry off the man of whom I speak. The nun, who judged that this marriage would be advantageous to him, advised him to accept it. "I would have fewer reservations about seeing you" she said to him, "for I always fear that I still want to take up your whole heart, and although mine has only innocent desires, and I believe yours to have the same, it seems to me that an honorable wife who loved you would be an even better guarantee of that innocence, and it is a protection that we would do well to give ourselves." "You have sufficient protection in the character of your soul, Madame," he said to her, "and in the character you have imprinted on my esteem for you. I look at you with an admiration that does not allow me to love you like another woman. You can judge, Madame, if I am not right to set you so much apart. I found you tender without being weak. You were vilely betrayed and did not despair. You have left a husband without his complaining about your conduct. You have driven your lover to despair without his being able to reproach you with anything. By a privilege that Heaven has given you, you are a wife, a lover, and a nun, without failing in any of your duties. How can I know you so well and leave any empty space in my heart for another woman. Do not order me to marry, Madame. An honorable woman who loved me would undoubtedly complain of the division of my heart, and, given my temperament, I would consider myself very unhappy if I could not make my wife perfectly happy."

It was this man, so passionate and so refined, who had been wounded in the siege of Cologne, and when I went to tell her my latest adventure, I found the poor abbess shedding the tears that he so well merited.

She found my tale so amusing that she gave herself a little respite from her sadness in order to hear it. And since it is my fate to find lovers and annoying people wherever I go, she gave me a story in return for my story and told me that Don Pedro had also fallen in love with me.

I had not noticed this, and I almost did not believe the abbess when she told me this news. But, Madame, it was not possible for me to doubt it. Because the abbess was pretending to be my aunt, he thought she was responsible for my conduct; so it was to her that he had spoken to reveal his love and to assure her that he had only legitimate and honorable intentions.

This did not gain him much credit with me, since in the mood I was in I hated lovers in the form of husbands just as much as in any other form. I needed the help of everyone, however, and I feared terrible effects from the resentment of this marquis if he found out what a cruel trick his heart had played on him.

I treated his rival, the marquis, more civilly than I would have done if I had followed my feelings. Since this constrained me a bit, and since I wanted either not to tolerate lovers at all or to amuse myself by making them ridiculous, I often took revenge for the constraint I felt through the questions I asked of my suitor and the roles I forced him to play.

He had gone into great detail with me about our business and had recounted to me all the things he had done to deprive me of the bequest of the marquise. This gave me the right to ask him sometimes for news of me, and you would have laughed too much, Madame, if you had seen how I persecuted him on this subject.

He did not know anything about me, as Your Highness can judge, but I pretended that he did and that he refused to say what he knew because he did not trust me. He did not want me to think that, so he told me the first story that came into his mind and in it made the most amusing things in the world happen to me.

One day, I remember, he said I had traveled through I do not know how many cities in Italy, disguised as a man, and attributed to me many adventures that we know happened to a beautiful lady of great quality, for whom I would certainly not be taken.

He told me one story, which I found the most amusing of all, and which would have suited me if I had been shut up in a convent where I was bored, and where I wanted to tire out the people who were holding me there. He said that this lady (whom he pretended to be me) was very fond of hunting and was very unhappy to spend a Saint Hubert's day without hunting, for it must have been around this date that she was in the convent.[8]

She expressed her chagrin to a gentleman of quality who had found a way to see her at the grate[9] and who, according to what people say, was quite taken with her. He sent her a live hare and several dogs to hunt it. I don't know if the hare escaped from the place where it was kept or if there was as much malice as desire to hunt in this matter, but this Saint Hubert took place in the middle of the night. The nuns were in their most profound sleep when they heard the barking of dogs and voices in their dormitory. They thought it was a troop of goblins and had the greatest fright they ever had.

The poor girls! They must have been very frightened indeed, and all that noise is a strange way for sleeping nuns to wake up. Our marquis asserted that this folly caused me much troublesome business, and you would have

---

8. Saint Hubert was the first bishop of Liege and the patron saint of hunters.

9. Convents were equipped with a door that had an opening covered by a grate, through which the nuns might converse with those in the outside world.

laughed a great deal, Madame, if you had seen the innocence with which he assured me that this had happened to me.

He acted out similar comedies for me every day, and I did as much as I could to keep him in his error, for the siege of Cologne was still going on, and it was more difficult than ever for us to enter that city without running great danger. I therefore hid myself from the marquis with great care. But, Madame, when chance takes control of things, it is useless to take precautions against it, and my identity was discovered as a result of a most unexpected incident, one that I could have least foreseen.

I have told Your Highness that when I passed through Lyon I had seen a friend of mine who was staying at the convent of the ladies of Saint Pierre and that she had no more reason to be pleased with men than did I. I have to explain to you some of the reasons why she was unhappy with them. For, besides the fact that this once again demonstrates men's flightiness, which I hate too much to spare them on this account, this little clarification seems required for the rest of my tale.

This friend had formerly had a great commitment to a man who was a minor and who, following the habit of the great majority of young men, repented of the promises he had made her and wanted to break them. This caused many lawsuits between this person and her lover, and since they did not turn out to her advantage, she retired from the world and put herself in the convent where I found her.

She seemed resolved never to leave there for the rest of her life, and I had very much encouraged her in that decision. For even though I do not like convents, I find them very happy places for those who like them, and I willingly advocate convents to those who can stay in them without great displeasure.

I had very strongly advised my friend to make this decision, and I thought that she had done so, for she had assured me of it when I departed. But, Madame, when a woman goes so far as to love in earnest and when a man is convinced that she loves him, he can make her do many things.

This same lover, whom she had understood to be so inconstant and so insincere somehow found a way to see her, and they were reconciled. He said that he had only acted as he had as a stratagem and in order to obey his guardian, whose goodwill he needed, but that he knew what his duty was and he would not fail to do it when he was his own master.

This poor girl believed him. They began to see each other again, and since after what had happened she did not dare see him publicly, she sometimes left her convent on the pretext of business, and they secretly went on little walks together.

They were not so secretive that the girl's relatives did not find out and become greatly angered, for this man had treated her very badly and she wronged herself in continuing to see him. Thus the relatives set traps for them, and having caught them at a meeting they had in a country home near Lyon, they wanted to carry off their relative, and they threatened nothing less than shutting her up in four walls. The lover strongly opposed their plans, an action for which he must always be praised. He killed a man in defending his mistress, and prosecution for this forced him to go away. He came to Flanders and his mistress joined him there, where she hoped to induce him to make amends for all his past faults. He firmly promised her he would do so. Whether he would have done so or not, I do not know. They were in Flanders and a lady whom she had met in that land took her to see the community of Maubeuge.

At that time I, along with my two lovers and five or six of the canonesses, was strolling in one of the gardens in which they entertain company. This imprudent woman, having recognized me before I saw her, ran up to me with open arms, crying out, "I am not wrong! It is Madame d'Englesac." She put everyone into a state of astonishment, which you can imagine.

My name was well known in Flanders, and the troubles I had had about the inheritance of Madame de Seville were still very recent. The canonesses with whom I was staying were not unaware of them. They remained in a state of surprise because of what they heard. One of them ran to others who were walking farther away, and soon everyone in the whole community knew what I had so much wanted to keep secret. I wanted to pretend that this woman had mistaken me for someone else, and I signaled to her to agree to this, but it took her too long to understand me, and her action had been too natural to leave any doubt as to the truth.

Imagine if you please, Madame, the surprise of the marquis when he had reason to believe that I was that Madame d'Englesac whom he had so persecuted, and the battle that raged in his heart between his love and everything that should have destroyed it. It was easy to judge his agitation by the changes in his face. I have never seen a more troubled one, and I expected some terrible consequence from his rage, for I saw him turn his back to us and leave the garden briskly before I had the time to say one single word to him.

I was distressed that he had left us in this way, and I would have liked to have seen what influence I had over him before he saw those people who could make him angry with me. I asked Don Pedro to go after him and bring him back if it was possible, but he did not find him. The marquis had already gotten on his horse, and for a long time afterward we did not know what had happened to him.

Madame, you would not believe the fuss that this affair caused in Brussels. Maubeuge is not, as you know, at much of a distance from there, and there is great communication between these two cities, for many ladies of Maubeuge have families in Brussels and go to spend the winter there. People soon found out that the Marquise de Menez, whom they knew as the Countess of Englesac, was in the area and that she had stayed there for some time under an assumed name. Since the people who make it their business to spread poison never go about it halfway, they attributed this disguise to all sorts of causes I had never thought of and never could have thought of.

The absence of the Flemish marquis made these rumors even more dangerous. The Count of Monterey was angry with him for having left without speaking to him. His wife was so chagrined that she was sicker than ever, and I was considered the cause of all this, for people did not fail to speculate on why he had been in Maubeuge for so long. They knew that he had seen me as often as he had wanted to. When they saw him leave half in despair and without having taken any measures against me, they figured out a part of the truth, and his relatives resented me terribly for it.

My abbess and I saw clearly that we needed to escape from their resentment, and we also thought that the ladies of Maubeuge seemed displeased that this comedy had been played out among them. But we did not know how we could manage to leave, for this was at the time when the King of France began the war against the Dutch.[10] The whole area was full of soldiers, and there were even some in Maubeuge, as a precaution to make sure there was no attack. Thus we did not dare expose ourselves to the danger of passing incognito among so many troops, and we dared even less ask for escorts and passports under our real names, for I feared some nasty trick on the part of Madame de Seville's heirs, and my abbess was kind enough to fear them for my sake as if for her own.

Under these circumstances, Don Pedro's love was a great help to us. He made no secret of it, for Don Antoine of Cordova had gotten over his anger with his mistress and had decided to bring about their marriage. This left Don Pedro entirely to me, and I pleased him no less as Madame d'Englesac than I had as the niece of the abbess from Cologne. On the contrary, I think that he had an opinion of me, now that he knew my identity, which delighted him even more than the one he had had when he did not know it.

Thus he came and very graciously offered us asylum in a castle he knew of in a neutral land and an escort to take us there. I confess, Madame, that this

---

10. The Dutch War (1672–78) began between the English and the Dutch in March 1672, while Louis XIV declared war on the Dutch in April of the same year.

offer pleased me a great deal, and that, despite my disdainful temperament, I was pleased with myself for being able to touch Don Pedro's heart. We accepted his asylum and his escort with pleasure. Initially we had every reason to be satisfied with it, for the castle he took us to was very pleasant, and we got there without any problem. It belonged to a lord from Liege who was one of his friends and who was at that time with the Prince of Liege, where an important post kept him. He had left there two of his sisters and another of his relatives who seemed to us to be very reasonable people.

Don Pedro left us with them and returned to Brussels, where his duty called him, but he promised to come and see us as soon as he could and, in the meantime, to keep us informed of all the news that had to do with my interests.

I only received unfortunate news, Madame, for the wife of our absent marquis had died after our departure, and people blamed me for her death as much as if I had killed her. Alas! I must not have contributed very much to it, for, if you recall, Madame, the first time that her husband talked to me about her, he said that she was in danger of dying soon. But they had found some letter or other that this man had written me in Maubeuge in which, they said, he made great promises of love to me. This woman had entered into transports of jealousy over it, and people claimed that this was what caused her death, rather than the mortal illnesses from which she had suffered for a long time.

The finding of this letter caused two or three bad effects. First it made the marquis's love pass for real, when previously it had only been suspected on the basis of some feeble conjecture. They asserted, as gossipmongers never fail to assert, that I had maintained this love through favors or hopes. This blackened my reputation again, and what I found most disagreeable about the consequences of this was that Don Pedro, seeing that he had a declared rival and knowing that the death of the man's wife made him the master of his actions, he feared what his rival might do and so had me kept in this castle as if I were a prisoner.

I was not at all aware of this, for I went out very little and, if I had gone out and seen soldiers, I would have thought they were there to defend us, not to act against my freedom. I therefore patiently awaited the end of the war of Cologne and, following the gaiety of my temperament, all I did was seek out, in the society of our people from Liege, ways to console myself over my new problems. I told Your Highness that these people were very reasonable, and indeed they were. They had been raised in Brussels, where people of quality are quite polite and have the manners of great lords. From this upbringing they had acquired more wit and more delicacy than the people of Liege usually have, and above all the relative was one of the sweetest and most cooperative people I have ever seen.

Her name was Angelique, and her mother had been the confidant of the loves of Monsieur the Duke of ——, uncle of the recently deceased duke,[11] with Madame the Countess of ——. This young woman and I became very close friends, and sometimes she told me what she had learned from her mother about those loves I have mentioned.

Without lying, Madame, those two lovers must have loved each other a great deal, and I am surprised that their love ended before their lives. Each felt a secret premonition that told them when the other would arrive long before they saw each other, and you will be able to judge, Madame, if this premonition was accurate.

The duke had become jealous of the Count of ——, who was in fact very much in love with the countess and who was known to be one of the handsomest men in the world. She did not love him at all, and, despite what people said, Angelique swore to me that Madame de —— loved only the Duke of ——. He, however, was not as convinced of his happiness as he might have been, and, since he kept getting messages every day that his rival was very assiduous and very passionate, he decided to question him without being recognized and for that reason came to Brussels incognito.

At that time there were great festivities honoring the birth of a Spanish prince named Balthazar.[12] The duke knew about this birth, for what man of quality does not know such things? He rightly judged that this would occasion public celebrations in that land, for the King of Spain is its sovereign; he thus thought this was a favorable time for his plan. He came to Brussels incognito, as I said. In order to better fool his mistress, he wrote her that he was leaving for a trip to France, the opposite of the one he made.

When he got there, he stayed in a very out-of-the-way neighborhood. Chance favoring him in everything, he found out that some young lords of that country were going to put on an Indian masquerade and that, dressed up in this way, they were going to go to the home of Madame the Countess of Cantecroix, where a great assembly was to be held. He had one of the costumes brought to him with little difficulty, since no one had suggested keeping them secret. He had a similar one made and, mixing in with the group of masked people, he entered with them into the dance hall.

He saw Madame ——, looking more beautiful in his opinion than he had ever seen her, and Monsieur the Count of —— near her, for he was pres-

11. The late duke is Louis-Joseph of Lorraine, who died in 1671 at the age of twenty-one. The present duke is the Duke of Guise (1614–64) (MC 343).

12. Balthazar Carlos, son of Philip IV (MC 344).

ent at every assembly and she could not prevent that, given the respect due to his rank. I think that, as my friend from Liege told me, Madame de —— was annoyed by this man, and it is even claimed that in this moment she was saying disagreeable things to him.

But even if she had been saying very sweet things, the duke could not have been witness to it, for, as soon as he entered the countess felt a certain emotion that his presence always gave her. She could not believe that it was fooling her, and, despite the fact that her lover had written to her about a trip he was supposed to be making, she looked for him carefully among those wearing masks, so carefully that she spotted him.

This made their relationship public, for, in her initial joy at seeing him again, she could not hide her feelings, and her lover was also so transported that he forgot the reasons he had to continue hiding his love. I will not tell you those reasons, for all of France found out about them, and you cannot be unaware of them. And, too, Madame, I am telling you all of this only in passing and only because it has come up.

I have seen the original letter from the duke on the subject of this shared feeling; it was, to my taste, one of the most beautiful letters that anyone could have written. In it he complained of the excess of his happiness, for he admitted that it was a very great happiness indeed to be thus found out by his mistress. But he said that this deprived him of the pleasure of seeing what was happening in her heart, without her wanting to show it to him. These sorts of discoveries were, to his mind, among the most perfect joys a lover could feel, and nothing appeared so touching for a sensitive soul as those displays of tenderness and sincerity in which art and prudence could not be suspected of playing a role.

Madame, I do not know how to express fully all that was in the letter I speak of. To do things right, I should be able to show to you the letter itself, and that is not possible. In addition to the fact that Angelique guarded it very closely, at that time other troubles came my way, and I had no more time to think about the affairs of others.

Cologne had been besieged, as I have told Your Highness and as you have undoubtedly found out from other sources. The siege had been rather obstinate at first, but in the end the city was reduced to doing whatever its prince chose to order. The taking of the city ended the war in that area, and so our abbess could resume her journey.

She was all the more impatient to do so since her wounded friend was still very ill, and it seemed to her that if she went in person to contribute to his recovery she would see his health restored all the sooner. She thus diligently prepared for her departure. However, Madame, we were surprised to learn from one of Don Pedro's officers that she was not free to take me with her and that she must decide to leave without me or stay longer in Liege.

Imagine if you can, Madame, how surprised we were by this disobliging news. There is nothing that we expected less than to receive such treatment from Don Pedro. Although I was persuaded that he loved me, and as a stratagem I had even encouraged that love with some hope, he had always seemed to me so honorable and respectful that I would never have suspected him of doing such a thing.

I did not want to believe that this was being done at his command. I accused the officer he had sent of stopping us on his own initiative in order to obtain a bribe for our release, and I told him that he would be punished for this as he deserved. But he had his orders in writing, and he even brought me papers in which the lord of the castle had ordered his sisters to give Don Pedro absolute power in his house and not to oppose any of his plans.

It was in vain that we complained to these poor young women about the violence that was being done to us. They could do nothing about it, though they seemed as touched by it as we were ourselves. Our abbess made a very great fuss about being treated in this way and threatened Don Pedro that she would complain to the Governor of the Low Countries and, if necessary, would take this matter to the Spanish Council. But she was told that she was not being kept there, that she could leave when she thought appropriate and that they would even escort her to Cologne if she wished. It was only me that they wanted to keep, for Don Pedro loved me too much to resign himself to seeing me escape his grasp without some assurances of my friendship. They said he would soon come in person, and that I was as safe in this house as in the convent in Cologne.

The abbess was not persuaded of this. She could not resign herself to abandoning me to the desires of a man who was in love with me and had absolute power over me. She seemed to me so torn between this act of generosity and the business that called her home that I thought a hundred times of telling her to leave and to let Fortune resolve my situation. But this same Fortune worked on my behalf without my thinking about it and got me out of this fix, as she had gotten me out of many others.

Angelique, of whom I have already spoken to you, did not normally live with her cousins. Her mother was in Liege and she had only come to this house to spend the summer months. A young brother of hers came to get her at the time when we received the message from Don Pedro, and this dear girl was so touched with my affliction that she undertook to bring about my rescue.

She had a very great influence over her young brother, for she was much older than he, and he respected her as much as if he had been her son. She convinced him to give me his clothes and to remain in that house in mine until she sent him other clothing.

The poor boy saw nothing more in this than a witty game in order to fool someone and provide amusement. He agreed without difficulty to what his sister wanted him to do, and everything was worked out between our abbess and ourselves, for you can well judge, Madame, that I did not do this without her participation. One morning I dressed in the young man's clothes and presented myself at Angelique's door as if I had been her brother, who they knew was supposed to take her home.

It was still very early in the morning, and I was the only person they had orders to stop. They looked very carefully at the woman from Liege, whom they recognized, and they paid no attention to me because they thought I was a boy, and they knew that a boy was supposed to leave with her. What can I say, Madame? We left that castle without a problem thanks to my disguise. Under the guidance of Angelique's mother's old valet, who had brought the brother and who knew the roads very well, we went to the home of the Baron of Roste. He is a great lord of Liege, and Angelique was related to him. She hoped to gain his protection for the purpose of having me brought to Cologne.

I could not thank this generous young woman enough or give enough thanks to heaven for having allowed me to encounter her so felicitously. We traveled quite quickly. For myself, I was a bit concerned for Merinville, whom I had left with the abbess for fear that she would cause me to be recognized. But we did not fail to laugh about Don Pedro, who was supposed to arrive perhaps that same day and who would be very surprised to find that his trip was useless.

We later found out that he had in fact arrived as he was expected to and that he was carried away with rage when he found out from the abbess that he should no longer look for me in that house. He said and did a thousand extravagant things. He wanted to kill the people who had done such a poor job of guarding me, and he almost lost all respect toward the young man who had lent me his clothes. But, after all that, he had no recourse but to be patient and go seek out among the beauties of Brussels something to console him for my loss. He wanted to send people after me, and he himself wanted to quarrel with me, but, in addition to the fact that he did not know what route I had taken, one cannot commit violence in a neutral country with impunity. If he had tried to kidnap me openly, there would have been people who, for the sake of maintaining their own privileges, would have tried to prevent it. All he could do was to keep Angelique's brother at his cousins' house to see whether someone would not send for him and whether in this way he could not find out where I was. But this precaution did us more good than he imagined, for we did not know what to do with this young man.

I thus arrived at the Baron of Roste's without any mishap, Madame, and although he was not at home, which disappointed us a little, we were so well received there by his mother that we thought we could wait for his return without impatience.

The baron had gone to Namur,[13] which is quite near this castle. The business that had taken him there was almost finished, and he was expected from one day to the next. Angelique thought that we should not reveal my identity to anyone but him, for women of the age of the Baronness sometimes take a rather dim view of adventures and disguises, and my friend from Liege feared being blamed by this good lady.

I think her fear was without reason, however, for the old Baroness really knew how to live, and one could see that she had not always been in the country. She was from Brussels and had been one of the greatest ornaments of that city when Monsieur the Prince was there.[14] Sometimes she recounted to us the gallantries and intrigues of that court and told us, among other things, that Marigny[15] had been among her close friends and that they still maintained a great correspondence together. I have always liked the way this man wrote, and I showed the Baroness so much curiosity about his letters that she was kind enough to show us some of them. I found myself mentioned in two or three of them because they consisted of all kinds of gazettes recounting the major events in Paris and at the court of France, and he had honored me with a place in his accounts. These accounts were neither too true nor too charitable, but I found them everywhere so filled with wit that I thought everything should be allowed to a man like that, and his expressions made me forgive his malice.

In the last of these letters I found a piece of news that saddened me a great deal and that I am sure will sadden Your Highness as well. It was that the Countess of Suze was suffering from an incurable disease, and people regarded her as already dead. In truth, it is a great shame that this person is dy-

---

13. Namur is the name of a Belgian province along the French border and also the name of a city in this province; the city is presently the capital of Wallonia, the French-speaking region of Belgium.

14. Monsieur le Prince is the Prince of Condé. He would have been in Brussels in 1653 (MC 355).

15. Marigny was a satiric poet and songwriter during the Fronde. Marigny had gone into exile with Monsieur le Prince (MC 355). For an explanation of the Fronde, see part 1, note 34.

ing so soon. She had a fine wit and wrote passionate verses. Marigny sent the
Baroness of Roste one of her elegies, which I do not think you have seen because Marigny said that it had not been seen by anyone. The baroness was
kind enough to let me make a copy, and I am going to send it to you, for I find
this poem admirable, and I think you will willingly forgive me for interrupting my narration in order to show you such a lovely thing.[16]

ELEGY[17]

He has at last departed, this incomparable man,
This Tircis,[18] whom my eyes found so dangerous.
No longer will I see him threaten my heart
With the deadly perils of his new ardor.
No longer will I see those tyrannical charms
Attack my pride with such rough alarms.
Act, O my reason, in a hundred powerful efforts,
Sustain my wishes and undeceive my senses.
Tell them that this manner, and this noble daring,
Draw all their graces from my bias.
Uncover, if you can, in these great sentiments,
Affectations and dissimulation.
Portray to me the sweetness that enchants me,
Less august, less tender, or at least affected.
In that charming mind, in that manner, in those features,
Find for me faults that have never been found there.
Seek out, speak, insist, tear out from my soul
The poisoned arrow of the first flames of passion.
The moment of absence is a happy time
For one who wishes to overcome a dangerous inclination.
Do not neglect such a favorable time,
Tircis may return, and return lovable.
But, fatal reason, with what painful blows
Do you beat down a heart, whose only hope was in you?

16. The origin of the poem is unclear. It does not appear among the works of Madame de la
Suze, and it is unlikely that Villedieu, a poet herself, would have published one of her own works
under the name of another (MC 355).

17. In the original, the poem is written in rhymed alexandrins. The alexandrin is a twelve-syllable
line used in formal poetry and in drama. In the translation rhyme and scansion have been sacrificed for clarity of meaning.

18. Tircis (or Thyrsis) is a name for a shepherd commonly used in pastoral poetry, drama, and
music in the seventeenth century. The name comes from the pastoral works of Theocritus and
Virgil.

Far from blaming my flame and far from its destruction,
You seem to speak only the better to seduce me.
In my unhappiness, to whom can I turn,
If you refuse me your rightful help?
To my senses, all enchanted with his charms?
To my pride, shaken by so many alarms?
Or to my heart, which seems made
Only to teach the art of loving and being loved?
I have already caught it, traitor to itself,
Making a supreme glory out of its chains,
And saying that, because of them, will disappear
The shame and regrets of all its past loves.
But it flatters itself in vain with a false hope,
Nothing can overcome the cold indifference
That that ungrateful one opposed to its tender desires.
And, my heart, you will waste your sighs and your vows.
How many have you made fruitlessly, without result?
I have given you no permission to sigh.
I have disavowed your indiscreet flights,
But I have felt them and know what inroads they make.
With this painful memory and sad thought,
My reason, can you still be obsessed?
Can you find remarkable attraction
In him who loves me not, and never will?
Are there virtues, talents, charms
Against which coldness provides no arms?
Ah! My Glory, let us pause and calm our fear,
This dangerous Tircis has no more charms for me.
To make me burn, I need a brilliant flame,
My heart wants a whole heart, my soul a whole soul.
Out of love or in love, I count everything for nothing,
And only the heart of a lover can buy my heart.
But how is it that, while I make such legitimate laws,
Secret emotions give my maxims the lie?
Something says to me that such a charming man
Is worthy of being loved for the sake of loving him alone.
No! I will not listen to this mad ardor.
Depart, fatal Tircis, depart from my thoughts.
I feel my pride bringing my heart back to me,
And this last transport is my last error.

We were reading this elegy on a terrace that overlooks the main road, and, as we finished reading, we saw a man pass on horseback followed by a valet. The baroness recognized him as one of her son's best friends and did not doubt that he had come to visit him.

She went to the avenue to meet him, and we followed her because it seemed that good manners required it. But, Madame, I did not follow for long, for, as the man approached, it seemed to me that I recognized him as that Flemish marquis about whom I have said much to you in the account of my adventures at Maubeuge.

It was indeed he, Madame, and I was not mistaken. We found out later that he had learned of his wife's death, and by chance the house of the Baron of Roste was along the route to Brussels, whither he was returning to settle his affairs, and the baron was, as I said, one of his great friends.

Imagine, if you will, Madame, what became of me when I saw that man whom I did not expect there, and from whom I was right to fear as much persecution as I had just suffered from Don Pedro. I hurried back into the house filled with fear, and the woman from Liege, having followed me because she saw from the change in my face that the arrival of this man upset me, asked me what the cause of it was.

Together we went into a garden that one entered through glass doors from one of the rooms, and I explained to her the worried state in which I found myself, and how, in saving myself from the clutches of one lover, I had now unfortunately thrown myself into the hands of another.

She was almost as distressed about this encounter as I was, for I never saw a young woman with a better heart, and she engaged herself in her friends' concerns as if they were her own. Together we thought over what we could do to get out of such a difficult situation. After a great deal of discussion we decided that the safest thing was for me to pretend I was ill and to hide until that man left.

For this reason, I went and shut myself up in my room, and Angelique went and told Madame de Roste that I had a migraine, something I was subject to, and that the best cure was not to talk to anyone. She said this so that no one would come looking for me. But, as for her, she came to see me from time to time, as if to find out how I was doing and to bring me some fruit and some preserves, out of which I made my supper that evening.

For, Madame, I have forgotten to tell you that I was still passing as that young woman's brother, and chance favored this pretense because the young man had done his military service in Antwerp, where he had an uncle, and scarcely anyone knew him in the region of Liege.

The Baroness of Roste knew that Angelique had a brother, but, for the reason I have just explained, she had never seen him, and although she knew that he must be about seventeen or eighteen years old, women look so young when they are dressed as men that she had no difficulty in taking me for him.

Thus she did not find it strange that Angelique spent part of the evening with me. She would have come herself had she not feared disturbing me. But, Madame, I might as well have let her come. The precautions I took were useless, and I would have done just as well to show myself as to keep myself so well hidden.

You can certainly judge, Madame, that we had to confide in the valet who accompanied us and that we could not let him see another person take the place of, and wear the clothes of, his young master without telling him at least part of our secret. We had taken all the precautions we could to make him promise to be discreet and faithful, but we had to run the risk of seeing him fail in this. Like us, he knew that I was a woman and that I was fleeing the violence of Don Pedro.

He had kept this matter secret at the home of the Baroness of Roste, and you have seen, Madame, that I had not been found out. However, he had previously served the Flemish marquis about whom I have just spoken to you. He had left his service only in order to get married, and he felt great affection for his former master. He did not think he had to maintain the same silence before him as before others. As soon as the marquis saw him and asked him what he was doing there, he innocently told him everything that had brought him there and everything that had happened before our arrival.

The marquis had not given up on Brussels and Maubeuge to such an extent that he did not get secret news of everything that happened there. Via letters written to him he had found out that Don Pedro had declared himself my lover, that he had taken me to Liege, and that the abbess from Cologne had gone there with me.

When he heard his former valet say that he was accompanying a lady disguised as a man and that she was fleeing a castle where she had been with an abbess and where a certain Don Pedro of Lara wanted to imprison her, he put that together with the fact that as soon as he had arrived I came down with an all too convenient malady in order to prevent him from seeing me. He had no doubt that I was the Countess of Englesac. Later on he told me that this idea greatly increased the esteem and the tenderness he had always felt for me, and that he could not hear without great pleasure that I had shown extreme revulsion for a love affair with Don Pedro, about which I have spoken.

He spent almost the whole night making I know not how many different resolutions. The next day, after having found out which room I slept in and having gotten someone to bring him there, he entered just as a servant, whom the baroness had sent to find out how I was doing, was leaving. I was quite surprised to see him there at my bedside before I could take any steps to prevent him from coming.

I was so upset by the sight of him that I could not say a single word to him. My silence allowed him to guess the state of agitation in which I found myself, and he said to me, "Fear nothing from my visit, Madame. I have not come here to reproach you with the errors into which you have thrown me and that you maintained with so many deceits and so much dissimulation. On the contrary, I come to assure you that to me your conduct is entirely justified and that it is up to you to decide if a very tender and very solid friendship can come after what has happened between us. I contested your right to the wealth of Madame de Seville because I was convinced that it was more mine than yours, and also because things were said about you that would not have allowed her relatives to have you as her heir without some shame. To these strategic and self-interested considerations was added the negative picture that had been painted of you. My heart assures me that this picture is not accurate, and it pleases me to believe so, for, Madame, I still love you, and I will love you in this way all the days that I live."

I shuddered again when I heard him make this announcement, and, interrupting, I said to him that he was undoubtedly in error and that he did not love me as much as he said he did.

"Forgive me, Madame," he continued, "I am not in error, and I certainly love you as much as I am capable of loving. But do not fear that this love will have the same effects as Don Pedro's. I am well aware that my wife is dead and that her death leaves me the absolute master of my wishes, but previously I said so many negative things about you that I cannot offer you the place she held, and I think so much good of you at present that I would consider it an injustice to offer you another place. What you have done to escape from Don Pedro's pursuits has touched me to the very heart and seems to me to be the behavior of a very virtuous person. You are undoubtedly such a person, Madame, and those who have spoken of you otherwise are evil people. A lady's virtue is not always that which men seek in her, but, as for me, I admit that I am very pleased to find virtue in you, and there is nothing I would not do to defend your virtue and give it due luster. Rely on my esteem and my friendship. They will never fail you, and I swear to you by all I hold sacred that if you have true trust in me, you will never be deceived."

I am naturally a rather trusting person and, when the marquis made this speech to me, sincerity was painted on his face. Nonetheless I could not believe what he said. I still feared that he was setting a trap for me in order to throw me into some new predicament. I think he would never have persuaded me, had Angelique not come to his aid.

Since she did not see things with the same mistrust as I did, her eyes could see the marquis's good faith much better than mine. She told me I was being unjust to this honorable man in believing him so ill-intentioned and dissimulating. He swore to me a thousand times that he was not so and that he had only done me evil on the basis of the false reports that he had been given about me. To this he added great promises to do right by me in the matter of Madame de Seville's legacy and then to take me to whatever part of the world I wished. In the end, what can I say to you, Madame? I accepted his proposals and his promises and began discussing with him everything I needed to do.

We agreed together that he would leave for Brussels that very day in order to see to everything he wanted to do in my favor. After having taken care of his business in that city, he would come back to get me, bringing women's clothing and everything needed to take me to Cologne, for, Madame, he had no success in suggesting other alternatives and in telling me he would make me able to live anywhere I pleased. I wanted to see our abbess again and make her understand by the rectitude of my conduct that she had not been wrong in having such a favorable opinion of me.

The marquis's opinion of me became more favorable each minute. I have never seen a man more full of esteem for a woman than he was for me. And, Madame, it was not an act; he really respected me, and in what follows he gave me great evidence of this, as I am going to tell Your Highness. He took it upon himself to look after Angelique's young brother, about whom she was beginning to worry. He gave us a valet to send to her mother to tell her not to worry about her children and that they were at the home of the Baron of Roste. He greatly reproached our valet for having so lacked discretion. He did more. To insure that in the future he would be discreet, he took our valet with him and replaced him with another who knew nothing about our business.

For, Madame, we had resolved that we would keep our affairs secret until the marquis's return or at least until the return of the Baron of Roste, whom he assured me was the most honorable man in the world, someone in whom I could have confided things of much more importance than the reasons for my disguise.

I did not have to confront this situation, for the baron's business led him to Namur, in the region between Sambre and Meuse, where he had a house and where he was obliged to stay during the passage of the troops for fear that, despite the orders the officers gave, the scouts might commit some outrages.

Thus it was only the old Baroness of Roste whom I had to manage, and that was not hard for me, for, Madame, she had acquired a great deal of goodwill toward me. She often told my alleged sister that I was the handsomest boy in the world and, when someone finds a person so charming in one sex, she is not likely to seek in him another.

She was not the only one in the house who took pleasure in this error. A young lady who was a relative of hers, whom she had raised from her earliest childhood and who was a very charming person, also found me much to her taste and would have wished, I think, that I was indeed Angelique's brother and that I liked her as much as she did me.

She did a thousand little things for me that went beyond what ordinary courtesy would have required. One day when we were playing *rever-quier,* which is the backgammon of that region, I said to her playfully that I wanted to gamble for her heart and try, if possible, to win it. "If you know, teach me, I beg you, what it is to win a heart," she said, "and how those who have lost a heart know it is lost." "There are many ways to win a heart, my lovely young lady," I replied, "but the most certain way is one in which chance plays a role, as it would if you bet your heart in *rever-quier* and a toss of the dice decided it." "But if I gambled with it and lost it," she added, "how would I know that someone had won it away from me?" "That is not difficult to know," I continued, smiling. "When you have lost your heart to someone, you always want to be with the man who has won it. One moment of his absence causes a thousand sorrows. You feel emotion when you see him and a chill when you no longer see him. It is useless to try to overcome these reactions; one can never do so, for one cannot live without a heart, and despite what one thinks, one follows along wherever it may go." "Let's not play any more," she said, blushing and casting aside her dice cup. "We have played enough, and I am so unlucky in gambling that I lose everything I bet."

The baroness entered as she said this, and we did not dare continue our conversation in front of her. For if the gratitude I owe her for her good hospitality allows me to say what I think, she praised me a great deal, and it seems to me that, coming from women, such great praises come more often from the heart than from the head.

But she was not always with us. We sometimes went for strolls together, this young lady and I. I took pleasure in seeing how her young heart became inflamed little by little. It could have let itself be led quite a distance had I been of such nature as to make it go that route. It seemed to me that I was once again at the home of my mother-in-law, Madame d'Englesac, and that I was witnessing the birth of that love between her son and myself, which has caused me so much adversity. These imaginings sometimes drew tears from my eyes. You would have been deeply touched by pity, Madame, had you seen how that poor child shared in my little sorrows and endeavored to put a stop to them.

I spent five whole weeks in that house, still awaiting the return of Baron of Roste or the Flemish marquis, neither of whom came back. I began to be so distressed by their long absence that I had resolved to confide in Madame de Roste and to beg her assistance to help me get to my convent. But as I was resolving to do this, the marquis came back, and not only did he get me out of my difficulties, but he also relieved Angelique's worries about her brother.

We had had no news of him since we had left him wearing my clothes in the house that I had fled, and we had not dared inquire about him, fearing that our hiding place would be found out if we did. Until we were assured of the Baron of Roste's protection, I always thought it was perilous for me to allow my hiding place to be discovered.

That poor young man had been very closely guarded in that house for some time, but as it became clear that no advantage could be gained by keeping him, he was let go. As good luck would have it, the Flemish marquis ran into him while the young man, very troubled to find out what had happened to us, was en route to Liege; he was recognized by Angelique's valet, who was accompanying the marquis.

The marquis left the two of them in a house he knew, and we joined them soon afterward. After he returned to Monsieur de Roste's, Angelique and I left, pretending that she had received letters from her mother that obliged her to return to Liege. The marquis came to see us the next day in the house where he had left Angelique's brother and her valet and where he had told us to meet him.

The poor young woman, about whom I told you, took our separation very hard. It also seemed to me that Madame de Roste was not impervious to it either. They both said very kind things to me, especially the young woman, who cried her heart out. But since both hoped I'd soon be back to see them, their grief was hardly comparable to what Angelique and I felt.

What a kind and generous young woman Angelique is, Madame! How indebted I am to her, and with what endearments did we part! She would have come to Cologne if she had dared, and I wished that she could have come with me. Although the marquis had brought me women servants so that I might travel more honorably, I still trembled when I remembered that I was putting myself at the mercy of a man who had once loved me and might well still harbor such feelings. But, Madame, we had to take this course, for I feared I would cause Angelique's mother to reject her, were I to take advantage of her tenderness by allowing her to come with me. It seemed to me that

involving her in such nasty business would have been a poor way of ac-
knowledging my obligations toward her.

I therefore left without her, Madame. She took the road to Liege, and I
the one to Cologne, where I have finally arrived safely and where Madame de
Seville's heir has kept all his promises to me so nobly that I find myself able to
lead a quiet and rather comfortable life in whatever circumstances I might
choose. But, Madame, should I remain in my present state of mind, I will
never choose a condition other than my present one. I find it sweet. The convent no longer seems what it had appeared to be from a distance. I might say
that my tranquility of mind lacks for nothing, save for being able to say to
you face to face, as I write it here, that no one in the world is as devoted to
Your Highness, with so much zeal and submissiveness, as your most humble
and obedient servant,

H. S. D. M.

SERIES EDITORS'
BIBLIOGRAPHY

Note: Items listed in the volume editor's bibliography are not repeated here.

PRIMARY SOURCES

Alberti, Leon Battista (1404–72). *The Family in Renaissance Florence.* Trans. Renée Neu Watkins. Columbia: University of South Carolina Press, 1969.

Arenal, Electa, and Stacey Schlau, eds. *Untold Sisters: Hispanic Nuns in Their Own Works.* Trans. Amanda Powell. Albuquerque: University of New Mexico Press, 1989.

Astell, Mary (1666–1731). *The First English Feminist: Reflections on Marriage and Other Writings.* Ed. and introd. Bridget Hill. New York: St. Martin's Press, 1986.

Atherton, Margaret, ed. *Women Philosophers of the Early Modern Period.* Indianapolis, IN: Hackett, 1994.

Aughterson, Kate, ed. *Renaissance Woman: Constructions of Femininity in England: A Source Book.* London: Routledge, 1995.

Barbaro, Francesco (1390–1454). *On Wifely Duties.* Trans. Benjamin Kohl [preface and book 2]. In *The Earthly Republic,* ed. Benjamin Kohl and R. G. Witt, 179–228. Philadelphia: University of Pennsylvania Press, 1978.

Behn, Aphra. *The Works of Aphra Behn.* 7 vols. Ed. Janet Todd. Columbus: Ohio State University Press, 1992–96.

Boccaccio, Giovanni (1313–75). *Famous Women.* Ed. and trans. Virginia Brown. The I Tatti Renaissance Library. Cambridge, MA: Harvard University Press, 2001.

———. *Corbaccio or the Labyrinth of Love.* 2nd rev. ed. Trans. Anthony K. Cassell. Binghamton, NY: Medieval and Renaissance Texts and Studies, 1993.

Brown, Sylvia. *Women's Writing in Stuart England: The Mother's Legacies of Dorothy Leigh, Elizabeth Joscelin and Elizabeth Richardson.* Thrupp, Stroud, Gloucestershire: Sutton, 1999.

Bruni, Leonardo (1370–1444). "On the Study of Literature (1405) to Lady Battista Malatesta of Moltefeltro." In *The Humanism of Leonardo Bruni: Selected Texts,* trans. and introd. Gordon Griffiths, James Hankins, and David Thompson, 240–51. Binghamton, NY: Medieval and Renaissance Texts and Studies (M RTS), 1987.

Castiglione, Baldassare (1478–1529). *The Book of the Courtier.* Trans. George Bull. New York: Penguin, 1967.

Cerasano, S. P., and Marion Wynne-Davies, eds. *Readings in Renaissance Women's Drama: Criticism, History, and Performance 1594–1998.* London: Routledge, 1998.

Christine de Pizan (1365–1431). *The Book of the City of Ladies.* Trans. Earl Jeffrey Richards. Foreword Marina Warner. New York: Persea Books, 1982.

———. *The Treasure of the City of Ladies.* Trans. Sarah Lawson. New York: Viking Penguin, 1985.

———. *The Treasure of the City of Ladies.* Trans. and introd. Charity Cannon Willard. Ed. and introd. Madeleine P. Cosman. New York: Persea Books, 1989.

Clarke, Danielle, ed. *Isabella Whitney, Mary Sidney and Aemilia Lanyer: Renaissance Women Poets.* New York: Penguin Books, 2000.

Crawford, Patricia, and Laura Gowing, eds. *Women's Worlds in Seventeenth-Century England: A Source Book.* London: Routledge, 2000.

Daybell, James, ed. *Early Modern Women's Letter Writing, 1450–1700.* Houndmills, England: Palgrave, 2001.

de Lorris, William, and Jean de Meun. *The Romance of the Rose.* Trans. Charles Dahlbert. Princeton, NJ: Princeton University Press, 1971. Reprint, Hanover, NH: University Press of New England, 1983.

de Zayas Maria. *The Disenchantments of Love.* Trans. H. Patsy Boyer. Albany: State University of New York Press, 1997.

———. *The Enchantments of Love: Amorous and Exemplary Novels.* Trans. H. Patsy Boyer. Berkeley: University of California Press, 1990.

Elizabeth I. *Elizabeth I: Collected Works.* Ed. Leah S. Marcus, Janel Mueller, and Mary Beth Rose. Chicago: University of Chicago Press, 2000.

Elyot, Thomas (1490–1546). *Defence of Good Women: The Feminist Controversy of the Renaissance.* Facsimile Reproductions. Ed. Diane Bornstein. New York: Delmar, 1980.

Erasmus, Desiderius (1467–1536). *Erasmus on Women.* Ed. Erika Rummel. Toronto: University of Toronto Press, 1996.

Ferguson, Moira, ed. *First Feminists: British Women Writers 1578–1799.* Bloomington: Indiana University Press, 1985.

Galilei, Maria Celeste. *Sister Maria Celeste's Letters to her father, Galileo.* Ed. and trans. Rinaldina Russell. Lincoln, NE: Writers Club Press of Universe.com, 2000.

Gethner, Perry, ed. *The Lunatic Lover and Other Plays by French Women of the 17th and 18th Centuries.* Portsmouth, NH: Heinemann, 1994.

Glückel of Hameln (1646–1724). *The Memoirs of Glückel of Hameln.* Trans. Marvin Lowenthal. New introd. Robert Rosen. New York: Schocken Books, 1977.

Henderson, Katherine Usher, and Barbara F. McManus, eds. *Half Humankind: Contexts and Texts of the Controversy about Women in England, 1540–1640.* Urbana: University of Illinois Press, 1985.

Joscelin, Elizabeth. *The Mothers Legacy to her Unborn Childe.* Ed. Jean leDrew Metcalfe. Toronto: University of Toronto Press, 2000.

Kallendorf, Craig W., ed. and trans. *Humanist Educational Treatises.* The I Tatti Renaissance Library. Cambridge, MA: Harvard University Press, 2002.

Kaminsky, Amy Katz, ed. *Water Lilies, Flores del agua: An Anthology of Spanish Women Writers from the Fifteenth through the Nineteenth Century.* Minneapolis: University of Minnesota Press, 1996.

Kempe, Margery (1373–1439). *The Book of Margery Kempe.* Trans. and ed. Lynn Staley. New York: W.W. Norton, 2001.

King, Margaret L., and Albert Rabil Jr., eds. *Her Immaculate Hand: Selected Works by and about the Women Humanists of Quattrocento Italy*. Binghamton, NY: Medieval and Renaissance Texts and Studies, 1983; 2nd rev. paperback ed., 1991.

Klein, Joan Larsen, ed. *Daughters, Wives, and Widows: Writings by Men about Women and Marriage in England, 1500–1640*. Urbana: University of Illinois Press, 1992.

Knox, John (1505–72). *The Political Writings of John Knox: The First Blast of the Trumpet against the Monstrous Regiment of Women and Other Selected Works*. Ed. Marvin A. Breslow. Washington: Folger Shakespeare Library, 1985.

Kors, Alan C., and Edward Peters, eds. *Witchcraft in Europe, 400-1700: A Documentary History*. Philadelphia: University of Pennsylvania Press, 2000.

Krämer, Heinrich, and Jacob Sprenger. *Malleus Maleficarum* (ca. 1487). Trans. Montague Summers. London: Pushkin Press, 1928. Reprint, New York: Dover, 1971.

Larsen, Anne R., and Colette H. Winn, eds. *Writings by Pre-Revolutionary French Women: From Marie de France to Elizabeth Vigée-Le Brun*. New York: Garland, 2000.

Marguerite d'Angoulême, Queen of Navarre (1492–1549). *The Heptameron*. Trans. P. A. Chilton. New York: Viking Penguin, 1984.

Mary of Agreda. *The Divine Life of the Most Holy Virgin*. Abridgment of *The Mystical City of God*. Abr. Fr. Bonaventure Amedeo de Caesarea, M.C. Trans. Abbé Joseph A. Boullan. Rockford, IL: Tan Books, 1997.

Myers, Kathleen A., and Amanda Powell, eds. *A Wild Country Out in the Garden: The Spiritual Journals of a Colonial Mexican Nun*. Bloomington: Indiana University Press, 1999.

Russell, Rinaldina, ed. *Sister Maria Celeste's Letters to Her Father, Galileo*. San Jose: Writers Club Press, 2000.

Teresa of Avila, Saint (1515–82). *The Life of Saint Teresa of Avila, by Herself*. Trans. J. M. Cohen. New York: Viking Penguin, 1957.

Travitsky, Betty S., and Anne Lake Prescott, eds. *Female and Male Voices in Early Modern England: An Anthology of Renaissance Writing*. New York: Columbia University Press, 2000.

Weyer, Johann (1515–88). *Witches, Devils, and Doctors in the Renaissance: Johann Weyer, De praestigiis daemonum*. Ed. George Mora, with Benjamin G. Kohl, Erik Midelfort, and Helen Bacon. Trans. John Shea. Binghamton, NY: Medieval and Renaissance Texts and Studies, 1991.

Wilson, Katharina M., ed. *Medieval Women Writers*. Athens: University of Georgia Press, 1984.

―――, ed. *Women Writers of the Renaissance and Reformation*. Athens: University of Georgia Press, 1987.

―――, and Frank J. Warnke, eds. *Women Writers of the Seventeenth Century*. Athens: University of Georgia Press, 1989.

Wollstonecraft, Mary *A Vindication of the Rights of Men and a Vindication of the Rights of Women*. Ed. Sylvana Tomaselli. Cambridge: Cambridge University Press, 1995.

―――. *The Vindications of the Rights of Men, The Rights of Women*. Ed. D. L. Macdonald and Kathleen Scherf. Peterborough, Ontario, Canada: Broadview Press, 1997.

Women Critics 1660–1820: An Anthology. Ed. The Folger Collective on Early Women Critics. Bloomington: Indiana University Press, 1995.

Women Writers in English, 1350–1850. 15 vols. New York: Oxford University Press. [Projected 30-volume series suspended.]

Wroth, Lady Mary. *The Countess of Montgomery's Urania*. 2 parts. Ed. Josephine A. Roberts. Tempe, AZ: MRTS, 1995, 1999.

————. *Lady Mary Wroth's "Love's Victory": The Penshurst Manuscript*. Ed. Michael G. Brennan. London: Roxburghe Club, 1988.

————. *The Poems of Lady Mary Wroth*. Ed. Josephine A. Roberts. Baton Rouge: Louisiana State University Press, 1983.

SECONDARY SOURCES

Ahlgren, Gillian. *Teresa of Avila and the Politics of Sanctity*. Ithaca, NY: Cornell University Press, 1996.

Akkerman, Tjitske, and Siep Sturman, eds. *Feminist Thought in European History, 1400– 2000*. London: Routledge, 1997.

Allen, Sister Prudence, R.S.M. *The Concept of Woman: The Aristotelian Revolution, 750 B.C.—A.D. 1250*. Grand Rapids, MI: William B. Eerdmans, 1997.

————. *The Concept of Woman*. Vol. 2, *The Early Humanist Reformation, 1250–1500*. Grand Rapids, MI: William B. Eerdmans, 2002.

Armon, Shifra. *Picking Wedlock: Women and the Courtship Novel in Spain*. New York: Rowman & Littlefield, 2002.

Backer, Anne Liot Backer. *Precious Women*. New York: Basic Books, 1974.

Barash, Carol. *English Women's Poetry, 1649–1714: Politics, Community, and Linguistic Authority*. New York: Oxford University Press, 1996.

Barker, Alele Marie, and Jehanne M. Gheith, eds. *A History of Women's Writing in Russia*. Cambridge: Cambridge University Press, 2002.

Battigelli, Anna. *Margaret Cavendish and the Exiles of the Mind*. Lexington: University of Kentucky Press, 1998.

Beilin, Elaine V. *Redeeming Eve: Women Writers of the English Renaissance*. Princeton, NJ: Princeton University Press, 1987.

Benson, Pamela Joseph. *The Invention of Renaissance Woman: The Challenge of Female Independence in the Literature and Thought of Italy and England*. University Park: Pennsylvania State University Press, 1992.

————, and Victoria Kirkham, eds. *Strong Voices, Weak History? Medieval and Renaissance Women in their Literary Canons: England, France, Italy*. Ann Arbor: University of Michigan Press, 2003.

Bilinkoff, Jodi. *The Avila of Saint Teresa: Religious Reform in a Sixteenth-Century City*. Ithaca, NY: Cornell University Press, 1989.

Bissell, R. Ward. *Artemisia Gentileschi and the Authority of Art*. University Park: Pennsylvania State University Press, 2000.

Blain, Virginia, Isobel Grundy, and Patricia Clements, eds. *The Feminist Companion to Literature in English: Women Writers from the Middle Ages to the Present*. New Haven, CT: Yale University Press, 1990.

Bloch, R. Howard. *Medieval Misogyny and the Invention of Western Romantic Love*. Chicago: University of Chicago Press, 1991.

Bornstein, Daniel, and Roberto Rusconi, eds. *Women and Religion in Medieval and Renaissance Italy*. Trans. Margery J. Schneider. Chicago: University of Chicago Press, 1996.

Brant, Clare, and Diane Purkiss, eds. *Women, Texts and Histories, 1575–1760*. London: Routledge, 1992.

Briggs, Robin. *Witches and Neighbours: The Social and Cultural Context of European Witchcraft*. New York: HarperCollins, 1995; Viking Penguin, 1996.

Brink, Jean R., ed. *Female Scholars: A Traditioin of Learned Women before 1800.* Montreal: Eden Press Women's Publications, 1980.

Brown, Judith C. *Immodest Acts: The Life of a Lesbian Nun in Renaissance Italy.* New York: Oxford University Press, 1986.

————, and Robert C. Davis, eds. *Gender and Society in Renaisance Italy.* London: Addison-Wesley Longman, 1998.

Bynum, Carolyn Walker. *Fragmentation and Redemption: Essays on Gender and the Human Body in Medieval Religion.* New York: Zone Books, 1992.

————. *Holy Feast and Holy Fast: The Religious Significance of Food to Medieval Women.* Berkeley: University of California Press, 1987.

Cervigni, Dino S., ed. *Women Mystic Writers. Annali d'Italianistica* 13 (1995) [entire issue].

————, and Rebecca West, eds. *Women's Voices in Italian Literature. Annali d'Italianistica* 7 (1989) [entire issue].

Charlton, Kenneth. *Women, Religion and Education in Early Modern England.* London: Routledge, 1999.

Chojnacka, Monica. *Working Women in Early Modern Venice.* Baltimore, MD: Johns Hopkins University Press, 2001.

Chojnacki, Stanley. *Women and Men in Renaissance Venice: Twelve Essays on Patrician Society.* Baltimore, MD: Johns Hopkins University Press, 2000.

Cholakian, Patricia Francis. *Rape and Writing in the* Heptameron *of Marguerite de Navarre.* Carbondale: Southern Illinois University Press, 1991.

————. *Women and the Politics of Self-Representation in Seventeenth-Century France.* Newark: University of Delaware Press, 2000.

Clogan, Paul Maruice, ed. *Medievali et Humanistica: Literacy and the Lay Reader.* Lanham, MD: Rowman & Littlefield, 2000.

Conley, John J., S.J. *The Suspicion of Virtue: Women Philosophers in Neoclassical France.* Ithaca, NY: Cornell University Press, 2002.

Crabb, Ann. *The Strozzi of Florence: Widowhood and Family Solidarity in the Renaissance.* Ann Arbor: University of Michigan Press, 2000.

Cruz, Anne J., and Mary Elizabeth Perry, eds. *Culture and Control in Counter-Reformation Spain.* Minneapolis: University of Minnesota Press, 1992.

Davis, Natalie Zemon. *Society and Culture in Early Modern France.* Stanford, CA: Stanford University Press, 1975. [See especially chapters 3 and 5.]

————. *Women on the Margins: Three Seventeenth-Century Lives.* Cambridge, MA: Harvard University Press, 1995.

De Erauso, Catalina. *Lieutenant Nun: Memoir of a Basque Transvestite in the New World.* Trans. Michele Ttepto and Gabriel Stepto; foreword by Marjorie Garber. Boston: Beacon Press, 1995.

DeJean, Joan. *The Reinvention of Obscenity: Sex, Lies, and Tabloids in Early Modern France.* Chicago: University of Chicago Press, 2002.

Dictionary of Russian Women Writers. Ed. Marina Ledkovsky, Charlotte Rosenthal, and Mary Zirin. Westport, CT: Greenwood Press, 1994.

Dixon, Laurinda S. *Perilous Chastity: Women and Illness in Pre-Enlightenment Art and Medicine.* Ithaca, NY: Cornell Universitiy Press, 1995.

Dolan, Frances E. *Whores of Babylon: Catholicism, Gender and Seventeenth-Century Print Culture.* Ithaca, NY: Cornell University Press, 1999.

Donovan, Josephine. *Women and the Rise of the Novel, 1405–1726.* New York: St. Martin's, 1999.

Erdmann, Axel. *My Gracious Silence: Women in the Mirror of Sixteenth-Century Printing in Western Europe.* Luzern: Gilhofer and Rauschberg, 1999.

Erickson, Amy Louise. *Women and Property in Early Modern England.* London: Routledge, 1993.

Ezell, Margaret J. M. *The Patriarch's Wife: Literary Evidence and the History of the Family.* Chapel Hill: University of North Carolina Press, 1987.

———. *Social Authorship and the Advent of Print.* Baltimore, MD: Johns Hopkins University Press, 1999.

———. *Writing Women's Literary History.* Baltimore, MD: Johns Hopkins University Press, 1993.

Feminist Encyclopedia of German Literature, The. Ed. Friederike Eigler and Susanne Kord. Westport, CT: Greenwood Press, 1997.

Ferguson, Margaret W., Maureen Quilligan, and Nancy J. Vickers, eds. *Rewriting the Renaissance: The Discourses of Sexual Difference in Early Modern Europe.* Chicago: University of Chicago Press, 1987.

Ferraro, Joanne M. *Marriage Wars in Late Renaissance Venice.* Oxford: Oxford University Press, 2001.

Fletcher, Anthony. *Gender, Sex and Subordination in England, 1500–1800.* New Haven, CT: Yale University Press, 1995.

Frye, Susan, and Karen Robertson, eds. *Maids and Mistresses, Cousins and Queens: Women's Alliances in Early Modern England.* Oxford: Oxford University Press, 1999.

Gallagher, Catherine. *Nobody's Story: The Vanishing Acts of Women Writers in the Marketplace, 1670–1820.* Berkeley: University of California Press, 1994.

Garrard, Mary D. *Artemisia Gentileschi: The Image of the Female Hero in Italian Baroque Art.* Princeton, NJ: Princeton University Press, 1989.

Gelbart, Nina Rattner. *The King's Midwife: A History and Mystery of Madame du Coudray.* Berkeley: University of California Press, 1998.

Glenn, Cheryl. *Rhetoric Retold: Regendering the Tradition from Antiquity through the Renaissance.* Carbondale: Southern Illinois University Press, 1997.

Goffen, Rona. *Titian's Women.* New Haven, CT: Yale University Press, 1997.

Goldberg, Jonathan. *Desiring Women Writing: English Renaissance Examples.* Stanford, CA: Stanford University Press, 1997.

Goldsmith, Elizabeth C. *Exclusive Conversations: The Art of Interaction in Seventeenth-Century France.* Philadelphia: University of Pennsylvania Press, 1988.

———, ed. *Writing the Female Voice.* Boston: Northeastern University Press, 1989.

———, and Dena Goodman, eds. *Going Public: Women and Publishing in Early Modern France.* Ithaca, NY: Cornell University Press, 1995.

Greer, Margaret Rich. *Maria de Zayas Tells Baroque Tales of Love and the Cruelty of Men.* University Park: Pennsylvania State University Press, 2000.

Hackett, Helen. *Women and Romance Fiction in the English Renaissance.* Cambridge: Cambridge University Press, 2000.

Hall, Kim F. *Things of Darkness: Economies of Race and Gender in Early Modern England.* Ithaca, NY: Cornell University Press, 1995.

Hampton, Timothy. *Literature and the Nation in the Sixteenth Century: Inventing Renaissance France.* Ithaca, NY: Cornell University Press, 2001.

Hardwick, Julie. *The Practice of Patriarchy: Gender and the Politics of Household Authority in Early Modern France.* University Park: Pennsylvania State University Press, 1998.

Harris, Barbara J. *English Aristocratic Women, 1450–1550: Marriage and Family, Property and Careers.* New York: Oxford University Press, 2002.

Harth, Erica. *Ideology and Culture in Seventeenth-Century France.* Ithaca, NY: Cornell University Press, 1983.

———. *Cartesian Women. Versions and Subversions of Rational Discourse in the Old Regime.* Ithaca, NY: Cornell University Press, 1992.

Harvey, Elizabeth D. *Ventriloquized Voices: Feminist Theory and English Renaissance Texts.* London: Routledge, 1992.

Haselkorn, Anne M., and Betty Travitsky, eds. *The Renaissance Englishwoman in Print: Counterbalancing the Canon.* Amherst: University of Massachusetts Press, 1990.

Hawkesworth, Celia, ed. *A History of Central European Women's Writing.* New York: Palgrave, 2001.

Herlihy, David. "Did Women Have a Renaissance? A Reconsideration." *Medievalia et Humanistica,* NS 13 (1985): 1–22.

Hill, Bridget. *The Republican Virago: The Life and Times of Catharine Macaulay, Historian.* New York: Oxford University Press, 1992.

History of Women in the West, A. Vol. 1, *From Ancient Goddesses to Christian Saints,* ed. Pauline Schmitt Pantel. Cambridge, MA: Harvard University Press, 1992; Vol. 2, *Silences of the Middle Ages,* ed. Christiane Klapisch-Zuber. Cambridge, MA: Harvard University Press, 1992; Vol. 3, *Renaissance and Enlightenment Paradoxes,* ed. Natalie Zemon Davis and Arlette Farge. Cambridge, MA: Harvard University Press, 1993.

Hobby, Elaine. *Virtue of Necessity: English Women's Writing 1646–1688.* London: Virago Press, 1988.

Horowitz, Maryanne Cline. "Aristotle and Women." *Journal of the History of Biology* 9 (1976): 183–213.

Howell, Martha. *The Marriage Exchange: Property, Social Place, and Gender in Cities of the Low Countries, 1300–1550.* Chicago: University of Chicago Press, 1998.

Hufton, Olwen H. *The Prospect before Her: A History of Women in Western Europe, 1: 1500–1800.* New York: HarperCollins, 1996.

Hull, Suzanne W. *Chaste, Silent, and Obedient: English Books for Women, 1475–1640.* San Marino, CA: Huntington Library, 1982.

Hunt, Lynn, ed. *The Invention of Pornography: Obscenity and the Origins of Modernity, 1500–1800.* New York: Zone Books, 1996.

Hutner, Heidi, ed. *Rereading Aphra Behn: History, Theory, and Criticism.* Charlottesville, VA: University Press of Virginia, 1993.

Hutson, Lorna, ed. *Feminism and Renaissance Studies.* New York: Oxford University Press, 1999.

Jaffe, Irma B., with Gernando Colombardo. *Shining Eyes, Cruel Fortune: The Lives and Loves of Italian Renaissance Women Poets.* New York: Fordham University Press, 2002.

James, Susan E. *Kateryn Parr: The Making of a Queen.* Aldershot: Ashgate, 1999.

Jankowski, Theodora A. *Women in Power in the Early Modern Drama.* Urbana: University of Illinois Press, 1992.

Jansen, Katherine Ludwig. *The Making of the Magdalen: Preaching and Popular Devotion in the Later Middle Ages.* Princeton, NJ: Princeton University Press, 2000.

Jed, Stephanie H. *Chaste Thinking: The Rape of Lucretia and the Birth of Humanism.* Bloomington: Indiana University Press, 1989.

Jordan, Constance. *Renaissance Feminism: Literary Texts and Political Models.* Ithaca, NY: Cornell University Press, 1990.

Kagan, Richard L. *Lucrecia's Dreams: Politics and Prophecy in Sixteenth-Century Spain.* Berkeley: University of California Press, 1990.

Kehler, Dorothea, and Laurel Amtower, eds. *The Single Woman in Medieval and Early Modern England: Her Life and Representation.* Tempe, AZ: MRTS, 2002.

Kelly, Joan. "Did Women Have a Renaissance?" In *Women, History, and Theory.* Chicago: University of Chicago Press, 1984. Also in *Becoming Visible: Women in European History,* 3rd ed., ed. Renate Bridenthal, Claudia Koonz, and Susan M. Stuard. Boston: Houghton Mifflin, 1998.

———. "Early Feminist Theory and the *Querelle des Femmes.*" In *Women, History, and Theory.* Chicago: University of Chicago Press, 1984.

Kelso, Ruth. *Doctrine for the Lady of the Renaissance.* Foreword by Katharine M. Rogers. Urbana: University of Illinois Press, 1956, 1978.

King, Carole. *Renaissance Women Patrons: Wives and Widows in Italy, c. 1300–1550.* New York: Manchester University Press, 1998.

King, Margaret L. *Women of the Renaissance.* Foreword by Catharine R. Stimpson. Chicago: University of Chicago Press, 1991.

Krontiris, Tina. *Oppositional Voices: Women as Writers and Translators of Literature in the English Renaissance.* London: Routledge, 1992.

Kuehn, Thomas. *Law, Family, and Women: Toward a Legal Anthropology of Renaissance Italy.* Chicago: University of Chicago Press, 1991.

Kunze, Bonnelyn Young. *Margaret Fell and the Rise of Quakerism.* Stanford, CA: Stanford University Press, 1994.

Labalme, Patricia A., ed. *Beyond Their Sex: Learned Women of the European Past.* New York: New York University Press, 1980.

Laqueur, Thomas. *Making Sex: Body and Gender from the Greeks to Freud.* Cambridge, MA: Harvard University Press, 1990.

Larsen, Anne R., and Colette H. Winn, eds. *Renaissance Women Writers: French Texts/American Contexts.* Detroit, MI: Wayne State University Press, 1994.

Lerner, Gerda. *Women and History.* Vol. 1, *The Creation of Patriarchy.* Vol. 2, *Creation of Feminist Consciousness, 1000–1870.* New York: Oxford University Press, 1986, 1994.

Levin, Carole, and Jeanie Watson, eds. *Ambiguous Realities: Women in the Middle Ages and Renaissance.* Detroit: Wayne State University Press, 1987.

———, et al. *Extraordinary Women of the Medieval and Renaissance World: A Biographical Dictionary.* Westport, CT: Greenwood Press, 2000.

Lewis, Jayne Elizabeth. *Mary Queen of Scots: Romance and Nation.* London: Routledge, 1998.

Lindsey, Karen. *Divorced Beheaded Survived: A Feminist Reinterpretation of the Wives of Henry VIII.* Reading, MA: Addison-Wesley, 1995.

Lochrie, Karma. *Margery Kempe and Translations of the Flesh.* Philadelphia: University of Pennsylvania Press, 1992.

Lougee, Carolyn C. *Le Paradis des Femmes: Women, Salons, and Social Stratification in Seventeenth-Century France.* Princeton, NJ: Princeton University Press, 1976.

Love, Harold. *The Culture and Commerce of Texts: Scribal Publication in Seventeenth-Century England.* Amherst: University of Massachusetts Press, 1993.

MacCarthy, Bridget G. *The Female Pen: Women Writers and Novelists 1621–1818.* Preface by

Janet Todd. New York: New York University Press, 1994. First published 1946–47 by Cork University Press.

Maclean, Ian. *Woman Triumphant: Feminism in French Literature, 1610–1652*. Oxford: Clarendon Press, 1977.

——. *The Renaissance Notion of Woman: A Study of the Fortunes of Scholasticism and Medical Science in European Intellectual Life*. Cambridge: Cambridge University Press, 1980.

Maggi, Armando. *Uttering the Word: The Mystical Performances of Maria Maddalena de' Pazzi, a Renaissance Visionary*. Albany: State University of New York Press, 1998.

Marshall, Sherrin. *Women in Reformation and Counter-Reformation Europe: Public and Private Worlds*. Bloomington: Indiana University Press, 1989.

Matter, E. Ann, and John Coakley, eds. *Creative Women in Medieval and Early Modern Italy*. Philadelphia: University of Pennsylvania Press, 1994. [Sequel to the Monson collection, below.]

McLeod, Glenda. *Virtue and Venom: Catalogs of Women from Antiquity to the Renaissance*. Ann Arbor: University of Michigan Press, 1991.

Medwick, Cathleen. *Teresa of Avila: The Progress of a Soul*. New York: Knopf, 2000.

Meek, Christine, ed. *Women in Renaissance and Early Modern Europe*. Dublin-Portland: Four Courts Press, 2000.

Mendelson, Sara, and Patricia Crawford. *Women in Early Modern England, 1550–1720*. Oxford: Clarendon Press, 1998.

Merrim, Stephanie. *Early Modern Women's Writing and Sor Juana Inés de la Cruz*. Nashville, TN: Vanderbilt University Press, 1999.

Messbarger, Rebecca. *The Century of Women: The Representations of Women in Eighteenth-Century Italian Public Discourse*. Toronto: University of Toronto Press, 2002.

Miller, Nancy K. *The Heroine's Text: Readings in the French and English Novel, 1722–1782*. New York: Columbia University Press, 1980.

Miller, Naomi J. *Changing the Subject: Mary Wroth and Figurations of Gender in Early Modern England*. Lexington: University Press of Kentucky, 1996.

——, and Gary Waller, eds. *Reading Mary Wroth: Representing Alternatives in Early Modern England*. Knoxville: University of Tennessee Press, 1991.

Monson, Craig A., ed. *The Crannied Wall: Women, Religion, and the Arts in Early Modern Europe*. Ann Arbor: University of Michigan Press, 1992.

Musacchio, Jacqueline Marie. *The Art and Ritual of Childbirth in Renaissance Italy*. New Haven, CT: Yale University Press, 1999.

Newman, Barbara. *God and the Goddesses: Vision, Poetry, and Belief in the Middle Ages*. Philadelphia: University of Pennsylvania Press, 2003.

Newman, Karen. *Fashioning Femininity and English Renaissance Drama*. Chicago: University of Chicago Press, 1991.

Okin, Susan Moller. *Women in Western Political Thought*. Princeton, NJ: Princeton University Press, 1979.

Ozment, Steven. *The Bürgermeister's Daughter: Scandal in a Sixteenth-Century German Town*. New York: St. Martin's, 1995.

Pacheco, Anita, ed. *Early [English] Women Writers: 1600–1720*. New York: Longman, 1998.

Pagels, Elaine. *Adam, Eve, and the Serpent*. New York: Harper Collins, 1988.

Panizza, Letizia, ed. *Women in Italian Renaissance Culture and Society*. Oxford: European Humanities Research Centre, 2000.

———, and Sharon Wood, eds. *A History of Women's Writing in Italy.* Cambridge: University Press, 2000.

Parker, Patricia. *Literary Fat Ladies: Rhetoric, Gender and Property.* London: Methuen, 1987.

Pernoud, Regine, and Marie-Veronique Clin. *Joan of Arc: Her Story.* Rev. and trans. Jeremy DuQuesnay Adams. New York: St. Martin's, 1998. French original, 1986.

Perry, Mary Elizabeth. *Crime and Society in Early Modern Seville.* Hanover, NH: University Press of New England, 1980.

———. *Gender and Disorder in Early Modern Seville.* Princeton, NJ: Princeton University Press, 1990.

Petroff, Elizabeth Alvilda, ed. *Medieval Women's Visionary Literature.* New York: Oxford University Press, 1986.

Perry, Ruth. *The Celebrated Mary Astell: An Early English Feminist.* Chicago: University of Chicago Press, 1986.

Rabil, Albert. *Laura Cereta: Quattrocento Humanist.* Binghamton, NY: MRTS, 1981.

Rapley, Elizabeth. *A Social History of the Cloister: Daily Life in the Teaching Monasteries of the Old Regime.* Montreal: McGill-Queen's University Press, 2001.

Raven, James, Helen Small, and Naomi Tadmor, eds. *The Practice and Representation of Reading in England.* Cambridge: University Press, 1996.

Reardon, Colleen. *Holy Concord within Sacred Walls: Nuns and Music in Siena, 1575–1700.* Oxford: Oxford University Press, 2001.

Reiss, Sheryl E., and David G. Wilkins, ed. *Beyond Isabella: Secular Women Patrons of Art in Renaissance Italy.* Kirksville, MO: Turman State University Press, 2001.

Rheubottom, David. *Age, Marriage, and Politics in Fifteenth-Century Ragusa.* Oxford: Oxford University Press, 2000.

Richardson, Brian. *Printing, Writers and Readers in Renaissance Italy.* Cambridge: University Press, 1999.

Riddle, John M. *Contraception and Abortion from the Ancient World to the Renaissance.* Cambridge, MA: Harvard University Press, 1992.

———. *Eve's Herbs: A History of Contraception and Abortion in the West.* Cambridge, MA: Harvard University Press, 1997.

Rose, Mary Beth. *The Expense of Spirit: Love and Sexuality in English Renaissance Drama.* Ithaca, NY: Cornell University Press, 1988.

———. *Gender and Heroism in Early Modern English Literature.* Chicago: University of Chicago Press, 2002.

———, ed. *Women in the Middle Ages and the Renaissance: Literary and Historical Perspectives.* Syracuse, NY: Syracuse University Press, 1986.

Rosenthal, Margaret F. *The Honest Courtesan: Veronica Franco, Citizen and Writer in Sixteenth-Century Venice.* Foreword by Catharine R. Stimpson. Chicago: University of Chicago Press, 1992.

Sackville-West, Vita. *Daughter of France: The Life of La Grande Mademoiselle.* Garden City, NY: Doubleday, 1959.

Sánchez, Magdalena S. *The Empress, the Queen, and the Nun: Women and Power at the Court of Philip III of Spain.* Baltimore, MD: Johns Hopkins University Press, 1998.

Schiebinger, Londa. *The Mind has No Sex?: Women in the Origins of Modern Science.* Cambridge, MA: Harvard University Press, 1991.

———. *Nature's Body: Gender in the Making of Modern Science.* Boston: Beacon Press, 1993.

Schutte, Anne Jacobson, Thomas Kuehn, and Silvana Seidel Menchi, eds. *Time, Space, and Women's Lives in Early Modern Europe.* Kirksville, MO: Truman State University Press, 2001.

Shannon, Laurie. *Sovereign Amity: Figures of Friendship in Shakespearean Contexts.* Chicago: University of Chicago Press, 2002.

Shemek, Deanna. *Ladies Errant: Wayward Women and Social Order in Early Modern Italy.* Durham, NC: Duke University Press, 1998.

Smith, Hilda L. *Reason's Disciples: Seventeenth-Century English Feminists.* Urbana: University of Illinois Press, 1982.

———, ed. *Women Writers and the Early Modern British Political Tradition.* Cambridge: Cambridge University Press, 1998.

Sobel, Dava. *Galileo's Daughter: A Historical Memoir of Science, Faith, and Love.* New York: Penguin Books, 2000.

Sommerville, Margaret R. *Sex and Subjection: Attitudes to Women in Early-Modern Society.* London: Arnold, 1995.

Soufas, Teresa Scott. *Dramas of Distinction: A Study of Plays by Golden Age Women.* Lexington: University Press of Kentucky, 1997.

Spender, Dale. *Mothers of the Novel: 100 Good Women Writers Before Jane Austen.* London: Routledge, 1986.

Sperling, Jutta Gisela. *Convents and the Body Politic in Late Renaissance Venice.* Foreword by Catharine R. Stimpson. Chicago: University of Chicago Press, 1999.

Steinbrügge, Lieselotte. *The Moral Sex: Woman's Nature in the French Enlightenment.* Trans. Pamela E. Selwyn. New York: Oxford University Press, 1995.

Stephens, Sonya, ed. *A History of Women's Writing in France.* Cambridge: Cambridge University Press, 2000.

Stocker, Margarita. *Judith, Sexual Warrior: Women and Power in Western Culture.* New Haven, CT: Yale University Press, 1998.

Stretton, Timothy. *Women Waging Law in Elizabethan England.* Cambridge: Cambridge University Press, 1998.

Stuard, Susan M. "The Dominion of Gender: Women's Fortunes in the High Middle Ages." In *Becoming Visible: Women in European History,* 3rd ed., ed. Renate Bridenthal, Claudia Koonz, and Susan M. Stuard. Boston: Houghton Mifflin, 1998.

Summit, Jennifer. *Lost Property: The Woman Writer and English Literary History, 1380–1589.* Chicago: University of Chicago Press, 2000.

Surtz, Ronald E. *The Guitar of God: Gender, Power, and Authority in the Visionary World of Mother Juana de la Cruz (1481–1534).* Philadelphia: University of Pennsylvania Press, 1991.

———. *Writing Women in Late Medieval and Early Modern Spain: The Mothers of Saint Teresa of Avila.* Philadelphia: University of Pennsylvania Press, 1995.

Teague, Frances. *Bathsua Makin, Woman of Learning.* Lewisburg, PA: Bucknell University Press, 1999.

Todd, Janet. *The Secret Life of Aphra Behn.* London: Pandora, 2000.

———. *The Sign of Angelica: Women, Writing and Fiction, 1660–1800.* New York: Columbia University Press, 1989.

Valenze, Deborah. *The First Industrial Woman.* New York: Oxford University Press, 1995.

Van Dijk, Susan, Lia van Gemert, and Sheila Ottway, eds. *Writing the History of Women's Writing: Toward an International Approach.* Proceedings of the Colloquium of the Royal Netherlands Academy of Arts and Sciences, Amsterdam, September 9–11, 2001.

Vickery, Amanda. *The Gentleman's Daughter: Women's Lives in Georgian England.* New Haven, CT: Yale University Press, 1998.

Vollendorf, Lisa, ed. *Recovering Spain's Feminist Tradition.* New York: MLA, 2001.

Waithe, Mary Ellen, ed. *A History of Women Philosophers.* 3 vols. Dordrecht: Martinus Nijhoff, 1987.

Wall, Wendy. *The Imprint of Gender: Authorship and Publication in the English Renaissance.* Ithaca, NY: Cornell University Press, 1993.

Walsh, William T. *St. Teresa of Avila: A Biography.* Rockford, IL: TAN, 1987.

Warner, Marina. *Alone of All Her Sex: The Myth and Cult of the Virgin Mary.* New York: Knopf, 1976.

Warnicke, Retha M. *The Marrying of Anne of Cleves: Royal Protocol in Tudor England.* Cambridge: Cambridge University Press, 2000.

Watt, Diane. *Secretaries of God: Women Prophets in Late Medieval and Early Modern England.* Cambridge, England: D. S. Brewer, 1997.

Weber, Alison. *Teresa of Avila and the Rhetoric of Femininity.* Princeton, NJ: Princeton University Press, 1990.

Welles, Marcia L. *Persephone's Girdle: Narratives of Rape in Seventeenth-Century Spanish Literature.* Nashville, TN: Vanderbilt University Press, 2000.

Whitehead, Barbara J., ed. *Women's Education in Early Modern Europe: A History, 1500–1800.* New York: Garland, 1999.

Wiesner, Merry E. *Women and Gender in Early Modern Europe.* Cambridge: Cambridge University Press, 1993.

———. *Working Women in Renaissance Germany.* New Brunswick, NJ: Rutgers University Press, 1986.

Willard, Charity Cannon. *Christine de Pizan: Her Life and Works.* New York: Persea, 1984.

Wilson, Katharina, ed. *An Encyclopedia of Continental Women Writers.* New York: Garland, 1991.

Winn, Colette, and Donna Kuizenga, eds. *Women Writers in Pre-Revolutionary France.* New York: Garland, 1997.

Woodbridge, Linda. *Women and the English Renaissance: Literature and the Nature of Womankind, 1540–1620.* Urbana: University of Illinois Press, 1984.

Woods, Susanne. *Lanyer: A Renaissance Woman Poet.* New York: Oxford University Press, 1999.

———, and Margaret P. Hannay, eds. *Teaching Tudor and Stuart Women Writers.* New York: MLA, 2000.

Printed in Great Britain
by Amazon

15981798R00130